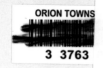

ASKING FOR IT

ASKING FOR IT

Lilah Pace

BERKLEY BOOKS, NEW YORK

BERKLEY

An imprint of Penguin Random House LLC
375 Hudson Street, New York, New York 10014

This book is an original publication of Penguin Random House LLC.

Library of Congress Cataloging-in-Publication Data

Pace, Lilah.
Asking for it / Lilah Pace.
pages cm
ISBN 978-0-425-27951-9 (paperback)
1. Man-woman relationships—Fiction. I. Title.
PS3616.A3255A85 2015
813'.6—dc23
2015002653

PUBLISHING HISTORY
Berkley trade paperback edition / June 2015

PRINTED IN THE UNITED STATES OF AMERICA

10 9 8 7 6 5 4 3 2 1

Cover photo by Scala / Art Resource, New York.

Penguin
Random
House

PROLOGUE

My fantasies always begin . . . normally. Whatever normal is.

The movie or TV show I'm watching features a sexy scene: a man and woman in a clinch, their lips silhouettes that almost touch. A ballad by Dinah Washington comes up on shuffle, raw and yearning. Hugh Jackman shows up shirtless on the cover of a supermarket magazine. The usual things get me started, I guess.

So then I'm in my boyfriend's bed (when I have a boyfriend) or alone between the sheets, or in the shower (when I don't). I close my eyes. I try to forget everything except the pulsing between my legs, the pressure and rhythm that's making my pulse race. The images in my mind jumble together, without narrative or emotion or sense—like a pornographic kaleidoscope of tongues and lips, cock and cunt, the heat of skin on skin. Usually I start to moan; I'm not one of the quiet ones. So far, so good.

But no matter how explicit and erotic the kaleidoscope gets, no matter how talented the guy's tongue is, or how constant my hand's pressure might be—it never, ever gets me off.

Only one fantasy does that.

I try not to think about it. I tell myself it's sick, it's wrong. A lot of times, when I'm with a guy, I just don't come. It's embarrassing to be this good at faking it.

When I'm alone—or when I'm with a lover and I want to get off *so bad* that I can't take it anymore—I have to go there.

In my mind, ropes wind around my wrists, my ankles. Or I'm rolled onto my stomach, hands pinned behind my back. Sometimes I'm blindfolded. Sometimes he makes me look at him. If I'm going down on a guy, I ask him to pull my hair, and the whole time I'm pretending that he's making me do this. Forcing me. In reality he says, *Baby* or *You're beautiful*; I imagine him saying, *Whore. Suck it, you cunt.*

I don't get off unless I'm imagining being raped.

Sometimes it's "softer"—a guy backing me against a wall at a party, or taking advantage when I'm sloppy drunk. Other times it's brutal. Tied down spread-eagled. Or in a ditch on my hands and knees.

At least I don't fantasize about weapons at my throat, or pointed at my head. Not yet, anyway.

I hate this about myself. I *hate* it. I've tried to change so many times; I've always failed. While I wish I could say I don't know why I'm wired this way . . . I do.

Maybe it doesn't matter. Lots of people have sexual fantasies they'd never act on, whether they're violent or perverse, silly or flat-out biologically impossible. If it's all in my head, and it makes me come, what's the harm?

(It makes me come *hard*.)

The harm is when the lines between reality and fantasy get blurred.

Like they did last night.

ONE

Highway 71 stretched in front of my car, black asphalt scrolling beneath my wheels. Seven hours into my drive back to Austin, I was wondering why I hadn't just flown Southwest.

Sometimes I like taking a long road trip by myself—listening to my music, relishing the freedom of knowing I absolutely, positively can't work on my thesis for a while. I'd enjoyed most of this drive back from New Orleans, but now that the sun had gone down and I still had an hour to go, I felt restless.

Maybe if you hadn't left your car charger at home, where it can do you exactly no good—

I groaned, thinking of my cell phone in my purse, dead for more than an hour now. Instead of putting on my favorite high-energy playlist for the final leg of my journey, I was at the mercy of the radio. Every station seemed dedicated to putting me to sleep.

Then again, it was late. After ten P.M. Most people were winding down, taking it easy as they listened to mellower music, maybe snuggling up to someone they loved.

A sultry Latin number began, soft guitar and thumping drums suggesting sensuality with every beat—and reminding me how long I'd been alone.

My last breakup had taken place four months before. Sometimes I missed Geordie, even though I knew splitting had been the right choice. At age thirty, he's still in party-hearty mode, while at twenty-five I already feel more grown-up than he probably ever will. We'd always been more friends than red-hot lovers anyway. Our sex life—well, I couldn't blame Geordie there. Probably most women would have been more than happy with what he had to offer. I was the one who had longed for something Geordie couldn't provide.

At least you told him what you really wanted. You finally trusted someone else enough to tell, and that alone counts for something, doesn't it? He just couldn't go there with you.

But I'd felt so shamed. So exposed. I'd confessed my deepest fantasies to Geordie, hoping he'd play along, and instead he'd freaked out. Oh, he tried to be sympathetic, all "But *why* do you think you feel this way?" That's what I pay my therapist for. What I needed from him was something a whole lot dirtier. A whole lot scarier. And gentle, funny Geordie couldn't give it to me.

Maybe I was being the rigid one. I figured I shouldn't condemn a guy for *not* getting off on the idea of forcing a woman. So I reminded myself, *Geordie gets to have limits too—*

The steering wheel jerked in my hands. I managed to keep my Civic from spinning out, but barely. It wobbled violently, pulling hard to one side as I guided it onto the shoulder. The hum of tires against highway gave way to jagged pops of gravel under my car. Once I'd cleared the road, I put the car in park, turned the key, and sat there for a moment, one hand held over my wildly thumping heart.

Shit. I've blown a tire.

I stepped out of my car, my sandals crunching in the roadside grit, as I inspected the damage. As I'd thought, the passenger-side front tire was completely blown out; strips of blackened rubber had peeled away, and it was already completely deflated against the ground.

Biting my lower lip, I glanced up and down the highway. I hadn't quite made it as far as Giddings, which was the closest thing to a real town in this part of Texas. The next outpost of civilization was probably at least half an hour's walk from here . . . in the dark, without even a streetlamp to guide me. Why hadn't I brought the stupid car charger? I'd have given a lot to have my cell phone with me so I could call for help. I could've bought another one in any gas station along the way; it wasn't like they were expensive. But I hadn't. So I was alone, in the dark, totally on my own.

Of course, as a modern, independent woman, I'd learned how to change a flat tire. I'd practiced so I'd be able to do it in a crisis. Except that the last time I practiced was eight years earlier, when I was a junior in high school.

I squared my shoulders. *Okay, Vivienne. You can do this. Let's make it happen.*

As I took the jack from the trunk, I decided to ditch the little cardigan I wore over my red sundress. In Texas in August, the weather was too warm to work hard while wearing extra layers, even this late at night. Besides, I didn't want to get grease all over my entire outfit if I could help it.

A truck's headlights appeared on the horizon, heading toward me. I was torn. *Wave for help or duck behind the car, so the driver doesn't see that I'm a woman out here alone?*

My fantasies were one thing. Reality was another. I wanted help really badly, but I walked behind the car.

Not that it mattered—the eighteen-wheeler barreled past me so fast my compact car rocked in its wake. The breeze blew my hair in my face and whipped the skirt of my sundress. Once the truck was well ahead of me, I took off my cardigan and tossed it into the front seat, then got down to business.

Okay. Obviously the first step was jacking up the car. I knelt beside the flat tire, angled the jack—and heard another car driving toward me.

Slowing down.

And stopping.

Headlights bathed me in their brilliance. I held up one hand, unable to see for the glare. Fear prickled along my skin. I took the lug wrench firmly in my fist as I stood, still holding my other hand against the light, and tried to keep my voice steady as I called, "Hello?"

"Looks like you've got trouble."

The driver stepped forward, the headlights silhouetting his tall, masculine form. As my eyes adjusted to the brightness, I could finally see his face.

Oh, my God.

All the adrenaline in my bloodstream changed. The fear was still there, sharper as I saw how broad his shoulders were, and the muscles in his arms—but now that fear was matched by excitement, raw and primal. This man . . .

He was tall, a couple inches over six feet. His jeans were slung beneath his almost impossibly tapered waist, which only exaggerated how muscular his thighs were. His black T-shirt clung to him tightly. Stubble shadowed his angular jaw, and his dark hair was cut almost military-short in a way that emphasized the strong lines of his face. His gray eyes raked over me, as I remembered why I'd worn the cardigan to begin with—my sundress was low-cut, and his gaze made it clear he'd noticed.

My hand tightened around the wrench.

"What seems to be the problem?" He took a step closer.

"It's just a flat tire. I've got a spare." I sounded breathless. Afraid. Would that encourage him to help me, or make it clear just how much power he had over me at this moment?

One of his eyebrows lifted. Clearly he'd picked up on the fact that I was nervous. It seemed to amuse him. "Can you change a flat?"

"Of course." That was possibly not the entire truth, but I figured I could manage if I had to.

"Do you have any help on the way? Triple A?" His gray eyes met mine again, but it was difficult for me to make out his expression with his headlights shining in my eyes. "A boyfriend?"

Is he trying to find out if I'm single, or trying to find out if anybody would know if something happened to me?

No one would.

I tried to smile; I probably failed. "Yeah. Triple A said they'd be here in—oh, another fifteen minutes or so." My voice sounded sharp, borderline rude, but I couldn't worry about that. All I could think was, *Why did I say that? Fifteen minutes was too long. Fifteen minutes is more than enough time for him to . . .*

His smile was a quick flash in the darkness, as hard-edged as a straight razor. "I can change that flat in five. That is—if you're not too proud to ask for help."

"Proud?" This guy had pulled over next to me in the dead of night, started interrogating me, and wanted to lecture me on my attitude? Fuck being afraid; I got mad. "Listen, if you think it's *funny* that I'd be worried about a stranger in this situation, I'm afraid you don't understand some very basic, sad facts of life."

He drew back, his gray eyes narrowing, almost like I'd slapped him. Had he taken my fear as an insult? Maybe it was one; I'd as good as said I thought he couldn't be trusted. However, when he spoke again, his deep voice was gentler. Meant to soothe. "I wasn't thinking. Here. Let me take care of this for you and get you on your way."

He held out his hand for the wrench. Obviously he'd need it to change my flat. But it was also the only potential weapon I had.

Do I trust this guy?

I took one step closer to him, squinting to see. Now his body blocked the headlights a little more, and I could examine his face more carefully. Strong brow. Firm, straight nose like a slash through his perfectly symmetrical face. A surprisingly full lower lip. He looked powerfully, almost aggressively masculine. Like someone who took what he wanted. And yet his eyes never glanced away from mine, as though he had nothing to hide—

Even though I wanted to trust those eyes, I couldn't. This man was a total stranger. What it boiled down to was this: If he was a good guy, then I could rely on him. If he was a bad guy, he could probably get the lug wrench away from me any time he wanted.

I hesitated one instant longer, then handed him the wrench.

He took it and stepped past me to get to work.

During the next few minutes, while he worked in silence except for the clanking of metal, I stood awkwardly in front of his dark sedan. Even now I found it difficult to relax around this guy. What if he was just toying with me? Trying to get me off my guard?

Oh, come on, I told myself. *Like any rapist on earth would go to the trouble of changing a flat tire first.*

But those fears weren't the main reason I found it hard to relax. What got to me was that I found my rescuer sexy as hell. And he'd been sexy to me even when I'd been scared of him.

Just what did you think he was going to do to you?

What did you want him to do to you?

As I watched him—his strong arms wrestling with the wheel, the headlights shining on the muscular expanse of his back or his stern profile—my mind filled with visions I didn't want to want. Visions of him bending me over the back of my car, pushing up the skirt of my sundress. Of him pulling me into the backseat, putting my hand on his cock, whispering, *Time to thank me.* His hands fisting in my hair as he towed me down on my knees—

Stop it.

I shook my head, pushing the loose strands of my hair back from my face. My cheeks felt hot. My pulse still raced, thumping in my chest, throbbing between my legs. I was turned on and confused and angry with myself. I wanted him to finish changing my flat so I could get back into my car and drive the rest of the way home, pretending I'd never had a bigger problem than crappy music on the radio.

Then I could also pretend he hadn't made me feel so hungry. So ashamed.

"Okay," he said. A few clicks of the jack, and my car settled back onto the ground. When he stood up, he had a smudge of dark grease along one cheekbone. "That should get you home. But it's just a spare. You need to buy a new tire right away instead of driving around on this one for too long."

"I know that," I retorted, stung.

"Sorry." His smile was knowing, almost disdainful. "I forgot I was talking to an expert."

Okay, so he's a smug son of a bitch, but he's the son of a bitch who just saved your ass. I swallowed my irritation. "Listen—thanks. Seriously. I don't know what I would've done without you. I owe you one."

His smile faded. "Then do me a favor. Don't try to be superwoman next time. Join Triple A, stay in the car and keep it locked, whatever you have to do to keep yourself safe." He handed me back the wrench. "You should be more careful who you trust."

His eyes searched mine again, and I hoped my face was in shadow—enough that he couldn't see how flushed I was. Then he turned and walked back to his sedan.

As his door slammed, I went to the driver's side of my Civic, legs trembling beneath me. I got back in and hit the locks. His car pulled back onto the highway, passed me, and kept on going. I sat still, watching the taillights shrink and pass out of sight as he drove away.

I needed to keep driving. But for a few moments I just sat there, one hand to my lips, and tried to stop shaking.

That's not what I wanted. It's not.

If only I could believe that.

TWO

Monday mornings mean Dr. Ward or, as she insists I call her, Doreen.

I've tried therapy before, but Doreen is the first psychologist who's made me feel like I might actually get somewhere. Everything about her and her office is comforting. Instead of a sternly neutral face and a crisp suit, she always wears a gentle expression and flowing, colorful knits. Instead of a cold, clinical office, she meets with clients in a room of her own bright, sunny house, filled with potted plants and the African sculpture she collects. Most importantly, instead of lecturing, she listens.

"I didn't know whether I was safe." I sit on the cream-colored sofa, my bare feet tucked under me. Doreen asks patients to leave our shoes at the door; supposedly it's to preserve her rugs, but really I think it gets us to let our guard down. "I could've been in danger, for all I knew. I didn't know that he wasn't going to hurt me. And I still fantasized about him . . . forcing me."

"He didn't hurt you," Doreen says calmly. "He helped you, and then he went on his way."

And he had an attitude about it. But that isn't the point. "We were still out there alone in the dark. The danger was *real*, and I wanted him anyway. It's like—like I wanted to get hurt."

Doreen raises an eyebrow. "Ever consider that you wanted him just because he was hot?"

I laugh despite myself.

She leans forward. "Let me tell you what I'm hearing here. You were in trouble. You were scared. A very attractive man helped you out. While he was doing that, you let yourself fantasize about him. That's not abnormal. In fact, I'd say it's the most normal thing in the world."

"What I fantasize about isn't normal."

"Rape fantasies are among the most common sexual fantasies women have," Doreen says, not for the first time. As ever, shame lashes me when she says the actual word. *Rape.* "Some men fantasize about being forced, too. That's not the same as actually wanting to get raped. Not all fantasies are things we want in reality."

"I should know."

That's my attempt at a joke. Doreen doesn't crack a smile; she's not so easily distracted. "One of the reasons you came to me was that you wanted to stop having this fantasy. I understand your reasons. But I don't think the fantasy itself is your most significant problem. I think your main problem is the way you beat yourself up about it." Doreen sighs. "That, and the reason you're fixated on the fantasy in the first place."

I can't talk about my reasons—not again, not now. My mystery man looms too large in my mind. His shadow falls across everything I say and do today. "If I'm having that fantasy at times when I might really be in danger—about men who really could—who might—"

"We've talked about this. Sometimes you tie yourself up in knots about what could have happened, instead of just dealing with the facts. For a little while, let's stick to the facts about last night." Doreen's tone is kind but firm. "This guy changed your tire, and then he went on his way. That's all."

Am I overthinking this? Maybe. With a sigh, I let it go—or
try to.

After my hour with Doreen is up, I take my Civic to the shop, buy a
new tire, and drive to the north side of town, up to a small town
house with empty packing boxes stacked by the curb.

"Anybody home?" I call as I walk up the path to the front steps.
"Because I feel the need to unpack something today."

Carmen appears at the screen door, a red bandana around her
black hair and a broad smile on her face. She wears a T-shirt dress
and rubber gloves; obviously I'm not the only one who wants to
help out. "Are you a glutton for punishment?"

"No more than you are. Besides," I say, gesturing to my cutoff
shorts and heather gray T-shirt, "I'm dressed to work."

"Then get in here and work, girl."

As I walk in, I see Carmen's younger brother Arturo with a
hammer in one hand. "Vivienne! I can't believe we didn't scare
you off for good on moving day."

I give him a hug. "Not yet, anyway."

Carmen and I were randomly assigned as roommates freshman
year, because I didn't have any friends attending UT Austin, and
because her best friend from high school changed her college
choice at the last minute. We were wary of each other at the start,
because two people more different would be hard to find. I'm from
New Orleans, from what my mother likes to call "old money"
even though not much of the money is left anymore. Carmen is from
a small town not far from San Antonio, the daughter of immigrants who worked their way out of poverty. I'm slightly taller
than average, slender, and, as Carmen has told me many times, the
whitest white girl in the world. She's short, curvy, and proud of her
Mexican heritage. My hair is honey-brown with just enough wave

to defy any style I attempt, and my eyes are an uncertain shade of hazel, like they can't decide whether to be brown or green or gold. Carmen's hair is a deep, shining, perfectly straight blue-black that I covet nearly as much as her dark brown eyes. I love literature and history, and I littered our dorm room with paperbacks. She loves mathematics, the harder and more abstract the better, and loathes clutter. We hardly dared talk to each other for the first few weeks—but somehow by Christmas break we'd become best friends.

When her younger sibling, Arturo, followed her to UT Austin two years later, I adopted him too. We took him to parties, made sure he studied for finals, even got him a fake ID. By now he's the little brother I've never had.

So I understood how protective Carmen felt when Arturo got involved with his first serious girlfriend. I just can't share her dismay about how it's turning out.

"Hey, Vivienne." Shay waddles down the stairs, her hands on the small of her back. Her Australian accent makes my name sound like *Viv-yin*. "Want a Coke?"

"Maybe in a minute, once I'm hot and sweaty," I say. "Then I'll be craving one."

Shay laughs. "Just get them out of the fridge! I swear, the cans are taunting me."

Shay's doctor told her caffeine was a bad idea during her pregnancy.

Yeah, Arturo and Shay are young to become parents—only twenty-two years old, still undergraduates. But it's as though they *glow* every time they look at each other. I don't think they got engaged because she got pregnant; I assumed a wedding was inevitable from the first time I saw them together. Sometimes you just know. Whenever I see Arturo and Shay together, I smile.

Carmen, on the other hand, scowls.

After we work in the kitchen for a while, unpacking dishes, I glance sideways at Carmen. She's staring out the window above the sink into the narrow backyard, where Shay and Arturo are giggling as they set up the charcoal grill. I say, "If you're not careful, your face will freeze like that."

She rolls her eyes at my dumb joke. "I'm just worried. That's all. A baby . . . I mean, Arturo used to forget to feed our *dog*."

I laugh. "He's not a little kid anymore! And he's got Shay to help him."

"Vivienne, get real. They're young. They don't have a dime. Even with their part-time jobs, they can only barely afford to rent a place big enough for a nursery." Carmen gestures around us.

The town house is modest, and I know Arturo and Shay already have to scrimp. That will only get tougher when the baby arrives in three months. Still—"Listen, if money solved every problem, my family would be the happiest in the world."

"I'm not being materialistic. I'm being realistic. Marrying young, before he gets his degree—it scares me."

"A lot of guys might drop out under that kind of pressure," I admit. "But Arturo's not 'most guys.' He'd never let anything stop him from taking care of Shay and the baby."

Carmen presses her full lips together. "I like Shay—I'm trying to love her, as a sister—but I resent what she's done to Arturo's life."

"She didn't make the baby on her own, you know. Remember, it takes two to tango."

"Oh, oh, gross. 'Tango' in that sentence means 'have sex,' and I know you didn't suggest my baby brother actually had sex." Carmen's smiling now, which counts as a positive sign. "They got pregnant via . . . osmosis."

"Definitely osmosis."

From outside we hear Shay's laughter, and we look outside to see Arturo dancing her around the backyard. Arturo is the male version of Carmen: compact, dark, attractive in a way that has as much to do with charisma as appearance. As for Shay, her bare feet are almost hidden by the high green grass as she spins around; her pixie cut is dyed to a shade of red that's almost maroon. She isn't easy to cast in the role of Evil Temptress. Instead she's straight-up Alternative Chick from her horn-rimmed hipster glasses to the roses tattooed around one ankle.

Carmen says, "I'm trying harder with Shay these days."

"Yeah, I can tell."

That wins me a glare. "I *am*. I even asked her to invite a few friends along to my party Friday night. You're still coming, right?"

"Are you nuts? Of course I'm coming to my best friend's party."

"Well." Carmen's expression turns guilty. "I should tell you I invited Geordie too."

I take a deep breath. "That's fine."

She gives me a look.

"I swear." Geordie and I promised we'd stay friends. After a whole summer away from each other, we ought to be able to hang out again. The party could be awkward as hell, especially if he drinks too much—but I can handle it.

"You agreed faster than I thought you would." Carmen grabs the box cutter to get us started on our next round of unpacking. "Have you been missing him? Thinking about getting back together?"

"No."

That isn't entirely true. I miss Geordie, not as a lover but as a person. Plus I miss sex. I really, truly, definitely miss sex. Maybe the lovemaking with Geordie wasn't the best, but at least it was *something*. Since the beginning of the summer I haven't even had that.

Our lack of chemistry in the bedroom isn't the reason Geordie and I split up, but it didn't help. Even though the sex was okay, he hadn't given me what I really want. What I need.

Once again I think of my rescuer—the tall, dark, dangerous man who'd had me at his mercy and walked away—

I shiver.

But Carmen doesn't notice, and I start talking with her about school, the weather, whatever. I try to sweep away my dangerous thoughts along with the dust on the floor.

The rest of the week goes like any other for a doctoral student at the UT Austin School of Art. Tuesday, meeting with my advisor and then going to the undergrad art history class where I'm a "teaching assistant," that is, the person who actually grades all the papers. Wednesday and Thursday, long hours at the School of Information downtown, where I'm doing some research on document preservation. Friday, some actual studio time with my prints—and I get a couple of really good prints of my favorite etching I've done so far this year, one of a man's hands cradling a dove.

Why does this image speak so strongly to me? I'm not exactly sure, and in some ways I'd rather not know. Art is mysterious, sometimes; unconscious inspiration is often the most powerful. I need nothing more than the image itself: a man's strong, large hands—rough, as if from years of labor or combat—cupped around the form of a dove, its bright eyes shining with both fear and life. The interpretation can come later, or not.

Once I'm done with my prints, I drive home to my little house, a tiny white one-bedroom place, small even among the modest, ramshackle homes just off First Street. Carmen says my place gives her claustrophobia, and Geordie always calls it "the dollhouse." But I like my snug little hideaway. Built-in bookshelves line the bedroom walls, and a freestanding brick fireplace divides the kitchen and the living room. My dream home, basically.

Anyone who walked inside would know a few things about me

right away. One, I'm a bibliophile—someone who collects everything from Jane Austen to John le Carré. Two, I'm a sensualist. Only someone in love with texture and color would buy a velvet couch on a grad-school budget, or drape richly woven throws over every other stick of furniture.

Three, I very much love a little girl named Libby, whose coloring-book pages decorate my refrigerator. One original drawing of hers I even framed and put on the wall. In each corner is the scrawled dedication: *To Aunt Vivi.*

No one could look around this room and guess that I don't see Libby very often, much less why. That remains unknown, which is exactly how I want to keep it.

What to wear tonight? I don't want to look too sexy, in case that makes Geordie think I want him back. But I don't want to look frumpy either. Finally I decide nothing matters more than the heat. In Texas in August, temperatures are scorching even after dark, and bare skin is your best friend. I slide into a denim miniskirt and a black camisole, trusting my silver strappy sandals and dangly earrings to dress it up a bit. Then I swing by the convenience store to pick up a six-pack of beer and head to Carmen's.

Her brick red bungalow is within walking distance of some of the great restaurants, clubs, and bars on Congress Street. I have to park my car more than a block away, because this party is one of Carmen's rare blowouts; as I walk up, I see about ten people laughing and talking on her back patio. No doubt a pitcher of sangria is already making the rounds.

Arturo shows me in, hugging me with one arm as he holds his beer with the other. Another two or three dozen people fill Carmen's tiny house, all of them talking and laughing at once, without quite drowning out the thumping of the music from her stereo. The lights are turned down, and a few candles flicker from atop the speakers and the coffee table. Through the glass door that leads to the back patio, I can glimpse a few of the solar torches lighting the yard as softly as fireflies. "About time you got here!" Arturo calls over the din. "We'll have to catch you up. Do you know everyone?"

"I don't think I know anyone." This is a little bit of an exaggeration—I recognize a couple of faces—but both Carmen and Arturo attract new friends with constant, magnetic appeal. Me . . . it takes me a lot longer to trust people. To let them in. I have my reasons, and I don't think it's a bad way to live, but it's lonelier sometimes.

Also, it makes parties awkward.

Shay comes up to me then, hugging me from behind; the swell of her belly presses against my back. "Introductions time! This is Nicole Mills—hi!—she works with Arturo. Then I'm sure you know Anna Dunham, from Carmen's department? And Jonny is one of Carmen's neighbors." I try to at least wave to everyone as they're introduced, but Shay is already guiding me toward the kitchen.

Carmen's tiny galley kitchen is cramped even for one person. In the middle of a party, with everyone trying to get to the fridge or the plastic cups, it's a tight squeeze. Laughing, I try to shimmy between two figures in the darkened kitchen, get pushed right up on some guy—and then go completely still.

Shay continues, oblivious. "And this is Jonah Marks. He's a professor in earth sciences. You know that's where I'm doing my work study this semester, right?"

The last time I saw him it was late at night, and headlights shone from behind him like a halo. Doesn't matter. I'd know him anywhere. Only one man ever made me go instantly hot and flushed and weak—or wore such a cool, appraising smile while he did it.

He's smiling at me like that right now.

Tall, Dark, and Dangerous is named Jonah. He's here with my friends, here in my life. And all my fantasies about the stranger on the road feel even scarier now that he's not a stranger anymore.

THREE

Our chests are pressed together by the crush of people, and I know he can feel my breasts through my skimpy camisole and the thin cotton of his T-shirt. He cocks his head slightly, and I know he recognizes me too. But he says nothing.

Shay blithely continues, "Jonah, this is Vivienne Charles. She's a good friend of ours, Carmen's old roommate."

I just nod. No words come to me. Once again that mixture of fear and desire surges through my veins, the same kind of fire I imagine injected heroin must feel like—an agony so sweet you'd do anything for it.

"We've met," Jonah says, never looking away from me.

"Oh, yeah? That's UT Austin for you." Shay grins, still oblivious to the energy between Jonah and me. "Practically the largest university in the country, but somehow we all cross paths."

"We met just the other night," I finally manage to say. "On my way back from New Orleans, I had a flat tire. Jonah changed it for me. Thanks again, by the way."

He inclines his head, acknowledging my words as little as possible.

"Hey, hey. Our hero," Shay says. "You never mentioned help-ing someone on the roadside, Jonah."

"It was no big deal." With that, Jonah finally breaks eye con-tact, turns, and walks away. I let out a breath I hadn't known I was holding.

If Shay notices my reaction, she misinterprets it. "Don't let Jonah get to you. He comes across as rude sometimes, but that's just his way. I mean, he's good to work for—doesn't treat me like his per-sonal servant, the way some of the professors do. But never once have I heard him laugh." Shay's expression turns thoughtful. "Huh. I'm not sure he even can."

"Why did you ask him here tonight? If he's so—cold."

"I asked a bunch of people from our department. Would've been mean to leave him out."

That's just like Shay. She'd invite someone she barely likes to a party before she'd hurt anyone's feelings.

Jonah's out of sight, and—for Shay, at least—out of mind. She resumes pushing me through the kitchen crowd. "Come on. Time to get you some sangria!"

It's not like me, going quiet that way. I've spent most of my adult life trying to teach myself to be more assertive, and . . . let's say I'm getting there. But seeing Tall, Dark, and Dangerous again—finding out that his name is Jonah Marks—he threw me off. Embarrassed me.

Correction, I tell myself. *He didn't embarrass you. Your fanta-sies about him make you ashamed. Not the same thing.*

Sometime later on, I'll find Jonah among the other partygoers. I'll say something simple and stupid. Basic party chatter. *Great song, huh?* That kind of thing. Then I'll thank him again, and it won't be weird anymore. After that I can walk away from this man for good.

Right now, though, I need to catch my breath.

Shay gets me sangria and grabs herself a ginger ale, and starts going on about how she wants to paint the nursery green, but Arturo prefers yellow. I'm excited about the baby and everything, but there's only so much nursery talk I can take. So I basically zone out, saying "Yeah" and "Of course" whenever she pauses for a moment.

Almost against my will, I steal glances across the room at Jonah Marks.

He's even more attractive than I remembered. Not *beautiful*, or *gorgeous*—any of the adjectives that would apply to a Ralph Lauren model or a boy-band star. Jonah's features are too rugged for that. Too stark. He looks like the work of a sculptor who didn't believe in polishing rough edges, who wanted you to see exactly where the chisel had struck. In some ways, he's aggressively masculine: the dark red henley he's wearing is tight enough to reveal the powerful muscles of his arms. But in others, Jonah looks strangely vulnerable. His waist is narrow, and his neck is longer than most men's. His whole body looks as though someone took the macho ideal of a masculine form and brought it almost to the breaking point. Strong—and yet strained, beneath the surface.

This is a man who could be broken, I think. *But he'd be more likely to break you first.*

Jonah moves deeper into the crowd, until I can't see him any longer. At first I wonder if I could extricate myself from Shay's nursery-decoration talk to find him; then I wonder why I feel like I need to do that this second.

Maybe I shouldn't seek Jonah out at all, if he shakes me up like this. Besides, what would I say? *It was incredibly nice of you to help me out the other night. Remember how I treated you like you were probably a serial killer?* Yeah, guys love that.

Then distraction arrives, in the form of Geordie Hilton, aka my ex-boyfriend.

"Vivienne!" Geordie's smile is absolutely genuine. In his eyes there's only the slightest flicker of doubt. He's glad to see me, but he's not sure I'll feel the same.

To my surprise, I do. "Hey, you. Come here."

We hug each other, the one-armed friendly hug that clearly says *We're not fucking anymore.* I'm aware of Shay studying us, and other people too; the first meeting of the exes is always an attention-getter. Right now they're looking at us half in relief (no fight), half in disappointment (no fight?). Shay sidles away, giving us as much space as this crowded party allows.

He says, "Did you have a good summer? You never post to Facebook, you know." Geordie is the kind of hyper-extrovert who considers avoiding social media nearly criminal.

"I had a quiet summer, which is exactly what I needed. You?"

"*Brilliant.*" Geordie lived in Inverness until he was sixteen, and occasionally his accent and slang give him away. "The internship went great. Seriously, beyond my wildest expectations. We won amnesty for *four* immigrants in danger of exportation to home countries where they'd have been killed, either for political protests or sexual orientation. Four in three months! The wheels of justice rarely spin so fast."

Most young attorneys who return to law school for an LLM do it to make even more money; Geordie's getting his LLM so he can better help people. I don't regret breaking up with him, but it's good to be reminded of what I liked about the guy in the first place.

Plenty of the eyes watching us are female. More than one woman at this party hopes to make sure I'm out of the picture with Geordie, so she'll have a shot at climbing into the frame. He's handsome—okay, *adorable*—with floppy brown hair, puppy-dog eyes, and a smile that can be warm, or sly, or both at once. With his white oxford shirt unbuttoned at the neck, sleeves rolled up, his frame looks less skinny, more wiry. He's the ideal hero of a romantic comedy.

But my life isn't a rom-com, and it never will be. That ship sailed long before Geordie came along.

Besides, standing within arm's length of Geordie does less for me than just glancing across the room at Jonah Marks.

Again I look toward the corner where I saw Jonah last, but he's not there. Did he leave the party already?

If he did, I ought to feel relieved. I don't.

Time to focus on Geordie again. "Good for you," I tell him, meaning it.

We chitchat about his time in Miami for a while, then go our own ways within the party. I manage to dodge Arturo's old room-mate, Mack, who always stares at my tits; he's one of those jocks with a thick neck and square head, like a canned ham in a Long-horns T-shirt. For a while I get to talk with Kip, the department secretary in my section of the art department, but then he receives some urgent text that sucks him into the cell phone dead zone. Mostly, even though I ought to be mingling and meeting new peo-ple, I hang out with Carmen. We're best friends for a reason, and besides, she has a new crush to describe in detail.

As for my crush—if you can use such an innocent word for what Jonah Marks does to me—I refuse to let myself look for him again. Nor does he seek me out. Either Jonah's on the patio or he blew out of here early, because I don't see him once.

What I do see is Geordie going back for a third glass of sangria.

And a fourth.

And a fifth. That's assuming I didn't miss any refills, and I might have.

It's on the fifth sangria that Geordie stumbles into the coffee table. A few people's drinks slosh onto the carpet, which makes Carmen swear under her breath; one of the candles rocks but doesn't fall over to start a fire. Barely.

People laugh, but there's an edge to it. Geordie's drunker than anyone else at this party, by far.

"Hey," I say to him as gently as I can. "Let's get you some air."

Even as she dabs paper towels against her carpet, Carmen defends Geordie. "It's all right! The rug's dark. It won't even show."

"No, Viv's right. She's right." Geordie must be smashed; otherwise he'd never risk my wrath by calling me Viv. "We should all listen to—to Viv—a little more often."

I get up and sling one of his arms around my shoulders. If he or anybody else misinterprets this, it's on them.

"Why don't I listen to you more?" Geordie stumbles against me, but I manage to keep us upright. "You're always so smart."

"That's me. The genius. Come on."

With my free hand I slide the glass door open and guide him onto the brick patio. Only a few people linger out there now, and I pay attention to none of them. Instead I get Geordie to the ice chest, where—amid several bottles of beer—I find a Dasani for him.

"Drink this, okay? You need to drink nothing but water the rest of the night. You should eat something too."

Geordie clasps the bottle of water, but he doesn't take a sip. Instead he gives me this sad smile. "I should've tried harder with you. I should've made it work."

Is he going to cry? Damn, Geordie's a sloppy drunk.

He just keeps talking. "I'm sorry I couldn't be the partner you wanted me to be."

"It's okay. Really. Please drink some water." I prop him against the patio table. Around us, a few people are snickering at Geordie; I'm still loyal enough to feel angry on his behalf.

"I mean, it's for the best. I know that. I do. But it hurts sometimes, doesn't it?" Geordie's slurring now. "We should've had more fun while we could."

"Less fun," I say. "More water."

Finally Geordie takes a sip, but it doesn't shut him up for long. "I just couldn't do that for you. Any of it. And, oh my God, I feel so bad about the rape thing—"

He did not say that. He did not start talking about this in public, at a party, with strangers standing around listening.

Except he did.

My face goes cold with shock, then hot with shame, as Geordie continues. "I mean, kink yay, right? Everybody should love kinks. And you get to have yours! You do. But it's not my kink. At all. Playing rapist freaks me out. But I shouldn't have been such a dumb cunt about it."

"We're not discussing this here," I manage to say. "Please stop."

It hits Geordie then, where we are and what he's done. The impact gets through all the booze. He sucks in a breath. "Oh, fuck."

I don't want to look at the faces of the people standing around who just heard that, but I can't help it. A few of them look shocked. Others look amused. That creeper Mack leers at me in a way that makes my skin crawl.

Worst of all is the one face that remains impassive—Jonah Marks, only a few feet away, who must have heard every word.

FOUR

Once, when I was thirteen, the bloody string of my tampon somehow hung out from the edge of my swimsuit. Jackson Overstreet—who I thought was so cute, with his blond hair and blue eyes, the boy I hoped would be the first guy ever to kiss me—he saw the string, pointed it out to everyone at my friend Liz's pool party, and laughed the loudest of all. Given how many people were shrieking in laughter at once, that was a hard competition to win. Jackson won it hands down. Since then I've believed that moment would probably be the single greatest public humiliation I'd ever feel.

Turns out it wasn't even close.

I stand at the edge of Carmen's yard by the tall wooden fence. The noise and light of the party are as far away as possible, which isn't nearly far enough. What I want most is to leave. But to leave, I'd have to walk through the crowd, and I'm not ready to do that yet.

Footsteps in the grass behind me make me cringe. When Arturo comes up beside me, though, his smile is kind. "You all right?"

This is Arturo; I can't lie to him. "If 'mortally embarrassed' counts as all right."

"Don't be like that. Everybody gets a little crazy in the sack once in a while, you know? I could tell you a few stories, if Shay wouldn't kill me afterward."

I give him a crooked smile. Probably everyone else who heard Geordie thinks what Arturo thinks: that he was talking about a bad night of role-playing, a one-time thing. They have no idea how deep this goes for me. To them it's a tremor, not an earthquake.

Arturo adds, "Geordie's a dick. Carmen shouldn't have invited him."

"He was drunk. That's all." I push my bangs back from my forehead. The night is sultry—hot and humid. "I'll take it up with him later. You guys stay out of it."

Arturo holds up his hands, a gesture of surrender, but I can tell he's not ready to let Geordie off the hook yet. My adopted younger brother is more protective than any real older brother could ever be. He's slow to anger, but once he finally gets mad—watch out.

Hopefully someone's driven Geordie home by now.

"You sure you're okay?" he says.

I nod. "Just give me a few more minutes, all right? By tomorrow maybe I'll be able to laugh about it." Fat chance.

"Sure thing." Arturo's hand touches my shoulder, a comforting pat, before he heads back to the gathering.

Nobody else knows the truth. If I'd been able to laugh off what Geordie said, chances are most people wouldn't have thought much more about it. I'm making it a bigger deal than it has to be by staying away from everyone else, so I should knock it off. Probably Mack's smarmy grin is the worst of the aftermath, and that's already over.

Geordie, you dickweed. I might keep Arturo from giving him hell, but that doesn't mean I'm not going to. *You couldn't have spent one single party drinking ginger ale?*

Footsteps on the grass again, but I don't turn around. "I'm coming back in, really—"

My voice trails off as I see who's come to my side.

Jonah Marks doesn't look directly at me; he stares in the same direction I do, right past the fence, but there's no missing the intensity of his focus. He is as vividly aware of me right now as I am of him.

"Sorry your ex embarrassed you," he says.

"He, um, he just had too much to drink." I hug myself a little tighter. "Guess we've all been there."

"I've never humiliated one of my lovers at a party. Have you?"

Wow, thanks for describing it as humiliation. "I just meant, I'm not angry with Geordie. You don't have to be either."

Jonah doesn't seem to think my take on this matters. "He should never have revealed something so private."

I remind myself: a tremor, not an earthquake. "That was just one thing Geordie and I talked about, one time. Don't read too much into it."

My best bluff. I even manage a smile. Most people would believe it. Jonah doesn't.

"If it were no big deal, you wouldn't be standing out here now," he says. "I knew the truth as soon as I saw your face. You want that fantasy. You want it more than you've ever wanted anything else." He looks directly at me for the first time. "You hate it, don't you? The fantasy. I do too. But it doesn't change anything."

I feel naked in front of him. Exposed, and vulnerable. I can't think about what he's saying; all I want is to get away. But Jonah's presence—the sheer heat of him—holds me in place, trapping me. "You—I don't want to talk about this with you."

"I think you do."

The presumption of the guy. "Excuse me?"

He takes a sip from his wineglass, utterly unhurried, completely and maddeningly calm. Then he says, "I want to tell you this now—tonight, while you're safe, and with your friends, and you know I'm not threatening you. What your ex said—if that's the fantasy you want, I can give it to you."

Did he just say that? He did.

It's like every sound turns into white noise. Like my brain won't process words any longer. The shock is physical. "You—you didn't mean—"

"Rape as fantasy. You'd like to play one role. I'd like to play another." Jonah's tone remains diffident, but his eyes tell another story. He stares at me so intently that I can't help picturing him in the role he wants to play. "On your terms, and within your limits. But I think we could . . . satisfy each other."

I can't even answer him.

Apparently I look as shocked as I feel, because Jonah says, "You're safe. You're with friends. Even if you were alone, you'd be safe with me."

There are a thousand objections I could make, from long outraged diatribes to a slap on the face he's surely earned. I go with, "I don't even know you."

"That's going to make it better for you," Jonah says. "With a boyfriend, you can pretend—but it's a joke, really. A game. Not the fantasy you really want. Me? I'm nearly a stranger. I can do more than fuck you. I can scare you a little. Just a little. Enough to make it what you really want."

I need to shut this down. "This is crazy. You know that, right? And it's never, ever happening."

"It's your fantasy, and mine. Chances like this don't come along often—two people twisted in the exact same way." Jonah smiles; it's a fierce expression, rather than a friendly one. "If we don't make something out of this, I think you'll regret it. I know I will."

I want to tell Jonah that he's wrong. I want to tell him to fuck off. I want to make it clear that I'm not the twisted woman he described—but I can't. This man has already seen right through me. "I can't believe we're even having this conversation."

"We can have a lot more than that. Think about it."

I can't help imagining it. Every fevered, violent fantasy I had about Jonah that night on the side of the road comes back to me, more vivid than most of my real memories. I wanted him to take me. Control me. Drag me down and force me.

The whole time, he was fantasizing about doing that to me. Maybe more than I even dared dream. Out there in the dark, when I was at his mercy, that was what was going through his mind.

Probably I should feel insulted, or scared. Instead I am powerfully, almost painfully turned on.

Turned on is not the same as suicidal. I say, "There's no way in hell I'm giving you permission to rape me."

"That's not what I asked for. I asked to play a role in your fantasy, just like I'm asking you to play a role in mine. Nothing happens you don't want to happen." His gray eyes are unfathomable. "We can work out a few details in advance, for your protection."

"Is this something you do with women?" I demand. Though I only mean it in terms of fantasy, I realize almost instantly that Jonah could have done this for real. I might be talking to a rapist. I could be a potential victim dangling in front of him like low fruit on a heavy branch.

"A couple of ex-girlfriends tried to act scenes out with me, but it was never quite right. They didn't want to play rough." His smile is as sharp and bright as a straight razor. "I think you do."

That ought to scare the shit out of me, except—he's right. I do want to play rough. I want the dirtiest, filthiest brutality, and I want it badly. Wanted it for so long. We still haven't exchanged more than a handful of words, but I already realize that Jonah's exactly the kind of man who'd give me what I need without any hesitation. Without mercy.

I don't want to want that. My fantasy is something I'm trying to escape from, not sink down into. If I try this and hate it, that would be beyond horrible. It might be as traumatic as a real rape, and I would have walked right into it.

That's not what scares me, though. What scares me is that I'll try it and love it. Maybe I really am that fucked up.

I'd rather not find out. "Listen. I realize this is—an offer. Not a threat. But we're having an extremely unnerving conversation, and I wish we weren't."

Something subtle changes about Jonah's expression. I remember the way I was thinking about him earlier tonight—that this was a man who could be broken. Some of that vulnerability is visible now, if you look hard. "I would never force a woman against her will. Never. If someone held a gun to my head, I'd tell him to shoot. That's not a line I'd ever cross."

"But you fantasize about raping women."

He raises an eyebrow. "You fantasize about being raped. You know the line between dream and reality. So do I."

How can he not see how different it is? My fantasy comes from a very dark place, but a very real one. For Jonah, this is probably just a way to get off.

I should walk away. I should suck up my pride, go back into the party, grab my purse and keys, and get home as fast as I can. Tomorrow I ought to call Shay and tell her not to invite Professor Marks to any more parties.

Instead I stand there, breath catching in my throat. Jonah's eyes crinkle at the corners, a smile too dark to show. He knows exactly how aroused I am. The shame I feel is just fuel for my desire.

"What about you?" Jonah says. "Have you done this before? I doubt it."

Not the way he's talking about. "No."

He cocks his head, studying me intently. "We could start slow. Not too much at first. We'd work up to what you really need."

Jonah knows what I really need. And I can't stand him knowing.

"This is crazy." I tuck a few strands of hair behind my ears and straighten my camisole, trying to pull myself together. But I can't help noticing that my nipples are obviously hard beneath the thin black fabric; even though I haven't caught Jonah looking at my breasts, I know he's seen that too. "Like you said, it's just a fantasy. I think we should leave it there."

"Too bad. Would've been a wild ride."

It takes a lot of gall to be that confident about something this outrageous. To hell with being intimidated; to hell with being polite. "Where do you get off, asking me to do something that kinky when I hardly even know you? We're supposed to make plans to fuck before we've even touched?"

Jonah doesn't answer at first. Then he cups my face in one hand, rough and possessive, and brings his mouth to mine.

His kiss is hard. Insistent. His tongue pushes my lips apart. I don't want to kiss him back, but I do. My head falls back as he steps closer, claiming me with an arm around my waist. I surrender to his touch. He wakes up every nerve in my body—like I hadn't known I was sleepwalking until this second. Desire sears my mouth, my breasts, my cunt.

Just when it feels like my knees might buckle beneath me, Jonah suddenly pulls back. It throws me off balance, and I nearly stumble. He must see that. He must see me flushed and breathing hard. This man already knows how much power he has over me, and he wants even more.

Jonah says, "The ball's in your court."

With that he strolls back toward the house, like what happened is no big deal. I can only stand there and watch him go.

FIVE

I can't sleep.

Carmen's party wrapped up a couple of hours ago. I made up
for my freakout by staying until the very end, until I was helping
Carmen scoop up beer cans and toss empty Tostitos bags in the
trash. If anyone made a joke about anything, I laughed, even if I
didn't think it was funny. More sangria? Sure. The life of the
party: That's me. I pretended Geordie hadn't spilled my secret, and
for the most part people either didn't know or didn't care. The
only one who put me on edge was Mack, who kept staring at me.
Then again, Mack always stares.

Jonah must have left right after he kissed me. I can imagine him
walking back into the house, then out the front door, without even
saying good-bye. Apparently no one saw our clinch in the backyard. That's a relief. The last thing I need is Carmen asking me if
I think he's cute.

Cute. Jonah is—handsome. Attractive. Overpowering. Hot
as hell.

Not "cute."

I go onto the UT website to look him up. Earth sciences, Shay
said. A professor. That's virtually the last profession I would have

guessed for him. Maybe—SWAT team member. Navy SEAL. Hit man. Not a *teacher*.

When I pull up his faculty page, the photo there isn't reassuringly ordinary, with Jonah in glasses or a cardigan or whatever else the PhDs usually wear in their official pictures. Jonah is shown standing outside—someplace rocky, with a broad expanse of sky behind him. He wears khaki pants, a white shirt with rolled-up sleeves, and a frown, like he wanted to punch the photographer. The frown doesn't make him any less attractive. He doesn't look like any professor I've ever seen, unless you count Indiana Jones.

Professor of Seismology and Volcanology, says the caption. That makes more sense. Now that I study his photo carefully, the rocks beneath his feet look like volcanic stone—that is, if I remember a damn thing from that geology class I took four years ago. I can picture him on the edge of danger, wearing gear that can only barely protect him from the forces nearby, walking straight toward lava flow or an eruption without hesitating.

With a shiver I realize—Jonah is a man who doesn't give a damn about danger.

No more. If I want to get any sleep tonight, I need to stop this. I turn off my tablet and try to settle down. My skirt goes back in the closet; the camisole gets tossed in the hamper. A thin white sleeveless undershirt and panties are about all I can stand to sleep in during weather this hot. The cotton clings to me, so that I can pretend it's a second skin. Sometimes I sleep naked, but tonight I feel like I want to be more covered up. Less vulnerable.

My neighborhood is safe, but tonight I double-check the deadbolt on the door. I go to every window to make sure each one is locked. Instead of turning off all my lamps, I leave one burning—the one by the window that looks out onto the street. If anyone drives by, maybe he'll think I'm still awake.

By anyone, I mean Jonah.

He wouldn't come after me, I think. Mostly I believe this. Jonah swore that he would never force a woman against her will. When he said it, there was something about his voice—something raw, something real. I trust my instincts enough to know Jonah was telling the truth.

But what if he thought he wasn't forcing me? He knows I fantasize about rape. He said he wants to give me my fantasy. Would Jonah break in, thinking I was waiting for him? We talked about acting everything out. Breaking in could be part of that. I want to think he wouldn't take it this far—but with something like this, the lines between fantasy and reality could get blurred much too easily. If I protested, even if I fought, Jonah might believe that was only part of the game.

He said the ball was in my court. Surely that means the next move is up to me.

Why am I thinking about the next move? I turn over in bed, restless beneath the thin sheet. This idea is insane. I told Jonah as much. When I said no, I meant it, and that's the end.

What I don't know is whether Jonah accepts that this isn't going any further. Whether a guy who gets off fantasizing about rape can even understand *No*. Whether I can trust him. This man asked me to be completely vulnerable to him, to put myself completely in his power.

And he's already proved he won't misuse my powerlessness.

Jonah's had me vulnerable and at his mercy before—last Sunday night, when he pulled over to help me with my flat tire. We were out in the middle of nowhere. When I told him that I had help coming, he had to know it was a lie. He's a big man, obviously strong. If he'd wanted to take me against my will, he could have done it. I'm not sure even that lug wrench would have saved me.

Now I know his fantasies were just like mine. He saw me. He desired me. He envisioned pulling me into the back of his car, pinning me under his weight—

But he didn't. Jonah had me exactly where he wanted me, and all he did was help me out and send me on my way.

Does that mean I could trust him after all?

I don't know. I couldn't know unless we actually tried this.

Which is crazy. Unhealthy. Possibly even dangerous. And it gets me hotter than anything else ever has.

I glance over at the window nearest my bed. That's one I don't have to worry about locking; over the past eighty years or so, the window's been painted shut so many times that it's practically part of the wall. Nobody's coming through there, not without slicing himself to shreds on broken glass.

That's what makes it safe to imagine Jonah just outside.

In my mind, the window slides open for him easily. I'm lying here in my skimpy tank top, breathing hard, paralyzed by fear. I imagine Jonah sliding through as easily as a cat burglar, his feet barely making a sound as he makes contact with the floor and stands up, looming over me. He doesn't say a word. He doesn't have to. In this fantasy, I know that I have to do whatever he says. What he wants to do to me, I have to take.

Don't, whispers the rational part of my brain, the part that knows I shouldn't go here even in my own mind. My rape fantasies about faceless strangers—those are one thing. Thinking about Jonah, the man who wants to tie me up and take me down for real: That's a whole new level of fucked-up.

But I seem to have reached that level at last.

I wriggle out of my underwear, and my hand steals between my legs. As my fingers start circling, I close my eyes, the better to dream of Jonah standing over me.

He has a belt, a rope, something, and he winds it around my wrists. He ties the other end to one of the bedposts, then tugs my body down so that my arms are stretched above my head. I whimper in fear. It just makes him smile. He pulls off my panties, pushes my legs open so wide it almost hurts. I hear the purr of his zipper. It's too dark for me to see his cock, but I feel the rigid head pushing against me—into me—

In my mind I keep replaying that, the moment he plunges inside, the first shock of penetration, Jonah's satisfied groan, my own desperate cry. Over and over again, the first time every time, as fast as he could actually thrust—and then I come so hard it makes me dizzy. Everything is blurred and humming, and I know nothing but the pulse of my cunt as it contracts, wanting the man who isn't there.

As soon as I can breathe again, I say, "Oh, shit."

If just imagining Jonah Marks playing this role for me gets me off that hard, what would the reality be like? I don't want to find out.

Or maybe I do.

Either way, I'm not going to be able to stop thinking about Jonah anytime soon. So much for sleep.

My entire weekend goes something like this:

Get up, eat breakfast, exercise. Resolve not to think about Jonah so much today.

Get some work done in the studio.

Break for lunch; head home for sandwich. Start thinking about Jonah.

Masturbate to the thought of him, right in the middle of the day, groaning and panting on my bed.

Put my clothes back on. Run an errand, or see a friend. Pick out a funny card at the store to send to Libby, so she doesn't completely forget her Aunt Vivi. Have trouble remembering what to

buy at the store, or what to say next in a conversation, because my
mind is still chained to the shadow of Jonah Marks.

Go home. Get myself off again. Toss my wet panties in the
hamper and put on a fresh pair.

Try to think of something fun to do in the evening. Play video
games with friends. Listen to music in a club. Spend the whole
time imagining Jonah's hands on my skin.

Get into bed. Tell myself there's no way I can possibly need
another orgasm.

Think about Jonah. Give myself another orgasm. Fall asleep.

At least I don't remember any of my dreams over the weekend.
Sleep is the only time I have away from Jonah. I go through six
pairs of panties in two days.

On Monday morning, I'm awakened by my iPhone, which offers
up the day's appointments along with the song that rouses me. Squinting, I scroll through the appointments on autopilot, until I get to my
usual therapy time. Today it says, *Remember: Doreen in Florida.*

My therapist told me a month ago that she would miss two
weeks to visit her son in Tampa. I put it in my phone and otherwise
forgot about her absence. It's been a while since I was so fragile that
even a two-week break from therapy seemed like a crisis. Now,
though, I feel a small shiver of dismay. Doreen would have talked
some sense into me. She would have reminded me that I'm trying
to get further away from this fantasy, not to wrap myself up in it
until it dominates my whole life. I would have walked out of her
office refreshed, stable, and ready to get back to normal.

Instead, Doreen is half a country away, and Jonah is very, very
close.

I throw on cropped pants and a simple white top, slide my feet
into sandals, tug my hair into a ponytail, and drive to the university.
As usual, merging into the thick campus traffic is a pain; we wind
up with a Los Angeles–worthy traffic jam virtually every day. UT

Austin is one of the biggest college campuses in the nation—more than fifty thousand students, nearly twenty-five thousand faculty and staff, with 150 buildings spread out across more than four hundred acres. All around me in traffic are undergrads driving to class. Even the lucky few who get to live on campus are sometimes so far from their classrooms that they take their cars instead of walking.

That said, every college is really a few hundred smaller colleges all wrapped into one. Each building, each department, has its own personality and its own cast of characters. I don't venture far from the School of Fine Art, as a general rule.

No doubt this is why I walk up to the building to see Geordie sitting on the metal bench out front. He holds a piece of paper, which he's crumpled slightly between tense fingers. When he sees me, his eyes widen. Even though he's clearly been waiting for me, he dreads what I'm going to say.

He should.

As I walk up to him, Geordie gets to his feet. "Vivienne, I'm so, so bloody sorry about Friday night."

"You ought to be." I cross my arms. "Do you even remember what happened? Or did Carmen have to tell you later?"

He scratches his head with his free hand. "I'm not denying it's a bit blurry. But I remember."

"That was personal, Geordie. As personal as it gets. No matter how drunk you were, you should never, ever have let those words come out of your mouth."

"I know that. I do." He looks so earnest. Almost heartbroken, like what he said hurt him more than it did me. Geordie always *wants* to do the right thing; he just doesn't always get there.

This time, though, I'm not letting him off the hook. "I don't discuss what our sex life was like. Not even with my best friends, and definitely not with strangers at a party. If we're going to stay friends, you have to do better than this. Do you understand?"

Slowly, Geordie nods. The two of us stand there in awkward silence for a few moments before he straightens out the piece of paper. "I felt so bad about this that I wrote you a poem."

". . . a poem?"

"Yes." He stands almost at attention, like a politician about to give a speech. "The title is, 'I Am a Complete and Total Shit.'"

I'm not going to laugh. I'm not.

Geordie reads: *"I am a complete and total shit / sometimes I act like a stupid git / when I become a blabbermouth / all my relationships go south / forgive this lowly wretched wanker / or I'll be sad, nothing rhymes with wanker."*

I can't help it anymore. Giggles bubble up inside me, and Geordie's worried face gentles into a smile of relief. I never could stay mad at him for long. "Please tell me there are no more verses," I say.

"I felt I'd achieved poetic perfection in just six lines. Less is more, you know?"

"Yeah. For instance, less intimate details about our relationship, more enjoyable parties."

He puts one hand on my arm—not a romantic move, just a reassuring one. "I swear to you, I'll never reveal anything that personal about us again. Never. There's not enough gin in the world to get me that drunk."

I sigh. "Okay. But you're on probation."

"My sentence is just and fair, Your Honor." Geordie squeezes my arm, then steps back. "So, I've got to get to class."

The law school isn't particularly close. "Will you have to run it?"

"Possibly. But we're all right?"

". . . sure."

With a grin, Geordie turns away to lope across the green. He's older than almost all the other students, but the way he moves—running, his longish brown hair flopping with every bound—he looks more like a kid than any of them. Shaking my head, I watch him go.

The teaching assistants all share a space on the fourth floor. The elevators only go to three. I take the steps the whole way—it's less irritating. Our designated office is as grand as you'd expect: a long narrow room that was probably originally designed as a closet, outfitted with the oldest, most beat-up desks that haven't already been thrown out as scrap. I don't really mind. Most of my work is done at home or in the studio anyway. Besides, even as low as I am on the totem pole, I still get to rely on the department secretary.

"Well, hello there," Kip says as I walk into the main office. "Not looking nearly as slinky as you did Friday night."

"Oh, no! I meant to wear lingerie to impress my two P.M. class." I smack my forehead with the heel of my hand. "Do you have any pasties lying around? Or a G-string?"

"Wouldn't you like to know?" Kip gives me a sidelong glance; his quick fingers never stop typing for a second. "I thought you might want to look nice for Geordie. Don't think I didn't see him out there, so spare me the sarcasm."

"Geordie and I are just friends now, remember?"

"Mmmm-hmm," Kip hums, making it clear he doesn't believe me.

When Kip Rucker joined our department last year, I wasn't sure what to think. Our previous secretary was a grandmotherly lady who wore appliquéd sweatshirts themed for every holiday, including Arbor Day. Kip, on the other hand, wears skinny jeans, oversized designer T-shirts, and nail polish. It takes courage to be as out as Kip is, here in Austin; we might be the bluest city in the great red state of Texas, but this is still Texas. So I admired his guts from the start, but couldn't imagine him fitting in. He has a big mouth and a bigger attitude and doesn't give a damn what anyone in the world thinks of him. Usually this is not great secretary material.

Within three weeks, Kip had restructured our entire office. Suddenly we'd become efficient. He turned around work faster and more effortlessly than any of us had dreamed possible. Even the old coffeemaker vanished, replaced by a newer model that produced actual coffee instead of blackish sludge.

When we asked him how he managed that, he said he knows people in food services. We soon learned that Kip knows people in every single department of the university. Somehow, all these people seem to owe him a favor. I think Kip could take over as dean if he set his mind to it. Possibly as dictator. I'm just glad he's on our side.

This morning, Kip's nails are cherry red. I take his hand for a second. "Nice shade."

"Thanks. You can borrow the bottle if you want."

"Not today. Maybe sometime."

I go through the side door into my skinny little suboffice. Neither of the other TAs has come in yet; Marvin's got class right now, and Keiko never puts in office time before noon. That means I have a little while to myself.

The computer chimes on. Our home page is the university's site, so it only takes a couple of keystrokes to get into faculty—and to bring up the page for Jonah Marks.

Once again I look at his picture. I've spent all weekend imagining his face near mine—giving me orders, calling me names—but the sight of him hasn't lost its power over me. If anything, he overwhelms me even more.

Maybe that's because he's closer than ever.

Before I can chicken out, I click the link for his university e-mail. A letter form pops out, Jonah's address at the top, ready for me to type. I don't bother putting anything in the body of the e-mail; everything I have to say to him fits in the subject line.

I type, Let's talk.

And then I hit send.

SIX

Here in Austin, most bars are raucous places meant to serve either the live-music scene, the crowds of college students with fake IDs, or both. This hotel bar, however, is more sophisticated, more low-key. Instead of the usual blaring alt-rock, R&B music plays softly from hidden speakers around the room. Pale leather couches and chairs cluster in various nooks to encourage conversation and create privacy. The other people here are mostly adults, and nearly as many people hold coffee cups as wineglasses.

I hesitate before I order my own drink. It feels important to keep my head—but I'm already nervous. Caffeine would tip me over the brink. Pinot noir it is.

The couch tucked in the farthest, most intimate area of the bar is available, so I claim it. I came here early on purpose, so I'd have a few moments to collect myself before Jonah arrives. Now I'm wishing I hadn't. While I sit here, I have nothing to do but freak myself out.

It's not too late to walk out of here. E-mail Jonah, tell him you can't make it, go out to your car and drive the hell away while you still can.

I don't move.

By now I'm used to the second-guessing. I've been doing that

ever since I sent that e-mail to Jonah two days ago. His reply was
simply this address, this day, this time—and the line, "Just to talk."
At first I found that maddening. He couldn't express surprise,
enthusiasm, doubt, *anything*? Not one question, not one detail,
about what he's thinking? Then I realized this conversation is one
that has to happen in person. We have to be completely clear about
this, in every detail. Otherwise everything could go terribly wrong.

Is it even possible for something this screwed up to go well? I
doubt it. Maybe I'll regret this. The dangers are very real, and I
haven't lost sight of any of them. This fantasy that dominates
me—it's sick, and it's twisted, but it's not going away. Fighting it
hasn't done any good. So I'm giving in. Surrendering.

I take a deep drink of my wine, close my eyes, and take a deep
breath, willing myself to be calm. It works until I open my eyes
again and see Jonah.

He walks straight toward me as if he'd known where I would
be sitting before he even came through the door. Like me, Jonah
dressed to fit in at this upscale place—charcoal gray slacks cut
perfectly to accentuate the taper of his waist, and a black linen
shirt that drapes across his powerful body. My hand goes to the
neckline of my plum-colored wrap dress. It's not that revealing,
but I feel exposed before his knowing gaze.

"I wasn't sure you'd show," Jonah says.

Hello to you too. If he can cut to the chase, so can I. "Nearly
bolted for the door a couple of times. But here I am."

That wins me his fierce version of a smile.

Jonah sits down beside me—but a couple of feet away, as though
I were a business colleague instead of the woman he wants to fuck.
Then again, this isn't foreplay. Nothing's going to happen tonight.
If we're going to go ahead, we need boundaries. Definitions. I
might be crazy enough to do this, but I'm not crazy enough to do
it without any rules.

"How was your day?" I say.

He gives me a look. Like he said at Carmen's, the less we know about each other's lives, the better. This is not a first date.

"Sorry." I take another sip of wine, then put down the glass. If I drink a little more every time I feel on edge tonight, I'll get plastered. "No details. No chitchat. We shouldn't go there."

"It's okay. This is difficult." He pauses a moment before adding, "Are you scared?"

Deep breath. Honest answer. "Yes and no. I believe you aren't going to do anything without my permission. But what we're doing feels a little like jumping off a cliff. I've had this fantasy since—since always, but I never thought I'd act it out with a stranger—"

At that moment, a waiter appears by our sofa. Why do bar waiters only show up when you least want them around? Offhandedly Jonah says, "Bring me whatever she's having."

I don't think he's even looked at my glass. What if I had some ridiculous tropical drink, the kind of thing served in a pineapple with pink straws and paper umbrellas? The thought of someone as serious as Jonah sipping one of those makes me smile. Finally I'm able to relax a little—but not much.

As soon as the waiter hurries off, Jonah turns to me. "What would it take to make you feel safe?"

I like that he asked this. But how do I answer?

Cut to the chase, I remind myself. Jonah's blunt honesty is the only way to go. "I'd need you to wear condoms. Unless you want to show me your medical records."

Jonah nods. "I can get those for you. Can you show me test results too?"

It hadn't even occurred to me that Jonah also might be concerned about that. "Um. Yeah, sure."

"No rush," he says. "I don't mind wearing a condom at first. Makes it last longer."

My cheeks flush as I envision Jonah inside me, pounding me, going on and on and on without mercy—

Jonah must know what I'm thinking, because he tilts his head as if he's relishing the effect he has on me. He murmurs, "What else?"

Another sip of wine steadies me enough to answer. "I wouldn't want you to tie me up. Not the first time, anyway."

He smiles. "I like that you're thinking about the future. I'll have plenty of chances to give you what you want."

It hadn't even occurred to me before today that Jonah might have been considering a onetime fling. Now that I think about it, that makes more sense than assuming we'd keep playing out this scenario. But I've wanted this too long, too much, to assume one night will be enough to get it out of my system. If Jonah's the right partner for this fantasy, then we have a chance I don't intend to waste.

Already I sense that one taste of Jonah Marks won't be enough.

"Yes." I meet his eyes evenly. "Assuming we decide we like it."

"I think we will." My God, his smile right now—it's hungry, and animal, and I know he's imagining having me. This instant. The knowledge shakes me in the best possible way.

The waiter shows up with Jonah's wine. We both fall silent just as long as it takes for Jonah to accept the glass and toss the waiter a twenty. "No change."

This wine was only $10 a glass. The waiter brightens. Me, I'm glad I bought my own drink. I don't want to owe anything to Jonah Marks. Yet.

As soon as we're alone again, Jonah says, "We should talk about what you don't want the first time versus what you don't want, ever. If we set the ground rules up front, it's going to be better for both of us."

That makes sense. I've been thinking this through ever since he made his audacious offer, and by now I think I know what to say.

That doesn't make it easy to get the words out. "Well. Let's see. I already said that I don't want you to tie me up the first time, and I guess we worked out the safe-sex thing . . ."

Jonah nods, a touch impatient. Although I never noticed him moving, he seems to have edged closer to me on the sofa. Our knees are nearly touching, now, and his gaze is locked on mine. My uncertainty is a turn-on for him, I realize. How could it be any other way?

Knowing he feeds off my fear makes me even more nervous. It takes me a few seconds to continue. "Okay. Some things I don't want you to do, ever—one, no weapons. If you have a knife or a gun or something, it's not going to be hot for me. It's going to scare me to death."

Jonah looks startled. He must never have considered that. "No weapons. Absolutely."

I count the next point off on my fingers. "Two, I realize I might get—banged around during all this, but please try not to actually injure me or cause me serious pain. I'm not a masochist; I don't get off on that kind of thing."

"I'm not a sadist, so that works."

Maybe he's not a sadist in the physical sense. Emotionally? He has to be. How can you dream about raping women and not enjoy hurting people, in soul if not in body? I guess if you don't understand what that does to a woman—how badly rape screws with your head, the scars it leaves—you could imagine that your pleasure wouldn't cause someone else lasting pain.

For a moment I'm angry. I want to tell Jonah everything he doesn't understand. Make him know how terrible it is.

But I need him to be fucked up, don't I? The only possible partner for these games is someone as bent as I am.

"All right," I say. "Third, you don't film this. You don't make an audio recording, and you don't take photographs."

He looks disappointed. That's something he wanted, then. "I'd never put anything like that online, or show it to anybody."

"I believe you, but stuff like that can fall into the wrong hands. Remember the scandal with all those movie stars last year? Some 'revenge porn' sites actually hack people's computers and cell phones. They steal the images if they can."

This is when I learn what Jonah Marks looks like when he's angry. His expression darkens, as do his gray eyes. His body tenses, like he wants to throw a punch but isn't going to let the guy know when it's coming. "Any man who would do that to a woman is scum."

I nod. It's so strange, the division within him—how he can simultaneously hate men who take advantage of women and yet fantasize about being one of them. "So no recordings, no pictures?"

He gives in gracefully. "None."

"Okay. Finally—this is my last not-ever thing, I think—" I glance around the bar to be sure nobody has wandered closer while I was distracted. Nobody has, but I lower my voice anyway. "Please don't come on me."

Jonah blinks, as if he's surprised. I guess he would be. We're talking about getting as kinky as anyone can, yet I don't want him to do something that ordinary.

I don't. I really, really don't.

At last he says, "Okay. I won't."

If he's not coming on me, he'll come in me. I imagine him in my mouth. Suddenly I want to taste him so badly I nearly moan.

I try to cover how flustered I am. "So. What about you? Do you have any limits I should know about?"

The answer I expect is *No*. He's going to be the one in control; what limits could he possibly need? Instead Jonah answers me immediately. "The main thing is that if we're ever discovered—if someone thinks what's happening is real and steps in or calls the police—you have to set them straight. I don't care if you're ashamed of this fantasy. You tell them the truth, no matter what."

"Of course. I would do that anyway." I hadn't even realized what a risk Jonah was taking. He studies my face carefully, and I know he's trying to figure out whether I'm being honest about backing him up. More gently I add, "We have to trust each other or this doesn't work."

"Right." Jonah goes back to his points like he hadn't paused. "I told you I wasn't a sadist. Well, I'm not a masochist either. Sometimes I realize you might want to fight back—and I might like that. If you struggled." The way he smiles at me makes me go hot all over. I shift on the sofa, and I can feel how slick I am between my thighs. "A few scratches, a slap, that's fine. A black eye or broken arm I have to explain to people, that's not fine."

"Got it." Like I could take out Jonah Marks. If we ever fought for real, he'd have me down within seconds.

He takes a deep breath. "Last thing, never call me Daddy."

I stare at him. It's all I can do not to laugh.

Obviously he sees my amusement. His scowl deepens. "Some women say that, in bed."

"I know." I swallow the last of my smile.

"If I ask you to talk, I'll tell you what to call me. And you'll say it."

The urge to laugh vanishes. In its place are other, more primal urges. I want this man to give me orders. I want him to tell me what to do.

If Jonah accepted my weird limit, I can accept his. " 'Daddy'— that's not one of my things. So we're good."

"And for the first time only—" Jonah considers for a moment. "I want to tell you what to say."

"Do you mean, like, a script?"

"No. I mean, I'll tell you to shut up, and you'll do it. You'll only

speak when I let you, and only say what I tell you to say. We can
get more—improvisational, as we go on. But this time, I want that
much control. Will you give it to me?"

Again I feel that quiver in my belly, fear and wanting inter-
twined. "Yes, I will." I've given him so much power over me
already. A few words won't make any difference.

Jonah nods, satisfied. We have our ground rules.

The waiter circles by again hopefully, but our wineglasses are
still half full. I've held true to my plan not to drink too much tonight.
Not only will I be driving home, but I also think it's important to
keep my head.

Then again, I'm here making plans for a guy I hardly know to
pretend to rape me. It could be argued I lost my head a while ago.

"We'll want a safe word," Jonah says.

I've heard of a safe word, of course, but I always thought it was
strictly an S&M thing. It makes sense for us, though. We're
already talking about scenarios in which I might be physically
fighting him off. Jonah needs to know what it would sound like if
I said no for real. "Silver."

"Silver?"

"That's the safe word. Silver." I chose it off the top of my head,
but now I like it. "What do we do if I want you to stop, but I can't
talk?"

Either because he has me gagged, or because his cock is in my
mouth . . .

"Then snap your fingers. You should always be able to do
that." Jonah smiles slowly. He knows he has me where he wants
me. "Even in handcuffs."

I can't speak. My breaths are short and fast between parted
lips. Part of me is terrified by the thought of this man putting me
in handcuffs. The other part of me wishes he'd do it this second.
Cuff me, drag me out of here and do God knows what for hours—

"Don't worry. Like you said, I won't use handcuffs the first time," he murmurs. "Or ropes, or any other kind of restraints. I realize that's something I'll have to earn."

My voice is husky as I say, "I'd like it if we got there. Someday."

"Me too. As soon as you're ready, but not before." Jonah extends his arm along the back of the couch. He doesn't put his arm around me. Instead he brushes the curve of my shoulder with his fingertips. The touch sets me on fire. "Anything else you don't want when we get together the first time? Be specific. Because there are a *lot* of things I want to do to you. If I should avoid any of them, tell me now, so I don't get my hopes up."

Once again I glance around; this is something else I don't want overheard. "This time—um—no anal sex."

I blush from even having said that out loud.

Jonah's fingers stroke the curve of my shoulder again. "That's a shame."

"Just not the first time or two. Okay? If this turns out to be too scary for me, too much, then I don't want that to be a part of it."

He nods, comprehending. "You haven't done that before, have you?"

"No," I whisper.

"But you'd give it to me eventually? That gives me something to work for. Something else to earn."

In all honesty, I find the idea of anal sex intimidating. It's not something I've ever wanted to do for my own sake. None of the guys I've dated had much interest in trying it, which was fine with me.

Still, in my fantasies, it's often there. A rapist wouldn't care what I wanted or didn't want. He'd make me take it.

Just like Jonah eventually will.

"Anything else?" Jonah says. When I shake my head no, he straightens, once again businesslike. "Friday night, then. Unless you have plans—you don't? Good. Here's what I want you to do. Go to a hotel; I'll let you know which one. I will have paid for a room in your name. Check in. Get comfortable. Then, around eight P.M., go down to the hotel bar. Have a couple of drinks. A couple too many." His eyes burn with intensity. He's thought out every word of this. "I'll be there. I'll try to pick you up. But you're not interested. When you walk out of the bar, I'll follow you. At the door of your hotel room, you try to ditch me. I won't let you."

It's as though Jonah has looked down into the core of me and seen exactly what I want. "What then?"

"That's up to me."

Oh, God. If I could come just from hearing a man talk, that would have done it. Hearing Jonah make plans for my body has me more turned on than most guys' foreplay ever has. "Up to you," I repeat.

"One last thing." Jonah leans even nearer, so close I think he's about to kiss me. Instead he murmurs, "How do I make you come?"

My cheeks burn hot, as if we'd been overheard by everyone in the bar. "That should, um, take care of itself." When he frowns, I have to explain. "Most women don't get off just on penetration, but I can almost always get there."

Of course, I get there by fantasizing about being raped by a man, even while my partner is still inside me. When Jonah and I are together, that fantasy will turn real.

"Perfect." He smiles. "By the way, that night? Don't wear clothes you're interested in ever wearing again."

Before I can even fully envision Jonah tearing my clothes off, he stands up. I'm caught off guard. "Wait. You're just—leaving?"

"Unless we have anything else to discuss." He tugs down the tail of his shirt—to cover his hard-on, I realize. Seeing how badly he wants me makes me want him back even more. Jonah, however, acts like he doesn't give a damn. "If you have any more questions, ask now."

I know this is the furthest thing from a first date. I know we agreed that the less we found out about each other as individuals, the better the role-playing would be. But I didn't realize he was cold enough to walk off like this.

Then again, cold is what I need. Cold and unyielding.

Yet one question is difficult to set aside. "Aren't you going to tell me why you want this?"

Jonah pauses, only for a moment. "Are you going to tell me why you want it?"

No, I'm not.

So I lift my chin. "Friday night at eight?"

"Friday night."

He turns and walks away without once looking back.

SEVEN

"Earth to Vivienne."

I realize I'm still sitting at Arturo and Shay's table, my half-finished dinner in front of me. Both of them are staring at me—half worried, half amused.

"Sorry," I say. "My graduate work is taking over my brain these days. Why not? It already took over my life."

The words come too quickly, too easily. That might be the only thing my mother ever taught me to her satisfaction: how to lie.

Arturo rises from his chair. "Sounds like someone needs a beer."

"No, really, I'm fine."

"I'm not," Shay chimes in. "Get me a ginger ale while you're up, would you?"

He sticks his tongue out at her, which makes her giggle, then goes to fetch her a can of Canada Dry.

It is not yet Friday night, I remind myself. It is Thursday. The hotel and Jonah and everything else that happens tomorrow is for *tomorrow*. Today you're with your friends. Act like it.

Shay is so proud of this meal, too. I'm their first dinner guest in their new place—"trying to make a home of a rented house," as the song says. She's into comfort foods these days, learning to make old-fashioned, Grandma's-house stuff like pot roast, pound cake, and tonight's chicken pot pie. Apparently that's a hipster thing, all the home-style recipes. This chicken pot pie is probably ironic. It's also delicious, though, so yay for hipsters.

We're eating at a card table set up at the far end of the kitchen. Whatever money they have for furniture is going toward the nursery. For the rest of the house, Shay says they'll decorate with Salvation Army and Goodwill stuff, or even dumpster diving. (That works better in a college town than it does most places. You wouldn't believe the things that get thrown out by nineteen-year-olds who didn't have to pay for it.) So far the house looks pretty bare.

Yet this place already feels like a home. It's illuminated by the way Arturo and Shay care for each other, the hopes they have for the future. I feel more comfortable here than I've felt in my parents' house—my childhood home—for a very long time.

I would say as much to Carmen, if she were here. Supposedly she has a bunch of test papers to grade. My guess is that she's still not ready to see Shay as the "woman of the house," but surely she's going to get over that soon.

"Are you sure you're all right?" Shay pats my shoulder. "I think you're pushing yourself. Not taking enough time to rest."

I try to put her at ease. "I'm in the heart of my research right now. It takes a lot of concentration."

Which is true. Which is why it's not exactly helpful to spend virtually every waking moment thinking about getting banged by Jonah Marks.

"I know you have to work hard," Arturo says as he returns to the table, putting Shay's ginger ale in front of her. "But that just means you have to play hard, too."

Did he just say—

"Are you choking?" Shay thumps my back. "Gone down the wrong way, hasn't it?"

"I'm good," I say, and I manage not to laugh.

By Friday night, I don't feel like laughing.

Whenever I let my mind rush ahead to the hotel room, my whole body trembles with fear and anticipation. I don't know which emotion is stronger. Right now I hardly know which way is up.

I've taken a couple of fail-safe steps. Carmen and I have made plans to go to the farmer's market tomorrow morning. If I don't show up at her place by ten A.M., she'll start looking for me immediately. I also scheduled an e-mail that will go out to her, Arturo, and Shay in three days, if I don't delete it. The e-mail reads: If something has happened to me, the police should look for Jonah Marks.

Of course I don't think that's going to be necessary. If I believed Jonah was definitely dangerous, I wouldn't go to the hotel in the first place.

. . . but he's a little dangerous. Enough for the fear to feel very real.

Rush hour. I drive against the traffic into the heart of downtown Austin, to the tallest hotel in the city, which is usually peopled by visiting celebrities, wealthy tourists, or corporate clients. Jonah didn't skimp. He's arranged an exquisite locale for his first attack.

"We have you for one night?" the check-in clerk says brightly.

"Yes. Just one key." How do I sound so calm? The role-playing has already begun.

The room is luxurious in a sophisticated, minimalist sort of way—a broad bed with a white duvet and half a dozen pillows, a long desk of polished wood for the business guests, and soft mood lighting shining from sconces carefully placed on the cream-colored walls. It's on one of the higher floors, and the windows look out over the cityscape. I admire the view while the sun sets, then close the curtains, so nobody can look in.

Getting here three hours early was overkill. Although I try to watch TV, my mind refuses to focus on the lights and sounds in front of me. Finally I give up and start getting ready. Tonight I want to take my time with it—to carefully put myself together so Jonah can pull me apart.

A long hot shower relaxes me slightly; the sugar scrub I brought softens my skin. I dry my hair upside down so that it will be bouncier and wilder than I usually wear it.

I'd contemplated getting a bikini wax but ultimately decided against it. Better if I seem—unprepared. Still, I use the electric clippers to trim everything neatly. Then I step into a pair of white lace panties. No bra.

For Christmas, my mother gave me this perfume she likes and I don't. It's one of those sultry, overpowering 1980s fragrances, the kind of thing that comes in a purple bottle. The scent might as well say *fuck me* out loud. Tonight is the first time I've ever worn it. I apply my makeup like my older sister Chloe taught me, the way I almost never bother with. Most days, powder, mascara, and tinted lip balm do the trick. Tonight, I go with a smoky eye and shimmery blush that contours my cheekbones. The lipstick I wear is dark glossy red.

I bought this dress online last year, on impulse, goaded by the deep final-sale discount and the website's red letters reading *Only One Left!* When it arrived, though, I realized it looked less glamorous, more trashy. The filmy, raspberry-colored fabric clings to every curve, and the hem barely covers my ass. Two slender straps hold it in place.

Should be easy for Jonah to tear through those.

Simple diamond stud earrings—anything dangly would just get in the way later. Finally I step into my silver strappy sandals. Done.

I stand in front of the mirror, trying to see myself as Jonah will see me when he walks into the bar. Everything about me says *sex*. This is the kind of outfit that jackass rape apologists say means a woman is "asking for it."

Tonight, I actually am. I'm asking for it.

In the hotel bar, I feel conspicuous. Certainly I stand out among the various travelers, most of whom are wearing dark, comfortable stuff that packs well. As I slide onto my bar stool, I have to cross my legs to keep from flashing the entire room. The bartender gives me an up-and-down look before saying, "What can I do for you?" Probably he thinks I'm a hooker searching for clients.

"I'll have a cosmopolitan, please." Not my usual poison. It seems like the kind of thing a girl in a trashy pink dress would order.

The bartender gets it to me quickly, just like he does the second one I order. I haven't yet eaten dinner, so that's more than enough to make my head swim. "Want another?" the bartender says.

I start to shake my head no, but then a deep voice says, "She'll have one more. On me."

Jonah is here.

How did he get in without my seeing him? Then I realize I've been staring at the way I came in—the entrance for hotel guests—and he walked through the door from the street. He's dressed more casually than I am, in black jeans and a long-sleeved white shirt, cuffs pushed up nearly to his elbow. Jonah doesn't look like a guy who's here to cruise for women. He looks ready for action. Ready for anything.

Am I ready? Now that he's here next to me, I don't know. Yet I stay where I am.

He's going to try to pick me up. My job is to shoot him down.

"One more cosmo for the lady?" the bartender asks, obviously giving me a chance to turn Jonah down. I don't say anything.

Jonah answers for me. "One more. And bring me a scotch and soda."

Once the bartender's busy making our drinks, I speak to Jonah for the first time. "Thanks."

He slides onto the bar stool next to mine. "You're visiting town?"

I didn't plan out a story for being here, so I keep it simple. "Just passing through."

"On your own?"

"Mmm-hmm." I turn my head from Jonah to accept my third cosmo. I don't dare drink much of it, but I lift the glass, clink it against his tumbler of scotch, and say, "Cheers."

"Cheers." Jonah's gaze rakes up and down my body, like he's already claiming me for his own.

The bartender hurries off to deal with other guests, which leaves us alone.

"Hard to believe, a beautiful woman like you alone on a Friday night," Jonah murmurs.

I shrug. One of the straps of my dress slides nearer the edge of my shoulder. "Happens to everybody, once in a while."

With two fingers, Jonah pushes the strap back into place. His touch is so hot it seems to burn. "You wouldn't have to be alone any longer than you wanted."

"Sometimes we all need to be alone."

"I can think of something else you need."

Arousal and fear both spike within me at once. My head reels. "I'm doing just fine."

Jonah smirks. "You must get this a lot. Attention from men, guys trying to pick you up. I think you like it."

"Why would you think that?"

"That dress doesn't say 'leave me alone.'" He looks down at my legs, exposed almost to my ass. "It gives a different message."

"The only message is—good night." With that, I take my one sip of that last cosmo, then hop off the bar stool. Although the floor is slightly unsteady beneath my feet, I'm able to walk out smoothly, as if I'm paying no attention to Jonah behind me.

But I can hear every footstep as he follows me out.

My heart is pounding so hard that you can *see* it—the front of my dress rising and falling with my pulse. My cunt is so tight and hot that it almost hurts. This is it. This is really it.

Then my brain suddenly wakes up and takes over, as if someone had thrown a glass of ice water in my face. *Are you really doing this? This is dangerous. You hardly know this man. Do you realize how fast your fantasy could become a very ugly reality?*

I push the elevator button as Jonah comes to stand next to me. He smiles slowly. "Headed up to your room too, huh?"

"Yeah." Nervously I tuck a lock of hair behind my ear. We're the only ones who get on the elevator. After I push sixteen, I glance at Jonah again. "Your room is on the sixteenth floor too?"

"They've got lots of rooms on the sixteenth floor. Right?"

I don't answer.

Silver. Say silver. End it here and now. Jonah might be pissed off, but he'd walk away. Wouldn't he? If he didn't, at least people would be around. I could yell and scream, and somebody would call hotel security. I could pay him back for the room. It's not too late to stop this. It's not too late.

We reach the sixteenth floor. I fish my key card out of my glittery evening clutch as I go to the door. Jonah walks right behind me, saying nothing.

I slide the key card in and out. The light turns green. As I open the door, Jonah leans against the wall just beside me. "Looks like you really are on your own."

It's not too late—

But it is. It's been too late for me for a long time. This is who I am. This is what I want. It's time to finally face it.

"Excuse me." I walk inside. As I'd expected, Jonah follows me.

He shuts the door hard behind us, and we're alone. I ought to protest. I should keep playing my role. Instead all I can do is stare at him, standing between me and escape.

Jonah stands there for a long moment, breathing hard. He's completely turned on—completely ready to claim me—and yet he says nothing. I realize he's giving me one more chance to speak up. One last out.

I don't take it.

"What are you doing?" I manage to whisper.

He grins, slow and hot. "Taking what's mine."

EIGHT

Jonah backs me against the wall.

"You like being a cocktease, don't you?" He slams his hands on either side of me, so that I'm imprisoned by his arms. His muscular body is only inches from mine. "Dress like a whore, get guys to buy you drinks, and then leave them hanging. That's your game. You're not doing that to me."

"Please—" I can't think of anything else to say. I've almost never been this scared, and I know I've never been this turned on.

"Shut up," Jonah says. His voice is quiet, contemptuous. "You don't talk. There are better things you can do with that mouth."

This is what he wanted—my total silence, his total control. I surrender without a word.

He grips my wrist. I can feel the pressure all the way through my flesh to my bones. A whimper escapes my lips; Jonah ignores it. He presses my palm against the erection that's straining the fabric of his jeans, then rubs it up and down the length of his cock. His flesh is hot even through the denim. "Feel that? You did that. You got me hard, so now you have to get me off."

Oh, my God, he's *huge*. Can I even take that inside me?

He's going to rip me apart. I ought to be scared. Instead I'm so wet it's slicking my thighs.

"Take it out," Jonah says. "Take my cock out of my pants. Do it."

My hands shake as I fumble with the zipper, open the front of his boxers. His cock slips free, jutting into my palm. He's thick, too.

"Lick your lips. I want your lips wet when they're on my cock."

My lips are still sweet from the cosmopolitans. As my tongue traces around my mouth, Jonah breathes out, hard, like I'd just punched him in the gut.

One of his hands fists in my hair. I wince, but Jonah just smiles. He pulls me down by the hair until I fall to my knees. His enormous dick is in my face.

He growls, "Open your goddamned mouth."

I have no choice. I have to obey.

Jonah pushes forward. His girth forces me to open my jaw all the way; it's all I can do even to get him inside my mouth. The velvety head is almost into my throat, and I feel like he could choke me like this. I can hardly breathe.

"Suck it."

I try. He's so huge that I can hardly use my tongue, but I bob my head back and forth, doing the best I can.

"Look at me." Jonah's voice is low. "You look at my face when you suck my cock, do you hear me?"

My eyes go up to his. He's breathing hard and unbuttoning his shirt with his free hand. The white fabric falls aside, exposing the muscles of his powerful chest. His jaw is set, his lips curled in a mocking smile. The hand in my hair tightens further, until his grip borders on pain.

"Harder. And use your fucking hands. Do me like you mean it."

I suck harder. Salty pre-come slicks the inside of my mouth, moistens my lips. With one hand I brace myself against his leg—his thigh muscles rock-hard. With the other I start working him, twisting my fist around him with every stroke, pumping his cock. I can feel every vein, every throb.

"I'm teaching you a lesson," he says. "You don't dress like a whore and go to bars unless you want to get fucked."

Pre-come floods my mouth, and I think he's going to finish any moment. Instead he pulls out, leaving me coughing and gasping for air. Jonah's so hard it's got to hurt—his cock swollen and dark—but he holds me there a few long seconds.

He doesn't want to come yet. That would be letting me off easy.

"Pull your dress down," he says. "I want to see those tits."

I tug down the front of my dress, just enough to expose my nipples. With his free hand he slaps at my breast. The impact stings, and I flinch.

Jonah laughs. "You don't like that? You're going to get a lot more than that before I'm through with you." He pushes his fingers between my lips, forcing them open again for his cock. "Now I'm going to fuck your mouth."

His other hand cups the back of my head, and he starts thrusting. I can't suck; I can't do anything but take it. He's so big that this almost hurts—makes my jaw ache. His cock fills me all the way to my throat. I gag around him, but he just keeps going.

"You'll think twice before you tease the next guy, won't you?" Jonah thrusts in harder as he tugs my hair. "Next time a guy treats you nice, you'll know how to behave."

Just when I think I can't take this one moment longer, he pulls out. As I gasp for breath, Jonah tows me upright by my hair. Once again I stand before him on shaky legs. My heavy makeup must be smeared all over my face.

With one hand he palms my breast and squeezes so hard it makes me cry out. Then he reaches under my dress, into my panties. Jonah's fingers push inside me, a touch meant to insult and bruise.

"Thought you were too good to go to bed with me?" His smile has never looked fiercer. "Then you don't get a fucking bed."

He pushes me backward so hard I nearly fall. I stagger against the desk, and Jonah shoves my shoulders down so that I'm splayed on top of it. The wood is hard against my back. Both of his hands grip the top of my dress, and he tears it almost in two. Pink fabric slides down on either side of my body, exposing me completely to his contemptuous gaze.

It only takes one hand to rip my panties apart.

Jonah works so quickly that I only realize he's putting on the condom when he's done. His hands shove my knees apart, and then the head of his cock bumps against my cunt. I realize he's teasing me with it. Making me more afraid. Making me want it.

He whispers, "This is what you get, bitch." And then he thrusts inside, savagely hard.

Oh, fuck. *Fuck.* He's so big—enormous—he's splitting me apart. The pain is greater than the pleasure, and I push ineffectually at his shoulders. Jonah just grabs my hands and pins them against the desk.

Silver. The word floats up in my mind again, and I nearly say it. But that's the moment when the pleasure eclipses the pain. Jonah's cock feels so good inside me, filling me up completely, blotting out everything else in the world.

He starts to move—slowly, at first. Still teasing me. My legs fall apart even wider; my whole body is giving in to him. Jonah owns me now.

He's speeding up, moment by moment. "You got what you deserved, didn't you?" he pants. "Tell me."

"I—I got what I deserved." My voice sounds dazed, drunk, like it's not my own.

"Thank me for teaching you a lesson."

"—thank you—"

Jonah laughs. It's a sound of triumph. Then he lets go.

I cry out again as he starts pounding into me, hard and fast and brutal. The desk shakes beneath me with each thrust. My breasts jiggle back and forth, and he stares down at them with undisguised satisfaction. The slap of his body against mine is as loud as it is savage.

The pressure and pleasure build inside me with every thrust. Every way Jonah's hurting me, humiliating me, only makes it better. I push against his hands, not because I think I can get him to let me off the desk but because the fight turns me on even more.

This. This is what I daydreamed about. What I've gotten myself off to for years. A man claiming me, using me like an animal, just like Jonah's using me now. Pumping into me harder, and harder, and harder—

A gasp, dizziness as everything else falls away, and then there's nothing left of me but the orgasm that takes me over. I clench around him, arching up involuntarily into his thrusts, as the world goes black.

It's never been this good. Never. Jonah Marks just made me come harder than I ever have in my life.

As I slump back onto the desk, reeling from pleasure, Jonah starts going even faster—so fast no man could hold back for long, and he doesn't. In moments he's shouting out, his eyes tightly shut, as his fingers dig into the soft flesh of my arms. His skin is as heated and sweaty as mine. He thrusts one more time, so deeply that he's buried in me, then goes still.

For a few seconds we stay like that, breathing hard and barely able to move. Finally Jonah pulls out of me, tugs me up from the desk, and tosses me onto the bed. Like I'm something he's done with and throwing away. I hear him sit down heavily in the desk chair, but I don't turn to face him. I just lie there sprawled across the covers, completely wrecked.

Always, I believed that if I ever acted out my rape fantasy the way I wanted, this would be the moment where I started to regret it. My pride would return. I wouldn't be able to believe I'd abased myself like this, that I'd let a man treat me like a possession he owned. No matter how good the sex had or hadn't been, I thought, afterward I'd be so ashamed it wouldn't be worth it.

I don't feel ashamed. Not at all. Even sore and bruised as I am, I've never felt better. Jonah is exactly what I always wanted.

"Hey," Jonah says. He's himself again. Role-playing over. "Are you okay?"

"Yeah." I manage to roll over to face him. The remnants of my dress don't cover my body at all, and I feel strangely shy in front of the man who just fucked me senseless.

I understand the impulse. In some ways, we've just seen each other for the first time.

"You're sure?" He leans forward, though he's careful not to come too close. Jonah is as sensitive to me now as he was brutal a few minutes before. I nod, and he frowns. "But you're shaking."

"—I can't help it."

He gets up from the chair. Jonah's still mostly dressed—his shirt flaps loose on either side of that perfectly defined chest, and once he's ditched the condom he tucks himself back into his boxers, zips his jeans. I can only lie there, boneless and exhausted, as I hear water running in the bathroom. Then Jonah emerges with a glass in one hand and one of the hotel bathrobes in the other.

"Come on," he murmurs as he helps me sit up. He holds the tumbler for me as I take a drink of water, then sets it by my bedside. With gentle hands he pushes the rags of my dress off my shoulders and drapes me in the soft white robe.

I never thought Jonah could be this caring.

He brushes a stray lock of my hair from my cheek. "Was that what you wanted?"

"Yeah." For the first time in my entire sex life, I don't have to lie. "That was exactly what I needed. Like you read my mind. What about you?"

"You were perfect."

His gray eyes meet mine. He doesn't smile, but his expression somehow gentles. Jonah leans forward. I tilt my head to meet his lips in a kiss.

This is nothing like the searing, almost punishing kiss he gave me at the party. This is soft, even tender. He kisses me as though I were something fragile and precious, only moments after he treated me like a whore.

I will never understand the contradictions of this man.

Then he pulls back, and just like that, he's cool again. He gets to his feet and begins buttoning up his shirt. It's as if he has an appointment later.

"Are you staying in the room tonight, or do I need to get you a cab home?" Jonah's voice is businesslike. Crisp.

I try to act casual. "I'm staying."

"You had a few drinks at the bar. You should eat something. Feel free to charge dinner to room service."

"I thought the guy usually bought dinner *before* the sex."

If Jonah hears my joke, he doesn't acknowledge it. He tucks in his shirt and glances in the mirror to check his hair. Some of my lipstick is smeared across his cheek. My torn panties lie crumpled on the desk; he uses the white fabric to wipe the lipstick away.

I feel stung. But why? Jonah and I agreed—the less we knew about each other, the hotter the sex would be. So far it's been scorching; that means we must have been on to something. He's playing this cool, and I should as well.

"Thanks," I say as I fold the robe more closely around me and burrow back into the pillows. "I enjoyed this."

Jonah looks back at me then, and he's not quite as stiff as he was a moment before. "I did too."

My body is still weak, but I have to ask, "Does this mean we'll get together again?"

"You can't get enough, can you?" He pauses for only a moment. "I'll be in touch."

With that, he's out the door. I'm alone with my torn dress, my sore body, and the aftermath of the most exhilarating rush I've ever known.

The weekend I thought would be filled with regrets is instead the best I've had in a long, long time. Room service delivers an excellent steak that night and an even better omelet the next morning. I drive home to my house singing along to the radio. After I've thrown away the ruined dress and underwear and deleted those "fail-safe" e-mails unsent, I meet Carmen at the farmer's market. She notices nothing but a small bruise on my arm that I write off to an accident in my art studio. That afternoon and evening, I'm even able to get some work done on my thesis. The distracting fever dreams of Jonah's hands on my body—for now, at least, they're at low tide. I'm completely sated, totally satisfied.

Sunday afternoon, Shay and I go to the movies. The comedy turns out to be fairly stupid, but I giggle helplessly at every dumb joke. "What's gotten into you?" she teases as we toss our popcorn box away at the end.

"Nothing." I shrug. My smile must look incredibly smug, but I can't help myself. "Just in a good mood today, that's all." Having the best sex of your life will do that.

The intensity of the pleasure I had with Jonah buoys me up. Even more important, though—I faced down my demons. I claimed what I really wanted. All these years I thought that fantasy would burn me. Instead I walked through the fire unscathed.

Take that, Anthony. You don't own me anymore.

But I try not to think too much about Anthony Whedon. He doesn't get to ruin one more day of my life.

On Monday morning, I'm still sore. I don't even care. Already I want to know when Jonah and I can play out our roles again.

"Look at you," Kip says when I walk into the department office. "What's got you so aglow?"

How is he so perceptive? It's like a superpower. I try to act nonchalant. "I went to the day spa. Had a facial."

"Likely story." Kip's phone rings, saving me from further questions.

I dart into my office and quickly type an e-mail to Jonah.

Subject line: Take Two.

Body: Should we talk sometime soon? Work out another night?

Only a split second after I hit send, my inbox chimes with a new e-mail. The bolded subject line is Out of Office Notification. Frowning, I click on it. The automatic reply text reads:

Dr. Jonah Marks is currently away from the office and will not be checking e-mail. Any questions should be directed to the earth sciences department.

Luckily there's a phone number for a secretary's direct line. I wouldn't want to call the office and get Shay. The less any of my friends know about my connection to Jonah, the better.

I hesitate one moment before dialing. Jonah did say he'd get in touch with me—which might mean he wants to make the next move. At this point, though, what's the point of being coy? Finally I decide I'll just find out when he's going to be back, whether it's tomorrow or three days from now, whatever. That way I won't drive myself crazy wondering if he's about to contact me. He can take charge when he returns. I smile, thinking about how good he is at taking charge.

Then my smile fades as the earth sciences secretary says, "Dr. Marks won't be returning to the university for some time. Can another professor assist you?"

"What do you mean, 'some time'?"

"Several weeks, I should think."

Weeks? Before I can catch myself, I blurt out, "He didn't say anything about being gone for weeks."

"He only alerted the department this morning."

So, a day or two after we acted out the most intimate sexual fantasy imaginable, Jonah got the hell out of town. He walked away from the university—away from his job—away from me.

I thought I'd found the perfect arrangement. The perfect sex partner. Instead I've been blown off and left behind.

NINE

The first couple of days, I can't fully believe it. I keep opening the e-mail with his out-of-office message, like I think it will say something different this time. It just seems impossible. How do you share something that intimate—demand that level of trust—and then walk off without even a word?

I don't let people in much. Seems like Jonah doesn't either. So I would have thought that what we shared—a *connection*, no matter how fucked up it is—I would've thought it would matter more to him.

Apparently not.

By the end of the week, I'm moody. Angry. For long hours I sit in my cramped office, grading papers without mercy, bearing down so hard with the red pen that occasionally I scratch through the paper. Nobody says anything to me about it, but Marvin and Keiko seem to give me more space in there than usual, and one afternoon Kip brings me a macchiato, placing it on my desk without a word.

Carmen calls, tempting me with a night of Tex-Mex and beer, but I tell her I don't feel like going out. I give the same answer to Shay and Arturo when they ask me over for a movie night, and to

Geordie when he tries to get me to accompany him to a wine tasting at Apothecary. For now I want the peace and quiet of my house. I want my walls around me, lined with books I can escape into, and no reminders whatsoever of Jonah Marks.

The following Monday, Doreen has returned from Florida, and it's time for me to face the music—in therapy terms. I don't hide things from Doreen; what would be the point of going to a counselor if I did? Although I don't describe the sex in detail, I go through everything else: Jonah's audacious offer, our erotic negotiation, and the night itself. Doreen must be in shock, because she keeps saying, "I see," over and over, which is how psychologists bunt. I have a feeling we'll be unpacking this for a while.

Two weeks after my night with Jonah, it all changes. The emotion I least wanted to feel creeps in, takes over.

Shame.

I let a near stranger pretend to rape me. I play-acted something so horrifying, so violent, that it ruins people's lives; I ought to know. Jonah came to me with the most indecent proposal of all, yet within a week I was in a hotel room, at his mercy.

A connection—is that what I thought we had? Now our encounter seems like nothing more than a sick joke. Maybe that's Jonah's game. He figures out what women want, whatever fantasy they're into, and uses it to get some no-strings sex. Then he walks off, looking for his next target.

(It's hard for me to really believe that. Whatever else Jonah might be, I don't think he's a player. But I don't trust my judgment these days.)

Besides, as outrageous as Jonah's behavior might be, as angry as I am with him. . . . I'm angrier with myself. For someone who's spent a lot of her life being guarded, I folded pretty fast when the right temptation came along. And that temptation is repellent. Wrong. I should have kept fighting it instead of instantly surrendering.

Every memory I have of that night with Jonah changes within my mind. At first it seemed so perfect. So liberating. So fucking hot.

Now I can only think I made a fool of myself.

About three weeks afterward, I finally decide to stop moping. Back to reality. I pick up an extra macchiato for Kip one morning, to return the favor. "I see your evil twin has finally left the premises," he says between sips.

"Yeah, she has a time-share in the Florida Keys. She tries to make the most of it."

"Good riddance." He smiles. "Welcome back, darling."

And maybe it's just that simple. I walk on, and I hold my head high. Nobody except me, Jonah, and Doreen will ever know what happened that night, so I can pretend it was just a really disturbing wet dream. Things would be easier that way.

Saturday night, I even go out.

"Oh, come on. It's almost sunset," Geordie says as he glances out at the bridge. "When are they going to get started?"

"Patience," Carmen says between sips of her wine. We're sitting on the grassy bank of the lake, a bottle of wine in the open ice chest at the center of our blanket—the perfect vantage point for the best free show in town. It always begins around the time darkness falls, but there's no predicting the exact moment.

My wineglass is cool against my palm; the sauvignon blanc gleams the color of candlelight. I'm wearing gray leggings, a long boho top, and more jewelry than I usually bother with. It feels like a special occasion, not that I can explain why to Carmen and Geordie. But I don't have to explain. I can simply enjoy the moment.

"So, how was your meeting with Dr. Ji?" I ask Carmen. The graduate program in mathematics is dramatically different from the art department—understandably—and I still don't quite get how it works. All I know is, Dr. Ji has a lot of say over whether Carmen gets to go on for her PhD.

She folds her arms in front of her, and her fingers tug at the sleeve of her peasant blouse. When Carmen fiddles with her clothes, it's a sure sign she's nervous. "Okay, I guess. He's so hard to read."

"But your paper is solid." Not that I'm a great judge of higher mathematics. Still, I know Carmen—how thorough she is, how bright. There's no way she would ever turn in anything less than top-notch.

"The work has to be more than solid," Carmen says. "It has to be brilliant."

"It's not like you've got to win a Fields Medal to get your PhD," Geordie says. When Carmen gives him a look, he laughs. "Yes, some of us math civilians know what the Fields Medal is."

I have no idea what that is, but it doesn't matter. "Come on," I say to her. "You've got this. You always do."

Carmen hesitates. In that moment, Geordie gulps down his wine and points to the bridge. "Here they go!"

At first we only see a couple of black shapes fluttering upward. Then a few more. Then a dozen. And then an enormous wave, dark, chaotic, and swirling like a tornado rising from the river—a hundred feet high at least, and spiraling outward, wider every second.

Geordie lifts his glass. "To the bats."

"To the bats," Carmen and I repeat, and we clink our plastic wineglasses together.

Years ago, when the bridge across Lake Austin was built, nobody realized that something about it would really, really appeal to bats. Now we have one of the largest bat colonies in the world. Sometimes their nighttime rush from the bridge results in guano raining down on the unwary. (We're sitting beneath a shady, broad-leafed tree for a reason.) But everybody loves the bats anyway. For one, they eat the mosquitoes that would otherwise bite all summer, which is definitely a public service. Mostly, though, they're just an essential part of the overall bizarreness of this town—one more reason our unofficial slogan is "Keep Austin Weird."

I always wish I could show Libby the bats. She would *love* that. But that would require a family visit to Austin, which means it's probably never going to happen.

The bats disperse for the evening's hunt. Geordie tells us a funny story about some court case where a house was somehow declared haunted as a matter of law. By the time I've finished my glass of wine, this actually feels like a good night.

"Thanks for the lift home. I know it's a hassle. Tell me, does anyone remember why I decided to live across the lake?" Geordie says as we head out onto the sidewalk.

"Oh, come on, it's not that bad," I say. My keys are in my palm, and I'm grateful that I'm the one driving. One glass of wine followed by dinner, and I'm okay to get behind the wheel. Geordie had three glasses, and he's weaving on his feet. "This time of day, I can get you guys home in . . ."

I'm parked in front of the bank. As we walk toward my car, someone steps out after a night run to the ATM.

And it's Jonah Marks.

". . . half an hour," I finish, without thinking. It's like my voice has decided to operate independently of my brain.

He's wearing jeans that hug his ass, outline his powerful thighs. His white T-shirt is cut in a deep V down his chest. Every ridge of his muscles shows through, reminding me of how powerful he is. How I turned myself over to him, completely.

I stop in my tracks. Geordie bumps into me from behind. He laughs and says something I don't even hear. At the sound, Jonah turns his head and sees me too.

He smiles. He *smiles* at me, like nothing ever happened. As if he's glad to see me.

But only for an instant.

I don't smile back. Jonah stiffens. His gray eyes turn stormy, and he turns away, stalking past us without a word.

"Earth to Vivienne," Geordie laughs. "Are you all right?"

". . . yeah. I'm fine."

"Are you sure you should drive?" Carmen gives me a worried look, then glances after Jonah. "Isn't that the professor Shay invited to my party?"

No way am I answering that question. "I'm fine. Let's go, okay?" I want to get as far away from this place—from Jonah—as possible.

"How could he act like nothing happened? I mean, was it that meaningless to him? That irrelevant?"

Doreen puts her hands up in the time-out sign. "I want you to take a deep breath, okay? Pause. Just for a moment."

I realize I haven't stopped ranting since my session began fifteen minutes ago. My cheeks are hot with pent-up anger and embarrassment. So I force myself to lean back on the sofa. Relaxing is out of the question, but at least I can calm myself.

When I know I can speak more rationally, I say, "I know you don't approve of what I did with Jonah. You probably think I deserve this. Getting blown off."

"Hey." She leans forward. The tagua-nut necklace she wears dangles from her neck, turquoise and brown. "It's not my place to approve or disapprove of your life. You get to make your own choices, Vivienne. All I do is try to help you see things clear."

"I let a near-stranger pretend to rape me. You can't tell me that's not fucked up."

"Honey, I spend all day, every day, listening to fucked-up. You're not even in my top ten. All right?"

I laugh despite myself. Although I suspect Doreen is lying—rape role-play with a guy who's practically a stranger has to make the top five, at least—I realize that she's telling me to stop beating myself up.

The worst part of the past three weeks hasn't been Jonah's rejection. It's been my own self-loathing. Maybe that's what Doreen is trying to get me to see.

She says, "It upset you, seeing him."

"Yeah."

"But you've been at UT for years without ever running into him before. So there's no reason to assume this is going to be a problem, going forward."

Now that I think of it, Jonah and I must have crossed paths several times before we met. Maybe we walked by each other on campus, or went to Whole Foods on the same afternoon. Although it's hard to believe I wouldn't have noticed a guy like Jonah anytime, anywhere, maybe I'm wrong.

Maybe I'm going to see him all the time from now on.

"I want to talk to him again," I say.

"What do you want to tell him?"

"I just want to ask why."

"In my experience, the answers to questions like that usually fail to satisfy."

Jonah could say that he didn't want me enough to do this again. That I disappointed him that night. Or he could have met someone else, somebody he wants more than me. But I keep thinking of the look in his eyes when he first recognized me. I keep thinking about his smile.

And about the way he laughed that night, as he thrust deeper inside me. The way he claimed me.

"There are valid reasons he could have gone off the grid," I say. This is the first time I've admitted this to myself; as usual, Doreen gets me to see the truth. "I worried that the fantasy would be . . . too intense, too much. It wasn't for me, but it might have been for him."

The dark, powerful figure he became that night—how he dominated me so brutally—that could have frightened Jonah. Maybe he's scared that's the person he really is, down deep.

I ought to be scared of that too.

"He may have his own limits," Doreen agrees. "Isn't it possible that what you're seeing is his reaction to the fantasy, and its place in his life, rather than his reaction to you?"

I nod, because I know that could be true. Still, though, I feel sure that's not the whole story.

Something else is going on in Jonah's head. Something I haven't even guessed at. And I want to know.

In the afternoon, I head onto campus. The undergrads have an essay due on Wednesday, which means my inbox is due to swell with requests for extensions, not to mention the reported deaths of a statistically unlikely number of grandmothers. As I walk in, Kip is on the phone, bartering what sounds like a deal to get our department a new copier. He gives me a wave—complete with blueberry-colored fingernails—which I return before going into my cramped little office. At least I've got it to myself for a while. I sign in to my university e-mail to see some of the expected excuses, a couple of campus announcements—

—and an e-mail from Jonah.

The subject line reads Re: Take Two.

He's answering the e-mail I sent three weeks ago, like nothing ever happened.

His reply contains only two words: What changed?

Between my sending this e-mail and our encounter Saturday— that's what he means. I know that much. But I don't understand anything else.

I know what Doreen would tell me to do. What Carmen or

Shay would tell me to do, if I'd confided in either of them about this. Any sane, rational person would say, *Write back, tell him you've thought better of it, and leave it there.*

Walk away.

My fingers tap out the message on the keyboard, and I hit send before I can think better of it. My reply: We need to talk.

I don't know what happens next. But I'm going to see Jonah Marks again.

TEN

Three days later, just after sundown, I'm back in the same wine bar where Jonah and I first met for "negotiations." I guess this is round two.

Tonight, however, the bar is less sultry, more rowdy. This is a home-game weekend, which means Longhorns football fans and UT alumni are already swarming into town. I didn't put on anything special this time—I'm wearing the same fawn-colored cotton dress I put on this morning. Yet I feel overdressed anyway, because I'm surrounded by a sea of orange T-shirts and football jerseys. It's like being trapped in a can of Fanta.

Somehow I know the moment Jonah walks in. I turn my head toward him even before he's fully through the door. His shirt and jeans are black, his gaze sharp as he instantly focuses on me. He doesn't smile as he comes closer, cutting through this raucous crowd like a knife.

"We can't talk like this," he says as he reaches me.

"Hello to you too."

But Jonah's right. Having an intimate conversation here is impossible. We'd have to shout to hear each other. Bad idea. "I think this place has a patio in back."

It does. Of course, the patio is crowded too—but it's not as awful, and at least here the talking and laughter around us isn't deafening. I can even hear soft Spanish guitar music playing. The heat that lingers even after nightfall curls around me; my skin is already moist, and strands of hair that have escaped my ponytail stick to the nape of my neck.

Jonah reaches toward me, like he's going to take me by the arm, but I don't let him lead me. It's not like I don't see where we're headed—the one empty corner. Strings of multicolored lights overhead sway in the breeze as we walk there together, to a small dark passage near the back door that leads into the alley. When I stop, Jonah does too, still a few steps between us.

"Let me repeat my question," he says. "What changed?"

"You took off without a word! That's what changed. How is that not obvious?"

I can see the muscles tense in his shoulders, his jaw. He's so built, so aggressively masculine, that I first think he's barely holding himself back from biting my head off. Yet his voice is steady, not angry. "I wasn't aware we had to check in with each other about our daily schedule."

"I didn't ask for hourly reports. You left for *weeks*, and you never even told me you were going anywhere."

"The point was to remain strangers. Wasn't it? To keep it . . . raw."

Something about the way he says that—*raw*—makes my breath catch in my chest. As angry as I am with Jonah, I can't forget the way his touch makes me feel.

I can't stop wanting him.

Jonah must sense my weakness. A slow smile begins to dawn on his face. Almost a smirk. "You can have neat, tidy, and safe. You can have tame. Or you can have what you really want. But you can't have both, Vivienne. And I think we both know which one you're going to choose."

Somehow I still have a scrap of pride left. "Where were you, that you couldn't send an e-mail or text or make a phone call even once in three weeks?"

"Antarctica."

Smart-ass. I could slap him. Then I realize—he's serious. Completely.

I repeat, "Antarctica?"

"Yes." Then his expression softens slightly, becomes less savage, more . . . human. "Well, Patagonia mostly. I was based in Punta Arenas, Chile. But from there I was able to charter a plane south for some flyover photography."

"Of Antarctica."

Jonah smiles, and it's not a smirk this time. "We discovered a dormant volcano beneath the Antarctic ice sheet a couple of years ago. I'm a research professor—I only teach a class once every two years or so. Mostly I analyze findings from all around the world, and sometimes I collect data myself. Like any other scientist. My data happens to be found near fault lines and volcanoes."

The one place in the entire world that's completely off the grid: That's where he was. I tuck another loose strand of hair behind my ear. "I have to admit, that's . . . a pretty solid excuse."

He leans against the nearby brick wall as he studies me. After a long moment he says, "I should have let you know."

"No, no, you're right. I'm not your girlfriend; you're not my boyfriend. You don't owe me explanations."

"No, I don't. But I owe it to you to protect you. After that night, you were vulnerable. I should've realized."

Just like that, Jonah's no longer the remote figure I imagined rejecting me with contempt. He's once again the man who asked how to make me feel safe, the one who brought me a glass of water afterward and kissed me as tenderly as any man ever has. I say, "You didn't abuse my trust. We had—a failure of communication."

"We'll have to do better," Jonah says. The smirk returns. "Besides, I had no idea you'd want to go again so soon. That e-mail came not even seventy-two hours after I left you."

The wounds to my pride are still healing, so I'm not going to let him get away with that so easily. I lift my chin. "Didn't you want it too?"

He laughs, low and rough. It's just the way he laughed when he was inside me, glorying in having thrown me down. Wetness wells between my legs, and I want him to touch me so badly it makes me weak.

"I thought about you every night," Jonah murmurs. "Most of the days. I dream about tearing that dress off your body. When I close my eyes I see you the way you were afterward. Wrecked. And what I want more than anything else is to wreck you all over again."

So much for Jonah "having limits."

Maybe I should feel powerful at this moment, when I realize that I affect him as much as he intoxicates me. Instead it's all I can do to keep from trembling. I brace my hand against the fence behind me, the one that marks the boundary between this loud, brightly lit place and the darker alleys of the city beyond.

This is when a particularly enterprising member of the wait-staff appears. "What will you two be having tonight?"

"Whatever the lady wants." Jonah's eyes meet mine as he smiles. "It's up to her."

Not fair, Jonah. I manage to answer, "We're still making up our minds."

Within another second we're alone again, and Jonah raises an eyebrow. "That just means he's going to come back."

"If I told him we weren't drinking tonight, he'd have asked us to leave." Sometimes it's hard to remember this is actually a place of business, not just a venue for indecent proposals.

"Maybe we *should* leave," Jonah murmurs. "Don't we have better things to do?"

Tonight? Now? He can't mean that. We're supposed to plan these nights in advance. Sane and safe.

But what's happening between us—that's not safe at all.

"We—we can't," I manage to say. "I want us to choose a night, a time, but not now—"

"What if I made it now?"

Jonah steps forward. With one hand he grips my chin, holding my face still as he leans closer. He's so tall that he seems to loom over me; the rest of the noise around us seems to fade away.

Yet as his eyes meet mine, I know . . . if I say the word *silver*, this will end in an instant.

I don't say it.

"I could back you into that alleyway," he whispers. "Just a few feet away. Five steps and we'd be in the dark, where nobody could see you, and nobody could stop me."

"I'd scream."

Jonah's eyes darken. He likes it when I play along. "I wouldn't let you," he says, as two of his fingers slide up to cover my lips. "I could cover your mouth while I pinned you against the wall. That would leave me one hand free. So I could reach up under that little dress of yours. Pull your panties down."

I'm completely caught in the spell he's weaving with his words. The low tone of his voice is like a hypnotic, drugging me. "I'd be so scared," I whisper. My lips brush against his fingers. "Too scared to scream, or to fight."

He breathes out sharply, as though I'd struck him. So dirty talk turns him on too. "I'd be able to get my cock out. It's already so hard for you. All I'd have to do is push your thighs apart—lift one leg up—"

"I couldn't stop you."

"But you'd push back."

"I would. But I wouldn't be strong enough to get away. I'd be helpless."

"And you'd be pushing against me the whole time I fucked you."

"Yes."

By now I'm dizzy. If Jonah pulls me into that alley for real, I don't care about the nearby crowd. I don't care how shameless it would be. I'm his.

Instead, though, Jonah slowly leans back and takes a deep breath. His knowing smile returns. "We'll choose a night sometime soon. Extremely soon."

He got me this keyed up and he's just walking away? I can see—just from the quickest downward glance—Jonah's as aroused as I am, so much it's indecent for him to be seen in public. "We—you and I aren't going to—"

Jonah shakes his head. "Not tonight."

"Oh, you son of a bitch." But I smile as I say it.

"It's a treat for you." He untucks his shirt. That's twice I've made him hide his erection in public. I should start putting notches on my lipstick case à la Pat Benatar. "I put you through three weeks of unnecessary confusion. So I'm making it up to you with a few days of suspense."

Suspense as a treat? Yes. Now that I know how good Jonah and I are together, the anticipation will drive me crazy.

(My shame has faded to a shadow next to Jonah, but it's still there. Waiting.)

The waiter reappears, eyebrows raised, eager to hear our drink orders. I want to wave him off again, but Jonah says, "A glass of pinot noir for the lady." He drops a twenty on the waiter's tray, and instantly the guy disappears, leaving us alone once more.

"Thanks," I say. "But aren't you getting anything?" I could remain here all night listening to him talk dirty.

Instead Jonah says, "I have to go."

"Are you kidding?"

"Nope."

I want to ask why he's going, and I sense Jonah might tell me, but that's one step over the line. We need to be totally open about our expectations and our limits. Our lives? Those, we don't share. Otherwise we'll stop being strangers. The fantasy will stop being what we wanted it to be. It would become . . .

I don't know what it would become, and I don't want to know. This is the arrangement, and we're sticking to it.

"So you'll pick the night?" I say.

Jonah nods. "And this time you get to pick the setting. The mood. When I call you, you tell me what you want. Be clear. Because once we meet each other—"

"—you're back in control. Completely."

Slowly he lifts his hand to my mouth. His thumb brushes the corner of my lips. Then he pulls back. "Good-bye, Vivienne."

After he walks away, I walk back into the noise and the hubbub of the bar to find the nearest empty chair. My heart is still racing, and I hardly trust myself to remain on my feet. How could I have gone from suspicion and hurt to exhilaration so quickly? But Jonah took me there.

Jonah takes me so many interesting places, I think, and I laugh to myself.

By now the sky overhead is dark, and the heat has faded to pleasant warmth. The waiter manages to find me; the red wine Jonah chose for me tastes earthy and rich. I indulge myself by hanging out on the patio for thirty minutes or so, drinking about half my glass. Once a guy comes over in hopes of hitting on me, but I wave him off. Happily he's a gentleman who can take no for an answer. All I want is to sit here luxuriating in the memories of Jonah's touch, and his words. In the promise of what's to come.

My phone buzzes from within my purse. Who would be texting

me? Maybe it's Jonah, determined to keep me hot and bothered all night long. I bet he's as good at sexting as he is at everything else.

A sly smile spreads across my face as I fish out my phone. Turns out it's not a text, just a voice mail. The name of the sender glows on the screen. My smile fades.

All the shame comes flooding back.

ELEVEN

"**Not answering. How** surprising." Chloe's voice is sharp, precise. Her words could cut diamonds. "I saw Liz at Art for Art's Sake. Imagine my surprise when she said you'd spent the weekend at her house not two months ago."

I grimace. Liz usually covers for me; my sister must have caught her off-guard.

Chloe's voice mail continues. "You know, I can't ask you to be a better daughter, or even a better sister, as apparently that holds no interest for you. But I wish you could be a better aunt. Libby loves her Aunt Vivienne, and she asks after you all the time. Colors for you, and makes me send them to you, even though I'm sure you just toss them in the trash. Maybe you don't understand children's feelings, since you don't have any of your own. But if you cared at all, you'd at least try to see your niece when you were in town."

My fridge is covered with Libby's drawings. I've kept every single one. Her photo smiles out from the picture frame beside my bed. On my last birthday, Libby called and sang to me on my voice mail, and I've never deleted that message. I play it when I'm feeling blue.

But I didn't go see her when I was in New Orleans in August. Seeing Libby means seeing the rest of my family.

"I'm giving you an ultimatum," Chloe says. "We expect to see you at Thanksgiving. My house, I'm cooking. All you have to do is show up. Do you think you could manage that much?" After a moment of silence, she adds, "No need to return this call. Come home for Thanksgiving, and we'll pretend this never happened. Don't, and as far as I'm concerned, my daughter doesn't have an aunt any longer. Because I'm not making excuses for you to Libby, not even one more time. If she asks where you are, I'll have to come up with something else to tell her. Not the truth, of course. That would be too hurtful. Just something that makes it clear Aunt Vivienne's not going to be around any longer. I'll see you in November."

She would have been so happy when the call went directly to voice mail. Instead of having an honest discussion, she got to issue a command: Thanksgiving or else. Chloe prefers to be confrontational in monologue. Face to face, or even voice to voice? Forget it. Everyone in my family is a master of the veiled threat, the cruel hint, the passive-aggressive twist of the knife that's deadlier than any stab.

I've spent the last five years or so learning how to deal with people in a more direct way. A healthier way. I'm getting better at it. But when it comes to my parents or my sister, it's like all that progress instantly collapses. Whenever I'm with them, within minutes, I sink into the sullen dysfunction that defines the Charles family.

Libby deserves better than that. Better than our dishonesty, better than my neglect.

Worst of all—beneath Chloe's anger, beyond the chill in her voice, I hear genuine hurt. Chloe and I got along well, growing up. She was five years older than me, and I thought she was the most sophisticated, glamorous person in the world. We sat on the bathroom vanity while she taught me how to apply mascara. She would hold my hand while we stood in line for sno-balls on hot summer days. Chloe didn't tease or bully me. I knew I had a good big sister.

We were never really confidantes; our ages were too far apart for that. And I doubt Chloe ever adored me the way I worshipped her. Still, we were sisters. Playmates. Friends. She doesn't understand what changed.

But I do.

Anthony changed everything.

That March I was fourteen. Just got my braces off. My breasts were finally making their belated appearance. Right before Christmas, I had finally been kissed for the first time (by Javier, an exchange student from Barcelona, which as first kisses go was pretty awesome). When I looked in the mirror, I no longer saw a gawky kid. I could glimpse the woman I would become.

Not that I was anything compared to Chloe. To this day she outshines me as brightly as the sun outshines the moon. She's a couple of inches taller, so she looks more svelte. Her hair is one shade lighter, but it's the shade that takes it from brown to blond. While my eyes are an uncertain hazel, hers are pure, piercing green. No doubt about it: Chloe's the beauty of the family.

But I'd finally realized that didn't make me ugly. Not by a long shot. I began playing with my hair more in the mirror and reviewing Chloe's makeup lessons more carefully. I thought of my prettiness as a tool I could use to get what I wanted.

(That's screwed up, right? Welcome to the world as seen by my mother.)

Then, that March, for spring break, Chloe brought home her first serious boyfriend. She was so proud of him, and I didn't blame her. Anthony Whedon wasn't especially tall—average height, no more and no less—but he was *built*. Turned out he was on the Sewanee lacrosse team. He wore the uniform of the Southern male—khakis and polo shirts—but they hung on his frame as though they'd been tailored for him. Sandy hair, a dimple in his chin, lips almost indecently full on a man: Anthony could get any girl he wanted. Clearly he wanted Chloe.

His arm was always around her waist. Her eyes were always on his face. To me, no celebrity couple had ever looked half as glamorous.

Anthony didn't treat me like the annoying brat kid sister, either. "Come on, Mrs. C.," he said to my mother. "It's just Frankie and Johnny's for some bell pepper rings. Not like we're dragging Vivienne out to Tipitina's with a fake ID."

"Well, I don't know," Mom said, but she was smiling. If Anthony had won me over, he'd *conquered* my mother. Though honestly, I think she was sold the minute she found out the Whedons were one of the wealthiest families in Tennessee. "You two don't want some time alone?"

"Aw, we don't mind taking her along," Anthony said. "It'll be fun. And Vivienne can tell me all her big sister's secrets."

"*Stop.*" Chloe shoved at him, but she was laughing.

That week I hung around them every chance I got. Occasionally I got on Chloe's nerves—but Anthony never seemed to mind. Chloe never stayed grumpy for long, either. I knew that was mostly because Anthony sneaked into her room every night.

On the last evening of their stay, though, Chloe didn't feel good. She'd had a headache all day, and around eight P.M. she announced she was going to bed. "To sleep," she said, with an emphasis that was only for Anthony. The message: No action tonight. I hid my smile behind my hand.

"No problem," Anthony said easily. "Vivienne and I can have a movie marathon 'til dawn."

Some cable channel was showing *Titanic*. Although I felt very grown-up, hanging out with a college boy until after midnight, mostly I was focused on the movie. In those days I had a serious crush on Leonardo DiCaprio.

Anthony kept talking to me, though. "Can't believe you don't have a boyfriend yet."

"I kind of had one." I figured Javier's kiss at the party counted. "But not anymore."

"How come a pretty girl like you isn't out there breaking all the hearts?"

I was so flattered. Blushing, I said, "I don't know. Talking to guys—it's hard. I don't know what to say. I don't know what guys like."

He laughed. "We're not that complicated, trust me."

It wasn't that I had a crush on him; Anthony seemed to belong to Chloe as firmly as Ken belonged to Barbie. But nobody had ever told me I was pretty before, much less a college guy. It wasn't even like I had on any makeup, and I wore just some old leggings and a giant T-shirt of my dad's.

For a couple hours more, I felt beautiful. Grown-up. Ready for the world.

Then—just after midnight, in my own home, with my parents and sister asleep upstairs—Anthony raped me on the living room couch.

It happened just after Rose jumped out of the lifeboat back onto the ship. While I was still focused on the TV screen, Anthony shifted closer to me, his hands going to my waist. I was innocent enough to think he was trying to tickle me. As I laughed and tried to scoot away, Anthony pushed me down, until he was on top of me.

When he pushed up my shirt, I honestly believed it was an accident. I yelped and tried to tug it down—but Anthony put one hand over my mouth as he tugged the T-shirt up even higher, exposing my breasts completely. "Shhhh," he said against my cheek. "You don't want them to catch us, do you?"

Catch *us*. Like any of this was my idea. But he'd made me afraid. If Mom or Chloe walked in, they would think I wanted to be with Anthony. They'd see me partly naked with a boy, and that meant I'd done something wrong. No, I didn't want them to catch us. So I didn't say anything, even when Anthony took his hand away from my mouth and slid it into my leggings.

"You want to know how to get all the boys to like you?" he murmured as he tugged my leggings down. I'd never been naked in front of a boy before, not even close. "I'm gonna show you."

He peeled my leggings off one leg; they dangled around my other ankle as Anthony pried my thighs apart. Only then did my stunned mind realize what was happening, and it seemed like it was too late to say anything. Why did I think that? How could I believe that it was ever too late to scream, or hit him, or just say no?

I don't know. But I believed it.

So I lay there, paralyzed with fear and confusion, as he got between my knees. He gave me his best good-ol'-Southern-boy smile. "Good girl," he said, and then he thrust into me.

It hurt. Not as badly as some of the girls at school had said it would, but still. My hands balled into fists at my side, hard enough that the next morning the indentations of my fingernails lingered as red marks on my palms. I started to cry. I thought when Anthony heard me he would stop. He didn't.

At the time it seemed to last forever—Anthony on top of me, panting, heavy. He was a twenty-year-old guy; probably it didn't take three minutes. But I felt like it was never, ever going to end. As I stared up at the living room ceiling, the fan dissolved behind a blur of tears. When the tears trickled down from the corners of my eyes, my vision would sharpen for a moment, then go liquid again.

Then Anthony started going slower, making these sounds that almost scared me—and he pulled out. I'd never seen an erect penis before, not even when he put it in me. When he came on my belly—the weird jerk and pulse of his cock, the thick white stuff spattering all over my skin—I jumped. It seemed like the grossest, most horrible thing anybody could ever do.

"There." Anthony smiled. "See, when the guy comes on you, you can't get pregnant. Bet you're glad I did that, huh?"

I nodded. Like I was *glad* about any of this. But all I could think about was the horror of getting pregnant. Then everybody would know, and I didn't want anybody to know.

Anthony grabbed a paper towel left over from our earlier snacking and wiped off my belly, like it was soda he'd spilled on the coffee table. Then he sat up and tucked himself in, straightened his shirt. I pulled my tee back down; it was long enough to cover my hips. As much as I wanted my underwear and leggings back on, I couldn't see how to put them on without flashing him, and I thought if that happened he might start again.

"You're a pretty, pretty girl, Vivienne. And now you know it." Anthony grinned, like we'd had a wonderful time. I guess he did. "This is our little secret, right?"

Numbly, I nodded.

He winked. "Don't worry. I won't tell Chloe. Wouldn't want to start a catfight."

Then he went back to watching the last bit of *Titanic*. I sat there, huddled on the far end of the sofa, leggings around my ankle, all the way through the end credits. When Anthony got up to go to bed, he ruffled my hair, like I was an adorable little scamp. He leaned close, and I winced at the heat of his breath against my face as he whispered, again, "Good girl."

It was maybe another hour before I dared to go up to my bedroom. The whole time I tiptoed past the guest room where Anthony was sleeping, I dreaded him walking out, or pulling me inside. I locked my bedroom door and sat on top of my covers, shaking. My mind kept replaying the last thing Anthony had said to me, over and over, until they seemed like the only words I knew.

Good girl.

I wish I could say that by then, at least, the worst was over. But it wasn't.

The worst came in the morning.

My mom kept calling me to come down and have breakfast. "Don't you want to tell Chloe and Anthony good-bye before they go back to school?" Even when my dad told me to get my butt down there, even after I heard Anthony's car revving up and backing out of our driveway, I stayed in bed, covers pulled up to my neck.

Mom finally came in a little before lunchtime. "Honestly, Vivienne, what has gotten into you?"

I didn't confide in my mother much. She always gave the impression that her problems were bigger than yours—more important—and that you were being selfish by even suggesting she needed to worry about you, too. I still hated the idea of anyone knowing about what Anthony had done. But that day, I felt so bad. I was sore between my legs, which I hadn't known could happen. I needed someone's arms around me so badly. So I reached for the lifeline. "Mom?"

Her hands were on her hips. "What is it?"

"Last night—something happened with Anthony."

She frowned. "What do you mean?"

That day, the word *rape* never came into my mind. Rape happened in dark alleyways, to women who wore short skirts and weren't careful. Rapists wore black and carried knives. I'd been on the couch with a guy who went right back to watching *Titanic* afterward. So to me it seemed like that couldn't be rape. But still, it wasn't right, and I knew it.

My voice shaking, I said, "Anthony made me—he did something wrong." That wasn't enough. "He made me have sex with him."

Mom stared at me for a few seconds, and then . . . she laughed. "Don't be ridiculous."

"What?"

"No such thing ever happened."

"But it did."

"Anthony Whedon is a nice boy," she said, starting to snatch up clothes I'd left lying on the floor. "He wouldn't do that to anyone, much less his girlfriend's little sister."

I'd known she might not hold me and comfort me. That's not her style. But I was totally unprepared for her not to believe me at all. "He pulled my leggings down. Mom, he did, for real."

She gave me a look like, *How stupid do you think I am?* "Don't you think we would have heard you screaming? You were just downstairs. That music woke me up three times."

"But I didn't scream."

"Well, there you go. You would've screamed, if you'd really been in trouble."

She was right. I hadn't screamed. Was it all my fault, then? Maybe Anthony was confused, and he thought I liked it. I'd been crying, but maybe lots of girls cried their first time. If I had screamed, he would've stopped. I felt so stupid for not screaming.

Finally I said, "I was scared."

"Of Anthony. The boy who took you out to Rock N Bowl with your big sister." Mom's whole body was tense now. This was how she got before she lost her temper and started shouting. I'd spent my whole childhood trying not to make my mother shout at me. "You have a crush on him, don't you? And you're mad that it's Chloe he likes and not you. So you're making up stories to try and get him in trouble. That's not very nice, Vivienne. You ought to know better."

I wanted to argue with her more, but if I did that, the shouting would begin. Sometimes she could back me into a corner and yell for fifteen, twenty minutes. When it was over I would feel like I'd been beaten up. That morning I knew I couldn't take it. So I said nothing.

"Now get your butt moving and clean up your room." She

dumped all my dirty clothes on the bed—on me, really. "Do some laundry while you're at it. You're old enough to help out around here, you know."

I got up. I cleaned my room. And I did two loads of wash. The whole time, I felt like Anthony had left with everything I'd ever been. Like I was the hollowed-out, used-up thing left behind.

A week later, Chloe sent me an e-mail.

> By the way, Anthony told me all about your little stunt the last night we were at home. Flirting with my boyfriend is NOT OKAY. You're just a kid, so of course he didn't take it seriously. But as your sister? I take it very seriously when you try to get together with my boyfriend.
>
> Anthony says young girls have crushes and we should put it behind us. I'm willing to do that. We can forget the whole thing, from this day forward. But don't ever do anything like this again.

Chloe believed Anthony. My big sister, who had known me my entire life and should've known what kind of person I was—she believed Anthony completely, even when he told her such a vicious lie.

Until I got that e-mail, I'd been considering telling my father. Afterward, I was too afraid. I thought if I told him too, then all three of them would hate me—my whole family—and that was more than I could bear.

Through the terrible depression of that spring and summer, I realized one important thing. Anthony had lied about me; that meant Anthony was scared of what I would say. So he had known I didn't want to have sex with him the whole time. All the flimsy excuses I'd made for him in my mind collapsed, and I knew how worthless and small he really was.

Once I could concentrate on hating him, I stopped hating myself as much. But that was before I'd realized how deeply he scarred me.

These days I don't hate myself for having been raped. I hate myself for wanting to act it out all over again.

"Ma'am?" The bar waiter leans closer to me, and I realize I've been sitting there motionless, wineglass in hand, for several minutes. "Are you all right?"

"Fine. I'm fine."

He doesn't buy it. "Would you like us to call you a cab?"

"I haven't had much to drink." My glass is still half full. "It's okay. I'm headed home."

I drive home, still in a daze. Doreen and I have worked hard on these memories, as I try to learn ways to deal with them without— going numb. Freezing up. By now, mostly, I can handle it.

But tonight takes me back all the way to square one.

TWELVE

When I arrive home from the wine bar, I dump my purse on the table and step out of my shoes on my way toward my bed. I collapse on top of my quilt, burying my face in the pillows. Merely remembering that night with Anthony has left me exhausted. My stomach clenches as if I were seasick, and I don't even have the will to get out of my clothes.

Okay. Doreen said that the next time I became overwhelmed about this, I should note down my reactions. Everything I felt, everything I thought. Then we could unpack it all later, in a session, while she's with me.

I push myself up on one elbow to search for my iPad. Like I thought, it's beside the bed. When I slide the bar across to wake the tablet up, I see that I have a new e-mail—and it's from Jonah.

Just wanted to say that I'm glad we worked things out tonight.
Looking forward to next time. —J

Next time. The next time I let Jonah pretend to rape me, and I get off on it.

It took me a while to realize how thoroughly Anthony had

screwed with my head. After the rape, I stopped masturbating. Completely. I didn't want to think about guys' bodies when the only one I'd ever seen aroused was my rapist. When I started having sex with my senior-year boyfriend, Derek, I flashed back to that night—every single time. It was like Anthony was back on top of me, inside me, turning me from a person into a body.

But my boyfriend was a good guy. He had no idea what was wrong with me, why I didn't seem to enjoy sex as much as he did. So he did his best. Went down on me, fingered me, took me in every position he knew and a couple I think he invented. Plenty of men never become as generous in bed as Derek was at seventeen; his wife must count herself lucky.

Bit by bit, my body woke up to the pleasure of touch. But every single time, I was thinking of Anthony too. Night by night, stroke by stroke, arousal and my rape were woven together. My mind turned the opposites into partners. I couldn't peel them apart any longer.

When Derek finally got me off, I was remembering a hand clamped over my mouth so I couldn't scream. And that orgasm— my first in three years—felt so goddamned good that I didn't care how sick my fantasy was. I only wanted it to happen again.

If Derek thought it was weird, the way I asked him to hold my hands down or pull my hair, he never said anything. Like most teenage guys, he was just thrilled I was finally into it. Even though I felt guilty every time I touched myself while fantasizing about being forced, I didn't stop. The only way I held myself in check was refusing to let myself think about Anthony anymore. Instead I came up with new scenarios, new kinds of violence—whether brutal or deceptive, as vicious as being bound and gagged or as commonplace as having a guy take advantage of me while I'm too drunk to fight him. The fantasies became more elaborate, just as I was learning how to bring myself off and how to teach a guy to take care of me.

And so here I am, twenty-five years old, only able to come when I think about being raped.

Believe it or not, I'm not the only one. Based on what Doreen has told me, and some psych books I've read, other victims sometimes find themselves having rape fantasies too. No, that's not the usual reaction. But it's not unheard of. Maybe that should make me feel better. It doesn't.

At least now I've accepted this about myself—my need to dive into this darkness, to claim my most secret and forbidden desires. And I've found the man who'll go there with me.

Already I know that I'll feel the sting of Chloe's anger, and the weight of those old memories, until I'm with Jonah again. Then I'll be in a place where none of it can touch me—every pain, every memory, everything that holds me back. Jonah can take me there.

"God, I miss coffee," Shay says, staring at my venti mochaccino with sorrowful puppy-dog eyes.

"Some pregnant women drink caffeine," I say as we claim the last available table in the campus coffee place. "I'm sure I've seen them do it."

But Shay shakes her head. "I had some spotting early on. It turned out not to be a big deal, but after that, Dr. Campbell said to knock off the caffeine completely. Doctor's orders."

"Look on the bright side. It's only another nine weeks."

Shay's face lights up, with a kind of glow that has nothing to do with old wives' tales about pregnancy and everything to do with happiness. "Before Christmas. I can't wait for baby's first Christmas."

"We'll all be spoiling him or her rotten," I promise. Shay and Arturo have refused to learn the sex of the baby; they say they want to be surprised. Personally, I'd think you'd be on such an

emotional roller coaster that day that the "surprise" would get
totally buried, but it's their call.

The two of us make an odd pair, I guess. I'm dressed up for a
departmental meeting this afternoon—pencil skirt, silky caramel-
colored blouse, and heels—while Shay is wearing some vibrantly
patterned 1970s pregnancy smock she must have thrifted and has
added a few blue streaks to her burgundy-colored hair. But she
wanted to meet up on our mutual free hour, and . . . well, since
Chloe's message, I've tried to avoid having too much downtime.
All I do with it is brood.

A happier idea occurs to me. "Hey, we need to have a baby
shower soon, don't we?"

For some reason, that wipes the smile from Shay's face. "Yeah.
Guess so."

"Hey. What's wrong?"

"It's just—" Shay bites her lower lip. She's curved both of her
hands around her bottle of water, looking at that instead of at me.
"My whole family's back in Perth, and they're not exactly thrilled
about this—"

Their daughter went off to school in America and informed
them via Skype that she was marrying a man they'd never met, no
older than her, and having his baby. As much as I love Arturo, and
as much as I believe in his relationship with Shay, I can see why
the Gillespies took it badly.

"—so I thought it would be my family here who would throw
the shower." She's staring down at our table, forlorn, completely
unlike her usual bubbly self. "I thought it would be Carmen. But
she hasn't said a word."

"I'm sure it just slipped her mind." Actually I'm not sure of that
at all, but saying so won't help. "She's been buried with her classwork."

"You know she doesn't like me."

"She does!" Not liking Shay would be the same as not liking

oxygen. It's impossible. "She's just worried about Arturo settling down so young, especially before you guys have finished your degrees."

"We can do it. If I didn't believe that, I would never have gone on with—" Shay can't finish the sentence. She already loves that baby too much to even say the words.

"I believe in you too. Carmen's just a little harder to convince. She's a numbers person, remember? They don't like soft squishy feelings. They like facts." I lean forward, hoping I'm getting through to Shay. "Even if Carmen has her doubts, she's with you all the way. You know that, right?"

Shay nods, but I can tell she's not convinced. Seeing her like this is like watching a dandelion wilt.

So I promise, "I'll throw the baby shower, because I count as family too. Don't even try to argue."

"I wouldn't." Her smile starts to return. "Yeah, you count."

"Carmen will pitch in too. Wait and see."

"Hope you're right. You'd just think—" Shay pauses, then says, "You'd think Carmen would be more excited about becoming an aunt. Weren't you thrilled when you found out Libby was on the way?"

Libby, whom I haven't seen since last Easter. Libby, who begged me to braid her long golden hair. I slid daisies into the plaits, and she thought that was the most magical, beautiful thing ever.

"My emotions were complicated, actually." I only say this because I know Shay realizes that I keep my distance from my family, and she doesn't snoop into the reasons why. "But I love her more than anybody else on earth."

I love Libby that much, and I never see her.

Shay and I have to get back to our respective departments, so I down the last of my mochaccino. She's back to her usual bouncy self, while I have to struggle to keep smiling. As soon as we part,

I let my face fall. The world around me seems to blur. I'm trapped inside my own thoughts, and my own regrets.

In my mind, I hear Libby singing on that voice mail I've saved. *Happy birthday, Aunt Vivi—*

Tears blur my vision. Undergrads swarm around me, a sea of ponytails and backpacks and laughter, but I feel alone. I push my way blindly through the crowd until I hear, "Vivienne?"

It's Jonah.

Amid the brilliantly colored T-shirts and jackets of the students around us, Jonah stands alone, stark in a crisp white shirt and dark jeans. He's the only one who stands still, the only one who's looking at me. The only one who knows who I am. Although he doesn't come any closer, his gray eyes search mine. I know Jonah didn't call my name just to say hello. He said it because he can see I'm upset.

I attempt a smile, badly. "Coffee's that way," I say, pointing to the Starbucks that must be his destination. "Talk to you later."

Jonah nods. I turn away from him to head toward the Department of Fine Arts. It takes about seven minutes to walk the distance. Seven minutes is how long I have to pull myself together. When I walk into the meeting, I have to be calm. Assured. Confident. Anyone but myself.

The department meeting goes well.

Like I said, by now I'm pretty good at faking it.

Nighttime.

Originally I'd planned to go get sushi with Carmen and some of her friends from the math department, but I text her to beg off. Worst headache ever, I type out, lying without guilt. She wouldn't really understand, anyway.

As much as I love Carmen, as close to her as I am, I've never told her about the rape. I never told Geordie, either, or Derek, or any of my other boyfriends. The one time I told people I love the truth about what Anthony did to me—that didn't end well.

I'm too tense and distracted to grade student essays. For a while I try to watch movies on Netflix, but none of them can hold my attention. Finally I take my frustrations out on the housework. Soon my little house smells like Comet and lemon Joy. With yellow rubber gloves on my hands, I scrub every dish, both sinks, the toilet, the tub, and even the grout between the tiles. By the time I'm done, this place will be spotless.

Just as I lean up to wipe sweat from my forehead with one arm, my phone rings. Generic ringtone. I strip off the rubber gloves as I go to answer. Probably it's one of the other TAs, but if this is another election robocall, I swear, I will not be held responsible for my actions. "Hello?"

A pause follows. Then: "Hi, Vivienne."

It's the last person I expected to hear from tonight.

It's Jonah.

THIRTEEN

I thought Jonah would call for only one of two reasons: either to let me know about some last-minute change in our plans—or to make new plans for another of our games.

But here I am, at nearly eleven P.M., listening to Jonah . . . being concerned.

"I wanted to check on you. When we bumped into each other today, you looked . . ." His voice trails off. How strange, to hear someone as sure and stoic as Jonah Marks sounding uncertain. "You didn't look good."

What am I supposed to say? A bad habit of mine—I try to think of what people want to hear, instead of just telling the truth. But I have no idea what Jonah wants.

"I realize I'm out of bounds here," Jonah says, and now he sounds more like himself. "Still, if I was any part of why you were so upset today—if what we're doing is turning out to be a problem for you—just say so. We can always call this off, or wait a while. I wouldn't want to be a part of anything you found disturbing."

Which is hilarious. From the first moment I laid eyes on Jonah, my life has been nothing but disturbing.

That doesn't mean I want to call it off.

"We're fine," I say. "What got to me today didn't have anything to do with you. I promise."

"Okay. That's good." To my surprise, Jonah doesn't hang up then and there. "Are you all right?"

"Yes and no."

We both fall silent. Maybe Jonah is afraid I'm going to start spilling my guts to him. Sharing my secrets. I have no intention of doing so. That kind of intimacy can't be a part of our arrangement.

Yet he stays on the line. He's giving me the option—or, more likely, can't think of a polite way out of this.

When Jonah finally speaks, he sounds steady again. Strong. His voice alone makes me flush with heat, from my cheeks to between my legs. "Do you want me to hang up now?"

I crave that steadiness, that strength. More than that, I crave *him*. Very quietly I say, "No."

"What do you want to talk about?" He's wary, but willing.

My bed is only steps away. I lower myself onto it, propping myself up on the pillows. "Anything. Just—distract me."

"Not the usual distraction, you mean."

I wonder what phone sex with Jonah would be like? There's something about the way he speaks—and it's not just his mesmerizing voice. Every single word seems to have been rationed. Measured. He reveals nothing he doesn't want to reveal. No emotion slips through unless he allows it. The totality of his control, his command of himself . . . it's even more intoxicating now that I know the intensity he's just barely holding back. And it reminds me of how fucking incredible it felt when he took control of me.

Phone sex with Jonah might be *amazing*.

But I still smell like cleaning products, and I'm wearing my grubbiest Longhorns shirt, and I feel about as sexy as Jabba the Hutt. If I'm going to get in to the mood, I need a moment.

Softly I say, "Not the usual . . . yet."

"Interesting." I can imagine his fierce smile as he says that. "So, what would you prefer as prelude?"

I notice that Jonah volunteers nothing. We aren't going to discuss our personal lives or our emotions—that would violate our covenant to remain strangers to each other as much as possible. So I need a completely neutral topic. The first thing that springs to mind: "Tell me about Antarctica."

"You want to talk about a place with no rain, little life, and temperatures down to a hundred degrees below zero. I wouldn't have guessed that was your idea of foreplay."

"I just meant—" I have to pause while I pull my T-shirt up over my head. "It's somewhere I'll probably never get to see."

"You don't have to apologize for being interested. I was teasing you." Jonah pauses, and I realize he's searching for words. "Antarctica is . . . brutal. But beautiful. Unlike anything else on earth."

I lie back on my bed. I'm topless now, clad only in my panties; the sweat on my skin could have been earned a very different way. "By brutal you mean the cold, right?"

"The cold, and the katabatic winds—those are the ones that scour the ground, stripping away all the snow."

"I thought Antarctica was covered in snow."

"Some areas are. But a lot of the continent is desert. The most desolate place on earth."

"So why do you call it beautiful?"

Jonah thinks for a few long moments before answering. "Weakness can't survive there. People live with as few possessions as they can manage, on the very edge of survival. Even the air is clearer. The sunlight can be almost blinding. It's the only place in the world with that kind of purity. That's why I call it beautiful."

For Jonah, savagery is beauty. I can believe that. "What else?" I ask.

"The aurora australis, I guess. That's beautiful."

I've heard of this. "Like the northern lights, but southern, right?"

"Right. They paint the sky green and gold, and the light surrounds you."

I wouldn't have thought of Jonah as someone who'd be enraptured by anything so poetic. Then again, maybe the aurora australis is truly exquisite. Even a man carved out of stone would be moved.

Though I know Jonah's not made of stone. Until this moment, I hadn't realized I knew that.

How much am I learning about him, as we go through this?

How much is he learning about me?

Then I feel uneasy once more—off-balance, unsure of anything. In the valley between tantalized and afraid. Which is just where I like to be, with Jonah.

"Maybe we should make plans," I say. "For next time."

If Jonah is surprised by my change of subject, he doesn't show it. But when his answer comes it's in a deep purr that's almost a growl. "Anything you want. As long as it's soon."

"How soon?"

"As soon as I can have you."

I suck in a deep breath. Already my nipples are hard, darkening even as I lie here on my bed, all but naked and alone.

He wants me to name the scenario. It's not that I don't know what I want from him; it's that the list is so long that I hardly know where to begin.

Besides, the control should be Jonah's. When I do this, I turn myself over to him, completely.

"When you imagine taking me," I whisper, "what is it like?"

"So many ways. Different positions, different speeds. Slowing down to pin you under me forever. Speeding up until I'm pounding you senseless."

Oh, God. I writhe atop my covers, my panties are already starting to get wet. "Yes," I say.

Jonah keeps going. "Sometimes I think about that night we met. I hated myself for the things I wanted to do to you, but I still wanted it. Wanted you."

"I wanted you too. I wanted you to—to make me thank you, or just push me into the backseat." Those fantasies tormented me so much that night. Now they're fuel for the fire building within me. "So let's do that."

"That's what you want next time? To act out how we met, and what we really wanted?" Jonah likes the idea; I can tell. "Whenever you want."

My cunt pulses so hard that for a moment I think I'm going to come right here. "Tonight."

After a moment of silence, Jonah says, "Now?"

I sit upright on the bed. "Now."

"We'll need thirty minutes." He sounds impatient; even half an hour is too long. "Meet me—in Zilker Park. On Columbus, past that first side road. Wear that little sundress again."

Am I really going to do this? Head out into the dark right before midnight, to turn myself over to Jonah?

"Yes," I say, and I hang up without another word. It's not like that was good-bye.

I take a two-minute shower so I won't go to our rendezvous smelling like detergent. My hair gets a quick comb-through, and I waste a few precious moments in front of my jewelry box, trying to remember which earrings I wore that night. In the end, I just grab some simple silver studs. The red sundress is clean, and without my bra, I appreciate the softness of the cotton more than ever before. Panties are probably a waste of time, but I bet Jonah's dreamed about tearing them off. When I met Jonah, I was wearing pretty simple sandals, but tonight I put on crazy high stilettos. Then I hurry to my Civic and drive to the rendezvous.

At this hour on a weeknight, even the streets of Austin are mostly bare. Downtown there would be some activity—but not out here. The city lights are invisible, hidden by the park's many trees. I pull my car off the main road, onto the gravel shoulder.

Nobody's likely to drive out this way. If someone does, we'll be able to see the lights far enough in advance to keep a passerby from seeing anything and . . . drawing the wrong conclusion. Jonah chose well.

I step out of the car. Dry grass crunches beneath my high heels. The only illumination close by comes from my headlights. The September night is as sultry as July, and the sound of cicadas shimmers louder, softer, then louder again. It's the sound of heat itself, of summer bearing down on you without mercy.

The last time I met Jonah like this, I had a flat tire. Puncturing it now would be taking reenactment too far. General car trouble will do.

Then, in the distance, I see a car driving up behind me.

At first I flush with excitement—and then I think, what if it's not him? What if some other person—some other man—is about to drive by and see me supposedly stranded and helpless on the side of the road?

Every danger I faced that first night comes to life again within my mind. The adrenaline pumping into my blood suddenly feels more like fear than arousal.

I take a couple of steps closer to the car door—I can get inside within seconds and drive away if need be. Then I stand there, breaths coming fast and shallow, as I try to make out the shape of the car coming closer.

A sedan, low and dark and long, like something a Secret Service agent would drive. It's Jonah after all.

The flush of fear mingles with my relief, and my desire. That hint of terror will make everything just real enough.

I take a deep breath and let it out. I don't have to control myself any longer.

I'll give myself to Jonah, and everything else—the things that worry me, that haunt me, *everything*—it will all fall away. Jonah will be the only one left.

FOURTEEN

He gets out of the car slowly, making me wait for it.

Before Jonah even looks at me, his gaze scours the area around us. He's looking for anyone who could see us—anyone who could stop him. But there's no one.

He's wearing cargo pants and an olive green T-shirt, both cut slightly looser than his normal attire. Yet his muscular body still shows through, as rugged and brutish as ever.

Finally Jonah's eyes meet mine as he steps forward, the outline of his body painted starkly by the headlights. He lifts one eyebrow. "Trouble?"

His voice is already low, husky. Like a man balls-deep inside a woman, on the verge. The intensity of his desire presses in on me like summer heat. My pulse flutters inside me, impossibly fast, like the wings of a hummingbird. I lift my chin. "Seems like it."

"Here," Jonah says, stepping past me. "I'd like to take a look."

He puts his hands on the side of my Civic. I expect him to just proclaim some vague sort of problem, but no. He walks around the entire car, studying it the entire way. My God, he's actually checking it out, like I might really have engine trouble.

At first I'm amused—is he going to go to all the trouble of

changing my tire again? Then it hits me. Jonah has committed completely to this role. To our game. When he goes into this mode, nothing can draw him out of it except the word *silver*. Unless I say it, Jonah will remain only a stranger who has me at his mercy. He will be the perfect embodiment of every dark fantasy I've ever had.

I remain silent.

The warm breeze tugs at the hem of my red sundress as I watch Jonah. He says, "Looks like you need some help."

"Sure could use a hand." My Southern accent normally isn't that strong, but it's come out to play.

Jonah likes my drawl. I can tell by the way his eyes darken as he studies me. "We ought to talk."

"Talk?"

"About how we're going to handle this." He nods toward the car. "You need a lot of work done, if you want to get moving again anytime soon. Work doesn't come cheap."

As long as I don't say the word *silver*, this is real. I'm stranded out here, alone, with this man so tall and strong he could overpower me in an instant. And he's my only chance of getting out of here—so I have to do anything he wants.

Anything.

"I—" My voice shakes with both anticipation and fear. "I haven't got much on me."

"Sure haven't." Jonah's eyes drop to my breasts, only barely covered by the low-cut neckline of my red sundress.

I blush so hot he can probably see it even in shadow. "I meant, I didn't bring my purse."

"No license? No phone? No cash? Not a very good idea."

"I guess not."

"Don't worry," Jonah purrs, stepping closer. "I've got you."

If only we could be sure nobody would drive along this stretch of road anytime soon. Then he could throw me down on the hood, rip my dress away, and take me as hard and mercilessly as he did the first time. My knees go weak, and I have to brace one hand against the car door. I bite my lower lip before I whisper, "I could give you my number. You could call me tomorrow, and I'd pay anything you wanted."

"I don't want your money." He nods toward his car. "Get in. Let's talk."

Slowly—as if reluctantly—I walk toward Jonah's dark sedan. My right hand trembles as I reach for the front passenger door, but Jonah steps past me to open the back door instead. I hesitate, breath catching, before I slip inside.

A lot of guys seem to care about their cars too much or not at all. Either they have sports cars or vintage numbers they fixed up, and they bore you with talk about horsepower and acceleration— or they have totally normal cars permanently littered with empty fast-food bags and junk mail, and they tell you to just kick that soda can on the floor out of your way. Neither scenario is attractive.

Jonah's sedan is long, sleek, and elegantly impersonal. Cream-colored leather covers the seats. It smells like he drove it off the lot this morning. The interior gives away nothing about what kind of person Jonah Marks might be. I scoot to the far end of the car, tucking the skirt of my sundress under me as Jonah slides in after.

He slams the door. The overhead light goes off. Now the only illumination comes from the soft blue glow of his satellite radio.

Jonah studies me for a moment. No doubt he's taking in the rise and fall of my chest, the way I'm already shaking. He makes me wait for several breaths before he says, "Kick off your shoes. Get comfortable."

I obey, letting the heels slip from my feet, even as I say, "I don't want to stay in your car."

"You want to get home, don't you?"

"I—I appreciate you helping me—"

"I'm going to help you, but you have to help me. See?"

This is—softer than our first time. Not an act of angry brutality. Instead Jonah's using coercion, putting me in a place where I say yes because I feel like there's no way out if I say no. Edging me closer and closer to a line that he'll then drag me over. It's an entirely different kind of force, but force all the same.

And it turns me on just as hard.

Jonah brushes one fingertip along my bare shoulder. I shiver as I pull back. He clucks his tongue and smiles. "So shy. That's no way to act with someone who's trying to be nice to you."

"I didn't mean—I'm sorry."

"That's okay. You're going to be nice to me too. Here. Give me your hand."

His fingers close around my wrist, his grip as hard as his tone is soft. He guides my hand down to his crotch, then presses my palm against his cock.

God, he's *so big*. I remembered that from last time—I couldn't forget it, ever—but still I marvel at the length of him. His cock jumps slightly at my touch, the pressure clear even through the thin fabric of Jonah's cargos. He starts moving my hand back and forth, the smallest, slowest strokes.

"See?" Jonah grins at me, openmouthed, already proud of himself for getting me into this situation. "I knew you could be nice if you wanted to."

If this were for real, what would I say now? What would I do? I whisper, "I just want to get home."

"You'll get home. But there's no rush. I like you when you're being nice."

"Nothing but this?" By now I'm shaking. "Just my hand?"

"You could do more with your hands. Why don't you show me? Maybe your hands are all I need, if you give me enough."

Jonah lifts his hand from mine, no longer pressing my palm

against his erection. He wants me to give him more—to bargain, in the hopes he'll demand nothing more than a hand job. So I have to give him the best hand job I can.

My fingers tremble as I clumsily unbutton his fly, then reach inside his boxers to draw out the length of his cock. It juts up, long and thick for me. Tentatively I close my hand around it. My reward is the first pre-come, slicking my fingers along with the head of his cock.

"Come on." Jonah doesn't sound so patronizingly reassuring any longer. Impatience grates in every word. "You can do more than that."

I begin jerking him off in earnest, tightening and loosening my fist as I move up the length of his cock. Now down again, and I begin using my wrist. He's hot against my palm, and so hard he must ache.

"I want it wetter," Jonah says. "Lick your palm."

So I do, quickly, before going back to my task. Guys have always told me I was good at this part—and I start giving Jonah what I'd give a regular lover. Twist and grip and stroke, teasing the ridge around the head of his cock.

He breathes out hard and lets his head slump back. I whisper, "This is enough?"

"Wetter." But when I lift my palm to my face again, he shakes his head. "Use your mouth."

"—but—you said—"

"I said you were going to be nice to me if you wanted my help. You want my help, don't you? Or do you want to stay out here all night? Somebody else might stop, and he might not be good to you like I am."

I wonder if Jonah will act out both parts. Whether he'll drive off and leave me stranded—then return in a few minutes as the savage attacker he's now using to threaten me.

Instead he reaches out as if to caress the side of my face—then fists his hand in my hair. His self-satisfied smile has vanished. "Play nice," he says. It's a warning.

I bend over, Jonah's hand still clutching my hair, until his enormous cock is in my face. Parting my lips, I take him in. I have to open wide.

Pre-come wells in my mouth, slicking my lips stretched around his cock. Salt is warm against my tongue. I start sucking—soft, slow little swallows at first. Then Jonah pulls my hair, hard enough for it to hurt. He wants me to work harder for my freedom, for my chance to get home.

So I do. I use my tongue, circling and licking, as I bob my head up and down. My hand closes around the base of his cock so I can pump him in time with my movements. The sticky stuff now trickling from the corner of my mouth tells me he loves this—that he's getting close.

But Jonah growls, "Dammit, hold still. *Now*."

I go motionless. His other hand grabs my hair too, and he pushes my head down, forcing himself so deep inside my throat that I gag.

He laughs slightly. "Yeah. That's it. Now you're giving me something."

Jonah takes control. His hands guide me, sometimes pushing no more than the head of his cock into my mouth, where I suck as best I can—then shoving me down again, making me deep-throat him.

"I like it when you start to choke," he whispers. "Your throat gets tight. Makes me think about how tight your cunt must be."

I whimper, the sound muffled by his cock in my mouth.

"Are you that tight inside? Huh?" Jonah jerks my head up and looks into my eyes as I cough and wipe my lips with the back of my hand. "Are you?"

My voice has gone hoarse. "Please—I'm already—you said this was what you wanted—"

"Never said it was all I wanted. Don't you want to be nice to me?

Don't you want to show me how grateful you are that I'm going to fix your car and send you home? Or do you want me to leave you here? That's right. I knew you didn't." Jonah's hand palms my breast through the thin red cotton of my sundress. His thumb circles the hard point of my nipple, and he grins. "Now take off those panties."

With trembling hands I reach beneath my skirt to wriggle out of my underwear. Jonah's hands circle me—not for an embrace, but to unzip the top few inches of my dress in the back. After I let the panties fall to the floor of the car, Jonah peels down the top of my sundress, exposing my breasts completely. He takes them in both hands and squeezes hard enough to take me to the edge of pain. When I pull back, his smile turns cruel.

"You can take more than that, can't you? I bet you can." He pushes me down until I'm lying on my back. The sedan is so wide that I can almost stretch the full length of it. "Now get those legs open."

"Please—"

"Do it!" The edge in his voice is meant to frighten. To terrify. The unspoken words are *or else*.

I let my left leg fall to the side, parting my thighs. Jonah angles himself between my legs as he pushes my right knee up so far it's almost against my chest.

Jonah takes a condom from the pocket of his cargos, which have almost fallen off his hips; his cock juts out like a knife. "See how nice I am to you?" he whispers as he slides the condom on. "I don't have to use one of these. I could just fuck you without it. But I'm a nice guy."

My arm is braced against the back of the seat. I'm splayed wide and helpless. Jonah's so large, so strong, that I couldn't push him off me if I tried.

"Aren't you lucky?" Jonah says, and then I feel the hard pressure of his cock against my cunt.

I bite down on my bottom lip as he slides inside—inch by inch, until it burns. He stretches me out, opens me wide.

"That's it," he whispers as he sinks the rest of the way in. "Just like that." Then he thrusts harder, filling me completely, and I cry out. He smiles at the sound and rocks his hips back so he can shove inside me again. I wish I could watch his cock going inside me, but I can't. The crumpled red folds of my sundress are in the way. I can't see; all I can do is feel.

Jonah keeps going, deliberately and almost cruelly slow. The tempo quickens without ever actually becoming fast. Every time he pulls almost all the way out, then plunges in deep and hard. Each time I have to gasp for breath, caught between pleasure and pain, because I'm on fire for him—reeling on the edge of orgasm, but he won't thrust fast enough for me to come. He's making this last longer, because he wants to revel in his power over me. Jonah wants to show me how helpless I am. Whatever he gives me, I have to take.

He lowers himself over me more each time, until we're so close I can feel the heat of his breath against my skin. His tongue laps at my nipple, and then he opens his mouth to suck at me. It only lasts a moment, but that's long enough to send a surge of pleasure ricocheting through me, brain to breasts to cunt.

I'm close. I'm so close.

"I can do this all night," Jonah pants. Again he thrusts, so hard I clutch at the car seat, my fingernails digging into the leather. "We can go slow and hard like this until you can't even walk. Or do you want me to fuck you faster and harder so I'll fix your car and let you go home? Which one?"

"You—just get it over with, please get it over with."

"But say it. I want you to say it." Jonah grabs my free hand around the wrist, holding it over my head. He's going to take whatever he wants. Making me ask for it is just one more way he proves he's in total control. "You want to get back in your car and go home? Then tell me. Tell me to fuck you as hard as I can."

Merely hearing the words brings me back to the brink. I'm dizzy and flushed, entirely helpless. My voice is hardly more than a whisper as I say, "Fuck me as hard as you can."

Jonah rams his full length into me. His hands go to my waist and grip me tightly as he starts to pump into me, each stroke as brutal as the last. I cry out—one long cry I can't control—as my blood rushes to my cunt. The sensation spirals, soars—and then my cry turns into a scream as I come. My head swirls in the rush of pure ecstasy, and I writhe beneath him as every muscle of my body surrenders to the intensity of my orgasm.

He knows what he's done to me. But Jonah just says, "I'm just giving you what you asked for." Then he speeds up, and the only sounds are his heavy breaths, my whimpers, and the wet slap of our bodies. By now I'm limp and dizzy, a completely passive body for him to use.

So he uses me. Jonah lifts my pelvis up slightly so he can thrust even deeper—I didn't think that was possible—and then grimaces. He slides in slower, once, then goes totally still. He shuts his eyes as his mouth falls open. Then his fingers sink into my flesh, and a shudder goes through him.

Already I know I love to watch him come.

After he sucks in a couple of deep breaths, Jonah pulls out. "Get dressed," he says roughly. "And get in your car. I'll see what I can do."

I pull up the front of my sundress but don't bother with the zipper. As I feel around the floorboards, my fingers find my panties, still wet. The red heels are easy enough to step into, but my legs wobble beneath me as I get out of Jonah's car and walk toward my own.

Had I ever thought that if we did it again, it wouldn't be as good as the first time? In some ways tonight was even better. Jonah knows how my mind works. Without my ever having to tell him, he knows how to be the dark, dangerous man of my fantasies. How many different scenarios could he play out?

I want *all of them.*

I sink into my car and shut the door. Leaning forward, I brace my forehead against the steering wheel and try to catch my breath. I'm flushed and woozy. Next time I should bring a cold bottle of water with me, for after.

But next time could be anywhere . . .

The passenger-side door opens, and Jonah gets in. At first I think he's going to role-play the end of it, telling me he's fixed my car so I can go home. Instead he gently brushes a lock of hair from my sweaty face. "Are you all right?"

I nod. "That was—amazing."

"Yeah. It was."

"It's like—like you read my mind that night we met. You did everything I dreamed you might do to me."

"And you gave in even more perfectly than I dared to imagine." Jonah's hand slides down my bare shoulder, a lover's caress. "God, you have no idea how good it feels. The way you trembled the first time I touched you—"

He gets off on my fear, or my simulation of it. Shouldn't that be enough to make me frightened of him for real? But I crave him just the same. Jonah pushes me past my limits, and I want him to.

I tilt my head and smile at him. "Not going on any more trips to the South Pole?"

Jonah laughs—the first natural, easy laugh I've heard from him. "No. I haven't got anything scheduled."

"So we don't have to wait a month for the next time?"

"I don't intend to wait nearly that long." His pale gaze drifts to the loose bodice of my sundress, like he might peel it off me again this second. "What do you want, next time? Where? When?"

There is no end to what I want from Jonah. We could fuck every night for a year and I still wouldn't have run out of fantasies for him to fulfill.

Yet the fantasy itself is about losing control. And Jonah knows me so well—or his desires match mine so closely—that I don't have to give him instructions. All I have to do is turn myself over to him, completely.

How can I best fulfill his fantasies? By giving him the most control. The most power.

"Next time," I whisper, "—surprise me."

"You mean . . . just find you when you're not expecting it. Take you wherever you are."

"And however you want."

Jonah doesn't say yes. Instead he leans forward and kisses me, a deep, searching kiss that tells me I've turned him on all over again.

Our mouths part. He whispers, "Good night, Vivienne."

I would tell him good night too, but he's already halfway out the door. It slams shut, sealing me back into my supposedly normal life.

But I don't feel lonely or rejected. I'm beginning to learn the rules. Besides, I can't stop smiling from both satisfaction and anticipation.

When he finds me next time, it's going to be *so fucking good*.

FIFTEEN

Even though I slept no more than five hours, when I wake up I feel refreshed. Energized. Ready for anything. Faint bruises on my hips remind me of how Jonah held me down, but they don't hurt. I run my hand over them and smile.

As I walk to the car, I remember the deal Jonah and I made. He could come after me at any hour—any moment—

But let's get real. It won't be this morning. Hopefully he's still sound asleep with a smile on his face. Me, I'm going to use this energy to work.

I indulge myself with a quick spin through Sorrento's drive-through for a café au lait, then head straight to the nearby studio where I create most of my artwork. Even though I'm studying to be a curator and historian of art, that doesn't mean I don't love doing my own work. It's been too long since I allowed myself to get lost in the flow of it. (Don't ask me how art school gets in the way of actually creating art, but sometimes it does.)

Normally I share this space with several other student artists, including my fellow TAs in the department. However, lots of creative types tend to prefer evenings to mornings, and today, at this hour, the studio is all mine. My faded thrift-shop chambray shirt hangs on a nearby hook; I slip it on over my clothes and get to work.

I create etchings. Although there are several different techniques, and I've experimented with most of them, every method of etching has the same fundamental process. You always start with a metal plate; you coat that plate with a waxy, acid-resistant material; you carve the design or picture you want to make into the wax, all the way down to the metal; and then you pour the acid. The acid bites into the metal, cutting your lines into it permanently. Then, when you ink the plate, you reveal a pattern you can print over and over—each piece of art identical and yet genuine, never faded by repetition.

Today, I'm making prints. Although I've done several etchings as part of my graduate work, this one in particular is special to me—that image of a man's hands cradling a dove. Every line actually looks precisely the way I envisioned it while I carved the wax—which you'd hope for every time, but that result is rarer than you think. The image also captures a theme I like to explore in my work: the juxtaposition of strength and fragility.

I remember Jonah gently brushing my hair back from my face before forcing me to deep-throat his cock. My fragility, his strength.

And yet there's that hunted, haunted quality to him too—and strength within me, which Jonah must sense. He wouldn't trust me to handle this fantasy otherwise.

His phone call last night tells me that my being okay with this is important to Jonah . . .

I pause. Inking while you're distracted is a bad idea.

And Jonah Marks is one hell of a distraction.

Since I don't have a class to teach today, I don't go into the office until afternoon, and I don't bother changing into one of my professional outfits. Instead I just ditch the chambray work shirt and head to campus wearing dark jeans and an apple-green wrap top. When

I walk through the door, Kip is deep in phone conversation with someone at FedEx about a professor's package gone astray, but he raises his eyebrows at me. This is Kip-speak for *We have to talk.*

I wonder what gossip he's dug up this time? Maybe Keiko's boyfriend finally proposed. He's been hinting around about it long enough. Whatever it is, Kip will have all the juicy details.

No memos are waiting for me in my department box, so I plop down in my rickety desk chair and check my work e-mail. Amid the flurry of essays turned in at the last minute by undergrads and the usual campus announcements, one line jumps out immediately—because this note is from Jonah. I sit upright and click.

Vivienne—

I loved your suggestion last night. For hours I couldn't think of anything else. Picturing it in every detail kept me awake half the night.

My toes curl inside my loafers, and I breathe out, hard. I think about Jonah lying in his bed, hand around his cock, already on fire to have me again, and the image makes me go warm all over.

Don't worry—I'm going to surprise you. But we need to lay some ground rules. You should know that I'm not going to approach you in any situation where you would normally be worried about your safety. Nor will I attempt to break into your house. You should always be ready to protect yourself, and you won't be if you assume anyone watching or following you would have to be me.

Jonah doesn't know me well enough to know I'm always ready to protect myself. My guard is always up. Still, I like that he considers my safety even in the maddened heat of our mutual fever.

On some level, Jonah is always in control.

I promise the next time won't be three whole weeks later. But that's
all you get to know—for now.

Jonah
P.S.—I don't think anyone actually monitors campus e-mail but we might
want to switch to our personal e-mail addresses. Just in case. Should've
thought of this before.

His e-mail is listed just after. The postscript makes me smile. I
hit reply.

Jonah—

Don't worry. I'll be ready for anything.

Vivienne

And I toss in my real e-mail in parentheses, after my name. No
sooner do I click send than a new boldface entry shows up at the
top of my inbox—but this one is from Kip.

V, my darling, duty calls. I'll be in the bursar's office the rest of the day—

What in the world could he need to do in the bursar's office?
No telling, but I have a feeling that by the end of the business day,
yet another university official will owe Kip a favor.

—but we absolutely have to talk. Free after hours? If so, come to
Sigmund's around 5:30. First beer's on me. See you there?

K

My first impulse is to refuse. Tonight I need to dig in to these essays; they promise to be excruciatingly bad, and the longer I put off grading them, the longer the task will hover over me like a gray, rain-fat cloud. More than that, though—I want to be alone with my thoughts. With my memories of Jonah, all of them, from the savage way he took me last night to the dark promises implied in today's e-mail.

But no. I've never been one of those women who cancels the rest of her life the first minute a guy comes onto the scene. This is no time to start. If Kip asked me to drop in at a bar we like on the average night, I'd probably go.

So, after a couple hours' worth of grading, I take myself off to Sigmund's.

Like pretty much everywhere else in Austin, the bar's atmosphere is casual with a side of wacky. Various graffiti artists were invited inside to tag the walls in brilliant Technicolor, and the tabletops have campy old advertisements from the sixties and seventies under the glass. I slide onto a bar stool at a table where the Breck Girl grins up at me from between her shellacked waves of golden hair.

Kip strides in only moments later, a brilliantly colored scarf around his neck. "You made it. And looking gorgeous too."

"Thanks." I tilt my head so Kip can give me a kiss on the cheek. "You don't look so bad yourself."

He touches the scarf at his throat. "This old thing? Glad you like. Aren't you glad the weather's finally turning chilly? At last we can layer and accessorize our outfits, as God intended."

In Austin, "chilly weather" means temperatures in the low sixties. Jackets and scarves emerge from the backs of closets to show up on the street once again. I smile at him and say, "I think you said something about buying the first drink?"

"Name your poison."

"Corona with lime. And thanks."

I needed something like this, I think. Some time to kick back with a friend and think about something besides my extremely unconventional sex life. Which is why it's so startling when Kip returns with our drinks, puts mine in front of me, and says, "Let's talk Professor Jonah Marks."

Although I don't do an actual spit-take with my beer, I come close. "Excuse me?"

"Sources report that you were apparently emotional and beside yourself in front of the campus Starbucks the other day—and Mr. Marks seemed to take pointed interest in this. As if, perhaps, he was the reason for your upset."

"He wasn't." Maybe Kip will let it lie there, but I doubt it. I try distraction. "What do you mean, sources? Do you own the baristas too?"

"Nothing happens on this campus that I don't hear about sooner or later. My eye sees all."

I groan. "You're like Sauron in *Lord of the Rings*."

"Except with less powerful bling. Now, fess up, darling."

"There's nothing to confess," I lie, then switch to the truth. "I'm not dating Jonah."

"Still merely considering it?" Kip nods, as if he expected this answer. From his Lisa Frank messenger bag he pulls a manila folder. "Good thing I took the liberty of preparing this dossier."

"A dossier? Kip, this is epic overkill."

"You don't get to be Sauron of UT Austin by half-assing it." He pushes the folder toward me, covering the Breck Girl's vapid smiling face. "Behold the many secrets of Jonah Marks."

Secrets? What does Kip mean?

No. Jonah and I have to trust each other. He hasn't broken his word or pried into my life. I won't pry into his. "I don't know how you dig up dirt, but I'm not interested in going through anybody's private information."

Kip scoffs, "This is hardly private. Almost all of this comes from CNN. A bit of Wikipedia too."

". . . why would Jonah be on CNN?" Did he appear as an expert on earthquakes, maybe? But Kip wouldn't bother showing me anything like that.

"It's not so much the man himself as his family. I suppose you hadn't realized Jonah Marks is of the Chicago Markses." When I look at Kip blankly, he adds, "The ones who own Redgrave House?"

"I have no idea what you're talking about."

"Do you not even glance at tabloids when you're in the super-market line? Never mind. I'll give you the swift overview." Kip rifles through the papers he printed out for me before presenting one that pictures a Victorian house nestled amid high-rises. Yet it doesn't look out of place; the house possesses a kind of dark glam-our and power evident even from this badly reproduced photo. Stone tile covers the outside, and the large door is flanked by enor-mous statues a story high, which have been carved as if they were struggling under the weight of the enormous arch between them.

"National Registry of Historic Places," Kip says. "Site of some of the juiciest stories in Chicago history, thanks to the wild and varied history of the Marks family. And our good professor's childhood home."

Now that I think about it, I *have* heard of Redgrave House— probably on some TV show about notable architecture. In that area of Chicago, so close to downtown, the lot alone must be worth tens of millions. Since Jonah's family has never sold the house, they must be able to leave that cash on the table.

It's not like I hadn't realized Jonah was well off; he drives a nice car, tips generously, and dresses better than any other straight man I ever met. Still, nothing about his possessions or demeanor ever suggested he had *this* kind of money. Was he one of those snot-nosed prep-school kids whose head is inflated by entitlement before age fifteen? Surely not. Somehow, despite being surrounded by riches and privilege, Jonah has maintained a sense of priorities. And he pursues a challenging field of study instead of just living off his trust fund, which shows character.

"Okay," I say, affecting even more nonchalance than I feel. "Jonah comes from money. What does that matter?"

Kip pushes more papers toward me. "The money doesn't matter unless you're out to marry your fortune, in which case, you're on the right track. But you're not that sort. You want the classic good guy, don't you?"

It's a rhetorical question. A few months ago, I would have said yes. But Jonah has taught me that I like a little badness too.

"Of course our professor isn't one of my intimates. No doubt you already know him much better than I do, so I don't want to judge him. And perhaps he's worked through all of his issues. Because the boy has issues, doesn't he?"

Oh, thank God it's too dark in here for Kip to see me blush. "Uh, we all do."

"Not like these." Kip points to the news story in front of me, and my eyes widen as I read the headline.

HALE: MY WIFE IS A DANGER TO
HERSELF AND OTHERS

At first I don't get it. "Isn't this—that guy Carter Hale?" I know him from the cover of business magazines—he owns some chain of luxury hotels, I can't remember which. And there's been some kind of gossip about his family lately, but how is that relevant here?

Kip answers my unasked question: "Carter Hale is Jonah Marks's stepfather."

Which means the woman in the headline is Jonah's mother.

This is Jonah's life. This is none of my business—or Kip's either. I glare at him. "Why are you digging all of this up?"

"For one, clicking the link on CNN's home page hardly counts as 'digging.' For two, people have a right to know if they're getting mixed up with serious Greek-tragedy shit. And for three . . . as far as gossip goes, this is *good stuff*. Better than anything Kim and Kanye have come up with in a while."

"Kip—"

"Will you just read the story already?"

I'm tempted to push the paper back and tell him where he can file it. And yet this was on CNN. National news. Jonah might assume I know about it already.

Don't I need to know as much as possible about this man I've given so much trust?

Lawyers speaking on behalf of hotel magnate Carter Maddox Hale today told a Cook County judge that Hale's wife, heiress Lorena Marks Hale, should be forcibly committed because she represents a danger to herself and others.

Testimony submitted to the court today reveals an incident in February of this year in which Mrs. Hale reportedly held a handgun on her husband for a period of nearly two hours, threatening to kill him and then herself. Mrs. Hale has previously been treated at inpatient mental health facilities for depression. He also alleges that she has made numerous threats to the lives and safety of those around her in the past several years.

However, Mrs. Hale's lawyers deny the February incident and point out that Mr. Hale made no police report then or at any other time during the marriage. Absent documentation of Mrs. Hale's criminal acts, legal experts say, a judge is unlikely to commit her against her will.

Even as the courtroom battle goes on, the couple continues to live together in the landmark Redgrave House near downtown Chicago—though reports indicate husband and wife now occupy separate floors.

Both Mrs. Hale's legal team and lawyers employed by her children from her first marriage to Alexander Marks argue that Mr. Hale is acting not out of concern for his wife's health but in an effort to gain sole legal control over the family's substantial financial holdings—which include Mr. Hale's hotel chains, Mrs. Hale's inherited wealth, and a substantive interest in Oceanic Airlines stock. Alexander Marks, Mrs. Hale's first husband and the father of her two adult children, cofounded Oceanic Airlines in 1975; she inherited a controlling interest in the airline upon his death in 1988.

Mr. Hale's adult children from his first marriage have thus far taken no legal role in the proceedings nor made public comment.

Beneath the article are the usual comments by the dregs of society, complete with one person convinced the situation is Obama's fault. This is of less interest to me than the photos tucked in beside the text. The first one shows Carter and Lorena Hale in happier days, the two of them standing together at some museum gala—him in a tux, her in a richly embroidered evening jacket, his arm around her shoulders and a glass of champagne in her hand.

The second one includes Jonah.

This shot isn't posed. Jonah is walking out of the courthouse, resolutely not looking at the phalanx of reporters clustered around the steps. Next to him are two other people—a woman with long dark hair that I instantly recognize as his sister, and a man with fair hair and broad shoulders who looks nothing like Jonah, yet seems to be part of the family. To judge by the coats and scarves they all wear, this picture must have been taken not long after "the alleged February incident."

Kip says, "You can't tell me that's not intriguing."

"You can't tell me it's any of our business," I say. Yet I'm already turning this sordid situation over in my head, spinning the facets as if Jonah's psyche is a Rubik's Cube I could solve.

I've wondered what could have led to Jonah's fantasy. He insists he would never, ever rape a woman for real, and I believe him. He's been fiercely protective of me, and of all women. Yet still, he's fixated on the idea of rape, forcing himself on a woman despite all her protests. I've watched his eyes darken as he tore off my clothes. I've seen him come inside me while he held me down.

Maybe . . . maybe he grew up with a violent mother. My mom dropped the ball, and I know it, but she never hit me. I never thought she would, even for a second. How much worse would it have been if she'd waved a gun around and actually threatened to kill me? I can hardly imagine the terror, or the sorrow. After something like that, you'd feel as if there were no safe place in the world.

So maybe, deep inside, Jonah has this anger at women. But instead of turning out to be a misogynistic shithead, he sublimated his rage into a fucked-up sexual fantasy. Made up for his powerlessness as a boy by imagining having total control over the object of his desire.

"You're interested," Kip said. "Knew you would be. Why don't I get us another round?" He's on his feet walking toward the bar before I can even tell him no.

As long as I'm already neck-deep in this, I might as well dive in. So I leaf through the other stories in Kip's folder. However, relatively few of them are about Jonah's immediate family, and those that are mostly date from before the legal battle about Mrs. Hale's sanity, or control of the company, whichever is really in dispute. Instead I see glossy, society-magazine stuff about the Hales' charitable giving, an *Architectural Digest* story about the renovation of Redgrave House, that kind of thing. One article mentions Jonah as a "track star," which I wouldn't have guessed. Runners always seem so skinny. Jonah's body would better suit a swimmer or a diver—lean but powerful.

The older articles focus on Redgrave House and what appear to be a centuries' worth of screwed-up people who have lived inside it. Suicide pacts, sex scandals, an alleged haunting: You name it, it happened there. This is probably the most famous house in the world that no one would *ever* want to live in.

Enough, I decide. This comes too close to prying for me to be comfortable with it. The CNN stuff, okay, whatever—but the rest of this is Google overkill gone bad. Jonah has respected my privacy, and I'm ashamed not to have respected his.

Now I'd like to leave, never mind the second round, but Kip is by now deep in flirtation with the bartender. As I learn when my Corona is presented to me, this sexy bartender turns out to be named Ryan, and he's the most interesting person Kip has met in forever so I *have* to stay to give Kip an excuse to hang around. I give Kip a look, but what the hell. I sigh, and drink my beer—slowly. Their mating dance continues for another half hour before Kip finally manages to get the guy's digits.

The way he carries on as we walk out onto the street, you'd think Kip had won the Olympic decathlon. "Come on, Ryan's hot. Scorching. *Radioactive*. And now he's in my phone. Normally it would take any amount of sexy groveling on Grindr to get that far."

"Sure. Ryan's gorgeous." Not my type, really—short, muscled, like lots of bodybuilders—but that hardly matters, since I'm not Ryan's type either.

Kip pouts. "Why aren't you celebrating my moment of glory?"

And there's the opening I was looking for. "Because I try not to meddle in my friends' love lives. Unlike some people."

"I wasn't *meddling*. Simply making sure you were informed."

"How did you even know about—that I'd gone out with Jonah

Marks? Whatever your barista source saw, it wasn't even about that, so . . ."

"I have other connections, as you should know." Kip's omniscience is one of the great campus mysteries. "In this case, one of the earth science grad students mentioned that she'd seen the two of you standing rather close at Carmen's last wingding."

Somebody witnessed my kiss with Jonah after all. "Kip—"

"No denials, Vivienne, please. They're so tiresome. Just tell me why you're trying to defrost that particular block of ice."

Ice? Maybe on the surface. Underneath, Jonah is pure fire. Not that I'm ever going to explain to Kip. "It's not serious, okay? Can you leave it at that? With Shay and I being so close, and Jonah sort of being one of her bosses—we'd rather not advertise it. Could be awkward, you know?"

He doesn't entirely believe me, I can tell, but he doesn't ask any more questions. "Fine, fine. This fling of yours with Jonah Marks will be but one of the many secrets I keep. At least you've finally discovered the joys of casual sex."

I shrug noncommittally. Jonah and I aren't in a relationship—but I wouldn't call our arrangement *casual.* "Why did you go digging up all this stuff anyway? Just for the sake of gossip?" Kip's all-encompassing curiosity has led him to snoop where he shouldn't, but never before did I feel like he was being judgmental about someone. Yet he seems wary of my connection to Jonah.

"Because," Kip says, "Jonah Marks is a cold man. And a hard man. He doesn't make friends easily, if at all. Not exactly the right type for you."

"Since when do you know what my 'type' is or isn't?" I ask.

"All I know is that you need someone who can be gentle with you." He sighs. "Because you have serious problems with conflict."

"No, I don't—"

"Liar!" Kip looks triumphant. "You can't bear it whenever people argue in department meetings; it's like you want to slither under the table. You're no pushover, but when you have to stand up for yourself? You always do it via e-mail if you can. Rarely on the phone, and *never* in person. When Professor Prasanna starts shouting about whatever's ticked her off recently, you *flinch*. You physically flinch as if you thought a five-foot-tall woman in her sixties was going to hurt you."

. . . I hadn't realized I did all that, but it's true. Kip sees even more than I thought he did.

He continues speaking, his tone gentler. "Geordie Hilton might be a lush, but at least he was always kind. You're someone who needs kindness, I think. And I don't know that Jonah Marks is the man to give it to you."

What I need from Jonah has nothing to do with kindness. The only cruelty he shows me is the type I desire.

I simply repeat, "It's not serious."

"Fine, fine."

Downtown Austin is quieter than usual tonight. Maybe it's the first chilly evening driving people indoors, to dig through the back of their closets for sweaters and jackets. Or maybe there's a more exciting place to be just a few blocks away. Whatever it is, Kip and I have this stretch of the street to ourselves, our footsteps echoing slightly from the tall buildings surrounding us. The setting sun paints the mud-colored capitol building a soft russet.

"Hey," I say softly. "I don't need you looking out for me—but I still appreciate the thought."

"I always think of you, Vivienne. Except when I'm thinking about my new future husband, Ryan."

Laughing, I get him to talk more about the many glories of Ryan. Inside, though, I'm deeply and unexpectedly touched. Kip can be a world-class meddler and gossip—but in the end, all he wants is to take care of his friends. To find us a bit of kindness in this world.

SIXTEEN

The next day, the suspense begins.

I sleep well, knowing Jonah won't come to my house—but from the moment I get in my car the next morning, every moment is charged.

Will he be waiting in the backseat? In the stairwell of the art department? Or maybe he'll be standing in the hallway leading to the restroom at my favorite restaurant. Jonah could find me at any time, in any way.

Sometimes I try to figure what he has in mind. If he's not following me, and not coming to my house, then how will this happen? I can't imagine what Jonah's planning.

Of course, that's the whole point. I won't know what Jonah's going to do to me until he does it.

Sometimes my curiosity piques as I'm sitting at my computer keyboard. It would be so easy to search for *Carter Hale Jonah Marks Chicago*. If I did, yet more chapters of Jonah's complicated personal history would unfold for me.

Then we wouldn't be strangers. We promised to stay strangers. So I don't look.

. . .

"Are you sure this dress looks okay?" Carmen says for about the fourth time since we left her place.

"You look *great*. Red is your color. Come on." I take her hand and tug her into the benefit.

The enormous theater has been decorated for the event in the spare-yet-elegant manner of most charity functions: Large plants in every corner, donated by a local nursery. Strands of lights hanging from the ceiling in graceful arcs. Bars in each corner, staffed by the usual grad students in white shirts and black vests. (If I hadn't won a scholarship, I might be one of them.) A lectern and microphone wait for various speeches, standing on the stage in front of the red velvet curtains.

We ran late because Carmen was still neck-deep in math when I came to pick her up, so the gala is already in full swing. Geordie must have been waiting for us the entire time, because he immediately waves and heads in our direction, weaving through the elegantly dressed crowd.

Tonight's cocktail reception benefits the public-interest law center Geordie sometimes volunteers with. Austin residents wear casual clothes almost all the time—but give us a chance to dress up, and we'll take it. Carmen's red satin sheath shows off her curves to perfection and fits perfectly with the tone of the party: cocktail dresses for the women, tailored suits for the men.

Me, I'm slightly overdressed. But I come from New Orleans, which means I usually wind up attending a Mardi Gras ball or two in the spring, which means I'm one of the few women who genuinely needs to own a full-length evening gown. This one is simple—emerald-green silk, spaghetti straps, skimming my body to the waist, then widening into a soft, flowing skirt. I adore this dress, and putting it on only twice a year always seems like a waste. Tonight seemed like a great excuse to wear it. However, I've already received a few glares from women who seem to think I was trying to show them up. Whatever.

"There you are!" Geordie holds a plastic glass of something amber in one hand but uses the other arm to hug me and Carmen in turn. His breath smells slightly boozy as his lips brush against my cheek. "Been wondering when the two most beautiful women in Austin would arrive."

Carmen laughs. "Let me know when they get here." Geordie shakes his head at her in disbelief, as if wondering how she could deny how gorgeous she is. I've got to hand it to the guy; he's a world-class flirt.

"So what do we do?" I say. "Walk around, talk about how great it is when lawyers do pro bono work, drink the free wine?" After you pay fifty bucks for a benefit ticket, they don't bother with a cash bar.

"That's pretty much the idea," Geordie says. "Mingle. Network. Definitely don't neglect the free wine. And check out the silent auction! Your print's the prize attraction, Vivienne."

I doubt this. As proud as I am of the etching with the dove, most bidders will be more excited by luxury spa packages, gift certificates to high-end stores, box seats for football games, the usual swag. Still, it's nice of Geordie to say.

The free wine turns out to taste like it *should* be free, so I don't bother after the first couple swallows. Instead I talk with a few of Geordie's law school friends and browse through the various artworks and gift certificates laid out for the silent auction. My print is prominently displayed—*Thanks, Geordie*—and for a moment I try to see it as someone would for the first time. Would they pay attention to the stark lines or the soft curves? The shadows or the light? You'd have to stand very close to notice that the ink I used isn't black, but a midnight blue.

I try not to be overly pleased with myself when I see that my print has already received a few bids. But I don't let myself look at the clipboard in front of the art too closely, because there's nothing like seeing someone bid five dollars for your work to drag you down. Better to enjoy the party. A smooth-jazz band plays at the far end of the room, so the murmuring of the crowd flows around the soft strains of piano and bass.

When I wash my hands in the restroom, a woman stands in front of the mirror, reapplying deep red lipstick. The red brightens her smile as she sees me. "I've been meaning to tell you all night," she says. "That's a fabulous dress."

"Thanks. So is yours." The white sequins are dazzling against her dark brown skin, and the high hem reveals her long, gorgeous legs. "And God, I wish I could carry off that haircut. You look amazing."

She laughs. Her natural curls are cut close to her scalp, making her come across as both feminine and bold. "Give short hair a try sometime. You might like it."

If I were ever going to be tempted by a pixie cut, it wouldn't be tonight. My hair is behaving for once, pinned into a messy updo with some rhinestone clips. I tuck one stray curl back into place, then head back out through the long hallway that leads to the front of the theater. Maybe I'll bid on that quilt I saw—

"Hey," says this guy whose name I can't quite recall. He's one of Geordie's friends . . . Albert? Alphonse? Fortunately, he isn't trying to start a hallway chat. "Your friend was looking for you— they told me to tell you to meet up backstage."

He must mean Carmen. "Oh, okay. Thanks."

What could have come up? If Carmen needs a private moment in the middle of a big bash, she must be upset about something. I can't imagine what, though. Surely this isn't about Shay's baby shower.

A side door seems likely to lead backstage. I go through it and see that I'm right—a few steps lead up to the wooden stage, where a couple of rehearsal items lie abandoned: a metal chair, a table, some water bottles people forgot to recycle. But I don't see Carmen.

I go up the steps, wondering if she's on the far side of the stage——and a hand closes over my elbow, hard.

In the first moment of shock, I try to pull away, staggering on my high heels. Then I realize who has me.

Jonah's other hand closes around my mouth. He pulls me close, his gray eyes staring into mine, as he whispers, "Don't scream."

The growl of his voice makes me shudder—deep and commanding. Even if I didn't know I could stop this in an instant, I might be too astonished and intimidated to cry for help. His grasp tightens—and all that does is get me hotter. He's brought me back to the line between fear and arousal.

And Jonah's going to hold me there as long as he wants.

He pulls me toward the back of the stage, farther away from the hallway, from anyone who might see or stop him. We're far behind the red curtain. Beyond the velvet, the muffled sounds of the reception swirl, laughter and music; here, there's no one but me and Jonah.

Nothing but the way he spins me around and shoves me against the back wall.

Jonah stands behind me now, both hands clutching my arms as he whispers into my ear, "You don't move. You don't talk. Do you hear me?"

"Yes—"

He presses his entire body against my back as he brings one hand up to cup my face. His fingers press against my cheeks. "No, no, *no*. Get it wrong again and you'll be sorry. *You don't move. You don't talk*. I don't want to hear a single sound from you. Do you understand?" I manage to nod, and Jonah laughs softly. "There we go."

When he releases me, I remain motionless against the wall. The plaster feels cool against my shaking hands and my flushed cheek. Jonah makes a small sound of satisfaction at my obedience.

His hands slide outward along my shoulder blades, curving down and around just enough for his fingers to brush the sides of my breasts. But when he realizes I'm wearing a strapless bra, he loses interest. Instead he traces my sides, the indentation at my waist, the swell of my hips. His fingertip teases the faint ridge of my panties, tugging it down slightly even through the thin fabric of my dress. Then he begins drawing up the long skirt of the dress, slowly, the rustle of silk the only sound besides our breathing.

As my legs and ass are exposed, I feel the sleek fabric of Jonah's trousers against my skin. He reaches around to slip his fingers down the front of my underwear, scissoring them just over my clit.

Pleasure arcs through me, and I gasp. Jonah shoves me against the wall again, and now I can feel the long pressure of his cock against my ass, straining through the smooth wool of his suit. He whispers, "You like this, don't you? I knew you'd like it. I could tell. Because beneath your fancy dress you're nothing but a whore." His fingers resume their massage, slow firm circles that spiral upward inside me until I'm dizzy. "I'm going to prove what a whore you are."

My breaths come sharp and shallow. Jonah knows exactly how to touch a woman—where to bear down, how fast to go. All the blood in my body rushes between my legs as my cunt gets hotter for him.

"Only a whore would let me do this," Jonah whispers as I start to pant. By now the sensation is almost overwhelming. "You want it now, don't you? I knew I could make you want it."

Warmth ripples through me in waves. My body tightens. I'm on the brink.

Jonah's breath is hot against the side of my face. "Don't worry. You're going to get it."

That's when he goes faster, presses harder, and I come. My orgasm crashes through me, long and hard and good. I try not to make a sound, but a soft cry escapes my lips.

He growls, "I fucking told you to stay quiet."

His hands go to the sides of my panties as he tears the fabric. I feel the remnants fall away as Jonah roughly pulls my thigh to one side, parting my legs.

"Hold your dress," he commands, pushing the fabric into my hands. "Let me see you. Show your naked ass off like the whore you are." So I stand there, silk clenched between my fingers, exposed before him like something he can decide whether to buy. I hear the sound of his belt being unbuckled, the purr of his zipper, the rustle of a condom packet opening. "I'm not done with you yet. And if I hear so much as a whimper, you're going to take it twice as hard."

Silently, I wonder whether I'd better keep quiet—or whether I want to find out just how hard Jonah can give it to me tonight.

Jonah must have one hand wrapped around the base of his cock, because he trails the head along the cleft of my ass, rubbing back and forth. Then I feel his fingers sliding in from behind me, knuckle-deep in my cunt. He pushes them in and out, obviously relishing the slick sound of it, before pulling his hand out again.

"So wet," he whispers. His hand curves around the front of my throat, fingers still warm and sticky. "I knew you wanted it."

And he thrusts inside, in one savage motion.

My entire body tenses. Jonah's width and length stretches me, tests me, makes me burn. His grip around my throat tightens, not enough to cut off my air, but enough to suggest the threat. Jonah holds me in place as he starts to move in long, hard strokes. My body still reels in the aftershock of my orgasm, and the renewed pressure of Jonah's cock inside me brings me back to the brink in mere seconds. As responsive as I am, I've never come twice this close together. But Jonah's going to bring me there.

From where he holds me against the wall, the side of my face pressed to the plaster, I can see our shadows painted blurrily on the floor by the few lights far overhead. Our shapes are elongated, stretched thin. As Jonah pumps into me, faster and faster, I watch the undulation of his shadow. I watch him dominate me. Use me.

Just beyond the curtain, people laugh and talk, completely unaware that only a few feet away, I'm spread out against a wall, being fucked mercilessly.

His breathing has become ragged. He tightens his hand around my throat—unconsciously this time, I think. Jonah's getting close. If I want to come with him, I need more, and I know how to get it.

My tongue traces my open lips before I whimper, "No."

This time the choke hold around my neck is real. As I gasp for air, Jonah says, "I warned you."

He spins me around, making me gasp, then forces me face-first onto the table. My feet remain on the floor; he has me bent at a ninety-degree angle, which means that when he yanks up my skirt again, I'm completely exposed to him. Then Jonah starts to pound into me, so hard it feels as if he wants to break me. He might. The table creaks and rocks beneath me; I grip the edges to hang on as his free hand once again finds my throat. I can breathe—barely— but his grip keeps me dizzy and light-headed. It sharpens the edge of my fear. Jonah fucks me, and he fucks me and then I'm coming again, pulsing hard around his cock as he remains totally still. My entire body shudders with the force of it. It's like I can't see, or move; if I were still pressed into the wall instead of on this table, I think I'd fall. Only after a moment do I get enough of my mind back to realize that Jonah's breathing slower. His cock twitches once inside me, and I realize he came at the exact moment I did.

Jonah's fingers release my neck as he leans back. Gently he strokes a soft cloth between my legs—a handkerchief, I guess— cleaning me before he pulls my skirt down. I sit up, my arms shaking. This time, when Jonah pulls me to him, his hands are gentle, his touch soft. I brace myself against his chest, letting my head loll back as I breathe slow and deep. By now a faint sheen of sweat covers my skin; he brushes loose tendrils of hair away from my forehead.

"All right?" he whispers. I'll never get over how much his voice changes when we shift from fantasy to reality.

"Yeah."

"Did you like your surprise?"

"Very much." I look up at him then, so that our eyes meet. Jonah's breathing as hard as I am, but his openmouthed grin is one of triumph. Why not? I would call this whole arrangement the definition of a win-win scenario.

We find a trash can for his condom and the remnants of my underwear. Then it's smooth, tuck, zip, check. When he's pulled together, he brushes the green silk of my gown with his fingertips. "Hope I didn't wreck your dress."

This man can go from pretending to choke and rape me one minute to worrying about crumpling my gown the next. "It's all right," I say, though honestly it is a bit wrinkled. Nobody's going to care, and at least it won't be wet. "You must've realized I would come to this, because of Geordie."

"No, I didn't realize your ex-boyfriend played such a big role in your life." There's an edge to those words, but Jonah moves on. "I saw you across the room. You looked so beautiful—that dress clinging to your breasts and your ass and even this little swell—"

His fingers slide between my legs, pressing the small mound there, rubbing one knuckle against my clit. I close my eyes and wish he could take me again right now, this moment.

But he won't. He always ends as soon as we're done. What if sometime I invited him to claim me for longer? To take me captive for an entire night?

Jonah must see how aroused I still am, but he draws his hand away. "I saw you and I knew it had to be tonight. Did my best to stay out of sight until I had my chance."

This was improvised? Damn, he's good. "What were you planning instead?"

He shakes his head, like I'm a naughty girl. "You'll find out when the time comes."

"You get to the pick the next scenario," I whisper. "Is that what you're going to give me? Another surprise?"

"I don't know yet." Jonah leans closer and frames my face in his hands. Our lips brush against each other as he says, "All I know is—next time I'm going to come in your mouth."

God, yes. Right now I want him in my mouth so badly that it's all I can do not to sink to my knees. Instead I nod, wordlessly accepting this and everything else he'd ever want to do to me.

"Perfection," he murmurs, and then he kisses me. It's a swift kiss, yet openmouthed, and our tongues touch for one instant.

But then Jonah steps back, turns, and walks offstage. I stand there alone.

Once I feel like I can walk straight, I pull myself back together. I find a bit of the campus newspaper to toss in the trash can, so the janitor or whoever won't be traumatized by the sight of Jonah's condom and my torn underwear. No small wet spots mar the green silk of my dress. Did Jonah bruise my throat? I doubt it— and even if he did, the marks won't show yet. So all I have to do is take a few deep breaths and walk back into the party.

Carmen and Geordie are talking nearby; Geordie spots me immediately and waves. I start heading in their direction, but I can't help looking around the room for Jonah. Probably, after this, he won't hang around long.

Sure enough, as I glance toward the exit, I see Jonah pushing the door open, about to walk out onto the street. But he holds the door a few moments longer, for someone else—

I recognize the woman in the white dress I spoke to briefly in the bathroom. She beams up at Jonah, whose arm slips around her shoulders as they walk out side by side.

She wasn't just someone he was being polite to.

That woman was Jonah's *date*.

SEVENTEEN

Jonah *smiled* **at** her.

That's the part that gets me. Jonah Marks comes across as cold, even forbidding, to most of the people he meets. I've seen another side of him—hotter than flame—but even when he's got his hands on my body, even when he's inside me, his smile is hard. Fierce.

To the woman in the white dress he gave a smile so warm that I know she's not a mere acquaintance. She's someone he cares about, deeply.

And yet he's fucking me.

I never asked if he was seeing anyone else. It seemed to go without saying. Now, however, phrases he said that first night we spoke at Carmen's ring louder in my memory—about other girls he tried this with, and how it never worked. *They didn't want to play rough. I think you do.*

At that moment, I should've asked whether there was someone else in his life. Maybe the mysterious woman in white had already rejected his fantasy. Is he cheating on her with me because she can't, or won't, give him what he really wants?

That's no excuse, even if it's true. But I can't stop wondering.

I realize I'm jumping to some conclusions here. There's no guarantee the woman I saw was Jonah's girlfriend, or that the two of them share any kind of committed relationship. I could've misinterpreted that smile. Possibly she's just a beautiful woman he asked out for a night.

Even that is too much for me.

In the morning I send Jonah a text: We need to talk, ASAP.

Unlike me, Jonah understands the rules of remaining strangers. He doesn't ask why, just gives me a time and place. So, just after lunch, I walk through one of the quads toward a bench where Jonah sits, waiting for me.

Even from a distance, I know him. We're surrounded by students, who slouch around in their ubiquitous sweatshirts and pajama bottoms. Jonah wears gray pants and a black shirt, nothing fancy, but still clothes that tell anyone that he's not an overgrown boy. He's a man.

I'm wearing jeans, a T-shirt, and a scarf wound around my neck—which looks casual but is there to hide the faint bruises of Jonah's hand on my throat. Yet he looks at me like I'm the sexiest woman on earth.

Even now he intoxicates me. I think he always will.

He rises from the bench as I walk to him, an old-fashioned, almost chivalrous gesture that touches me in a way I can't define. As we sit down together, he says, "Is everything all right?"

"No." I take a deep breath. "Jonah, I can't keep doing this. Meeting you. Playing out our—scenes. It has to stop."

At first he says nothing. His expression remains cool. Is he that controlled? Will he just get up and walk away like none of it ever happened?

But it couldn't have ended any other way.

Finally Jonah speaks. "You weren't unhappy with—what I did at the benefit."

"No." God, no. When I think about the way he slid his fingers inside my panties, I want to take back everything I've said, grab him by the collar, and drag him into the nearest building for a quickie in the stairwell. It would be as scorching hot as every other time Jonah's put his hands on my skin.

And it would only be delaying the inevitable.

I take a deep breath. "This isn't about anything you did wrong. Okay? You've kept every promise. You made me feel safe at moments I don't think any other man could have, ever. And you—" My voice breaks. Dammit. I pull myself together. "You saw something in me I've always hated and made me feel less ashamed of it for a while. So thanks for that. And the sex. Definitely thanks for the sex."

My crooked smile doesn't fool him for a moment. Jonah leans forward; he brings his hand closer to me, as if he'll touch my shoulder, but rests it on the back of the bench instead. "Vivienne, what's wrong?"

This is normally where I bunt. Where I take the gentlest, easiest out for everyone involved, so we can walk away with no hurt feelings, no unresolved conflicts.

I've always thought of it as consideration, or poise. Doreen says it's dishonesty, and asks me what would happen if for once in my life I just told the ugly truth and let people deal with it.

Jonah already knows one of my uglier truths. What the hell.

"I thought I could have sex outside a relationship, with no strings attached," I say. "I did in undergrad, like anyone else. Probably I could do it again with someone else. But you and me— it's not a normal situation. Not only because of, you know, the fantasy—" I glance around, but few students walk anywhere near us, and every single one is either wearing earbuds or absorbed in their cell phone. "It's more complicated than that."

"Our arrangement is simple," he says flatly. "We were very specific about what this would be and how we would handle it."

"This isn't about logistics." I look upward at a pale gray sky, the kind you see when the clouds have claimed the entire sky. *Truth. Tell the real truth.* "Jonah, every time I'm with you, it's more than sex. Every time, I turn myself over to you, completely. I have to give you total control, and total trust."

"I haven't abused that trust, have I?"

Shaking my head, I say, "No. But don't you see? I don't just fuck you, Jonah. I *bare my soul* to you. Then we go back to being almost strangers to each other. The disconnect is getting to me, and I don't think I can handle it anymore."

Despite all our rules and resolutions, I have begun to have feelings for Jonah. To feel jealous of other women he might touch. To want to have not just his body but his heart. That means I want too much. Which in turn means I have to get out, now.

Jonah's gray eyes become distant. The steel wall he keeps between himself and the rest of the world now separates us too. "If that's how you feel."

It's not. I'm still drawn to this man in a way I've never felt for anyone else. While I thought that connection was purely sexual, I reveled in his power over me.

But now I want more from Jonah, and I have no idea what *more* would be. All I know is it's not what either of us said when this began.

Goddammit, I'm going to cry. Not out here in the quad. Not in front of Jonah. I don't have the strength for that kind of honesty; I'm all out. So I stand up. "This truly doesn't have anything to do with you, okay? You were—my ultimate fantasy. Thanks for making that come true."

Then I walk away. I never look back; I never stop hoping he'll
call my name, or run to my side, catch my arm, and keep me from
leaving.

He doesn't.

"You feeling okay?" Arturo says that evening, as we hang out in front
of one of our favorite food trucks.

"Sure." I scrape my shoes back and forth in the gravel beneath
this red picnic bench. All around us, groups of people are eating
the best fish tacos in town from small plastic baskets, using their
cups to hold down brown paper napkins that would otherwise
flutter away in the breeze. Shay's gone to the truck across the lot
to get us some churros for dessert. Nearby, a grackle hops toward
our table and cocks his head in the hope we'll drop a bit of food
he can steal. Overhead, strands of kitschy multicolored lights with
big, fat, 1970s-style bulbs stretch between the trailers and the tall
tree near the road.

Arturo gives me a look. "That was the least enthusiastic 'sure'
I've heard in a while."

"I'm fine. Really. Just—having a down day."

No doubt Arturo knows better than that, but he also knows
when to let something go. "We all have those sometimes. You
know what fixes down days? Tacos. So get to work, girl."

"I think I'd rather fix today with churros," I reply, because I see
Shay walking back toward us. But then I realize she doesn't have
the churros. She has one hand to her forehead and is walking
slowly.

Getting to his feet, Arturo puts a hand out to support her.
"Feeling light-headed again?"

"Yeah." Her smile is weak and watery. "You know, I don't
want to stick around for dessert. Can we just go home?"

"Sure, honey," Arturo says. I mean to tell them it's fine with me too, but that's when I happen to glance downward.

When I see the red droplets of blood on Shay's white tennis shoes.

"Shay—" I get up and support her other arm. "Don't freak out, but—"

"Oh, my God." Now she's seen it too, and as we stare downward, another drop falls onto the gravel. And another.

"We're going to the hospital," Arturo says. "Don't move, okay? I'm driving the car right here. You've got her, Vivienne?"

"Yeah, of course, go!" As Arturo runs for the car, I squeeze Shay's hand. "You should probably sit down."

"I'm okay," she says faintly, as if nothing in particular is happening. I realize she's on the verge of shock. So I put my arms around her to hold her steady and upright until Arturo gets to us—he's already in the car, best to let her stand so we can get her into the vehicle and on the way as fast as possible. Shay's head rests against my shoulder; the skin of her forehead is cool and clammy.

I'm scared, or so I think, until I look down and see the bloodstain spreading across her white skirt, darker and wider every moment. That's when I discover just how scared I can be.

"Please, can Dr. Campbell come?" Shay pleads as the orderlies wheel her stretcher down the hospital corridor. Arturo and I jog beside them; he's determined to stay with her until the moment they physically pry him away, and I want to be with him when that happens. "Is she coming?"

"An obstetrician will be here any second," says a nurse in yellow scrubs.

"But I want my own doctor—" Shay's voice is so faint. It sounds like she might pass out at any second.

As they get her into a room and strap a fetal heart monitor around her belly, Arturo clasps her hand. "It's going to be okay," he says. "It's got to be."

Please, I pray to a God I believe in but rarely speak to. *Please let Shay be all right. Please let the baby live.*

I'm ushered out just as the OB-GYN runs in, and I hear Arturo say, "Dr. Campbell!" before the door shuts. So her doctor was the one on duty anyway. Maybe that's proof God's looking out for the baby after all. Or maybe it's just dumb luck. Either way, I'll take it.

For the next couple of hours, I have two jobs. The first is to sit in the waiting room and try not to cry. The second—and worst—is to call Carmen and tell her what's happening. Carmen arrives about ten minutes after she hangs up, in the faded jeans and ratty T-shirt I know she only wears when she's working on her thesis. When she sits beside me, I hug her tightly; now we can only hang on.

Carmen whispers, "They think I don't want them to have the baby, and if they lose it—"

"They're not going to. And you're going to be a great Tia Carmen. Wait and see. Hey, you want to help me throw the baby shower? Shay would love that."

Slowly, Carmen nods. So I start talking about presents and party games and cupcakes and everything else I can think of that could possibly be at a baby shower, in the hope that all that pink and yellow and baby blue will erase the memory of dark red blood.

Finally Arturo walks into the waiting room. He looks exhausted and pale—but not broken. "She's okay."

"*Dios mío.*" Carmen jumps up to embrace her brother, and he hugs her back tightly. "What happened?"

"Something about the placenta—we have to watch it, but for now it's okay. Shay can even come home soon." His smile is crooked. "And the baby's just fine."

Carmen starts crying harder, and Arturo starts too. I might be an informally adopted sibling, but I realize sometimes I need to butt out and let them have a minute.

I walk out into the corridor and catch the attention of the nearest nurse. "Can Shay Gillespie-Ortiz have visitors yet?"

The answer comes from someone standing behind me, "Not right now."

I turn around to see the obstetrician, a young woman wearing a doctor's long white coat with the name tag *Dr. Rosalind Campbell*. She's smiling, which ought to be the only thing that matters. But it isn't.

I've seen this woman before. She was wearing white then, too. I saw her the night of the charity gala, first when we complimented each other's dresses—and then when she left, with Jonah's arm around her.

EIGHTEEN

At first all I can think is, of *course* she's a doctor. Rosalind Campbell, the woman in Jonah's life, is stunningly beautiful, has impeccable taste in clothing, is friendly with strangers, *and* practices medicine. Couldn't she at least have a wart or something?

But concern for Shay and the baby quickly eclipses my pettiness. "Arturo said she had something wrong with her placenta—isn't that serious? Does she have to stay in the hospital?"

Rosalind puts her hand on my shoulder for a moment as she begins walking, tactfully leading me farther away from the patient area. "I realize you're a close friend, but I can't divulge a patient's personal information to anyone but her next of kin. However, if you want to know about placenta previa in general—it's what happens when the placenta is located wholly or primarily in the lower part of the uterus. At this later stage of pregnancy, the placenta can rub against the unfolding uterus, and bleeding can occur. The condition occurs in varying degrees of seriousness, from mothers requiring immediate C-section to those we can monitor on an outpatient basis."

Arturo already said Shay could come home soon, so she must be on the less dangerous end of the scale. I breathe out in relief. "It helps to know that. Thanks so much."

"You're welcome," Rosalind says. "And—forgive me, but do I know you? I can't shake the feeling that we've met before."

"Um. Yeah." *Until very recently I was acting out violent sexual fantasies with your boyfriend.* "We ran into each other at the public interest law benefit last weekend. In the restroom. We had mutual dress envy."

Instantly Rosalind's eyes light up. "That gorgeous green silk. Of course! Do you know, I looked for one like it online? No luck so far." Politely she holds out her hand. "Rosalind Campbell."

As we shake hands, I say, "Vivienne Charles."

Rosalind's smile widens, and her fingers give mine a tiny, conspiratorial squeeze. "Oh! So *you're* Jonah's Vivienne."

She knows who I am. She's not angry. She called me *Jonah's Vivienne.* "Excuse me?"

"I'm the guilty one who stole him as my date the other night." Rosalind shrugs, smiling. "Hope you didn't mind. What a pity we didn't run into you together—we could've met then, under less stressful circumstances."

Rosalind was Jonah's date, but she knows Jonah and I have been together, and she doesn't mind, and I understand exactly zero of this. "We need to talk. Do you have a minute?"

Although Rosalind seems surprised by my question, she nods. "Sure."

She leads me into a nearby examination room, empty and awaiting its next patient. Rosalind closes the door behind us and—perhaps by habit—I sit on the patient's table, while she claims the doctor's chair. It's like I've come to her for a diagnosis.

"All right," Rosalind says, "what's this about? You don't look like you're about to tell me where you bought your gown."

"It's about Jonah—"

"Oh, no." She holds her hands up to ward off my next words. "I don't give romantic advice to anyone. Never turns out well."

"That's not what I meant. Just—Jonah obviously told you about me, but he never told me about you. I didn't see you with him until the two of you left the benefit together, and—I guess I don't understand your relationship."

Her eyes widen. "Oh, no, no! Jonah and I are *friends*. That's all."

"Just friends?" My voice sounds more skeptical than I meant for it to. It's hard for me to imagine any woman being near Jonah and not wanting to rip his clothes off.

Rosalind begins to smile. "I happen to be very much in love with one of the best chefs in town—and luckily for me, she's not the jealous type."

She. Well, that explains why Rosalind doesn't want to jump Jonah's bones.

"Candace and I have lived together for more than a year now," Rosalind continues. "But the down side of being involved with a chef is that they're unavailable several evenings a week. Since babies don't keep to a timetable, my schedule is unpredictable as well. So I often find myself alone on a rare free night when I'd like to see a movie or go to a party, and sometimes I enlist Jonah to come with me."

"Got it," I say. "And I'm feeling pretty stupid right now."

Rosalind laughs, but not unkindly. "It's all right. I hope I didn't start a lover's quarrel."

"Not exactly."

Maybe I should feel elated. Jonah doesn't have a girlfriend. He wasn't using me to cheat, or having sex with somebody else, any of that.

But Jonah's behavior isn't the issue. My jealousy is.

The envy and fear I felt when I saw Jonah and Rosalind together told me a truth I'd wanted to deny: I want more from Jonah. More than sex, more than this twisted fantasy that imprisons us both. I have no idea what *more* could mean, for us.

Nothing, probably. Jonah made it very clear from the very first time he suggested our arrangement that he wasn't looking for romance.

And it terrifies me that I feel this way about a man who pretended to rape me.

Rosalind says, "I'm not one bit surprised he didn't get around to telling you about me yet, much less introducing us. Jonah's one of the most private people I've ever met."

I nod as I realize just how strong those steel walls around him truly are.

"So, if I've set your mind at ease, I should get back to work." She rises and goes to the door, but pauses with a hand on the knob. "One last thing—"

"—yeah?"

"Jonah almost never talks about his personal life. But he talked about you."

My reckless heart aches and warms at the same moment. "What did he say?"

"Very little. Your name, that you were someone he'd spent time with. He spoke about you just today, actually, when we grabbed a quick dinner—he worried he'd upset you. That's about it," Rosalind says. "Which is more information than he's given me about any other woman in his life in the four years we've been friends. Whatever else is going on—you're important to him." Rosalind gives me a crooked smile. "So if *I'm* what you were upset about, no more worries, all right?"

I want to believe her. I want it too much. Right now I might make myself believe anything if it meant going back to Jonah.

More lightly, Rosalind says, "Good-bye, Vivienne. I'm sure we'll see each other around, one way or another."

Then she's gone, and I sit alone in the examination room for a few long minutes, feeling a kind of pain no medicine can cure.

Once I've pulled myself together, I go back to the waiting room. Arturo and Carmen are still in tears, but after some more hugging and lots of Kleenex, Arturo returns to Shay's side. Carmen and I make an emergency Target run.

"She'll want socks," Carmen says, pushing the red shopping cart toward the women's section. "Soft fuzzy socks, so her feet won't be cold. And could we get her a maternity nightgown, or does she have to wear that stupid hospital one the entire time? I bet she does. Well, would she want any pillows? Maybe the ones in the hospital suck. Anyway, everybody likes extra pillows."

"Calm down, okay?" If I don't stop her, she's likely to walk out of here with half the store's merchandise. "Shay only asked for some snacks and something new to read. Let's just grab that and get back to her before visiting hours are over."

Carmen looks like she might start crying again. "I just want to take care of her."

"I know. And Shay knows that too, okay?" I give Carmen a quick hug around the shoulders.

She isn't convinced. "I dug myself a pretty deep hole."

"Well—yeah. But you can't shop your way out of it. Let's listen to Shay and Arturo for a while. Take your cues from them."

Finally Carmen nods. "But I still think the socks are a good idea."

"They are, aren't they?" So we pick up some of those, too.

Our visit to Shay's bedside is necessarily brief—visiting hours are ending, and she's clearly tired and emotional. Carmen babbles on about the stuff we bought, while I set the granola bars and cups of applesauce nearby, where she can reach them. Arturo keeps his hand in Shay's the entire time.

As I drive home that night, I keep thinking about the way Arturo and Shay held hands. Today they faced unbelievable pain and fear, together. Arturo kept himself together for Shay's sake even when he must have been on the verge of panic—and in the hospital room afterward, even as she lay on the brink of exhaustion, Shay somehow summoned the strength to comfort Arturo too.

Their ages don't matter. Whatever it is that binds people together through a lifetime—the kind of love that allows them to transcend themselves for the sake of someone else—Shay and Arturo have it.

As for me? I have complicated feelings for a complicated man. Rosalind says some of those feelings might be returned—but all Jonah told her was my name.

When I walk through my front door, I breathe a heavy sigh of relief. Even the silence sounds sweet. My little home has never felt more like a cozy shelter from the rest of the world. I ought to prep next week's lectures, but forget doing any constructive work tonight. Every nerve I have is fried. I'm going to change into a T-shirt and leggings, warm up some soup for dinner, and spend the next couple of hours curled on the sofa rereading an Agatha Christie. Maybe then I can fall asleep.

I wiggle into my leggings and throw on the tee before I realize how long it's been since I checked my phone. Right now I couldn't care less about answering any work e-mails—but I ought to turn the ringer back on, in case Carmen or Arturo calls during the night. So I do that and quickly scan through the e-mail to see if there's anything I should answer.

And there's a note from Jonah.

The subject line reads only, On my wall.

What's that supposed to mean? I open the e-mail—which has a file attached—and the first line reads, Take a look.

I can't imagine what Jonah might have sent me. My first thought is that he broke his word—that he secretly recorded us having sex after all—but no. He wouldn't do that. Then what? Jonah's not the dick pic type, thank goodness.

So I click on the attachment, and gasp.

There, hanging on an exposed brick wall, is the etching I donated to the charity benefit. It's already been framed in simple dark pewter that highlights the lines and shades of the etching itself. The strong hands cradle the little dove tenderly, brutish power devoted to the safety and protection of a fragile thing.

I liked the etching before. Obviously, since I made it. But seeing it in Jonah's possession moves me on a level I would never have expected. The image means even more to me than it did before—because it has revealed something inside Jonah's heart.

The rest of Jonah's e-mail reads:

This caught my eye at the auction even before I walked over to make a bid. Imagine how I felt when I searched for the artist's name and saw yours there. I put in a bid large enough to discourage any further competition—with success, as you can see.

You're exceptionally talented, Vivienne. This is a side of you I never got to see. Every time I look at this etching, I'm reminded of how much I never learned about you.

I won't ask you to resume our arrangement. I've always agreed that the moment you said stop, it would all end, and I intend to keep my word. You're safe from me, Vivienne. You always were, but I wanted to say it again.

If you ever want to talk, you know how to contact me.

—Jonah

If I talk to him even once more, we'll start over. It won't be a week before he has me back in his thrall. In my mind, his ragged voice whispers, *Next time I'm going to come in your mouth.*

He still wants that. He's still thinking about that. He can write this, look at this tender image, and still daydream about forcing a woman to her knees and raping her mouth.

How can those two parts of him coexist? How can I yearn for Jonah while I continue to fear the darkness inside him?

Doreen would ask why I'm even reading this e-mail. Common sense would too. I walked away with my dignity—or whatever's left of it after I let Jonah fuck me senseless in his car. Everything is clear between us. No hurt feelings. No further complications.

The best move is not to answer him, now or ever.

I click reply.

NINETEEN

One of my favorite restaurants in town is the Elizabeth Street Cafe. Technically it serves Vietnamese cuisine, but the mood of the place is far more eclectic than that. The waitresses all wear floral cotton dresses as they serve up classics like pho ga, or local variations on traditional dishes, like the rice noodle bowl with ranch flank steak.

It's a good place to eat. More to the point—they have tables outside, reasonably far apart. If you want to have a private conversation over dinner without being overheard, this setup is ideal.

Which is why I asked Jonah to meet me here.

I get there a little early; he gets there a couple minutes late. Although we both smile as he joins me at the table, the moment feels undeniably awkward. I know how to negotiate with this man. I know how to surrender to him. Now I have to figure out how to talk to him like a normal person. That might be the hardest part.

The picnic table I chose is at the far end of Elizabeth's outdoor section, so we'll have as much privacy as possible. We look like any other patrons—both of us in jeans and long-sleeved T-shirts, mine white, his black. Normally Jonah's cheeks bear some stubble, but he's completely clean-shaven tonight. I realize he did that for me.

"I'm glad you e-mailed," he says, instead of hello.

"Same here." It was Jonah's e-mail that changed things. I want to tell him that, but words don't come. He doesn't speak either, though he looks completely cool and at ease. I bet I don't. The silence stretches between us until, embarrassed, I try to laugh. "It's so hard to know how to begin."

"We haven't had much opportunity for small talk."

I laugh again, for real, and am rewarded with a small smile. "No. We haven't." Okay, we've got to begin somewhere, so we might as well plunge in. "I'm glad you like the etching."

"It's extraordinary." Jonah doesn't say it like he's trying to suck up to me. He sounds like he's describing artwork in a museum. As if this were objective fact instead of his opinion. "It's . . . precise. Complicated. I can only imagine the hours of work it took. Yet the image doesn't feel stiff or unnatural. Instead it's like—like you captured a moment in time."

People have praised me more effusively, including guys trying to get into my pants. None of them made me feel as flattered as Jonah just did. "Thank you," I say, tucking a loose strand of hair behind my ear. "You really bid on it before you saw I was the artist?"

"Technically, no, because I read the label before I wrote my bid down. But I intended to bid from the first moment I saw it across the room." Even in a more casual setting, his smile remains fierce. "I might have bid sooner, if I hadn't seen you first. After that I was . . . distracted."

The two of us locked together, hidden from the world by red velvet, Jonah buried inside me up to the hilt—the memories bring a flush to my cheeks. It would be easy to let myself get distracted, to start planning the next time.

But there I go again, dodging a hard truth. Better to just say it. "That night, at the benefit, I saw you with a woman I thought might've been your date."

"What?" Apparently Rosalind hasn't spoken to Jonah about our conversation. When she said she didn't meddle in her friends' romantic lives, she must have meant it. "No, no. I went with a friend."

"I realize that now. Even when I first saw her, I knew she might not have been someone you were romantically involved with, or interested in. It just didn't matter." Saying this out loud is so hard. "Our arrangement was supposed to be sex only. You and I were supposed to remain almost strangers. So I shouldn't have cared so much whether someone was in your life. I mean—I don't cheat, and I don't spend time with guys who would be cheating. But that wasn't the part that got under my skin. I was *jealous*. I didn't want another woman anywhere near you. It's that simple."

Jonah remains quiet for a few long moments. Then he says, "Your ex was there. Geordie, is that his name?"

"Yeah." I'm surprised Jonah knows that. "We're not involved anymore. We never will be again."

"I know. But when I saw you near him, and I knew that he'd had you—that he'd slept with you more times than I ever had, that he's gone down on you, that you've come for him—I wanted to put my fist through a wall."

That shouldn't turn me on nearly as much as it does.

"Normally I'm not the possessive type," Jonah continues. As coolly as he speaks, I can now glimpse the uncertainty deep within those gray eyes. "With you, I'm jealous of everyone who ever touched you."

Should that be a huge red flag? Maybe. But when I saw him with Rosalind and didn't understand the truth about them, it made me crazy.

I can't blame Jonah for irrational jealousy when I'm in its grip myself.

"We haven't spoken that much outside our—games," he says.

"We both obeyed the rules. So I shouldn't feel close to you. Not this close."

After a long moment, I reply, "Really you only know one important thing about me. But the *one thing* you know is the single most intimate, private thing I've ever shared with anyone. That's why I said I bared my soul to you, every time. That's why this relationship feels like—"

Like what? I don't have the words for it . . . or I'm afraid to say them. Maybe Jonah's afraid too. He says nothing, but he nods. I tell myself it's enough that he understands.

"You're the only woman who ever fully realized what I wanted from this fantasy." Jonah meets my eyes more evenly than I was able to meet his. "I always thought any woman who would understand that would be—"

"Frightened?" I ask.

Jonah nods again, even though suddenly I feel certain that's not at all what he'd planned to say. But he continues, "I think we both made some assumptions about each other that aren't true. But you're right. Doing what we've done, sharing what we've shared— we've revealed more than we planned. So we feel more bound to each other than we ever meant to."

Bound to him. Yes. That's it. Even though I still wonder what kind of man Jonah is—even though the roots of his fantasy continue to puzzle and unnerve me—I am already bound to Jonah Marks.

For better or for worse, he's bound to me too.

"How do we keep going?" I whisper.

There's his fierce smile again. "You still want to play."

"Yes." A thousand illicit dreams remain unfulfilled inside me. Jonah can make them come true. I want that as much as I've ever wanted anything.

"Then we have to go back to square one."

"What does that mean?"

Jonah's smile changes. Gentles. "I guess we go out on our first date."

"First date?" Now? After we've already fucked like animals? As absurd as it is, the idea charms me, and I realize I'm grinning back at him. "Do you mean tonight?"

"No." He seems almost offended by the idea. "We'll make a whole evening of it. Talk and walk around town and—"

"Act like normal people."

He nods. "If we can."

I start to laugh. Jonah doesn't, but he's smiling down at me, and I know—we're actually going to try this.

It's all delightful fun until you have to explain your life choices to your shrink.

"To say I have mixed feelings about this," Doreen said, "would be putting it lightly."

"You're not supposed to give opinions about my life. That's not what therapists do, right? They listen."

Doreen shoots me a look. "Have we ever had a traditional patient-therapist relationship?"

"No," I admit.

"And I doubt we're going to start now. Besides, I gave you my opinion when you asked whether I could 'believe this.' If you weren't uncertain about your decision, you wouldn't have asked."

She just poked through the bubble of giddiness I've floated in since Jonah and I spoke two nights earlier. All the concerns I had—that I still have—become clear once more.

She says, "I have to admit, I feared your meetings with Jonah would prove destructive, and they haven't. The shame you've carried about your rape fantasy has diminished to some degree. Both he and you took precautions to ensure your safety. Best-case scenario, I'd say. But you need to be aware what you're doing now—merging your fantasy life and your emotional life; that's about a thousand times more complicated."

"What's going to be so different?" I snap.

"You tell me."

I hate it when Doreen makes me answer my own questions, mostly because I usually do know the answers. They're just answers I don't like. For a moment I fidget on the couch—pushing up the arms of my white cardigan, curling my feet beneath me. But I can't postpone replying for long. ". . . I still wonder what kind of a man has such powerful fantasies about rape. When we play our games, he knows exactly what would scare me. He knows how to be cruel. He's thought about that a *lot*."

"That's a valid consideration."

"How can I judge him for that when I have rape fantasies too?"

"You know why you're so fixated on them. You don't know why he is."

I want to tell Doreen my theories about his family—about his anger with his mother, the way her threats might have taught him about violence. However, I remain quiet. Doreen would simply say that it's only a theory, with absolutely no proof to support it. She would be correct.

More gently, Doreen says, "Have you ever considered telling Jonah the truth about your rape?"

"No." The word comes out more sharply than I intended.

"You've still never told anyone besides your mother and me, have you?"

I shake my head. "Nobody else."

One time, years later, I tried to tell Chloe the truth about that night. But she shut me down before I'd even revealed the whole story, telling me I'd always been jealous of her, asking whether I'd come on to any of her other boyfriends. It wasn't exactly a moment for the Sisterly Bonding Hall of Fame. So Chloe still doesn't know. "Refusing to believe" is the same as "not knowing," right? For my sister, it might as well be.

"It's your secret. A piece of your life that's yours to share or not to share, as you see fit. You never have to tell a soul if you don't want to." Doreen has never tried to make me feel ashamed of my own silence, for which I'm deeply grateful. Sometimes I see courageous rape survivors on television or the Internet, braving clueless commentators or vicious trolls to speak out about their experiences, and my admiration of them is mirrored by my own sense of cowardice. She continues, "But keeping this secret from Jonah—giving him that kind of power, without knowing how deep your wounds lie—"

"I've handled it so far," I say. Which is true.

So far, though, Jonah and I have played "softer" games. Ones where I could easily reassert myself at any second. I want more than that from him, though. I want him to tie me up. I want him to fight me, to defeat me.

I want him to *own* me.

When the sex between Jonah and me turned out to be so freaking amazing, I thought maybe I'd disarmed Anthony's power over me, for good. What if I only buried the bomb deeper? As Jonah and I dig further into my darkest fantasies, we might be getting closer to the fuse.

Doreen says, "Your involvement with Jonah so far has worked well because you set boundaries. Without those boundaries—what happens?"

"I don't know," I admit, but I lift my chin. "I guess I'll find out."

"Come on," Shay gripes Thursday afternoon, as Carmen fusses around her. "Dr. Campbell put me on bed rest. Not in traction."

"Still, the closer all your stuff is, the better." Carmen steps back to admire her work: a semicircle of remotes, magazines, and snacks all around Shay's place in bed. "The iPad is at one hundred percent, but the charger is here on the nightstand when you need it. And here's my Netflix password! So you can watch movies all you want. Now, do you need some ginger ale? Maybe some apple juice?"

Shay gives me a slightly helpless look, and I stifle a giggle. She's gone from having not nearly enough of Carmen's attention to having way too much of it. In the long run, I think this is a good thing; Shay can no longer doubt how much Carmen truly does care about her. But right now, Carmen is getting on both our nerves.

I take Carmen by the shoulders. "Enjoy the Netflix," I say. "And let us know if you need anything. Now Carmen and I have work to do."

"But we'll be back tomorrow!" Carmen promises. "As soon as our last classes are over!"

Looks like I can't put this off any longer. ". . . I won't, actually."

Carmen looks at me, stricken, as if I'd shot Bambi's mom. Shay simply smiles. "Got a hot date?"

She's joking. Why did she have to pick *that* joke? "Well, yeah."

"Really? You've been holding out on us!" Shay perks up, excited for me—and probably relieved to no longer be the center of attention. "Who's the guy? Anyone we know?"

"Well, you know him, Shay. And I guess you might've met him at the party, Carmen. Do you remember Jonah Marks? He's one of the earth sciences professors?"

Carmen might be distracted by Shay's condition right now, but her sharp mind never forgets a single detail. "The guy with the great arms."

I have to laugh. "They're pretty good, yeah."

Shay, meanwhile, stares at me as if I'd suddenly begun speaking in Hindustani. "Jonah . . . Marks," she repeats. "The same one I know."

"The one and only." I feel so shy talking about him, as if I were going out on my first date ever. "Remember how I told you Jonah helped me with that flat tire? Well, we talked some at the party— and then we ran into each other again at the charity event for Geordie's organization—and tomorrow night we're going to get some dinner."

Each and every word I said was the truth. Just not the whole truth.

"Okay. Wow." Shay blinks, then pulls herself together. "I've never talked to him much, but like I said, he's pretty cool to work for. He's so *quiet*, though. Hardly ever says a word."

Already I feel protective of him. "He's not a cold person. Just reserved."

"Oh, sure, definitely," Shay says, nodding quickly. She'd never trash-talk anyone. Already, I can tell, she's trying to see Jonah through my eyes. Thank God she can't.

Carmen says, "Jonah's quiet? Hardly seems like your type."

I shrug. "Turns out we have a lot in common."

They'll never know what that means. Now I have to find out if what Jonah and I share can bring us together, or whether it's destined to tear us apart.

TWENTY

Every other time I've dressed for Jonah Marks, my main concern has been whether to wear underwear.

Tonight, I have new priorities.

He's seen me in everything from the professional stuff I wear to teach in to trashy pink dresses to plain old T-shirts and jeans. Even though I've never actually been fully naked with Jonah, he's seen every part of my body. So why am I trying on the entire contents of my closet in an attempt to find the perfect outfit tonight?

Makes no sense. But here I am.

After putting on and then rejecting at least ten other possibilities, I settle on something simple: a pleated black skirt, white button-up shirt with the sleeves cuffed, ballet flats, and a simple chain around my neck. It's laid-back and pulled together, but not fancy, and, well, not that sexy.

I mean, I think I look good in this. I wouldn't wear it if I didn't. But this outfit doesn't show off my legs, my ass, my cleavage, anything like that. This is the first night Jonah and I have ever spent together that isn't totally about sex. Tonight we'll . . . talk. Somehow that feels scarier than our role-playing.

For once I'm ready ahead of time, which means I have to find a way to wait that makes it seem like I'm not waiting. So I open Spotify and click on my contemporary jazz channel; Cassandra Wilson starts to croon, and her voice melts over me like caramel. I sink into my plush white sofa and take slow, deep breaths.

Just for tonight, I won't ask where this is heading. I won't try to reconcile our sexual fantasies with the kind of people we are. I won't bring my enormous load of emotional baggage with me.

Tonight, I'm going to find out just what kind of person Jonah Marks really is.

The music keeps me from hearing the car's approach, so I startle when I hear the bell. But the song and my new resolution calm me, and I smile as I open the door. "Hi."

Jonah simply nods. This man isn't big on hello. He doesn't smile, either, but his voice is warm as he says, "You look beautiful."

"Thanks." *So do you*, I want to add, because he does. Simple black pants that nonetheless hug his taut waist and skim past muscular thighs—a midnight blue shirt turns his gray eyes the shade of a less stormy sky—and a heavy platinum watch around one wrist, the first sign of real wealth I've ever seen from him. But men never understand when you call them beautiful.

I see him glance past my shoulder, perhaps curious about the place where I live. Or maybe he's figuring out how to get in, some night. He says only, "So—should we go?"

Jesus, he's ripped the clothes off my body and we've fucked like animals, but suddenly neither of us knows what to say. I laugh a little, and when Jonah gives me a look, I explain, "I was smoother than this at my junior prom."

"Same here." A smile slowly dawns on his face. "Should I have brought a corsage?"

"Next time. Come on, let's go."

. . .

We go to a restaurant on Congress, not far from my place. Most Italian restaurants serve up the classic spaghetti and pizza, but here, the emphasis is on authentic northern Italian cuisine: roasted lemony chicken, pale white cheeses, and light, crisp Soave wine. Just inhaling the scent of the air is more delicious than most meals I've ever had.

That gives Jonah and me something to talk about for approximately twenty seconds. After that, we're sitting across the table from each other, hardly knowing what to say.

What if I don't like this guy at all? I wonder. *What if we have nothing in common besides our kinky fantasies?*

Just when the silence is about to go from awkward to pathetic, Jonah says, "What made you decide to draw that picture? The one in the print I bought. The man holding the dove."

"I like to portray—contrasts. Duality. So I look for images that express two very different concepts at once."

"The strength of the hands," Jonah says. "And the fragility of the dove."

"Exactly." Should I ask this? Might as well. "You said you were drawn to the etching even before you knew I made it. Why?"

Jonah remains silent long enough that I wonder if he was lying about his interest in it. But then I realize he's not stumped for an answer; he's searching for the right words. "There's so much tension there—you can sense the energy, even in the muscles. So I thought he'd imprisoned the dove in his hands. That he was on the verge of hurting it. But then I saw how careful he was—that his grasp is gentle. He wants to keep the bird alive. The drawing surprised me, and I liked that sense of surprise. A simple image turned out to mean more than I first thought."

"Wow. Thanks." Don't get me wrong—it's nice to be told that people think your work is beautiful, or lifelike, that kind of thing. But there's no compliment an artist loves more than someone telling you your work made them *think*.

"When did you start drawing?"

"Well—first of all, I've always loved to draw. But the work you bought isn't a drawing. It's an etching."

Jonah has relaxed slightly as we settle into conversation. So have I. He says, "What's the difference?"

So I start explaining about etching—the processes, the materials, the history of it all. He's genuinely interested, and every minute is easier than the last, and suddenly our evening together takes flight.

No, Jonah's not hugely talkative. His explanation about why he liked my etching is the longest he talks about anything the entire dinner. But he listens well. Instead of planning the next anecdote he can share, he responds like someone who genuinely wants to know more about my work, and more about me.

Of course he's naturally curious, I remind myself as we leave the restaurant. Instead of heading straight back to his car, we begin wandering along Congress, side by side. The guy's a scientist. Curiosity is his fuel.

"Enough about me," I say as the Thursday-night bustle flows around us—college kids heading to bars, stores open late to take advantage of the foot traffic, guitar music and drumbeats audible from the door of every club. "What about you? What made you decide to study earthquakes?"

"And volcanoes," he adds.

"Can't leave out the volcanoes," I say, and am rewarded with a small smile.

"Well, when I was about ten years old, my mother and stepfather took the whole family to Hawaii."

Stepfather, I note. Jonah could have no memory of his real father, and Carter Hale's been married to Jonah's mother for almost three decades. Most kids in that situation would wind up calling their stepfathers Dad. Not Jonah.

He continues, "Like most tourists in Hawaii, we went out to see the volcanoes. I hadn't imagined you could get that close to the lava flow. When I saw it—glowing orange with heat, pure liquid stone—" To my surprise, he grins. "I was ten, so I thought it was *totally cool*."

I laugh out loud. "So that's how you picked your scientific specialty? Because it was cool?"

"Any scientist who tells you something different is lying. If you're going to spend your entire life studying something, it needs to thrill you. Volcanoes and earthquakes thrilled me when I was a kid, and they still do. Even after all the studies and the dissertation and months of looking at nothing but seismograph readings. I get a charge out of it every time."

"Hey, they always say that if you do what you love, it doesn't feel like work," I say.

"Which is a crock." When I raise an eyebrow at Jonah, his smile regains some of the fierceness I know so well. "If you spend twelve hours in a row doing something—anything—it feels like work."

Laughing, I admit, "Okay, yes. The studio's my favorite place to be, but there are times when I feel like if I go in there one more time, I'll tear my hair out. Still, I'd rather go crazy making art than do anything else."

Jonah nods. "That's it exactly."

"So you get to spend your whole life chasing lava."

"And you'll spend yours making art."

"Yes and no," I say. "After graduation I'm hoping to go into museum work. Preserving old etchings, curating important pieces, even using original plates from centuries ago to make new prints."

He gives me a look. "You should do your own work. Not worry about taking care of someone else's."

"It's not either/or. I'll never stop creating my own work. But even if I set the entire art world on fire, it'll be years before I can support myself through my etchings alone—if ever. So there's going to be a day job for a while, probably a long while. Should I do something boring that sucks my soul away one day at a time? Or should I surround myself with some of the greatest etchings of all time, and help other people understand how amazing they are?"

After a moment, Jonah nods. "When you put it that way, okay. I see it."

Then his hand brushes against mine. At first I think he's drawing me aside as we go past a group of college kids drunkenly weaving along the sidewalk. After they pass, though, he adjusts his grip, twining our fingers together.

Jonah Marks has screwed me hotter and dirtier than any other man ever has—and yet my heart flutters like a girl's as he holds my hand for the first time.

We browse the various shops for a little while, mostly for the pleasure of remaining hand in hand. Cowboy boots are available in every color, every size; these days in Austin, college girls wear them more often than ranchers do. Other stores offer Mexican crafts—thick woven serapes, kitschy wrestler's masks in red and gold satin, bins filled with beads painted like the skulls of *Dia de los Muertos*, tin hearts crowned with flame.

"These are called *milagros*, right?" he asks as he traces his finger around the sharp edge of one of the hearts. "Miracles?"

"Exactly." An enameled image of the Virgin Mary is at the very center of the heart. "The flame symbolizes the Holy Spirit, touching hearts, making us change."

Jonah gives me a look; I seem to have surprised him. "Are you a believer?"

"I think you'd have to call me a 'hopeful agnostic.'"

"I'm less hopeful. But when I see things like this—the feeling in them—I envy that kind of faith. The world must look so different, through those eyes."

I *like* this man. Once you break through his cool reserve, he's . . . engaging. Intelligent. Even fascinating. He may be guarded, but it's possible to get past his gates. I've only just begun learning who Jonah is, besides my ultimate sexual partner; now I realize I want to find out everything there is to know.

Finally the shops begin to close, and Jonah drives me the short distance home. We don't speak. I suspect Jonah's mind is full of many of the same questions now rushing through my mind about what happens with us later. Can two people so sensually connected by a very specific fantasy have any other kind of sex? Am I ready to find out? Strange though it seems after everything Jonah and I have done, making love as ourselves—not playing any roles—feels far more intimate, and even more scary.

But when Jonah walks to me to the door, he stops. "Aren't you coming in?" I ask.

"Not on the first date." At my surprise, he smiles that fierce, knowing grin that turns me to jelly. "What kind of man do you think I am?"

I squeeze his hand. "You're right. Wouldn't want to rush things."

"Wouldn't be proper," Jonah murmurs as he draws me closer. Two of his fingers trace along the side of my face, painting my skin with the warmth of his touch.

"We couldn't have that."

"Absolutely not."

"But what about kissing?" I tilt my face up toward his. "Do you kiss on the first date?"

"Not usually." Jonah pulls me into his arms. "But sometimes I make an exception."

He nuzzles my cheek, my chin. Tilts my head back slightly so he can brush his lips against my throat. I breathe out—a sigh that makes him tighten his embrace. My fingers stroke the back of his head, his short hair soft against my palms. Then I trace his neck and the broad planes of his back. I could worship this man's body for hours. The powerful muscles I feel beneath my hands make him seem like he was created to give pleasure, or pain. Maybe both.

When Jonah's mouth meets mine, his touch is feather-soft. My entire body reacts—flushing warm, getting wet, wanting more. I part my lips, and he kisses me again. Only the tips of our tongues touch, but it's enough to make me reel.

But then he pulls away, his arms slipping to my sides, and I know he's about to go. That's all? I want to smack him. I want to kiss him again. And yet this is perfect. For our first date, we're leaving each other wanting more.

Jonah's voice is husky. "I enjoyed tonight."

"Same here."

"We can do this again sometime?"

"Sometime soon."

He smiles, leans forward, and gently kisses my cheek. "Good night, Vivienne."

"Good night."

I don't shut my door until he's started his car. Once I've closed and locked it, I literally slide down to the floor. My laughter sounds giddy. What was erotic fascination has become infatuation—and I *love* it.

How long has it been since I felt this kind of elation after a date?

Never. Not unless you count the one kiss from that Barcelonan exchange student. This is about a thousand times better.

I'm still beaming when I lie down in bed and turn out the light. It feels like I could even smile in my sleep.

. . .

My subconscious has other ideas.

Someone's knocking on the door. "I'm tired," I moan. "I don't want to come down for breakfast."

The knocking continues. Gets harder and louder. It turns into pounding.

"Jonah?" I sit upright, unsurprised to find myself back in my childhood room. My bedspread is trimmed with eyelet lace. The stuffed lamb I loved as a baby, Woolly Bully, still sits on a bookshelf, ratty and gray and yet adorable. "What are you doing here?"

The next slam against the door makes the wall shake, and I hear someone roar, "*Let me in!*"

That wasn't Jonah.

I scramble out of bed. In my haste I trip myself up in my own sheets and fall on the floor, so I try to crawl to the closet. If I hide in the closet he won't find me—

The door breaks, pieces flying against the wall. I scoot to the back of my closet, hanging clothes swinging against my shoulders and head, thinking, *please no please no please*—

"You can't hide from me," Anthony says as he comes toward me. His fist closes around my wrist, and by now I'm screaming, but no one can hear. Nobody ever hears. "Come on. Get on the bed. Be a good girl."

"I won't," I shriek. "*I won't*—"

Then I'm awake, in my own bed, gasping for breath. I realize I woke myself up screaming in my sleep.

TWENTY-ONE

After that nightmare, sleep doesn't come easy. I give up around six A.M. If I have to be awake this early, I might as well get in some more studio time.

Carmen texts me around eight, supposedly just to see what's up—but I know she wants to hear about my night with Jonah. I'm reluctant to explain, for a few reasons, but I've admitted he's in my life. Besides, if I can talk Carmen into swinging by the studio to chat, I might be able to persuade her to pick up coffee on the way.

"One café au lait," she announces as she comes in the door. "So spill. Good date or bad date? Not a *great* date, I'm guessing, since you're here instead of at his place."

"Oh, come on. I don't usually move that fast." Jonah doesn't figure into the equation; he's an outlier. "Just faster than you."

"I can't help it if I'm an old-fashioned girl."

Carmen smiles as she says it, but it's only half a joke. She dated the same guy throughout high school, and another guy through most of our undergrad years, so she has almost zero experience with sex outside a committed relationship. Not for lack of chances, though: Carmen gets more male attention than any other woman I've ever known. Cute as she is, she'd be the first to admit she's not any kind of supermodel—but she radiates warmth and fun, which is more attractive than anything else.

"Out with it," she says as she perches at a drafting table in one corner. "What did you guys do? Were you able to get more than two words out of him?"

"We went to dinner. It took the conversation a while to get rolling, but soon it was fine. Better than fine. Great. Jonah's not cold or unfriendly. He's guarded until he gets to know people, that's all."

Not really. Something else lies behind Jonah's silences, his darkness—something that began at Redgrave House in Chicago. But I wouldn't talk about that part of Jonah's life even if I understood more about it. His troubled relationship with his family is none of my business, and even less of Carmen's.

"Who knew? I guess everybody has, I don't know, hidden depths." She blows a bit of her cappuccino's foam out of the way. "When did you get interested in him, anyway?"

I'm torn. Carmen is my best friend; I don't make a habit of lying to her, beyond the occasional fib like, *You look fine, nobody's going to notice you spilled coffee on your skirt.* But how can I possibly explain the whole truth about this? The only two human beings who come anywhere close to understanding are Doreen and Jonah himself—and even those two don't have the whole picture.

Finally I decide to start at the beginning and see how far I get. "Well, you remember that I met Jonah when he changed a flat for me—"

"Chivalry's not dead!" Carmen chirps.

I remember Jonah forcing me to my knees, growling, *Look at me when you suck my cock.* Even that quick flash of memory gets me hot. "Then he was at your party, thanks to Shay, and—" Maybe I can lead into the truth like this. "—after Geordie, uh, embarrassed me out on the deck, I was pretty freaked out. Then Jonah talked with me. Distracted me."

"Oh, right. Arturo said Geordie started oversharing about

your relationship. What did he say?" Carmen's eyes widen. "Did Geordie talk about your sex life?"

Dammit. I thought every single person at that party knew! That was the reason I hid out at the far end of the yard in the first place. When so many people heard Geordie drunkenly apologize for not fulfilling my rape fantasy—well, I thought that was the kind of gossip that flowed through a party even faster than sangria. Arturo heard it, I know. But apparently nobody told Carmen.

I ought to be grateful. Instead, I'm chagrined. If someone had told her the truth then, I wouldn't have as much to explain now. I say, "Yeah. Geordie got seriously personal, and I was pretty embarrassed."

Carmen shrugs. "Come on. You guys went out for more than six months. It's not like people didn't know you two were sleeping together."

"That's not the point. Geordie, um, gave specifics."

"Oh, my God. Was he talking about your body? I would *die.*" She gives me a look. "Do you think that's why Jonah got interested in you? Because that would weird me out."

I can't tell her. I can't. Carmen's so far from realizing what I'm talking about, and I don't want to bridge the gulf between her relative innocence and the kind of kink Jonah and I have indulged. Explaining feels impossible . . . or, at least, uncomfortable. "Not quite like that," I say, not meeting her eyes. "Jonah didn't want me to feel embarrassed. So we wound up, uhh, talking when we saw each other at the charity benefit. And guess what? At the silent auction, he actually bought my etching."

"No way! Really?"

I smile back. "Even better, he decided to bid on it before he knew it was mine."

Then Carmen and I are talking easily about the fact that Jonah's interested in my art, and how cool that is, plus it's pretty hot for a guy to be flying all around the world to study volcanoes, and so on. I ask her whether she's made a move on her latest crush, but she claims she's too busy with schoolwork. Has she suddenly turned shy? Maybe this particular guy brings out her bashful side. Our conversation widens as we spiral further away from the dark truth I'd rather not tell.

Doreen's voice echoes in my memories. *Pay attention to the secrets that you keep. You don't have to share everything with everyone—but sometimes the very things you hide are the things you least need to keep locked inside.*

The secret Jonah and I share is different. Surely it belongs to us alone.

Carmen has a ten A.M. class, so before long she's headed to campus, as blissfully ignorant of my warped sex life as ever. I need to get into the departmental office soon, so I should follow her, but I linger awhile, restless and unable to focus.

Instead I pace the length of the studio. People will start coming in soon, but for another few minutes, the space is mine alone. My footsteps on the concrete floor echo in the empty space. The air smells like paint. I'm surrounded by drafting tables, a potter's wheel, easels, X-Acto knives, pots of ink. A few long poles stretch from floor to ceiling, lingering evidence of the spiral staircases that were here back when this was a warehouse. Masking-tape labels proclaim this brush or that canvas to be the property of one of the artists who pays for the studio's use.

I wish the studio belonged to me. Only me.

Because then I could ask Jonah to meet me here.

He would rip open my work shirt. Cover my mouth with his hand. Thrust against me so that I felt the length and hardness of his erection against my belly. I imagine him using the ragged remains of my shirt to tie me to one of the poles—pulling so tight I can almost feel the pressure. My breaths quicken as I imagine him taking one of the artists' knives and cutting away my jeans and panties. Then he could force my legs apart and—

"Hey!"

Startled, I spin around to see Marvin—a painter, one of my fellow TAs at the UT department of art, and the guy who told me about this studio in the first place. "Oh! Hi. Hi there. How's it going?"

"Fine." Marvin gives me a look as he hangs his messenger bag on one of the wall hooks. "You okay?"

"Sure! Of course."

"You look a little flushed, that's all."

"Just got done working hard." Wow, that could not have sounded less convincing if I'd tried. Hastily I head for my own bag. "Heading out. Anything you need me to take care of at the office?"

Marvin shakes his head, bemused. "It's all good."

Honestly, I think as I drive to campus. *You went out with Jonah. You've told your friends. The two of you are—normalizing this.*

He's not your mystery lover anymore.

But the whole day, I can't stop thinking about Jonah. Not the conversation we shared—not the tender kiss at my front door—but endless fantasies, overlapping each other and blurring every other thought I have. Over and over, I imagine him taking me as roughly and brutally as possible.

Concentrate! I tell myself, as I sit through a department meeting, as I grade papers, as I talk to Geordie on the phone about a mutual friend's birthday dinner. It doesn't help. My erotic imagination has taken over, and there's no room left in my head for anything else. Even when I guest-lecture in the Renaissance Sculpture class, I linger too long on the slide of Bernini's *Apollo and Daphne*. It's as if I'm drinking in her fear, his lust, and her hands reaching skyward for escape.

I want Jonah to chase me. To catch me. I want it *now*.

As I walk back to my office after class, my phone vibrates in my hand. I'm expecting Geordie to call back with the final word on the restaurant, so—for once—I don't look at the screen before I answer. "Hello."

"Oh. Vivienne." Chloe sounds dismayed to have gotten me instead of my voice mail. That makes two of us. "How are you?"

"Fine. And you?"

"Very well, as it happens." *As if you care* remains unspoken. "Mom's decided to get rid of the armoire on the second floor. You know, the one that used to belong to Aunt Mignon? It would look just perfect in my guest room . . . but of course I've taken the last few heirlooms. So I thought I ought to ask you whether you were interested before I became greedy."

Sounds generous, doesn't it? Of course, Chloe's fully aware that I live in a two-room house that barely has room for my books, much less more furniture. "You should have it," I say. "Besides, then the armoire will be Libby's someday."

"Of course. Well." A silence falls. She wants to know about Thanksgiving, but she doesn't want to ask.

I'm so, so tired of jumping through hoops—but if I don't visit Libby this Thanksgiving, how long will it be before I see her again? Chloe couldn't keep me from her forever, but she could separate us for a long time. So I stifle a sigh. "I'm planning on coming home for the holidays. For Thanksgiving and Christmas." That last is only partly true. Christmas day with my family, I can endure. The entire break? No way in hell.

"It's good to know how many to plan for," she says primly. But then, with what seems like genuine interest, she says, "I don't suppose you'll be bringing anyone? Are you still seeing that adorable Scotsman?"

"Geordie and I decided we were better off as friends. But I'll tell him you said he was adorable. It'll make his day." The one time

Geordie and Chloe met, they hit it off. Of course, Geordie hits it
off with nearly everyone.

"A pity you two broke up. He suited you, I thought. There's no
one else on the horizon?"

I let the silence go on too long before I say, "I'm not bringing
anyone to Thanksgiving." Jonah and I might be trying to find our
way back to normal, but I doubt he's the holiday-dinners type.

"Sounds like there's a story there," Chloe says, but she doesn't
ask further. That would come too close to having a meaningful
conversation. "Well, be sure to let us know what night you'll come
in from Austin."

"Will do. And tell Libby hi."

"Of course." In her voice, there's not even a hint that she
recently threatened to keep Libby away from me permanently.
"Thanks for being so understanding about the armoire."

"Don't mention it," I say, knowing she won't.

This makes for a solid three minutes I've spent thinking about
something besides Jonah Marks. But I don't make it to four,
because as soon as I open my e-mail, there's a note from Jonah.

The subject reads, Complete Disclosure.

My pulse quickens as I click, wondering if I'm about to read
some confession—the truth about Jonah's fantasy, whatever dark
place it comes from, all his inner secrets. The answer proves to be
more prosaic than that.

We said we would exchange these. I feel strange sending them
after our evening out together, but you need to know now more
than ever.
    I can't stop thinking about the way you kiss.

My heart does a dizzy little flip when I read the last line, which softens the moment when I open the attachment to see a lab report—Jonah confirming that he's free of any STD.

Ah, modern love.

Well, I asked. And I need to get my own records to send to him too. Then we can stop with the condoms. Our fantasies can be even freer—our scenes more spontaneous. More savage.

I remember what I imagined he whispered to me the night of the charity benefit. *Next time I'm going to come in your mouth.*

Next time can't come fast enough.

It's Doreen's job to be a wet blanket sometimes. That doesn't mean I enjoy it.

"You're being obstinate," I say during our next session. "You were all, ooooh, be scared, this date is going to be the worst date in the history of dating—"

"You know full well those words never came out of my mouth." But Doreen is laughing.

"No, but I bet you were thinking them. Instead, Jonah and I went out and had a really good time! He's smart, Doreen. He's—insightful, and patient, and interesting." I hug my knees to my chest. "Plus he has great taste in art."

"I believe you about the art," she says. Doreen has another of my etchings, one I gave her as a Christmas gift last year. It hangs in her foyer; I walk by it every time I come to a session. "The rest, I'll take your word for. I'm glad to hear that he's a person you're drawn to on levels beside the physical."

Gloating is too much fun to stop so soon. "You're glad to hear you were proven wrong?"

"No, I'm glad to hear that you're having the most honest sexual relationship of your life."

That stops me short. I hadn't thought of it that way—but she's right. "Jonah knows what I want. What I need. It's what he needs too."

"Do you still feel guilty about the fantasy? Like it's something bad you should be ashamed of?"

I listen to her clock for a few moments, the slow *tick-tock* punctuating the silence. "Less."

"Less means yes."

"It also means less." I readjust myself on the sofa, so I'm sitting up like an adult instead of hugging myself like a girl on her best friend's floor. "The fantasy feels different when—when it's shared."

"Then why do you think you continue to feel some shame?"

We go over this, and over this. I'm so fucking tired of answering this question. "Because I'm getting my rocks off on something horrible. Something criminal. There are women who get raped—even men who get raped—who never want to have sex again after that. I don't know why it wasn't like that for me, or why it was the exact opposite. It just *is*, and now—now I get turned on by the same thing I hate Anthony for." I have to swallow hard. "If I hate Anthony for raping me, but I keep putting myself through all these fantasy rapes in my mind—and finding Jonah, going into this arrangement we have—maybe I should hate myself too. Because I do it to myself."

That's the first time I've uttered those words. The first time I've even allowed myself to think them. Doreen's endless patient questions finally connected and broke me open.

"There's a world of difference between your fantasies and what Anthony did, because *he raped you*," Doreen says. "You *choose* your partner in the fantasy—whether that's a figment of your imagination or a willing lover like Jonah. You didn't choose Anthony. He took that choice away from you."

"I know. I know." Tears have started to well.

That's Doreen's cue to tell me that I shouldn't beat myself up over my fantasies, but today she goes in a different direction. "You still haven't told Jonah about your rape?"

"God, no."

"Do you think keeping this secret from Jonah is different than keeping it secret from others?"

"Jonah's the last person I could tell."

"And why is that?"

The answer is obvious, but Doreen wants me to say it out loud. Fine, then. "I'm scared he'd get off on it."

Doreen sits back in her chair. "Vivienne, I want you to think about what this says about the trust between you and Jonah. You've given him a great deal of power over you; so far he hasn't abused that. But how much trust can there be when you're afraid he would enjoy hearing about your real-life rape?"

I have no answer for her. The clock ticks on, measuring the silence.

Those words of caution linger in my mind, but they don't make me stop wanting Jonah.

No, I'm even more turned on than before. That's how fucked up I am.

But Doreen reminded me that, on some level—one that goes deeper than a nice dinner out, or his admiration for my artwork—I'm still a little bit frightened of Jonah Marks.

The fear is what makes it so good.

I get home just at sunset. As soon as I've shut and locked the door behind me, I call Jonah.

"Are you all right?" he says. Still no hello.

"Yeah, I'm fine."

"Is this about my e-mail earlier? Maybe that was—abrupt."

"No, it's good that you sent it. I'm glad, really. My records will be headed your way as soon as I can scan them." I run one hand through my hair, restless as I pace my floor. "Are you free tonight?"

". . . I can be."

"Do you want to play?"

He knows what I mean. I can tell by the long silence that follows, and the huskiness of his voice as he finally answers, "Yes."

Tonight, I'm going to test my limits.

I'm going to prove how far I can trust Jonah Marks, and how far I can't.

TWENTY-TWO

Quarter 'til ten.

Keiko's pottery—put that away. Breakables have no place out in the open, not tonight. *What about the lamp? If I move it to the center of the table, that's probably okay.*

I took a shower just after a light dinner of toast and eggs, plus the last of the peaches I bought a few days ago. The juice was still sticky on my chin and fingers as I stood under the hot spray of water, rubbing in something that promises to be "ultra-moisturizing." My skin feels soft, anyway, and the faint lavender scent lingers.

I wonder if Jonah will even notice. Probably not. If tonight goes according to plan, his mind should be on other things.

"Unlock your door at ten P.M. No earlier. I don't want you to do anything unsafe."

Protecting me as he plans to terrorize me. This is the paradox of Jonah Marks.

Nearly everything that could break during a struggle has been put away. Now what? Lights on or off? He'll want to see me—and I want to see him—but the dark would sharpen the edge of my fear. Finally I turn down one of the floor lamps in the far corner of my living room, so only a faint shadow of amber-tinted light falls across my bedroom floor.

"I should warn you," I said. *"When I said I'll fight, I meant it."*

Jonah's low voice made me shudder. *"Struggle all you want. It won't matter."*

My hair is down. Wearing makeup would be sort of ridiculous, but if I went to bed like it really was any other night, I might have acne cream on my chin. Let's not. I settle for clean-scrubbed skin and cherry ChapStick. My shoes have all found their places in my closet, instead of their usual line near the side of my bed. This tank top is a soft shade of apricot—seemed like a good idea on the clearance rack, but it doesn't really match anything else I own. It's been sleepwear for a while now. My nipples are just visible through the thin ribbed cotton.

Simple cotton panties. If they get torn, so be it.

I should probably shop at the Salvation Army for more clothes I wouldn't mind being destroyed.

"If I haven't come in by ten thirty, something's held me up. Lock your door and wait for me to call."

Five until ten. On the back of my bedroom door, I've hung a series of hooks, which gives me a handy place to keep belts, scarves, accessories like that. I run my hands through the scarves, feeling the various fabrics against my skin—then close my fingers around pale pink cotton. This scarf is sturdy enough to stand up to some abuse. Yet thin enough to serve as a makeshift rope—if that's something Jonah wants.

I'm about to find out.

"You remember the rules I gave you, back when we began? About what I didn't want the first time?" I put my hand to my chest, as if my touch could slow my fluttering heart. *"You can consider those suspended."*

"Fewer limits."

"Mmm-hmm."

Jonah growled, "Good."

Ten o'clock.

I almost never go to bed this early, but tonight is about setting the stage. So I drape the pink scarf across the foot of my bed—a careless temptation—then walk into my kitchen. By now I can feel my pulse in my throat, in my cunt, in the soles of my feet.

Slowly, I turn the lock, then slide back the deadbolt. Anyone could come in now.

I walk into the bedroom and turn off the one lamp on the nightstand. Now there's just the dim light from the living room slanting across the floor. Lots of people might leave that much light on so they could find their way around in the dark, if they wanted.

Now Jonah will be able to find his way to me.

Every second is exquisite torture. I lie on my side, covers tucked up around my ears, as if I could possibly pretend to be asleep. Really I've never been this awake in my life. Every sound seems unnaturally loud in this silence—the wind through the trees outside, the distant rumble of a truck on the road, the soft creaks in the walls natural to any old house. Surely I'll hear Jonah's car pull up . . .

. . . but no. Jonah's sedan was out front before ten o'clock; I know that as surely as if I'd seen it myself. He would be watching my door from the first moment I unlocked it, to make sure no one else tried to get inside.

A creak from the kitchen first seems normal enough, until I hear another. Footsteps. My entire body tenses in the best possible way. He's here, now.

Should I get up to investigate? Surprise him in the front room? No. This time I want him to find me in bed.

I close my eyes.

The footsteps come closer. He's wearing soft shoes, or none, because he walks so quietly that I think if this were real, I'd sleep right through it. By now adrenaline courses through me, setting every single nerve ending on fire.

If I even put my hand between my legs—just that contact, not even a stroke—I swear I'd come this second.

Now the footsteps are right next to me. I feel the foot of the bed sink down, the unmistakable sensation of someone sitting on the mattress. It's so hard not to open my eyes, so hard to pretend—

His hand closes over my mouth, hard.

My eyes fly open to see Jonah leaning over me. He's dressed in black, and his face is almost unrecognizable. This is hardly a human being I see. This is . . . a predator.

He hisses, *"Don't scream."*

I don't scream.

I strike.

My hands close around his wrist, yanking it away from my mouth, and I pull both knees up to my chest, then kick. My feet thud into Jonah's chest, knocking him completely off the bed.

Instantly I scramble across the mattress, as if I were trying to reach my cell phone (charging in its dock, a few feet away). But Jonah's hand closes around my ankle and tows me back toward him.

"You hurt me." His hand pulls at the strap of my tank top, yanking it down to expose one of my breasts. "You're gonna pay for that."

"No!" I shove my hands against his chest, hard, and then the battle is on.

No broken bones. No visible wounds. Those are the rules we agreed on in the beginning—permanent rules, which neither of us will ever, ever break. But that doesn't mean we can't fight like hell.

I shove him away again. Slap him hard across the face.

Jonah slaps me right back. The force is enough to send me staggering against the wall. Hearing the thud, feeling the sting of my skin, shakes me—*this is so real, so fucking real*—and for the first time since our inaugural night at the hotel, the safe word comes to the tip of my tongue. *Silver.*

I don't say it.

Instead I run at him for a full-on tackle. Jonah didn't expect that; I can tell by the way he staggers backward. We both land on the bed. I use my momentum to roll me over him until I fall off the far side. Now I'm free, and—holy shit, will I actually get to the phone? Not sure what to do then—

But Jonah's up. He grabs my arm and throws me bodily onto the bed. Before I can scramble backward, he's on top of me, his knees pressing down on my arms. I try to kick at him, but from this angle it's almost impossible. So I writhe, twisting from side to side, until one of Jonah's hands closes around my throat.

Instantly I go still.

"Now you're going to behave." He laughs, a sound as sharp as any switchblade. "You're not as dumb as you look."

Would he like it if I begged? "Let me go. Please."

"Why would I do that?"

"You—you can take my phone, and my laptop. My purse, too, and I've got a lot of cash in my wallet. Just take it and go. I won't be able to call the police, because you'll have my phone. So you could get away."

"I'm going to get away just fine." Jonah straddles me, his erection clearly straining at the fabric of his black sweatpants. I can feel his balls against my belly; they're tight, ready. "You don't get away. You do what I tell you."

"Please don't. Please."

"Will you ask me politely?" Jonah's hands find my breasts—both exposed now as he plays with them, squeezing hard, then soft, then hard again. He tugs at one nipple, forceful enough to make me whine.

"What—what do you—"

"We'll make a deal." He leans over; I realize he's seen the scarf I left out for him. "If you can suck me off, I won't put it in your cunt."

Next time, I'm going to come in your mouth. I want him to. But I want to get fucked too.

"No," I say. "I won't do it, I won't—"

Jonah slams down on top of me, hard enough to make me cry out in genuine shock. "You *don't get to say* what you will and won't do. That's not what this is about."

I'm shaking so hard. My panties are soaked. I want to cross my legs, just cross them, because I think I could come by merely clenching my thighs.

Yet I keep fighting. I thrash beneath him, frenzied enough to make him swear in what sounds like genuine frustration. Then Jonah grabs the scarf. I think he'll tie my hands, but instead he winds the scarf around my throat. One hand closes around the fabric right in front of my windpipe as he tugs me off the bed with the other, until I tumble off the bed onto the floor.

I use my feet to push myself away from him, but Jonah drags me back and slaps my face again. The very real pain brings tears to my eyes, but it only sharpens the desperate hunger inside me. His grip on the scarf around my neck strengthens.

"You fight me, I'll tie this tighter," he says. "Are you done?"

I nod, defeated. All I can do now is lie on the floor and wait for whatever Jonah has planned next.

His cheek is flushed from where I struck him. My face must be too.

As I pant for breath, my exposed breasts rising and falling with each gasp, Jonah starts going through my nightstand. To my astonishment—and embarrassment—he pulls out my dildo.

My lone sex toy. It was a gift from Geordie. We tried using it a time or two, but mostly it made us crack up laughing. It's been languishing at the back of the drawer for months.

"You don't get enough dick?" Jonah says as he inspects it. The thickness and length of the hot pink silicone would intimidate most men, but Jonah puts that toy to shame. "Well, you're gonna get some tonight. You're gonna take it all."

"Please," I beg. He likes it when I beg. "Please, no."

"I *said*, you're going to take it."

That's when he pushes down the front of his black sweatpants, revealing his erection—blood dark, fully stiff, jutting out at me and wanting release.

He's even more turned on than I am. I didn't think that was possible.

Jonah shoves one of my legs up until my knee nearly touches my chin. Now my crotch is exposed, and his hand closes around that wet strip of my panties and pulls it aside. Two of his fingers push inside, and I whimper. He won't stop for a condom this time; this will be the first time he fully feels how wet he makes me. How hot.

"Not enough for you, huh? You want some cock?"

"No—"

"No? You don't? Too bad I don't give a damn what you want. Shut the fuck up before I shut you up."

Jonah lowers himself over me and pushes inside.

"Oh, God," I whisper against the floor as he starts to thrust. Though I try to brace myself against the floor, every move he makes rocks me. My legs splay open wider, as if that will somehow make my body ready for the enormous length and girth of him. Nothing could do that. "Please—please—"

"Please more?" Jonah shoves himself in harder, and I cry out. "Or do you like the deal I gave you? Are you ready to suck me off yet?"

"No—"

"Then take it."

Jonah starts giving it to me good. This angle makes it harder for me to get fully stimulated, but the fantasy is so good that it pushes me the rest of the way. And the images—the muscles of Jonah's abdomen and pelvis working with every thrust, the thatch of dark hair above his cock, the grimace of ecstasy on his face—

Within seconds I'm panting; within two minutes, I'm at the brink. When Jonah thrusts even deeper inside, the sensation arcs inside me, cunt to heart to brain, and I can't hold it back. The world turns upside down, inside out, and I come, moaning desperately as I clench around Jonah's cock.

He knows what he's done to me—he always does—but he says, "You ready to suck me off yet? Or you want to get fucked some more?"

I don't answer. The breath won't return to my lungs. I lie dazed, openmouthed, against the floor.

"You won't choose," Jonah pants. "So you get both."

When he pulls out, I expect him to immediately get his cock into my mouth. Instead, Jonah takes the dildo and slowly pushes it inside me. My cunt, still tight from my orgasm, spasms around the thick silicone.

"You want me to use this on you hard? Or are you ready to suck?"

I want both. But I nod, half in a daze, unable to resist his will any longer.

Jonah rolls me onto my back, and I prepare myself for the blow job he wants—opening my mouth, wetting my lips with my tongue. But when he straddles my chest, he doesn't move any closer to my face. Instead he cradles my breasts, then pushes them tightly together and thrusts his cock between them. He's already so slick with pre-come and my wetness that each stroke is frictionless.

"Has a guy fucked your tits before?" When I don't answer, Jonah pants, "Tell me!"

"Yes." It's the truth. Derek and Geordie both did this, though not to completion.

Because I asked them not to come on me, I asked Jonah not to come on me either, that's a forever rule. Please don't come on me and make me think about Anthony, please, please.

"Yes?" That wasn't what Jonah wanted to hear. "You'll give it up to anybody, won't you? About time you gave it up to me."

His thumbs rub against my nipples as he thrusts faster. My breasts ache from the pressure, and I can see nothing but the swollen head of his cock pushing toward me over and over again.

Jonah stops—perhaps catching himself on the brink of orgasm. Then he rocks back and forth, very slowly. His voice is a ragged whisper, now, all the more frightening for its quietness. "You're gonna give me your throat. Say it."

"I will."

He pulls back, and for a moment I can only suck in a deeper breath, freed from the pressure across my diaphragm. My aching arms tingle as blood rushes back into them.

Then Jonah grabs me by the hair as he stands up, towing me to my knees. As I sit, the weight of my body forces the dildo deeper into me. It's going to be like I'm getting fucked in both ends at once.

No doubt he sees me writhe around the unfamiliar sensation between my legs. His smile is smug—self-satisfied—and all I can think is, *I didn't fight hard enough.*

My eyes narrow. "Fuck you."

He stares at me. "*What* did you say to me?"

"Fuck you. You think you're so tough—surprising me when I'm asleep. But you're not. You cheat. You *cheated.* I don't see how anyone can stand you, you fucking coward."

That did it. I can feel Jonah's anger in the way he pulls my hair. "Just for that, you're gonna swallow it all."

He steps forward, his glistening cock right in front of my lips.

His voice is hardly more than a whisper, but it shakes with rage. "Now open your goddamned mouth."

The fist in my hair doesn't leave me any choice. I open, and Jonah pushes inside.

This time he doesn't wait before he starts fucking my mouth. My head is held between both of his hands, inexorably tight, and I cough and struggle for breath as he thrusts in and out, shallow and then deep. My body rocks back and forth with each thrust, and I feel the dildo shift within me. He's close to finishing—so close I feel his cock pulse once against my tongue.

"You want this over with?" Jonah sounds breathless, but still totally in control. "Then suck."

I go to work on him, giving him everything I have. The abandon with which I start going down on him—the way I relish the salty taste on my tongue—it totally goes against the fantasy of force. But Jonah's too far gone to notice that now. His breaths come shorter and sharper, each one just short of a moan. Slowly I rotate my hips in a spiral, enjoying the thickness of the dildo inside me. And when it hits me right there . . .

Oh, God, I'm going to come again already.

So I move faster, rocking my pelvis at just the right rhythm, as I feel the head of Jonah's cock swell between my lips. Sensation shivers upward through me, strengthening by the moment—

My second orgasm isn't as strong as the first, but it's better. Slower. It ripples through me in waves, claiming my whole body in white-hot ecstasy. I groan around Jonah's cock, and the vibration must push him over the edge. He shouts out, and then he comes, filling my mouth with heat. Quickly I gulp it down, every drop, the action almost lost in the spasms of pleasure still echoing through me.

Jonah pulls out. His cock—still half-hard—dangles in front of my face. A thin line of come trickles down the side of my mouth, and Jonah's finger catches it. "There," he murmurs, and already the scene is over.

He eases me onto the bed, unties the scarf. As I lie there, rub-

bing my tingling throat, Jonah gently parts my thighs, slides the
dildo out, and readjusts my panties. Then he stretches out beside
me and pulls me against his chest.

We've never held each other in bed, after sex. Such a simple
thing, but new to us. Even now we're more or less clothed. Yet this
is a more intimate moment than I've shared with any other lover.

"Was that okay?" he whispers against my temple.

"Yeah. It was amazing. Was it for you?"

"Every time." Jonah kisses my cheek, then my mouth, not shy-
ing away from the taste of his own semen the way some guys do.
"You destroy me every time. Completely."

I'm the one who gets slapped around, thrown to the floor, tied
up. But I'm the one destroying him? To anyone outside this bedroom it wouldn't make sense. Doesn't matter. Jonah and I understand.

He turns my face by the chin, examining me carefully. "I didn't
slap too hard, did I?"

"No. It was just right." I pull back enough to give him a look.
"Sometime I want to fight you a lot harder."

"Oh, yeah." There are no words for the wicked anticipation in
Jonah's smile. "Maybe on a night when we don't have to be on
campus the next morning."

"That would work."

Postorgasmic drowsiness has begun to tow me down. I can stay
awake a long time after coming once—but after the second cli-
max, sleep beckons fast. I yawn against Jonah's chest, and he cud-
dles me closer.

He says, "Do you want me to stay?"

That's what most people would do now. We're dating. We just
had sex. We're lying together in my bed, worn out and deeply satisfied. What could be more natural than asking him to spend the
night?

And yet I can't.

"Not this time." I prop up on one elbow. "After this—just not after this."

Jonah's disappointed, I can tell, but he takes it well. "I understand that. It's going to take a while to—to make both sides of our relationship fit together."

"Exactly." I feel more relieved than I should. "You don't mind?"

He shakes his head no as he looks down at me. "You've shown me so much trust, Vivienne. More than any other woman ever has. However slowly you need to take this, it's up to you. Always. All right?"

"All right." And in that moment, I like Jonah so much that I nearly ask him to stay anyway.

But I don't.

He locks the door on his way out. I can still hear his car pulling away as I drift into deep, fathomless sleep.

TWENTY-THREE

Maybe it's not a big deal that I didn't ask Jonah to stay over the first night we had sex at my house. But the fact that it was the first time since we admitted we might mean something to each other—since I realized Jonah was a man I could come to care about deeply—

That feels important.

Usually this is the kind of thing I would share with Doreen. On Monday I might. But I already know where this will lead. Doreen will ask lots of leading questions meant to tell me what I already know: If I want to have a meaningful relationship with Jonah—an honest one—I have to tell him the whole truth about my rape fantasy. What an extreme fixation it is for me, how dirty it still makes me feel sometimes, and worst of all, what happened with Anthony.

I'm not ready to talk about any of that yet. I don't think I'll be ready to talk about Anthony ever.

So for now I just have to carry this weight around, and hope Jonah wasn't too offended by my asking him to leave.

He shouldn't be, though. I get the sense Jonah likes to run into locked doors once in a while, for the pleasure of kicking them open.

. . .

The next morning, when I park my car near campus and do the usual postdrive phone check, I see a text from Jonah: Call me when you get a chance.

Rather than walk to my office, I sit down on the nearest metal bench. It's still strange to me that Jonah's in my contacts. That he's a guy I call in the middle of the day, like any other important person in my life.

Jonah answers almost immediately. "Vivienne."

Still no hello. "Yeah. What's up?"

"I just got a call to consult on locations for a deep-sea rig in the North Atlantic, off the coast of Scotland."

"Wow. That's the kind of thing you do in person?"

"Not necessarily. But they offered to fly me out there, and Scotland is one of the places I visit whenever I can. I'll leave tonight."

Jonah's going away again. I'm glad he told me. I feel a pang at the thought of being without him, even for a few days. And yet I'm slightly freaked out that I already want him around all the time. "Thanks for letting me know. How long will you be gone?"

"About a week and a half. Do you think you could get some time off?"

"Wait. What?"

"I was asking if you'd like to come with me."

"To *Scotland*?"

"An island just off the coast of the Highlands." Jonah acts like he just invited me to the movies. "I realize it would take a couple of days for you to get things in order and join me—and I'll be working—but we'd have some time away from it all."

I can't think of what to say. "I'm sorry, you surprised me. Seriously, you want me to come meet you across the Atlantic in a few days?"

"On the Isle of Skye. It's a beautiful place, Vivienne. Stark and wild. Not everyone appreciates it, but I suspect you would."

"But—a transatlantic flight—"

"It's on me," Jonah says. "I have the miles."

You shouldn't waste them on me, I nearly say, before I remember that one news story I read about his family. His late father was one of the founders of Oceanic Airlines. Not only is Jonah not short on money, but he also probably gets to fly himself or his friends for free whenever he wants.

That makes this invitation less of a splurge for him—but no less of a leap for us both.

I laugh in surprise. "You really know how to step it up for the second date."

"I realize it's unusual. But I wanted to ask."

This is impossible, of course. I have a class to help teach, a dissertation to write, Shay to look after—

But a reckless whisper in my head answers, *You've covered tons of classes for both Marvin and Keiko; they owe you, big-time. You ought to turn your dissertation over to your advisor for a preliminary look soon anyway. Shay's not due for nearly another month. Arturo and Carmen are taking good care of her—Rosalind too—*

Somehow I find myself saying, "Let me see if I can reschedule some things."

"You'll come?" Jonah sounds surprised, but in a good way.

"If I can make it work."

He speaks with a knowing, arrogant assurance that should infuriate me. Instead it curls my toes within my ballet flats. "You can."

"We'll see!"

Five minutes later, as I walk into the departmental office, Kip glances over from his computer, eyebrow arched. "Well, well, well. I hear you're painting the town red these days."

"Huh?"

"A friend of mine who waits tables in the area reported seeing you and Jonah Marks strolling along Congress this weekend. Quite lovey-dovey, at least for Professor Marks, which means he seemed to acknowledge you were there."

Does he have spies everywhere? The "campus Sauron" comparison is starting to feel a little too accurate. "Yeah, we went to dinner."

"If he's treating you right, I withdraw my earlier objections," Kip says as he types something so quickly his orange nails fly across his computer keyboard. "But let it be known, if he breaks your heart, he'll regret it."

From anyone else, that would be pure bluster—some guy threatening to punch Jonah out, knowing full well this battle will never take place. From Kip? It means Jonah could find himself reassigned to a smaller office, denied a campus parking sticker, and God only knows what else. Could Kip derail Jonah's chance at tenure? I wouldn't put it past him. "Hey. Jonah's been great, okay? No need to break out the nuclear option."

"Yet," Kip says with relish. "He remains under watch. Is he taking you on some other outing soon? I want to spy on you."

Note to self: Never set up one of our "games" at any location where we could run into Kip. "Actually, now he wants to take me to Scotland. Can you help me clear next week?"

I really should've pulled out my phone before I said that, because the look on Kip's face would make the greatest Vine ever.

"Wait. Hold everything." Kip clasps the desk as if he thinks he might fall down. "Did you say he wants to take you to *Scotland*?"

"He's going tonight, but he wants me to meet him over there in a couple of days. Probably I could leave on Saturday, if I get somebody to cover my classes early next week. But getting out of the departmental meeting, making sure I can move my appointment with Dr. McFadden—"

"Scotland as in another country, across the ocean?" Kip shows no sign of recovering from the shock anytime soon.

I shrug. "I realize it's kind of extravagant for a second date."

Kip is one of the only people who might realize that Jonah and I have a connection that dates further back than our evening out on Congress, but he's too bowled over to catch it. "Kind of? He wants to whisk you away to foreign parts for glamorous locations, uninhibited vacation sex—"

Jonah and I don't wait for vacations to be uninhibited. I have to smile. "He's traveling for work, so I'll probably be on my own most of the time. Still, I'd like to go. Can you help me out?"

"Of course I can, sweetie. Just give me a moment." He pinches the bridge of his nose and takes deep breaths, like someone trying not to faint. "My God. You've ensnared the most elusive man in Texas. Tamed the untamable. It's like I'm talking to the big game hunter who brought down the yeti."

"He's not the yeti!" By now I'm laughing.

"Then he's George Clooney, and you're Austin's answer to Amal Alamuddin. But . . . this is a big step for you two. It's not too big, is it?"

"What do you mean? It's just some time away—a little farther away than usual."

"Sometimes what looks like generosity can be control." Kip speaks more quietly now, and something in his tone tells me he's speaking from experience. He's made some allusions to a significant love affair in his past that ended badly, but this is the first time he's ever suggested any of the real details. "You think you're being swept up in this big romance, but really it's all about separating you from your own life."

That's not what's happening at all, I want to say—but I can't deny that Jonah likes control. I've been wondering whether the change in our relationship would take away the sense of danger that excites us both. Maybe I should have been wondering if the danger would instead become real.

Being with Jonah is a risk. It has been since day one. Someday I might flinch—but not today.

"You're overreacting," I say. "This is a trip. Just a trip, and one I'd love to take. Come on, Kip, work your magic."

Kip shakes his head, as if to clear it. "For this, darling? You get the full-on Dumbledore."

Unsurprisingly, everything falls into place just the way Kip said it would. Within the day, I'm able to e-mail Jonah: Hope you were serious about that invitation, because I'm coming.

Which is how I wind up spending Saturday night thirty thousand feet in the air, suspended between the sea and the moon.

Until now I've spent my aviation life in coach, so first class feels surreal—more like *Inception* than real life. Flight attendants and passengers alike speak in hushed tones as we recline in large, cream-colored seats that turn into perfectly flat beds. Free champagne arrives the moment anyone lifts a hand. We're given blankets softer than the ones on my bed, face masks that feel like silk. Even though a transatlantic trip is already a long journey, this feels like even more daring—like traveling from one world to another.

I am flinging myself into the unknown, and trusting Jonah to catch me.

Jet lag means my arrival in Scotland is no more than a blur, just like the driver who brings me into the Highlands, onto the ferry, across the water to Skye. Somehow I manage to stay awake until we reach the bed-and-breakfast, where the kindly manager shows me to Jonah's room, gives me the key Jonah left behind. Then I collapse into bed for a three-hour nap of the sweetest, most perfect slumber, like returning to the womb.

When I open my eyes again, I feel as if I've awakened from hibernation, and I'm more vividly aware of my surroundings than I've been in a long time.

Our room is small, and just barely on the right side of the line that separates "cozy" and "tacky." A blue-and-green quilt covers the bed; the paintings on the wall show Highland hills blooming violet with heather. Jonah's square, hard-sided suitcase stands in the corner, next to my lilac duffel bag. I've seen his stuff before I see him. It feels strange to be in Jonah's room without him, to have come to an entirely different country to be with him and still remain alone.

Yet my solitude doesn't feel lonely. It feels dreamlike. All my other responsibilities have fallen away. Every other source of tension is gone.

I put on jeans and a heavy gray sweater that doesn't get much wear in Texas or Louisiana. Then I walk out from the B&B to see a wild, rocky stretch of coastline in front of me—and behind, endless rolling hills. Only a few scrubby patches of heather linger this late in the year, but the purple is beautiful just the same. Aside from a small stone cottage near the dock, not another house can be seen for miles in any direction. Even the nearby road is too narrow for more than one vehicle at a time. The breeze off the water is cool; the air smells of salt. Splashing at the shoreline makes me look for fish, but to my delight, I instead see two otters scampering in the shallows.

Some artists believe in creating every single day—writing, painting, doing whatever it is you do—to stay productive. Others believe in a concept called "filling the well." This means stopping for a while to just take in something new, whether it's a book you've never read, an activity you've never tried, or a place you've never been before. The new experiences sink deep into your consciousness and take your creativity in new directions.

If I didn't already believe in filling the well, the stark, wild beauty of this place would convince me.

I packed a sketchpad, thinking only to fill the hours when Jonah was working. Now I can't wait to spend every spare hour drawing. The rugged landscape—the rocky shoreline—even the way our B&B seems to snuggle against the nearest hill: I want to capture every detail, forever.

From across the water I hear the sound of an engine and the choppy impact of waves against metal. Somehow I know, even before I turn to see the white boat coming nearer, that this is Jonah's return. When I wave in greeting, I see him lean out—no more than an outline, at this distance—and raise his hand.

I'd thought seeing him would shatter the dreamlike quality of this place. Instead it seems as though Jonah has entered my dream.

"What did you tell your friends?" Jonah asks that night over dinner.

Unlike most B&Bs, the one we're staying in serves food and drink throughout the night—mostly, I think, for the fishermen gathered at the other two tables. Jonah and I sit at a beat-up wooden table, near a crackling fire, with lamb stew and dark beer. The firelight illuminates the harsh planes of Jonah's face; sometimes the flickering shadows make him look almost demonic, but at other moments, he looks as beautiful as I've ever seen him.

This is one of those moments.

"I told my friends the truth," I say. "They were surprised, but Carmen and Arturo are excited for me. And Shay . . . she's trying to wrap her head around the fact that you aren't always as, um, reserved as you come across in the office."

"She thinks I'm cold."

"No, no! It's not like that." Shay would never be that bluntly unkind. "One of the first things she ever said to me about you was that you were the best professor in the department to work for."

Jonah thinks that over, then nods. As well as he's concealing it,

I can tell—Shay's opinion means something to him. I doubt he ever goes out of his way to ingratiate himself with people. So if he cares about what Shay thinks, it's because he realizes Shay is a person whose respect is worth having. This, in turn, makes me realize he's a good judge of character.

"What about you?" I say. "Did you tell your friends about bringing me along?"

"Most of my close friends are from undergrad. We don't communicate every day. But I told Rosalind."

I remember the way she smiled at me when she realized I was "Jonah's Vivienne." Her respect is worth having too. "What did she say?"

"She said it was about time I 'stepped up my game.'" Jonah says this so seriously that I can't help but laugh. Slowly, he smiles too—and yet he's wary about something else. "You didn't tell me how that ex of yours reacted."

"Geordie? He said you were making him look bad, because he never took me anyplace fancier than Ruth's Chris Steak House." I would giggle at the memory, but Jonah's expression seems to forbid it. He's become stony again, and I wonder if the emotion he's holding back is anger, or jealousy. "You realize there's nothing between me and Geordie any longer."

"So you've said. But you spend a lot of time together."

We do. I've been surprised how easily Geordie and I transitioned into a platonic relationship. Then again—"We were always closer to 'friends with benefits' than any red-hot love affair," I say. "You know, we tried romance on, it didn't fit for either of us, and so now we stick to what *did* work. Our friendship."

"Does he understand that?"

"Definitely." Truth be told, Geordie looked a little wistful when I told him about this trip, and the fact that I was seeing Jonah Marks—but no more than that. "You sound jealous."

"I am," Jonah says. He looks straight into my eyes and speaks with a calmness that belies every word he says. "I'm jealous of every man who ever touched you."

Just hearing him say that brings the heat to my face, to my solar plexus. Our eyes meet, and I know he wants to grab me, right now. To knock everything off this table, lay me down on it and take me . . .

But that's not a fantasy we can act out here and now, not without giving these fishermen the free porno show of their lives.

Jonah keeps speaking as though he didn't know I was already crazy hot for him. "You're better at that than I am. Staying friends with exes."

Lightly I say, "Why is that, do you think?"

This is where most guys would give me a canned speech about how it's better for the past to be the past. Or, worse, that talk about how their ex-girlfriends *went crazy*, which in context always means she dared to express anger at some point. Jonah, on the other hand, thinks for a few long moments before answering. "I tend to . . . compartmentalize. To keep the different aspects of my life separate from each other. So I don't want to change my exes into the friends they never were. When it's over, it's over."

Sounds sane enough. I'm pretty good at handling ex-lovers, but I also realize I'm unusual in that way. Some people need to lock the doors behind them. Clean breaks aren't the worst idea.

But then Jonah adds, more quietly, "I'm trying to do things differently with you."

Wait? When we break up?

No, of course not. Jonah invited me to join him here in Scotland. He brought me into another part of his life. I'm the one he wants to change for.

He slides his hand across the table until our fingers touch. I take a deep breath and look into his eyes. The intensity of the desire I see there—the need to own me not just in bed, but in every possible way—it thrills me. And terrifies me. I can't say which emotion is more powerful.

This is the moment when I realize what tonight means. Jonah won't want to play out a scenario tonight. The sex won't be any fantasy rape. It will just be us, him and me, literally and emotionally naked.

Either I'll have to fake my way through it, or I'll have to tell Jonah the truth.

It shouldn't be scarier than the dark fantasies Jonah and I have shared—but it is. It is.

TWENTY-FOUR

As soon as Jonah and I enter our room, he closes the door and reaches for me. Neither of us even turns on the light.

I sink into Jonah's embrace and feel his lips brush against mine. As he winds his arms around me, our kiss intensifies. This isn't the hard, punishing kiss he first gave me, or the gentler one we've shared after sex or at my front door after our first date. This is desire without violence. Passion that comes not from any fantasy but from the emotions we've kindled in each other.

Jonah's hands slip beneath the hem of my sweater, and I feel his fingers brush along the small of my back. "I never get to tell you how beautiful you are," he murmurs. "How much I love just looking at your body. Do you know how fucking gorgeous you are?"

"You're the gorgeous one." Which is true. I'm attractive, but no more so than any number of women the average person sees on the average day. Jonah? He's a breed apart.

Like no one else, I think as I unbutton his shirt—pausing only to let him lift my sweater over my head and toss it aside. The firmness of his abdominal muscles, the unreal disparity between the broadness of his shoulders and his taut, trim waist, even those storm gray eyes—Jonah is extraordinary. Anyone attracted to men would want him desperately.

But they couldn't share his fantasy. Couldn't give him what he really needs in bed. That's only me.

Jonah's fingers find the front clasp of my bra and click it, so that the lacy cups slide sideways, exposing more of my breasts. He pushes the straps over the curve of my shoulders. "Look at you," he whispers as he starts caressing me. "I don't get to do this enough."

I kiss the line of his jaw, his throat. His stubble is rough against my lips. "Mmm. Do what, exactly?"

"This."

Jonah lifts me just enough to toss me on our bed, then impatiently pulls off his shirt and lets it fall. He crawls onto the bed, his arms and thighs caging me beneath him. His kisses are warm against my skin as he moves from my neck to my breasts.

I whimper as the warmth of his mouth and tongue close over my nipple. Jonah sucks—he licks—he kisses—and he keeps going, drawing out the pleasure. Too many guys rush this; not Jonah. By the time he shifts to my other breast, I'm already writhing beneath him. Even as he sucks harder, his hand reaches for the button of my jeans.

"So—fucking—beautiful," he murmurs as I help him get my jeans past my hips. Jonah sits up to tug them away, then sits there at the foot of the bed for a moment, gazing at me. I lie naked in front of him, my nipples hardened and glistening, my breaths coming fast. Slowly, so slowly, he slides my legs apart and stares at me even more intently. "I never get to do this either."

Which is when he lowers his mouth to my clit.

Oh, God, he's good at this. He's really, really good at this. Jonah's tongue laps at me, circles me, and then he starts to suck in a rhythm that brings me to the brink almost instantly.

But it's not going to make me come.

Only the fantasy does that.

Pretend, I tell myself desperately. My entire body trembles. *Pretend he's forcing you to do this. That he told you to lie here and let him do whatever he wants or he'd make you sorry.*

Usually that works, but tonight I can't convince myself. Jonah's face is buried between my legs—and I can tell he's lost to anything but the desire to taste me, to make me come. The broad muscles of his shoulders work beneath my knees, nearly as sexy as the slight bob and turn of his head. He's giving everything to me. Serving me. And I love it, I do, but even as I hover at the dizzy edge of orgasm, I can't let go.

"I want you inside me," I moan. "Please, Jonah, fuck me."

He pulls back a bit, kisses my cunt one more time, then shoves himself off the bed to get rid of his jeans. I lie there, splayed out for him, panting hard. Jonah can't move fast enough.

Then he's atop me again, the hardness of his erection pressing insistently against my belly as we kiss. I take his cock in my hand and guide it downward; Jonah closes his eyes in pleasure as he feels how wet I am.

"Now," I whisper, and Jonah pushes all the way inside me with one long, slow thrust.

Yes. I arch my back, close my eyes. Now I can imagine anything I want.

"You feel so good," he murmurs. "So fucking tight. I love feeling you wrapped around me."

I ought to enjoy hearing him say that. On some level I do. But his praise only cuts into the fantasy I need.

As Jonah begins driving into me, I fill my mind with images of what we've done before. If—if maybe that first night at the hotel, when he threw me on the bed—if he hadn't ended the scenario then. If he'd kept me there, calling me a whore and a slut, until he could fuck me again—

—it might have felt like this—

As I get close, my entire body tenses against his, and he feels it. Jonah starts thrusting harder. Answering me. I fill my mind with the memory of that hotel room, the savage way he took me, not so unlike the way he's inside me now. I can't think anymore, can't see. I belong only to him, only ever to him.

The world goes white-hot as I clench around him. My orgasm hits me so hard I think for a moment I'll pass out. I manage to stifle my cry of ecstasy against Jonah's shoulder, and I hear him sigh with satisfaction.

"Vivienne," he groans, and then he's there with me. Pleasure shudders through Jonah's body as he grips me closer, and there's nothing better than this.

Or there shouldn't be.

But I can't forget that I still had to fantasize about rape to get myself all the way there.

"At last," he murmurs as we lie together in the aftermath. Jonah spoons behind me, drowsily kissing my neck and shoulders. "I got to take my time enjoying you. Now I get to sleep beside you."

"I should warn you—sometimes I talk in my sleep."

Jonah chuckles, the vibration of his laugh resonating against my back. "What do you say?"

"Nothing intelligible, apparently. Just mumbling."

"Doesn't matter. I could sleep through a tornado."

"My perfect guy," I say. I mean it as a joke—thinking of how Geordie used to grumble about my waking him up in the middle of the night. But once I've said the words, I realize how true they might be.

Some men would hear that and instantly panic. Jonah simply kisses the nape of my neck and holds me tighter.

I should be so happy right now. And I *am*—in so many ways— but the dark weight of doubt lingers deep inside. Whatever else my sexual relationship has been with Jonah, it has been completely, utterly, honest.

Tonight, for the first time, I hid the truth from him. When I indulged in that fantasy without him—in a way, I lied.

But the only thing worse than lying to Jonah would be telling him the truth.

The rest of our time in Scotland is as beautiful and unearthly as the beginning. Jonah spends most of his days out on the water, getting readings about the nearby ocean floor that I would need at least a master's in seismology to understand. Meanwhile, I hike along the coastline, almost never seeing another human being save for the driver of the occasional truck that rumbles by on this lone, deserted road. Sometimes I run into sheep. Here, a flock is as close as you get to a crowd.

This landscape is both beautiful and strange. Not a single tree grows as far as I can see. The ground only lies level right next to the water; otherwise, the land bows and buckles into countless rocky hills. Although low clouds cover most of the sky, it only rains on me once, and then when I'm close enough to the B&B to make a dash for it.

Each day, I fill my sketchbook with more drawings. Sometimes I try to portray everything as far as my eye can see. Mostly, though, I concentrate on smaller details—the delicate, fading heather next to weather-worn stones, or the slim dark shapes of otters just beneath the water.

Each evening, Jonah returns to me, and we eat and talk in the small, darkened dining room of the B&B. He never opens up about his childhood, or really about anything else truly intimate— but even the simpler conversations we have about books we like or places we've been carry their own weight. Jonah isn't someone who reveals himself easily, I realize. These smaller confidences aren't his version of small talk; this is how he builds a bridge. Slowly, gradually, stone by stone.

Besides, I can't be impatient with him for holding back when I'm doing it too.

Every night, we make love. Jonah's caresses only become more tender, more fervent. I treasure every kiss, revel in the way we learn to move together. Finally I get to see his entire perfect body and worship it with my hands and tongue.

But there always comes a point where I have to imagine the rape. It's easier to pretend he's forcing me when he fucks me from behind, so I ask for that a lot. Jonah seems to love it. Even when he's on top of me, though, I can close my eyes and lose myself in yet another fantasy.

No harm done, I think, until our last night in Scotland.

"C'mere," Jonah murmurs in the middle of foreplay, pulling me atop him. "Haven't had you like this yet."

"I thought you didn't like woman-on-top," I say, which is not exactly true but at least believable.

Jonah grins. "I like you any and every way I can have you. Come on. I want to watch your beautiful body move."

It feels good to straddle him, better to lower myself onto his rigid cock. And it's amazing to look down and see him sliding in and out of me—to feel his hands massaging my breasts as I move—and to watch Jonah's face, his openmouthed smile of desire and wonder. I control the pace; I have the power.

Which is what makes it impossible to sink into the fantasy again.

I keep going, riding him hard. My breasts bounce with every move, and Jonah's fingers find my clit. It's not enough. Why can't it just once be enough?

"Come for me," Jonah whispers.

I should fake it. What's one more lie, after the others I've told this week? But my unspoken fantasies were only lies of omission. Faking it for him is a kind of dishonesty I won't stoop to, not with Jonah. "I can't—like this—"

"What do you need?" He grips me more tightly around the waist. "Whatever you need, it's yours. Just say the word."

He means it. I know he does. Maybe I can at least trust him enough to take him at his word. "Push me down. Take me hard. Like in our games."

Jonah stops moving. His gray eyes search mine, and I have no idea what he finds. All I know is that the warmth of his expression fades. Once again he becomes the forbidding, controlling figure of my darkest fantasies.

He flips me over so fast I gasp in surprise. Jonah pulls out, rolls me over, gets behind me, pulls my hips up to meet him. One of his hands closes over my mouth as he thrusts inside me again.

Oh, God, yes. Jonah takes me hard—so hard he brings me to the edge of pain—and the grip of his fingers around my face completes the illusion. I imagine him breaking into my house again, gripping me like this, telling me I have no choice but to take it. My cunt tightens around him; I know he can feel it. I know he can tell how close he's brought me already.

Jonah's the only one who knows me like this. The only man who's ever fucked me the way I wanted to get fucked.

Each stroke gets better, and better, until I come, groaning against his palm. Even as I swoon from the dizzy pleasure of it, Jonah slams into me harder, determined to live the fantasy through to the end.

He's silent when he comes, this time. I only know he's finished from the way he tenses and goes still. After a moment, Jonah slides out of me, and I feel warm wetness slicking my thighs. Now that we're past using condoms, sex with Jonah is a lot messier. Hotter, too. "That was perfect," I murmur as I collapse onto the bed.

"Was it?"

Jonah sounds so . . . cool. I look over at him, but he's already closed his eyes. After a moment he rolls over onto his side, away from me.

It's almost as if he's angry with me for wanting the fantasy. But that's absurd. Jonah never judged me for wanting it before, and besides, he loves it too.

Maybe the man's just tired. He just fucked you six ways from Sunday. Eventually he was bound to fall asleep immediately after.

Makes sense. I'm tired too. And I refuse to think about it any further than that.

But this is the only night in Scotland that he doesn't hold me as I go to sleep.

"And you haven't spent time with Jonah since returning to the States," Doreen says the next Monday, as I sit on her sofa, fighting to stay awake despite jet lag.

"I wouldn't have expected to," I say. "It's going to take me days to get through the Category Five storm that is my inbox, and I'm sure Jonah is at least as slammed as I am, if not more."

Doreen simply nods, her hands folded in her lap. "Has he called you on the phone? Have you texted?"

"He texted after we got into separate taxis at the airport, to make sure I got home safe. Then earlier this morning I e-mailed to ask him to come to Arturo and Shay's Halloween party, and he said yes."

"Halloween party?" That makes Doreen smile a bit. "Not that I've ever met the man, but Jonah Marks doesn't seem like the costume-wearing kind."

"I know." I have to grin too. "Still, the natural next step is introducing Jonah to my friends. Well—not introducing, they've all met him—but having all of us spend time together. Making sure everyone can get along."

"And if they can't?"

"They can." In all honesty, I'm not sure how Jonah will react to my friends—particularly Geordie—or how they'll react to him. But Jonah's default mode is cool courtesy, which means even in the worst-case scenario, everyone will be able to manage. "Hopefully I'll spend time with Jonah and Rosalind sometime soon. She seems great."

Doreen is too smart to pursue the conversational detour I just offered. As ever, she sticks to the point. "So everything is going well."

"Exactly."

"Then why did you tell me you were feeling uneasy after that last night in Scotland?"

I sigh. "I shouldn't even have said anything."

"Vivienne." Doreen's voice is soft. "We've made a lot of progress these past couple of years because you've learned to be truly open with me. Be a shame to lose that now."

"We aren't losing it," I reply—which is maybe not one hundred percent true, if I can't open up to her about this. "It's just that so many things about my relationship with Jonah are difficult to put into words."

"He's proved himself trustworthy. You enjoy spending time with him even in a nonsexual way. Jonah Marks has turned out to be an interesting, intelligent person."

I nod.

"But you feel that he reacted badly on that final night, when you expressed your wishes during sex."

"I think so. I'm not sure." I am, though. Something about the silence between us has been—too empty. "He wouldn't freak out about that, though. Not when we've acted out that fantasy in so many other ways."

"Does that feel like the whole truth to you?"

With a sigh, I admit, "No."

"What else might be bothering him?" Doreen cocks her head. "I think you have an idea."

She's right; I do. Really I've sensed this all along. "I guess it could be that—when I admitted what I wanted—he realized that I was fantasizing about it every other time we had sex in Scotland. Pretending he was forcing me, even when he wanted us to make love in a more romantic way."

She says, "Why do you think that would disturb him, when it's a fantasy he shares?"

Finally I say what I know Doreen's been getting at the whole time. "Jonah wouldn't be angry about the fantasy. He'd be angry about the lie, because that's how he'd see it. As a lie."

"How do *you* see it?"

My rationalizations about "lies of omission" seem flimsy now, and I'm embarrassed to even speak them out loud. ". . . I guess it *was* a lie."

How do I even start to tell Jonah the truth? How can I find the right parts to tell?

All I know is that I'm never telling him the whole story. No matter what else might come between Jonah and me, I can't confess the truth about my rape. I hate even saying the name Anthony.

And then I would have to discover how Jonah reacts when the rape isn't only a fantasy. When he has to confront the fact that this dark, twisted scenario that gets him off is something that—in the real world—scars people for life.

Once he understood that, either Jonah would come to hate his fantasy, or—or he wouldn't care.

Either way would mean Jonah and I could never play our games again.

And I can't give them up.

TWENTY-FIVE

Why did it have to be Halloween?

As I sit in front of my mirror, braiding my hair, I tell myself that I'd have been nervous about introducing Jonah to my friends at any time. This is the next big get-together. Ergo this is when I take him to hang out with the whole gang.

But Halloween seems so . . . silly. Like the kind of thing Jonah wouldn't be into at all.

Then again, I *am* into Halloween. The crazier the theme party, the more I like it: That's the New Orleans in me. Might as well find out if Jonah can deal.

Just as I finish buckling my Mary Janes, I hear Jonah's sedan pull up out front. I open the door to greet him, and when I see him step out of his car, I have to grin. "You wore a costume!"

"That's the whole idea of a costume party, right?" Jonah pauses, glancing down at the scrubs he's got on. The pale blue, loose-fitting pants and top don't disguise the phenomenal physique underneath; he looks just like a doctor. A *hot* doctor. The surgical cap over his dark hair is the finishing touch.

"Yeah, we're supposed to dress up. I just didn't think you'd actually do it."

"Rosalind borrowed these for me from the hospital supply cabinet." He says this as if it explains everything. Probably it does. I can hear her telling him you can't go to a costume party in your everyday clothes without coming across as a total killjoy. "Nothing as elaborate as what you've got on."

"Oh, this old thing." My getup was sold as "Oktoberfest Fräulein"—short poofy skirt, peasant blouse pulled down off the shoulders, high socks, and faux-Teutonic embroidery around the edges. The pigtails aren't long enough, or blonde, but I left most of my wigs at my parents' house, so this will have to do.

Jonah laughs. "You wear this often?"

"At least a couple times a year since I bought it my first semester in college."

"You're not kidding, are you?"

"If I didn't already know you'd never lived in New Orleans, this would prove it," I say as we walk to his car. "Between Halloween, Mardi Gras, and various theme parties, you *need* a few costumes in case of emergency. A lot of people there have what we call 'costume closets,' so you can put together an outfit or help a friend."

"Do you have a costume closet?"

I shrug. "Just a pith helmet, a couple cloaks, a couple wigs, some go-go boots, and this."

"New Orleans," he says, as if it's another planet. He's not that far wrong, actually. His eyes drift toward the cleavage revealed by the tugged-down peasant top. "You look sexy as hell, by the way."

"Thanks. So do you." It's all I can do to keep from fondling his ass right here in the driveway. I take pity on my neighbors and restrain myself.

It's a relief to hear him laugh, and for conversation to flow freely between us. In the days since we got back, Jonah's coolness has lingered. He only e-mailed twice: once to make sure I had settled in well, and then again to accept my invitation to Arturo and Shay's party.

He had a lot to do, I remind myself. *Remember how you had to bust ass all week to get back up to speed?*

True. Still, I can't shake the feeling that something has changed between us, and maybe not for the better.

Arturo opens the door in his Star Trek redshirt getup. I get a big hug, and Jonah gets a handshake. Not the warm, half-hug, hetero-guy handshake good friends often share—more businesslike—but surely Arturo's grin makes up for it. "Good to see you again, Jonah. What's your poison?"

"I'm driving tonight," he replies.

"Which means *I* get to have a glass of wine," I interject.

Arturo laughs. "Not a beer? It would match your costume better."

"Not unless you've got the steins to put it in." With that, I lead Jonah into the party.

Already a large crowd has gathered. Arturo and Shay can't entertain quite as extravagantly as Carmen does, but their friends trust them to provide a good time. (Plus, to judge by the umpteen six-packs and bottles lying around, it looks like at least half the people here contributed to the refreshments.) Décor is at a minimum—mostly a couple of white drapes in the windows stained with "bloody" handprints and slash marks. But a few candles burn here and there, and the stereo is thumping with a Latin beat. There's that creep Mack wearing a neon-green "pimp suit," complete with zebra-striped lapels. The costume is as repulsive as the guy himself. Carmen, on the other hand, looks radiant—a long skirt, peasant blouse, and embroidered shawl in brilliant colors, her thick black hair braided atop her head and pinned with paper flowers, and for the finishing touch, a penciled-in unibrow to make her a perfect Frida Kahlo. I spy Kip in the corner, one of two guys dressed up as punk rockers. To my delight, the other one turns out to be Ryan the bartender from a few weeks ago. Kip must not have wasted any time after getting Ryan's number.

As Arturo leads us toward the bar area, I catch sight of the person I've been most nervous about seeing. At least his getup gives me a ready opening line. "That does *not* count as a costume."

"I beg to differ," Geordie says. He's in full Scots regalia: kilt, high socks with ribbon, velvet evening jacket, and even a sporran hanging in front. Like any true Scotsman, he somehow manages to look manlier while wearing a skirt. "Yes, back in Inverness, this would be evening wear appropriate for any wedding or formal function. Here in the U.S.? It's a costume."

"If you say so." Deep breath. "Geordie, I think you might have met Jonah Marks, from the earth sciences department? Jonah, this is Geordie Hilton. He's getting his LLM here in Austin."

"Pleasure," Geordie says, with enough gusto that it passes for sincerity.

Jonah nods. "Vivienne speaks highly of you."

Geordie smiles in surprise. "Does she, now? Then she's being too kind."

With his impeccable sense of timing, Arturo appears with a glass of wine in one hand and a can in the other. "This is for you, and can you take the ginger ale to Shay?"

"We'd love to," I say, seizing the graceful exit Arturo has provided. "We'll catch you later, okay, Geordie?"

Geordie smiles, somewhat stiffly, then turns to start pouring himself more wine.

In the town house's living room, Shay holds court from the sofa. She's lying there comfortably, while different guests come by to say hi or chat for a while. Her face lights up when she sees Jonah and me. Or maybe it's the ginger ale. "Tell me honestly," she says as I hand her the can. "Isn't this the most boring costume ever?"

"Of course not," I tell her. "The pregnant nun is a classic."

She sighs as she pushes the black wimple back from her face. "I was going to go in drag as Santa, or maybe Homer Simpson if I could find the mask. But in the end Arturo just had to grab something from the costume shop. And hullo there, Jonah."

"Hi," he says, and his smile is easier than it's been the rest of the night—even with me. "We've missed you in the department."

"Have you?" Shay's cheeks pink with pleasure. "Sometimes I think they don't know what to make of me."

"They talk about hiring you full time, when you're ready for that," Jonah says. "Don't tell them I told you."

"Really?" Shay beams even more when Jonah nods, and finally I relax a bit. At least one of my friends can get along with Jonah just fine.

I decide to help things along. "Turns out Jonah is a good friend of Dr. Campbell's."

Her eyes widen. "*My* doctor?"

"Don't worry. Rosalind would never betray a patient's confidential information." Jonah grins, fierce as ever, but at the moment not intimidating at all. "Now, the same rules don't apply to me. So if you want to hear any embarrassing stories about *her*—"

"Spill it!" Shay starts to laugh. "She makes me tell her how I *poop*. So I need to even the playing field."

Jonah makes a face, but a good-natured one. Then they're deep in an anecdote about the time Rosalind talked Jonah into going on a hike, then sprained her ankle at a point where he had to carry her piggyback about six miles back to the car.

Finally I can really relax. I mix and mingle, never losing sight of Jonah for long. Mostly he stays by Shay's side; after a while, Arturo joins them, and as they talk, Arturo's smile broadens. He's winning them over.

Carmen whispers, "He's hotter than I remembered."

"Oh yeah," I say.

"The sex is great, isn't it? I can tell just looking at him."

"You have no idea."

Geordie keeps his distance, never straying far from the bar as he flirts with every unaccompanied girl who shows up. I wish he didn't feel so awkward, but hey. Maybe he'll find someone, and we can finally complete the last stage of "moving on."

The only dark spot on the evening comes when I see Carmen and Arturo exchange a few sharp words. He frowns, and she hugs herself the way she does when she's feeling hurt. But I don't interfere. Sibling relationships can be complicated.

I think of Chloe and inwardly groan. *Can they ever.*

When I cycle back to Jonah, he's completely at ease—the way he was in Scotland on our best nights. I sit next to him, near Shay's feet, and drop a kiss on his shoulder. "You seem to be enjoying yourself."

"More or less," Jonah replies, like he can't quite believe it. "You have good friends. I've always thought that was the best measure of a person."

"Never looked at it that way before—but you're right." How better to judge someone than by the people they choose to have around them, the ones who love them best? "So when do I get to spend time with Rosalind?"

"Soon." Jonah turns to kiss my cheek. His eyes are gentle as he looks at me, and my heart turns over in my chest as he touches my hand. Everything's all right between us again. Maybe it always was. At any rate, I can stop freaking out.

I whisper, "Let's not stay too late. I wouldn't want to tire Shay out." A wicked smile spreads across my face. "I want to tire *you* out."

"—and we're leaving." Jonah gets to his feet.

We're almost to the door before I run into Kip, who has sprayed his hair into a pink faux-hawk for the occasion. He's had even more to drink than Geordie, which is why he folds both Jonah and me in a sloppy embrace. "My darlings. My most surprising lovebirds. How are you?"

"Great." Gingerly I try to extricate myself from Kip's arm. "Not as good as you, though."

"He's sex on a stick, isn't he?" Kip throws a coquettish glance over his shoulder at Ryan, who waves. "As are you, Professor Marks. Oh, no need to make that straight-boy terror face. I'm well aware I'm not your flavor."

Jonah is clearly at a loss for what to say. I don't blame him. Finally he comes up with, "Okay."

"So glad it's all working out! Scotland and the rest of it." As Kip lets us go, I breathe a sigh of relief. Too soon. Because the last thing Kip says to Jonah before he staggers off is, "Shouldn't have even bothered playing spy."

Instantly Jonah's expression darkens. I take his hand. "Come on. Let's go."

But as we walk away from the house, Jonah demands, "What did he mean by that?"

I want to say I don't know—but that's too direct a lie. "Kip looked up all this stuff about you when he realized you and I might have something going on."

Jonah stops in his tracks. "How do *you* know about it? Did he tell you later?"

Time to confess completely. "He printed out all these stories about your family and showed them to me. I read some. It wasn't that big a deal."

"If it wasn't a big deal, why didn't you tell me about it?" His eyes are blazing.

I might submit to Jonah completely in the bedroom, but in real life? It's a different story. "Because it's awkward as hell! Because I thought you might overreact—*no idea* where I got that from. So you grew up in a big house! Who cares?"

"That's not all you read."

"No. Do you really want to talk about the rest right now?"

"I don't want to talk about it *at all.*"

"Then why are you angry with me for not saying anything?"

We glare at each other for a long moment. Then Jonah's hand closes over my forearm, hard enough to bruise. "We're going to my place," he says, his voice low and rough. "And we're going to play."

My entire body responds. Arousal lances through me so sharply I gasp. "Yes. Let's play."

We say almost nothing on the drive. It helps preserve the angry mood.

At one point, though, Jonah mutters, "You know you can say the safe word at any moment."

Silver. "Of course I know."

He's going to give it to me *rough.* Right now I want him so badly I can taste it.

Up until now, I've had no idea where Jonah lives. He drives us into the heart of downtown, to the edge of Lake Austin. A few high-rises here host luxury apartments, the kind of accommodations most students can't afford—or most professors, either. I've never even walked inside one. Jonah grabs a bronze-colored card from his sun visor and buzzes us into the parking garage almost without slowing down.

All the vehicles here are sports cars, status symbols; Jonah's sedan looks modest compared to the Mercedeses and Jaguars parked in each spot. Yet one garage is very like another. Once we're parked, we walk through the same dark, echoing concrete you'd see anywhere else.

He grabs my arm again, pulling me along faster. "It's quiet. This late, nobody would see. Should I fuck you here?"

It's Halloween. People will be out and about—which means they'll be coming in at all hours. "No. We shouldn't—"

Jonah pushes me against the nearest pylon, hard enough that I have to steady myself to stay on my feet. "I'll fuck you here if I want to. It's not up to you, is it?"

The game has intensified. We're working out something through our fantasy, even though real anger should probably never play a role in what we do. But that edge of anger only makes me want him more. "No," I whisper. "It's up to you."

Apparently satisfied, Jonah drags me with him into the building. He turns a key so we can ride the elevator to the penthouse floor. When the doors slide open, they reveal the large, shadowed space of his apartment; Jonah is the only one on the top level.

So I can scream or struggle all I want. No one will hear.

"Take your goddamned clothes off," Jonah says. He starts stripping off his scrubs, right there in front of the elevator door.

I obey. The space is too dark for me to see much, besides the city lights of Austin shining through the windows. I can tell his apartment is enormous, though, open-concept—so I'm standing in the middle of a vast, murky room I don't know. Trembling, I ditch my shoes and socks, push my skirt down to the floor, then lift my peasant blouse over my head. Now I'm only in a strapless bra and panties.

Before I can remove those too, Jonah steps close to me and grips both my arms, holding me fast. He's stark naked, his erection jutting between us. The dim light from the city outside shows me little more than how big he is, how muscular—how futile it would be for me to fight him. That, and the anger in his eyes.

Tonight, for the first time, Jonah's fury is absolutely real.

Surely this is when he'll start calling me names. *Slut. Whore. Bitch.* In my mind I can hear his voice growling those words.

But tonight I learn that when Jonah is truly angry, he falls completely silent.

His silence is scarier than anything he could ever say.

The hardwood floor slams against my knees when he shoves me

down. He grabs my hair, hard, to hold me in place as he pushes his cock inside my mouth. If he would slow down, I'd try to suck him off, but nothing I do is enough for Jonah. He keeps thrusting, relentless, going deep enough that I cough and sputter for breath around his cock.

Jonah could hurt me. He wants to hurt me. Say silver, or snap your fingers. Make him stop.

I don't.

The sheer force Jonah uses on me stuns me. All I can do is kneel there, mouth open, letting myself be used. I whimper in both fear and desire. That's when he pulls out and yanks me to my feet again.

"Jonah—" But I can't think of what to say, and he doesn't give me a chance to say it. Instead he pushes me forward until I make contact with something low and leather. A bench or ottoman, maybe.

He tugs me against his chest and whispers the first words he's said since the garage. *"On your knees."*

By now I'm shaking. But I do what Jonah demands. I climb onto the bench and kneel there, waiting. Everything around me is darkness.

I feel something slide around my arms—a belt, I realize, as the leather tightens. Jonah has bound my wrists behind me. Never before has he bound me; the thrill of fear I feel only sharpens my desire. By now my fear and arousal are so overpowering that it's as if I'm drunk. He yanks back on the belt, nearly knocking me off balance, and I cry out. His hand slides down the center of my back, a touch that I know means possession.

Jonah owns me now, and he knows it.

He pushes between my shoulder blades, so that I nearly topple over. When I'm bent like that in front of him, one of his hands seizes my hip and he shoves his cock inside.

Jonah takes me with a ferocity I've never experienced before. One of his hands closes around the belt, holding me in position by

my arms; the other releases my hip to fist in my hair, and he pulls
back hard. Jonah pumps me, so fast and so hard that my breasts
shake and my entire body starts to sweat. My knees and wrists
ache—my shoulders feel like they're being pulled back too far—
and yet there's nothing I love more than the slap of his body
against mine, the feel of his cock filling me up. Jonah vents his full
fury on me, inside me.

Yes, I think, *fuck me. Punish me. Make me take it.*

Desire sharpens inside me. Peaks. The darkness seems to be
turning red, and my heart thumps so hard I think I can hear the
rushing of blood in my ears. Ragged cries escape my lips; I couldn't
hold them back if I tried.

And then, in a blinding rush of pleasure, I come. For the first
time in my life, my orgasm makes me scream.

Jonah doesn't stop. Doesn't even slow down. He just fucks me
harder, so hard he must want to break me—but then he comes too,
shouting out as he pumps deep inside me and stiffens. We spend a
couple seconds locked together, too stunned to move.

Then he slides out of me, hot and wet. The belt around my
arms loosens and falls away. I try to get to my feet, but I can't; I'm
still shaking too hard for that. Instead I slump onto the nearby
couch.

Jonah stands above me, a black, featureless shadow. Everything
I ever told myself about fearing this man comes back to me, and I
wonder what happens after this. If he's still angry, if what he just
did to me isn't enough—

But my eyes are adjusting to the darkness, and I see an expanse
of white on a nearby brick wall. A square, in a silver frame.

The etching. The man's hands cradling the dove. That's what
I'm looking at.

And in that instant I remember that whatever twisted fantasies bind me to Jonah, our connection goes beyond that. Or it can, if we figure out how.

I whisper, "Hold me?"

Jonah pauses, but then he sits by my side and folds me in the warmth of his embrace. He is as gentle now as he was cruel a minute before.

Slowly he lowers us to lie on the sofa, and I curl next to his chest. I say nothing else, and I don't look at Jonah's face. Instead I stare up at the etching, trying despite the darkness to make out the lines of the dove's fragile wings, and the man's strong hands.

TWENTY-SIX

Few things could be more embarrassing than taking the Walk of Shame dressed like the St. Pauli Girl. So Jonah lends me a T-shirt and some workout shorts with a drawstring that allows me to cinch them around my waist.

I almost don't remember the moment when, half asleep, I let Jonah carry me into his bedroom. But this morning I woke up next to him in an enormous, king-sized bed, and since then he's been considerate. Almost courtly. The total opposite of last night.

As Jonah scrambles some eggs for us, I walk around, taking a look at his place in the daylight. His bedroom and bathroom are the only fully enclosed spaces, occupying a bricked-in area at the center of the enormous open space that forms the rest of his apartment. Stainless steel shines in the kitchen, yet the dining table nearby seems to be made of reclaimed woods, rustic and yet somehow perfect here. I circle around to see low bookshelves beneath the wide windows that look out on Lake Austin and the rest of the city—a space defined as the living room by low leather sofas, a Turkish carpet, and the ottoman I remember. Turns out it's dark red. At the far end of his apartment—the part where I've nearly circled back to the kitchen—is a home office with books stacked around his computer, and a seismograph sitting on a small end table. All the lines move slowly and easily—no tremors today. I step around a treadmill to reappear in the kitchen, where Jonah is spooning our finished breakfast onto our plates.

He's wearing nothing but boxer briefs and a white tee so tight and thin that he might as well be shirtless. Even after weeks of screwing around, this man's body takes my breath away.

Jonah gives me a sidelong look. "Feeling okay?"

"Yeah, sure." I take a sip of the OJ he's poured into a sleek glass tumbler. "I only had one glass of wine last night."

"That's not what I meant." His hand finds mine, and I watch him examine my wrists, looking for burns from the leather he strapped around them last night. But there's only one small bruise, no larger than a fingertip.

I meet his eyes evenly. "When you go too far for me, I'll tell you." After a moment, he nods.

I only wish I knew just how far "too far" would be.

When we sit at the table, I have a good view of my etching, which hangs on the brick inner wall. Jonah catches me looking at it and smiles. "Is that the right place for it?"

This is your apartment, I want to say, *hang it wherever you want*—but the truth is, as an artist, I kind of *do* care about where my work ends up. "That spot is perfect, actually. You get enough light to see it clearly, without so much sunshine that the inks could fade." It's in a place of pride, too, which is always an enormous compliment.

Jonah uses his fork to push his eggs around his plate. "I'd like to ask you a question. Feel free not to answer."

"Um, okay."

"What else did you read?" He can't meet my eyes. "From the stuff Kip gave you."

"I learned you ran track. That your house is supposed to be haunted. And—and I learned that your family's having a tough time." That seems like the most tactful way to put it. He'll have to realize how much I know; the guy can't be blind to the way the press seizes on his family's troubles.

Jonah finally looks up at me. Once again, I see a sliver of that deep-buried vulnerability. "What the media reports—that's not the whole story."

"I never figured it was." I rest my hand on Jonah's forearm. "You can tell me what you want, when you want. I'm not going to pry. I shouldn't even have read the stuff Kip gave me."

"No. If it's in the papers, it's fair game."

"Well, I haven't pried any further than that, and I won't."

He nods, but I can tell he doesn't entirely believe me. At first I'm offended—but then I wonder whether anyone has ever respected Jonah's privacy. He can't believe anyone would willingly give him space and solitude, because he was denied it before. I remember the news stories about a mad mother—my own theories about his anger with her—and feel a pang deep inside as I realize how long Jonah's been building these walls around his heart.

Can those walls ever be torn down?

Not by anyone hiding behind walls of her own.

We eat breakfast in silence, lovers who have told each other everything and nothing.

Jonah drives me back home, kisses me gently before I get out of the car. We're all right—at least, as close to it as we ever were.

Time to figure out what all this means later. Right now, I need rest.

So I nap for a while longer, take a long, hot shower, and change into jeans and a sweater. A party as epic as Arturo and Shay's would need a volunteer cleanup crew the next morning even if Shay could help. Since she can't, the earlier I get over there, the better. Tidying up will take my mind off the tangle of emotions between Jonah and me.

When I pull up in front of the town house, Carmen's car is already parked out front. I expect to get teased about sleeping in—and then maybe about who I slept in with. So I brace myself to face the inquisition.

I'm not prepared for what I find instead.

Arturo opens the door without even looking at me. "What business is it of yours?"

"If you get evicted, who else are you going to move in with?" Carmen's voice is shrill and sharp—unlike her. "That makes it my business!"

"We're not going to get evicted!" Arturo's face is flushed. This argument has been going on for a while.

"You spent almost a hundred dollars on *beer*," Carmen says as she stomps through the living room, grabbing cans and tossing them in a trash bag she has clenched in one fist. "With a baby on the way! That's irresponsible!"

It's a measure of how close I am to Carmen and Arturo that they think nothing of letting me in while they're having a bitter argument. Doesn't make it any less awkward for me. "I'm going to check on Shay," I say, before hurrying up the stairs. The sounds of their squabbling follow me the whole way.

I find Shay propped up in bed, holding the new crochet needles and soft white yarn I gave her at her bedside baby shower a couple days after I returned from Scotland. But she's not working with the yarn, just sitting there teary-eyed. She tries to smile when she sees me, but it doesn't really work. "They've been going on like this for at least half an hour." She wipes at her cheeks with the back of her hand. "I can't stand it."

"Hey, hey. Every brother and sister fight sometimes." This is true, but I feel like a liar saying it. Neither Carmen nor Arturo is the type to shout, especially not at each other.

Shay sniffles. "It was like Carmen was mad at me for getting pregnant to begin with, and then as soon as she got over that, she turned on Arturo. We saved up for one last party before the baby! Everything besides the beer, other people brought! We weren't being stupid—were we?"

I sit on the bed beside her. Despite the fact that she's a married woman on the verge of motherhood, she looks so much younger than me right now. More like a girl than an adult. "You've got all the furniture for the nursery. You've started a savings account for college, and this kid is still a fetus!"

"But there's day care to pay for too—because I've got to finish my degree, or else I'll just be a lead weight around Arturo's neck—" By now Shay is breaking down completely.

"It's going to be fine," I promise her. "Okay? You guys aren't going to get derailed by one last party."

"Did war break out downstairs?" Surprised by the voice behind me, I turn around to see Geordie standing in the doorway, shirtless but still clad in his kilt. He winces at the light coming in through Shay's bedroom window. "Also, is it November first or have I been out for longer?"

"You passed out around two A.M.," Shay says between sniffles. "Arturo put you on the nursery floor."

"Kind of him." Geordie slumps against the doorjamb. His complexion has taken on a ghastly shade of green. "I'm afraid I may be on the verge of getting sick in your toilet."

Shay waves her hand toward the bathroom. "Go ahead," she says miserably. "I've vomited in it often enough the past couple months. Someone else ought to get a turn."

As Geordie stumbles into their bathroom, I hear Carmen yell, "Yes, you *do* have to justify this! You're going to be a father, Arturo! You have to justify everything you do that isn't about taking care of that baby!"

I squeeze Shay's hand. "I came here to help clean up. But what if I got Carmen out of the house instead?"

"Oh, God bless you." Shay leans back on her pillows, gone limp with relief.

So I hurry downstairs, grab Carmen's purse, then point to her. "You. Me. Brunch. Now."

Carmen and Arturo freeze, midargument. It would be funny if I hadn't seen Shay crying. Finally Carmen manages to say, "How can you think about brunch at a time like this?"

"On a weekend morning? It's pretty easy. Come on."

She doesn't say a word as we leave, or on the drive to Magnolia Café. But while we wait in line outside, Carmen mutters, "You could have just told me to cool it."

"Would it have worked?"

Carmen doesn't answer. She just hugs herself more tightly against the chilly breeze.

"What were you freaking out about?"

"The way they spend money—"

"They threw *one party*, Carmen. Otherwise they've been more careful with their money than you or I have ever been." Arturo is one of the genius-freaks who started an IRA at eighteen. "That's not what's actually bothering you."

"How would you know? You can't read my mind. You don't have to ask yourself what it would be like if you had to help support your brother and his wife and a baby—"

"That's not going to happen!" Even if I didn't have so much faith in Shay and Arturo, the Ortiz family is reasonably well off. Carmen and Arturo's parents aren't rich, but they're in a position to help out if the new baby needs anything.

Carmen hasn't even heard me. "—you don't have to ask yourself if you're going to get derailed, because you don't have any responsibilities like that. You can just keep working on your thesis, and going to the studio. You're going to make it no matter what. It's not like that for me."

"Of course you're going to make it. You're a math genius."

"No, I'm not." Her voice breaks. "I was really smart on the high school level. And the undergrad level. But now? At this point? I'm falling behind—I can tell I'm falling behind, and my advisor says I have to buckle down or—"

Carmen starts to cry. A few people in the brunch line are staring. Well, let them stare. I hug her tightly. "You're not scared for Arturo. You're scared for *yourself*."

"One of us has to make it," she whispers as she hugs me back. "I don't think it's going to be me."

Her behavior over the past several months finally makes sense. All this time, Carmen's been dealing with this incredible anxiety by pushing her fears onto her brother. First she resented Shay for weighing Arturo down with responsibility so young; this morning, she turned on Arturo. But really she's scared to death that she'll fall and no one will be there to catch her.

"Listen to me, okay? You're going to get through this. Yeah, graduate work is difficult. It's supposed to be! But you were smart enough to get there, and you're smart enough to make it through."

Carmen shook her head against my shoulder. "I don't know."

"Sometimes life is like a video game. When things get harder, and the obstacles get tougher, it just means you leveled up."

She laughs brokenly. "Except I suck at video games."

"I know." Carmen never even figured out how to steer her car in Grand Theft Auto. "But you don't suck at math. Come on. Deep breaths."

She keeps crying it out for a while, though, and is still teary when we finally get seated. Still, one of the great truths of life is that any situation can be improved with coffee. By her second cup, she's perked up a little—and when her waffles arrive, she's calm again, enough to notice my relatively empty plate. "Hey, why didn't you order anything?"

"I got tea and toast."

Carmen gives me a look, no doubt remembering my ability to slaughter a stack of pancakes.

"Well," I admit, "Jonah might have made me breakfast this morning."

"Oh, yeah? He stayed over?"

"I stayed over."

Carmen's eyes are still red from crying, but I can tell she's glad to have something else to think about for a while. "You've been so quiet about this guy. When you first met Geordie, you told me everything."

I'll never be able to explain why I didn't tell her about Jonah at first, or why so much of our relationship will remain secret. But if he's going to be a bigger part of my life, I have to open up about him a little more. "Jonah's a very private person," I say. "I respect that."

"*Fine*. Be mysterious. It doesn't matter, because obviously this relationship is the definition of a whirlwind romance. And you're totally into him. I mean, you went to Scotland with him! How much was that ticket at the last minute?"

She isn't asking for real—just trying to get me to prove I'm head over heels for Jonah. Still, this might be the moment to be totally candid about the Scotland trip. "He got me the ticket."

Her eyes go wide. "Jonah bought you a ticket to Scotland? Oh, my God, Vivienne. That's huge!"

"Not really. His dad actually was one of the cofounders of Oceanic. So he's got an in with the airline."

This doesn't have the effect I expected. Carmen frowns. "You said Oceanic?"

"Uh, yeah. Why?" Was there a crash today or something?

Instead Carmen says, "So . . . Jonah's part of that screwed-up family in the tabloids."

I gape at her. "How do you know that?"

"If his dad founded Oceanic, and his name is Jonah Marks, that means his dad was Alexander Marks, right?"

"Since when have you heard of any of these people?"

Carmen makes a face. "The usual! TMZ, sometimes the news, supermarket tabloids—I mean, come on, you have to read those once in a while, right? What else can you do while you're waiting in line?"

"I check my phone and talk myself out of buying candy bars, like a normal person!" Great. Everyone in the *whole world* pays more attention to gossip than I do. So much for keeping Jonah's secrets. Calming myself as best I can, I say, "I think Jonah tries to keep his distance from all that."

"He didn't even say anything about his mom this morning?" Carmen winces. "I bet he hadn't heard yet."

"Hadn't heard what?"

Even the most serious news sources print sensational headlines for this story. There's no way to describe it that isn't lurid.

CHICAGO "MAD HEIRESS" ARRESTED
FOR ASSAULT ON STEPSON

Everything from the *Wall Street Journal* to *OhNoTheyDidn't* has differing accounts of what happened. A few blurry camera-phone videos have been posted to YouTube, but none of them reveal much beyond distant movement in the dark, and the sound of a woman shouting. As near as I can piece together, Jonah's mother left Redgrave House—already unusual, for her—and went to The Orchid, a downtown club and restaurant so chic even I've heard of it. The Orchid's owner turns out to be Maddox Hale, Jonah's younger stepbrother. When Jonah's mom accosted Maddox, an argument ensued, and apparently she hurt him—though nobody can agree whether she knifed Maddox through the hand, only slapped him, or something in between. I don't get a good look at Jonah's mother at any point on the videos, but I do hear a man saying, "She doesn't know what she's doing. It's all right. I don't want to press charges."

So Maddox would have let it go, whatever it was she did. The police feel differently.

All I know for sure is that Jonah must feel so torn up inside. And I understand instinctively that he will never, ever talk about it with a single soul—not Rosalind, not me, not anybody.

Maybe I should call him or run back by his apartment. Not to make him open up if he doesn't want to, just to be there with him.

Yet that feels like . . . too much. Like acknowledging his pain would be too intimate. How can we be this close and yet this distant? I want to bridge the gulf between us, but maybe that's impossible.

The entire day, I wait for him to call. I don't expect Jonah to vent about his family's sorrows, but he might turn to me for companionship. For understanding.

He doesn't phone that day. Or the next. No e-mail either.

Whatever hell Jonah is going through, he seems determined to go through it alone.

TWENTY-SEVEN

On Thursday, Jonah finally calls while I'm shopping at the supermarket.

Even after five days, I don't get a hello. Instead he says, "Sorry I've been—off the radar."

"That's okay. Sometimes we all need some space." That's my invitation to him to tell me why he wanted his solitude.

The invitation is declined. He says only, "I had an idea."

"Yeah?"

"For our next game."

I'm standing in the produce aisle between the cucumbers and the persimmons, but just hearing his low, rough voice talk about our games makes my body respond instantly. Fire kindles deep inside, and I cradle the phone closer to my face so no one will overhear. "Tell me."

"When I have you, I want to *own* you."

"You always do," I whisper.

"Not completely," he says. "Until now."

Doreen's hair seems to have gone gray at the temples in the past couple of months. I wonder how much of that is due to me.

"You and Jonah haven't spoken about his family issues at all,"

Doreen says. "Even with their goings-on splashed on every website and newspaper in the country."

"He doesn't want to talk about it." I shrug. "Sometimes I don't want to talk about things either. So we respect each other's privacy. Isn't there a quote about that? About how the best love is two solitudes that border, protect, and greet one another?"

"We'll discuss Rilke some other time." Doreen's dark eyes never leave my face. "You say Jonah never mentioned his mother's arrest. Instead he called and asked you to 'play' again."

"That's right."

"You realize he may be compensating for feelings of powerlessness."

At that I have to laugh. "You don't need a psychology degree to figure that out."

"What do you think you're compensating for?"

"I'm punishing myself by indulging myself. When I indulge my rape fantasy—when I surrender to that fear and helplessness—I'm punishing myself for wanting it. Don't you see?"

"I doubt it's as simple as that."

Is she kidding? "Nothing about this is simple."

Doreen leans forward, and when she speaks to me, genuine emotion comes through in every word. "There is no reason for you to punish yourself for this fantasy."

"I want to relive the worst thing that ever happened to me? What Anthony did to me? It's sick."

"Again, many women have rape fantasies. Some men do too. It's not always a response to trauma. Most of the time, I don't even think there is a specific reason."

A thousand times, Doreen has said this. But what she says next explodes in my mind like she'd thrown a hand grenade:

"You might have had this fantasy even if Anthony had never raped you."

"No." I shake my head. "He did this to me. You know he did."

"Anthony raped you," she says. "The fantasy comes from that, *and* from a culture that eroticizes violence against women, *and* leftover puritanical guilt about sex that tells us we're not allowed to choose it and want it for ourselves, and from God only knows where else."

I'm furious with her. I want to cry. My cheeks are flushed with shame. Every emotion I've ever felt about this is bubbling up at once. "But it's the only thing that gets me off. I can't come any other way! Does that sound normal to you?"

Doreen looks at me steadily. "Exactly. The fantasy isn't your problem; it's the extremity of your fixation on it. Who is it who won't let you find sexual satisfaction any other way?"

Me. She means me.

And only at this moment do I realize Doreen has been building to this moment for a very long time.

I grab my purse. "This is over."

"This session, or our counseling relationship?"

She said this knowing I might break from her permanently. Right now I want to. But I've found too much solace here in the past to let Doreen go that easily.

"For now," I say. "But I'll be back."

I go out the door without waiting to hear her reply.

As I walk to my car, trembling, I think of what I meant to talk with Doreen about. We weren't supposed to unearth the roots of my fantasy today. We were supposed to talk about this weekend. What Jonah wants from me. How much further we're going than ever before.

It doesn't matter. No matter what Doreen said today, it wouldn't have stopped me.

What Jonah asks of me, I'm going to give.

Preparations:

I set up an automatic e-mail response at both my school and

personal accounts, letting everyone know I won't be able to reach them until Monday morning at the earliest.

I tell Carmen that Jonah is "taking me away for a weekend," just to a cabin in the state park, nothing major. She thinks it's something romantic and sweet; more to the point, she won't worry about me. Won't look for me.

Kip hears that we might go hiking, Jonah and I. Although he raises an eyebrow at my choice of recreational activities, he believes me. Why wouldn't he? That way, when I come back to the office next week, Kip won't think anything if I'm scratched or bruised.

Water the plants. Pack an overnight bag.

And on Friday, I drive to the place where I'll be held captive.

I want to kidnap you, Jonah said.

I want to keep you tied up, away from the rest of the world, for days. I want to use your body in every way it can be used, over and over, until you can't take it anymore. But you'll still have to take it. And I want you to know there's no place you can run to, no one who will hear you.

You will be completely mine.

When we could think straight again after that, we worked out the logistics. As aroused as I am by the thought of Jonah actually grabbing me and dragging me into his car, we can't risk it. We might easily be seen, which means someone could either call the police—or worse, play vigilante, which could get Jonah arrested, badly hurt, or even killed. The places where we live offer some privacy, but I'm too familiar with them. Too comfortable. Both of us want the illusion of ultimate control to be as complete as possible.

So Jonah found a place, a rental cabin near the edge of the state park. He's given me an address and a time to show up there Friday afternoon. By another hour on Sunday, he'll set me free.

The rest is completely unknown to me. I'll be in Jonah's hands.

I wear the clothes I bought at the thrift store specifically to be destroyed—a faded cotton skirt, a T-shirt too thin for November weather. While I can't saunter in carrying my suitcase without destroying the illusion, I've packed a duffel bag Jonah will bring inside from my car at some point. It contains a change of clothing for Sunday and my cell phone. Anything else I need, or want, I'll have to earn.

This late in the season, we're probably the only ones who've rented a cabin for the weekend. Even if we weren't, none of the other cabins are within three miles. Every minute I drive reminds me of how remote our location is. How all-encompassing this fantasy will be. My palms are sweaty against the wheel of my car. Songs play on the radio but I don't hear them. There's only my pulse, my nervousness, and my desire.

Sunset stripes the sky violet and orange as I reach the cabin. Gravel crunches beneath my tires while I take the long, narrow road away from the highway and the rest of civilization. Finally I see the cabin—a small, rustic place with bare-wood walls and a low ceiling—and Jonah's sedan parked in front.

He will have heard me pull up. That's his cue.

I get out of my car. My legs feel weak and wobbly beneath me. I drop my keys on the hood of my car, turn away from the cabin, and listen. Every rustle of leaves in the trees makes my ears prick, and—not for the first time—I think, *This is crazier than anything else you've done. You're crossing a line. Are you ready for that?*

Then I hear the cabin door open, and I run.

Twigs and branches snap across my chest as I hurl myself into the woods, running as though my life really did depend on it. My world has become a blur of trees, dirt, the pale sky above. The uneven, rocky ground makes me stumble once, twice, again—but I keep my footing. I have to. I have to try to get away.

And I can hear him behind me. His footsteps coming faster and louder. Even his ragged breath. Jonah's chasing me with all his strength.

We are both too good at our games.

I reach a clearing and attempt to run faster, but that's when I'm tackled from behind. We fall to the ground, and I put up the best fight I can—kicking, wriggling, trying to get out from under him—but Jonah has me. All my struggles do no good.

He gets his knees on my arms, puts his weight on my chest. Jonah is breathing hard, dirt smudged across his cheekbone and his forehead. He pants as he looks down at what he's caught, and I feel the rise and fall of each breath beneath my trembling body. I am powerless to do anything but lie beneath him.

Slowly, Jonah smiles.

"I've been waiting for you."

Jonah has dragged me inside this cabin—which is bare-bones, so far as I can tell. One of his arms pins both of mine behind my back as he pulls me onward so fast I stumble. I glimpse only a few sticks of wood furniture, a rag rug on the floor, before Jonah pushes me into the bedroom.

The bed is the only piece of furniture in the room. Barely even a double, with a metal frame that has tarnished to dingy mercury gray over time, and covered only with a stark white fitted sheet— but what catches my attention are the ropes.

Jonah has wound pale ropes around each of the four posts of the bed. They wait for me.

He shoves me onto the bed. One shoe I lost in the doorway; the other falls off now. I try to push him off, but it's futile. Jonah straddles me and smiles in slow satisfaction as he spreads my arms wide. "Shhhhh." He pushes one of my wrists through a loop of rope—it's soft, silky, like the stuff that holds back curtains, but when he tightens it, I'm bound as inexorably as I could be by hand-cuffs. "This will go so much easier if you stop fighting me. Much faster. Don't you want it to go faster? To be over?"

"Let me go—"

Jonah thrusts my other hand into its binding. "Shut up," he whispers. "Or I'll gag you with your own panties."

No.

Yes.

He slides off the foot of the bed and pulls one of my ankles to the post. Within a moment I'll be tied down, spread-eagled, open to him and whatever he wants to do to me.

He ties the other foot. That's it. I'm completely helpless. Only the word *silver* could save me now.

As he stands at the foot of the bed, between my legs, Jonah runs his hands up my thighs. "I wanted a pretty one. A girl like you. One I can keep."

Silver, I think wildly. *Silver*. But that's not what I say. "Please let me go. I won't tell anyone, I swear. You could drive me somewhere—let me out, so I don't know where you are—"

Jonah shakes his head slowly. "I warned you."

He reaches under my skirt and rips my panties away. As I watch in a crazed mixture of horror and desire, he wads the cotton into a ball, then climbs atop the bed. One of his hands forces my jaw open, and he stuffs what's left of my panties inside. I can taste my own wetness, my own need.

As he kneels between my parted, trembling thighs, Jonah takes my T-shirt collar in both hands and rips it open. I went without a bra, so my breasts are exposed to him. As he cups them, he pinches my nipples and smiles as they harden to his touch.

"Let's see what else I caught," Jonah says. His strong hands tear through my skirt as if it were made of tissue paper. Now I'm naked, as exposed to him as a person could be. "Oh, I can think of lots of things to do with you."

By now I'm crying. It's not acting, not completely.

"What?" He looks at me, mock-innocent. "Do you have something to say?"

He pulls my panties from my mouth for the pleasure of hearing me beg.

"Please," I whisper. *"Please."*

"Why should I? Are you a virgin?"

"—no—"

"Then you're a slut. Anyone can use you. Now it's my turn to use you."

I try to turn my face away, but he stuffs my underwear back into my mouth. For a few moments he watches me, writhing and helpless. My cunt is completely exposed to him—every part of me is laid bare—and I can hide nothing. Prevent nothing.

"So many things I can do to you," he murmurs. "First I need my toys."

Toys? That could mean anything. I told him not to cause me serious pain—so not a whip, probably—but the list of things he could use to bind or humiliate me is endless. They run through my mind, a kaleidoscope of sexual perversion that lights me up inside.

I hear him outside, then at the door. What else could he have brought?

When he walks inside, he casually tosses a bag near the foot of the bed, then smirks to see me there, tied so that he can see my exposed cunt. Jonah steps closer and thrusts his fingers inside me. He works his hand in and out, slowly, then steps back. His grin is wicked as he unzips his pants.

I don't want to want this, but I do—I do—

"You want to beg me some more?" Once more he tugs the

panties from my lips. I think he likes this, shoving them inside, silencing me.

"You don't have to do this." My words come out shaky.

Jonah laughs. "Say anything you want, bitch."

Then he climbs atop me, his blood-dark cock thick between my legs for the moment before he pushes inside.

It burns. It aches. It's so fucking good I could scream.

His cock fills me, inch by inch—he's taking it slow, tormenting me with how long it will take. "Yeah," he whispers as he sinks in deeper. "That's it."

He's in me all the way now, and starts thrusting, still going slow—but strong, so strong he pushes my body upward on the bed, and the ropes around my ankles strain. I groan in mingled satisfaction and pain.

"Shut the fuck up," he says. His hips rock forward, so that he's buried in me to the hilt. "Or I'll pound you harder, 'til you bleed."

Jonah slides into me. Out of me. Every stroke burns; every move aches. My traitorous body responds to him, wanting more even as the ropes bruise my wrists.

"Taking it slow," Jonah says. "Do you know why?"

I shake my head. My hair is stuck to my forehead with sweat

"Because I'm not going to come in you yet. You have to wait for it. Soon you'll beg for it, because that's the only way I'm going to stop." He pushes in again, burying himself deep inside me, and whispers against my shoulder, "Stop for now, I mean. I'm going to fuck you again. And again. I'm going to fuck you blind."

"Don't—"

"I told you to shut the fuck up."

Jonah pushes the panties back into my mouth, and this time he won't take them out again. He pumps into me, his hips pistoning faster and harder until the force of it feels like it's going to rip me apart. He's spread my legs so far apart that I can see where he sinks into me, the faint glistening of my wetness against his rigid cock as he slides in and out and in again. My ragged cries are muffled by the cotton in my mouth, and I can tell he loves how I try to scream, and fail.

When I'm on the verge, I can't help rocking my hips up to meet his—but that's when he pulls out, denying both of us release.

For a moment he kneels there, his cock jutting forward as he looks at his prisoner. He reaches up to cup my breasts, squeezing hard.

Then he slides off the bed.

He goes for his bag and pulls out something small and white, U-shaped. What in the world?

"I'm going to roll you over," he says. "You're not going to kick me, or fight, or do anything else stupid. If you do, you get spanked. Understand me?"

Nobody's ever tried to spank me before. Is Jonah talking about light, playful pats, or something more brutal?

Probably the latter. I mean to find out.

When he loosens one of my ankles, I do nothing more than flex my foot. Renewed circulation sends blood rushing through my heel and arch and toes, tingling in a way both painful and welcome. But when he releases the other, I use my newfound traction to push myself farther up the bed and kick at him.

"Bitch." Jonah lunges over me and sinks his teeth into my shoulder. Pain ripples through me—has he broken the skin?—and I freeze. This is what he wanted. He turns me over as best he can. While my arms are still tied to the posts, most of my body lies on my left side, and he's now scooting down the bed to tug my legs to the opposite bedposts.

He's turning me over just enough to expose my ass.

"That's right," Jonah murmurs. "Lie still instead of fighting. You want to make me happy, don't you? If you make me happy, I can be nice to you. Give you something to eat. Let you sleep in this bed instead of on the floor."

Oh, God, oh, God. What is he going to do to me? I fear it as much as I thrill to it. Is there no danger, no humiliation, that can ruin this fantasy for me? Or will it own me forever?

It owns me. Jonah owns me.

I shake my head yes, silently affirming that I'll do what I can to "make him happy."

He grabs my hair, lunges close. "Good. You've learned that you have to do whatever I want. And now I want you to wear something."

Wear something? Confusion only adds to my fear as he pulls away again and grabs the small white device. Now that I see it more clearly, I can see that the ends of the U are flatter, the center more cylindrical; it seems to be coated in silicone. Then I feel him slide it inside me— one end within my cunt, the other pressing against my clit.

"You're not just going to take this," Jonah says. "You're going to like it."

I hear a soft click—and the device inside me begins to vibrate.

This is a vibrator? I've only seen the rabbit ones, not counting the enormous things they sell at the pharmacy as "back massagers." I come so easily that I've never bothered buying one.

It feels good, though. Great. I realize now that this is perfectly designed to be worn during sex; the end inside me is slim enough that Jonah could push his cock in there too. Maybe the sensation will do something for him, too. But I don't know why he thinks I'd need a vibrator to enjoy it when he fucks me . . .

Just at that moment, Jonah slides two fingers inside my ass.

My entire body tenses, clenching around him. His fingers seem to slide up so deep inside me; the pressure kindles primal shame within. I start to shake, individual muscles in my legs and my ass trembling like the strings of an instrument being played. As Jonah

turns his hand inside me, I can feel the pressure of his knuckles—
the roughness of his skin against my hole—and I feel myself blushing so strongly that my skin seems to be on fire. Jonah chuckles,
low and hot; he must see that I've gone scarlet with shame. He
pulls out his hand, but he's not done.

I called off my limits. Why did I do that? Because now he's going
to do something to me no other man ever has. Jonah is going to fuck
my ass.

"You're going to *love it*," he whispers as he ties one of my legs
to the bedpost, then the other. I couldn't turn over if I wanted,
now. Jonah's fingers push back inside me—not so slow, this time—
and he starts working his fingers back and forth. Yet the vibration
against my clit keeps doing its job, turning me on even more.
"You're going to come hard while I'm in your ass, and that's going
to prove how much you love it, slut."

Oh, God, oh God, oh God, oh God. I told him this was no
longer forbidden, but only because I knew it was something that
could happen in a real attack. Nobody's ever put it in my asshole
before. It's going to hurt. It would hurt if *anyone* did it, but Jonah's
massive cock will split me in two—

"You're going to come so hard, it'll be the best it's ever been."
Jonah pushes another finger in me. Tender flesh stretches. By now
I can tell he's slicked his hand with something, oil or some other
kind of lube, but it doesn't lessen my panic. I don't want him to do
this. I want out of here.

And yet I don't.

I can't say *silver*, not with my underwear jammed in my mouth.
Still, I could stop him by snapping my fingers. Even bound as I am,
I could manage that. But the vibration is starting to profoundly
affect me. Spirals of arousal spin through my head, dizzying me
completely. My cunt throbs and aches. But it's my ass Jonah is working hard.

One last plea: I shake my head. Jonah laughs. "What, do you want to beg? I like hearing you beg." With that he tears the wet rag of my panties from my lips and throws it aside, done with it at last. "Beg me, baby."

"I—" I choke out the word. "Please, not that. Anything but that. I'll do anything else you want."

"You're going to do everything I want anyway, bitch."

And then Jonah pushes inside.

I cry out. The pain is undeniable—and yet it lessens quickly as Jonah holds still, stretching my body to fit him. Shaking, I try to wriggle away from him, but I can't move. All I do is push the vibrator more forcefully against my clit, and then there's no telling the pain from the pleasure.

Jonah starts to move, taking my ass the way he's wanted to since the beginning. I hear him groan in satisfaction.

He's tearing me apart—no. He's fusing us together. There's no me any longer, no him. There's only the way Jonah pumps into me, every move turning us into one.

Jonah's the only man who ever made my entire mind splinter like this. Because I can't speak. I can't think. I don't know what to feel. All I know is that he's pumping me hard now, so deep inside me that it seems like—like there's nothing left of me except my body, and my body is completely his—even the arousal arcing inside me, more and more powerful, that belongs to him too—

My cunt contracts, and my orgasm crashes over me, through me, a tidal wave of pure ecstasy. My ass clenches around Jonah's cock, and I hear his low, cruel laugh of triumph. He did this to me, fucked me up the ass and made me come long and hard and good while he did it.

That's it. He's won. He could never own me more than he does right now. And I glory in my own defeat.

Jonah plunges into me again, his hands pressing into the mattress on either side of me. "Not done yet, baby. Not nearly done yet."

And the vibration isn't done with me either. Already I feel arousal building inside me again. Surely I can't come again this fast. I *can't*. Yet the vibrator's inexorable stimulation continues rippling through me, demanding my response.

He keeps pumping into me. Stretching me out. Violating me in the most degrading way a man can force a woman—and making me love it.

Every single flutter of the vibrator between my legs brings me closer to the brink.

"Oh, God," I whisper against the mattress, in mingled surrender and shame. "Oh, oh—"

It crashes into me like white noise and white light and oblivion. I come so hard it makes me convulse beneath him, and Jonah laughs out loud in his triumph.

No one else could ever master me like this. Only Jonah.

He whispers, *"Slut."* And then he grunts and shoves inside me to the hilt, shuddering as his own orgasm takes him.

For a moment I lie there, vibration now almost painful against my overstimulated clit. But Jonah leans back—slides out—and slips the vibrator out too.

"You'll beg me for that again later. You're going to beg me for all kinds of things." He unleashes my ankles and turns the vibrator off, setting it aside. I'm too limp and weak to resist or even to move. "Now you're going to shower for me. I want to watch you. Then you'll come back here and get tied with your legs open again. So anytime I want to use you, I can."

Jonah slips my wrists free, drags me to my feet—

—and my cell phone rings.

The sound of that ringtone—the one I assigned to Chloe after our last awkward phone conversation—jolts me almost entirely out of the fantasy. He must have brought in my duffel bag when he walked away for a few seconds, because the ring is close, maybe by the door. Jonah's growl of frustration is completely real. How could I have forgotten to turn the ringer off?

"Are your friends wondering where you are?" Jonah runs his hand over one of my breasts, pulls at my nipple. "They're never, ever going to know. I'm going to shut off your phone so we don't get disturbed again."

The ringing stops. Thank God. Chloe will leave her voice mail, and Jonah and I can slip back into the fantasy. He walks me through the living room into the bathroom, which is basic tile, stark and white. Trembling, I step into the shower where I'll have to perform for him——which is when the damned phone rings again. And it's still Chloe.

Chloe would always rather leave a voice mail. Always. She wouldn't keep calling back if this were any ordinary call.

This is important.

Something's wrong.

"Silver." I turn to Jonah and repeat the safe word. "Silver."

Instantly he releases my arms. His expression shifts in an instant, no longer the angry, brutal master. Now he's Jonah again, and I'm me. "What's going on?"

"My sister. She never calls twice like that."

I head toward the sound of the ring. My legs are still shaky; my breathing is still too quick. I slump to my knees on the floor before I unzip my duffel. Although the ringing stops in the instant before I grab the phone, I immediately hit the key to return her call. She picks up instantly. I say, "Chloe? It's me. What is it?"

"Thank God I got you." Chloe doesn't sound sarcastic. She's totally sincere. This is bad.

"What happened?" I whisper. "Tell me."

"Dad had a cardiac arrest. Tomorrow they have to do open-heart surgery. They don't know if he's going to live."

TWENTY-EIGHT

I was shattered before Chloe called. Now I'm—I don't know what I am.

"It's after seven o'clock," I say as I put on my underwear, yank on a bra. "I couldn't get to the airport before eight or eight thirty. They never have leftover seats anymore, especially not for the flights at the end of the day."

Jonah has refastened his jeans. He holds his hands out the way a groom might try to soothe a skittish horse. "You can fly out first thing in the morning. We can buy your ticket over the phone."

I shake my head. "That's too long."

"They have to operate right away," Chloe said. *"He's scheduled for a valve replacement first thing in the morning."*

There's no way I could spend the morning up in a plane, phone shut off, waiting to land so I can find out whether my father is alive or dead.

"Wait," Jonah says. "Are you going to drive it?"

"I've driven from Austin to New Orleans before." It's eight hours, usually—but late at night I can make better time. I might be able to cut that down to six. I could get to my house before dawn. Then maybe I could see my father first thing in the morning, before the surgery.

Jonah doesn't look convinced. "That's one hell of a drive."

"You meet the most interesting people that way." My laugh sounds strangled in my throat. "So don't knock it."

"Vivienne." He steps closer to me. "You're shaken up and worn out. Driving through the night—you could fall asleep at the wheel."

"While I'm freaking out about my father maybe dying any second? I seriously doubt I'm in danger of dozing off." I yank on my sweater, step into my jeans.

Jonah's hand closes over my shoulder, a gentle touch that seems to flow into me like a slow, deep breath. "At least eat something," he says softly. "It won't cost you ten minutes, and you'll be in better shape for the drive."

I can't imagine a snack would make any difference in how I feel. But I realize Jonah's trying to be helpful. To at least act like the lover he might someday be for me.

When will that be? After all your secrets are told. So, never. My illusions have been overshadowed by harsh, cold fact.

"If you can give me something to take with me, that would be great." I kneel to pull on my socks. "But I have to get out of here."

By the time I'm ready to go, Jonah has a plastic grocery bag filled for me—a chicken sandwich, a banana, even a plastic bottle of orange juice. Provisions for his hostage, I guess.

"You're positive you're ready to drive?" he asks.

I nod. I'm ready because I have to be.

"Your family—" Jonah hesitates for a long moment. "Are they going to take care of you?"

He's seen between the lines. As little as I've told him about Chloe and my mother, he already knows they don't have my back. Not even a crisis like this is going to seal the rifts between us.

Jonah's a perceptive man. That doesn't change anything.

"You don't talk about your family. I don't talk about mine. We figure how much we can share, and how much we can't. Aren't those the new rules?" I pause and take a deep breath. "Thanks for the food. And—this setup was great. Some other time."

He simply nods. The man is no better with good-bye than hello.

When I sit behind the wheel of my car, lingering soreness reminds me of how perfectly Jonah fucked me only minutes ago. I was exhilarated. I was shaken to the core. But all of those emotions have been wiped away. Only dread remains.

I'm on the verge of losing the last adult person in my family who hasn't betrayed me.

"Sugar, you aren't acting like yourself," my dad said so many times that spring and summer. "We need to take you to the doctor. I think you have mono."

"I don't have mono," I would say. "I don't need to go to the doctor."

Even if I'd been miserable with strep throat or stomach flu, I wouldn't have gone to the doctor then. For months afterward, I was convinced that my next medical exam would somehow reveal I was no longer a virgin. That wouldn't make Mom believe me about Anthony. Instead she'd have assumed I'd slept with a boy from school, told me I was fast, grounded me for months. Then I'd never be able to leave my house. I'd be stuck staying in, having to sit on that sofa and pretend I hadn't been raped there.

My father had no idea about what Anthony Whedon had done to me. My mom didn't share my "lie" with him, and Chloe wasn't the type to admit to anyone that she was worried about her little sister "flirting" with her boyfriend.

And, of course, I never said a word to Dad myself. He wouldn't have been as unkind as Mom or Chloe—but he wouldn't have believed me either. I'd heard the things he'd said when he heard news stories about a girl found unconscious in an athletic dorm, or someone trying to prosecute the five guys who videotaped what they did with her while she was passed out. *If a girl gets that drunk—if she goes to a young man's dorm room—she knows full well what's going to happen. She wouldn't have done any of that in the first place if she wasn't looking for sex. Now she's been caught and doesn't want people calling her a tramp, so she's making up stories. Ruining those poor boys' lives.*

I hadn't been in a dorm. I hadn't been drunk. I had been watching a movie on my own sofa. But I sensed there were other excuses to be made for Anthony, excuses that would come too readily to my father's tongue.

Hearing those words would have destroyed what little sense of security I still had. The surest way never to hear them was never to tell, and I didn't.

Instead I clung to him tightly. To some extent, I'd always been "Daddy's girl" while Chloe stayed closer to Mom, but that summer I spent more time with him than ever before or since. Although I never cared much about sports, I pretended to develop an interest in the Zephyrs, so he'd take me to the home games. We'd sit up in the stands, cheer on the antics of the team mascot (a guy in a nutria suit, called Boudreaux), and eat peanuts. I still remember Dad sitting next to me, one hand holding his beer, the other around my shoulders. In moments like that, I almost felt like a little girl again.

Not quite. But almost.

I can't lose my dad. If I do, then the slender thread that binds me to my family will snap. As insane as Mom and Chloe make me sometimes, even though I've never forgiven them for taking Anthony's side and never will—I don't want to be completely alone in the world.

Then I will never, ever be able to make it up to Libby . . .

Tears blur my vision, and for a moment the road seems to vanish. Fiercely I wipe my eyes and force myself to focus. This is no time to have a wreck. I have to make the best time I can without being pulled over by the highway patrol. Even if they did pull me over, I could tell them what happened to Dad. The cops would know I was telling the truth just by looking at me. So I press down on the accelerator, and my car speeds faster into the endless black landscape ahead.

My phone rings. My entire body goes cold. It's Chloe calling to tell me Dad's already gone—

—but it's not her ringtone. It's Jonah's.

I scoop the phone between my chin and shoulder. "Hey."

"Vivienne," he says. "Where are you?"

"Outskirts of Houston."

"Listen—what you said back at the cabin—"

I try not to talk on the phone while I'm driving. Right now, I don't need any more distractions. "What?"

Jonah says, "You're right. I haven't told you enough about my life, and I haven't listened to you about yours."

"That's not all your fault." It's not like I haven't kept certain doors locked.

As significant as this conversation could be, it mostly just makes me crazy. I can't think about Jonah right now. I need to focus. Is this really the best time for a heart-to-heart about our relationship?

But then Jonah speaks again. "If you want things to go on like they have been, we can do that. But when I saw you leaving tonight, and you were hurting, and I couldn't help you— Vivienne, I want something different for us."

Despite my frustration and fear, Jonah's words touch me. "Exactly how do we get there from here?"

"I don't know. All I can say right now is—if you need me, I can be there for you. I want to be with you. If that's something that would help—if you'd take any comfort from that—just say the word. I'll get on the first flight to New Orleans tomorrow morning."

"*Jonah,*" I whisper. Tears threaten to overcome me again.

"But if this is the wrong time—I know you have other things on your mind, and I don't want to intrude on your family—"

"Come." The word comes out as a sob. "Please come."

He takes a deep breath. "You want me there with you?"

"Yes. I do."

Although Jonah sounded so unsure a few moments before, he turns decisive in an instant. "Okay. Next time you're at a service station, text me your parents' address. I'll send my flight info as soon as I've booked the ticket."

"Thank you," I whisper.

"And please tell me you've practiced changing a flat since we first met."

My laugh is more like a sob. "I did. Arturo went over it with me."

"Good." He pauses. "I should let you go so you can concentrate. But if you need to call me at any moment, then call."

"I will."

The line goes dead. This time I don't mind the lack of a good-bye, because I know I'll find Jonah again at the end of the road.

How did this man with the power to terrify me also become the one person who truly makes me feel safe?

Our home is in the Garden District of New Orleans. It was built by a distant ancestor back in the 1890s. Since then it's been remodeled for the basic modern comforts of AC, cable, and indoor plumbing, but we retain the cast-iron scrollwork on our gallery, the thick, ten-foot-high doors, and even the "carriage stone" out

on the sidewalk—an old, white step that once made it easier for
people to step into and out of horse-drawn carriages.

This neighborhood has always been one of the most desirable
in the city. A few movie stars have houses here, though they tend
to appear only around Mardi Gras and Jazzfest. Our home is on
one of the less fashionable streets, inhabited by the merely well-off
rather than the mega-rich.

Neither term has applied to my family in a couple of generations
now. My parents keep up appearances, but at the cost of their savings. For years now I've wondered what they're going to retire on, if
anything. They could sell the house for millions, but that will never
happen. For my mother, giving up this desirable address would mean
admitting defeat.

I cross the Lake Pontchartrain Bridge around four in the morning. The only other vehicles on the road are semis driven by truck-
ers who are probably sky-high on speed. As soon as I exit the
highway for local streets, the endless bumps and potholes in the
road tell me I'm home for real.

When I reach my parents' house, I click the plastic box clipped
to my sun visor. Slowly the metal gate in front of the driveway
begins to slide open. I take the moment to check my phone. Jonah
replied to my text of my parents' address: FLIGHT ARRIVES 10:45
WILL CATCH TAXI.

For a moment it seems like there's still a way this could all turn
out okay. If Dad makes it through, and Jonah's here—I can bear
this. I can.

I walk to the front door. At first I think no one has waited up for
me, but at the last moment before I go for the bell, the door opens.
"There you are," Chloe says. She's wearing designer jeans, a form-
fitting cashmere sweater, and gold-knot earrings—glamorous even
at a moment like this. "You made good time."

"Any change?" When Chloe shakes her head, I breathe out in relief. The only change that could've happened overnight would've been bad.

As soon as I walk into the hallway, I see Mom coming down the winding oak stairs in a thick white robe, the pocket monogrammed in red. "Vivienne, darling." She hugs me too tightly, as if we were being watched by someone she wanted to impress. "It's all so terrible. I still can't believe it's real."

"Me either," I say. Maybe the hug is genuine. Even my mother is vulnerable at a moment like this.

Our house was built for a grander age. Twenty-foot ceilings on the first floor, French windows that stretch almost as high as the walls. In every downstairs room but the living room, my mother has decorated for that era instead of our own. Our dining room could seat twenty-four. If you don't look too closely, you won't notice that the long velvet drapes have become a bit shabby, or that dust has collected in the crystals of the chandelier.

The long, low sofas are overly grand as well, but right now they look perfect, because one of them has been draped with a quilt to cover a sleeping little girl.

"Libby," I whisper. I want to brush my hand over her golden curls, her chubby cheeks. But of course I don't want to wake her. "Why is she sleeping on the sofa?"

"Dozed off down here, and we thought we might as well not move her." The answer doesn't come from Mom or Chloe. It comes from Libby's father.

I straighten and take a deep breath before I turn around. "Hello, Anthony."

TWENTY-NINE

Sitting beside Anthony at the breakfast table makes my skin crawl.

I tell myself what I always do: *It's not as bad as being a brides-maid at their wedding, is it?*

No, it isn't. But this still sucks.

I took a quick nap around dawn, but now I'm here, drinking café au lait with my family as we pretend my father isn't being wheeled into surgery this very moment.

"He was on the golf course," Mom says as she sips her coffee from a china cup. "They say he simply fell over. Not a word. Bud Teague didn't call me until they were already at Touro. Wouldn't you call a man's wife first thing?"

"I'd call an ambulance first thing," I say. "Which Mr. Teague did. He might've saved Dad's life, Mom. So maybe don't worry about the etiquette."

My mother gives me a wounded look, as does Chloe. It's my sister who reprimands me as she primly spoons a slice from her grapefruit half. "We're all upset. I think sometimes it's easier to fret about little things than the big things."

That would almost be wise, if it came from someone who didn't take it to the point of living in total denial.

"Do you want some Cocoa Krispies, Aunt Vivi?" Libby believes us when we tell her that her PawPaw is going to be just fine, so she's as bright and chipper as ever. "'Cause look, I have Cocoa Krispies, and then we would be alike."

"Aunt Vivi would rather have some bacon, wouldn't you, darlin'?" Anthony always smiles when he calls me *darling*. He knows I hate it. He also knows I can't shoot him down for it without roiling waters we've all allowed to lie still.

"I'll have Cocoa Krispies," I say, to make Libby smile. Besides, I'm operating on about two hours' sleep, so I could use the sugar rush.

"Better watch it with that kind of junk," Anthony says. "Don't want to lose that pretty figure, do you?"

How dare he examine my body. How dare he act as if he should get to control me. I say only, "You're one to talk. That's your fourth piece of bacon." And I cast a pointed glance at his softer middle, but then I wish I hadn't. Even looking directly at him revolts me.

He and Chloe broke up and got back together endless times during undergrad. Each time they split filled me with hope. Maybe this time he'd go away for good; maybe Chloe would be so angry with him that she'd think again about what I'd told her, and realize it was the truth.

But Anthony sweet-talked his way back into her life over and over again. My mom did what he couldn't, encouraging Chloe to take him back. I know Mom was thinking more of the Whedon family fortune than anything else. If only the same were true for Chloe. Instead she actually loves the son of a bitch.

I can tell Anthony's trying to think of a comeback to my "bacon" remark, so I decide to move the conversation along fast. "When can we visit him?"

"Once he's in the recovery room."

"Not before surgery?" So much for my hopes of seeing him before the operation.

"No, not until after." Mom looks stricken, and for a moment, the real love she feels for my father eclipses everything else. I feel like her daughter, the one who trusted her so much. Despite everything I still want to trust her. "We'll all go in together."

"Not Olivia," Chloe says hastily. "She's too little. It will frighten her."

"I'm *not* too little!" Libby insists. She would say this no matter what we'd just suggested, whether it was visiting the hospital or steering a fire truck. "And I want to see PawPaw."

Mom says, "I tell you what, Chloe. Vivienne and I will go in first. If Thad seems up to talking, you can bring Olivia in with you. If not, she can stay with Anthony."

Libby looks like she might cry. Anthony chucks her under the chin. "Cheer up, sunshine. I'll take you someplace nice."

She smiles at him. This little girl I love so much adores her father. To her he can do no wrong.

Someday, no doubt, Libby will learn that's not true. But she'll never learn it from me.

The mundane has a way of intruding on the extraordinary.

Mom runs out of bread, and Libby will want some milk later on, plus I don't have any extra underwear with me. (Thank goodness I can write this off to packing in a hurry.) So around ten A.M.—even while our dad is lying on an operating table—Chloe and I make a Walgreens run.

"I feel so guilty," I say as I grab a package of cheap Hanes bikini briefs from the drugstore wall. "I know it doesn't make any difference whether we're in the waiting room, or at home hoping the phone will ring, but—buying panties and groceries seems so trivial."

"It's trivial until you're hungry," Chloe points out. "Besides, what would be the point of the waiting room?"

This isn't as heartless as it sounds. We live not even a five-minute drive from the hospital, which means the house is as logical a spot to wait as anyplace on-site could be. I know my parents stayed at the house while I was getting my tonsils out; they sat with me on the upstairs gallery while Chloe was in labor.

And if we get bad news, Mom would rather fall apart in private. Even then, she would care about appearances. Then again, I'd probably rather be at home too. Then I wouldn't have to think about driving back, or pulling myself together to talk to doctors, or anything. I could just let go.

Listen to yourself, I think. *You're telling yourself how to react if your father dies.*

Which is when Chloe's phone rings.

We both freeze. She and I stare at each other, stricken. This is too early for them to be calling, isn't it? Too early if it's good news—

Chloe fumbles in her purse for her cell phone. As she lifts it to her ear, she holds her other hand out to me. For this moment we are sisters again, sisters only. Daddy's little girls.

"Momma?" Chloe's voice shakes. I can just make out my mother's voice—high, tremulous—but the words escape me.

Then Chloe smiles, and I let out a breath I hadn't known I was holding.

Thank God. Thank God.

I hug Chloe tightly. She hugs me back like nothing had ever come between us, or ever could.

This truce lasts all of seven minutes.

After we cry our eyes out standing in the Walgreens cosmetics aisle, and Chloe relates the details (went even better than expected, new valve is functioning perfectly), we check out and head back home. As Chloe steers her beige-gold Lexus down Napoleon Avenue, she asks, "What else do we need to do for him? He's got his bag. We can bring him a couple of books—"

"And his slippers." We forgot to pack those this morning. Then another idea occurs to me. "We ought to move some of his stuff downstairs and fix up the guest room for him."

The guest room is a small, closetless space on the first floor separated from the living room by some old sliding doors. It's not the most luxurious place on earth, but it's comfortable enough.

Chloe stares at me. "Why would Daddy move into the guest room?"

"He can't climb those stairs every day right after heart surgery, Chloe."

"Who said anything about every day? We'll get him upstairs and take care of him from then on."

"It might be weeks. Or months."

"Then we'll hire someone to stay with him."

My mother can't afford that. Anthony and Chloe can, though. Maybe I should be thankful for their generosity, but—"You're not thinking this through. Dad would hate being stuck up there for forever. He'd much rather be able to eat in the dining room, or go out on the porch swing when Libby's playing in the yard—"

"You come home twice a year, if that." Chloe snaps the turn signal, refusing to turn toward me. "It takes an emergency to get you here. Then, when you decide to grace us with the honor of your presence, you think you know what's best for everyone."

Count to ten, I tell myself. *Deep breaths.* "It's like you said this morning. We're all upset and tired, so we're all picking at little things."

Chloe doesn't take the graceful way out. "You could be more a part of this family than you are, if you really wanted to be. Obviously, you don't. It's fun for you to play with Libby every once in a while, but otherwise you don't care whether you see us at all."

That's not true. But it's close enough to the truth to sting.

She keeps talking as she steers the Lexus onto St. Charles Avenue. "I don't know why we bother asking you. All you do is see the worst in things. You're always looking at the negative. Like now, when you assume Daddy's going to be an invalid for the rest of his life."

"That is *not* what I said." Looking at the negative? For Chloe, that means I acknowledge reality. "You know what? Let's ask Dad what he wants once it's time for him to come home. Then we can do whatever he'd like best."

Chloe's shrug means she'll consider it. By now, however, she's too invested in our argument to let it drop so easily. "You're not going to graduate school on the dark side of the moon. You're in Austin. Why don't you ever come home, if you care about us so much?"

I cross my arms in front of my chest. The edge of the seat belt rubs uncomfortably against a raw spot on my wrist. "I'm busy. The coursework is demanding."

Which is true, and yet not true. I cleared a few days to visit Jonah in Scotland. If I wanted to get back to New Orleans more often, I could.

Yes, I'm the most emotionally honest member of my family, but that's not saying much.

Chloe actually laughs at me. "Is your 'coursework' the reason you didn't come see us the last time you were in New Orleans?"

"Chloe—"

"No, tell me. I want to know. You used to like me. I remember how we used to play, and how I put your hair in curlers for you—" Her voice has become hoarse, and I realize she's on the verge of tears. "When did you start hating me?"

"I don't hate you. You're my sister, Chloe. I love you."

"Then why don't you ever come home?"

Something inside me snaps. "You know why!"

For a few moments we drive along in silence; the only sound is Rihanna on the radio. Then Chloe shakes her head. "I can't believe you're still hung up on Anthony after all these years."

I swear to God, right now I could put my fist through the windshield. "Never, *ever* have I been 'hung up' on Anthony."

"Then why did you make up all those vicious stories about him?"

"They weren't stories."

This is as close as Chloe and I have come to discussing what Anthony did since the week before her wedding, when I made the mistake of bringing it up. I thought I might be able to talk her out of making the worst mistake of her life. No such luck. Even before I'd gotten the whole story out of my mouth, she became even more convinced that I was a liar, one who had it out for her beloved Anthony.

Maybe I should try again, this moment. Simply start with Anthony and me on the sofa, *Titanic* on the TV, the beer can in his hand. Tell her every detail, from the way he yanked down my leggings to the way he called me a "good girl" for simply lying there and crying. Would she recognize any of that? Or does Anthony save his cruelty for women who aren't his wife?

Down deep, though, I know it will do no good. Chloe believes Anthony. She doesn't believe me. Second verse, same as the first.

"You're right," Chloe finally says as she parks on the street in front of our house; she's so ready to get me out of her car she doesn't even bother with the driveway. "We're all upset and tired today. Let's forget about this."

Everyone else in my family chooses to forget. I'm the one cursed to remember.

The weight settles over me. I feel ungrateful, childish, for caring about anything else after I just found out Dad's going to make it—but even that happiness doesn't shield me from the hard truths: My family remains as toxic as it ever was. Anthony will be waiting for me back at the house with a grin on his face, and for Libby's

sake, I will have to be polite to my rapist, again. My exhaustion
and my sorrow bear down on me at the same time, and suddenly
I feel too heavy and sad to even get out of the car.

But there's Libby, waving both arms as she runs around in the
yard. "Aunt Vivi! Come and swing with me!"

So I get out. When I open the car door, it bumps the white
carriage stone. Sure enough, there's a small scuff on the golden
surface of Chloe's luxury car. She breathes out sharply through
her nose but says nothing. Instead she jams her hands into the
pockets of her quilted vest and heads straight up the walk, her
golden hair swinging behind her as she goes. Even at a difficult
time like this, her jeans are neatly pressed, her boots match her
Prada bag, and her nails are perfect. Chloe doesn't let anything
touch her. Her shell is her shield.

As much as I want to despise her for that, I envy it, too. I could
use a shield around now.

I follow her up the path to my parents' front door. Anthony
leans against one of the tall columns in front, watching. Probably
Chloe thinks he's looking at their daughter, but he's looking at me.
His smile always makes me remember the things he said that night.

You don't want them to catch us, do you?

Good girl.

My steps falter. Struggling for composure, I turn toward Libby
instead. She's running in circles around the oak tree in the front
yard, and I try to summon the energy to chase her. Before I can,
though, she stops and points. "Who's that?"

I lift my head to see a taxicab pulling off, and Jonah standing
on the sidewalk, his dark suitcase by his feet.

It's not as if I forgot he was coming. But until this moment, I
didn't realize how badly I wanted him to be here. How much I
needed him. At this moment, I feel safe—from Anthony, from my
screwed-up family, even from the ghosts in my own mind. It's as

if I had been drowning until this moment, when I finally broke the surface and breathed in fresh air.

Jonah came here for me.

I take one step toward him, another, and then I'm running. Jonah steps through the gate in time to catch me in his arms. I don't speak. I don't cry. I just let him hold me. It's enough.

THIRTY

Jonah whispers in my ear, "Your dad?"

My breath catches in my throat, but I manage to answer. "He made it through. He'll be okay."

"Good." Jonah brushes my hair back, kisses my forehead. "That's good."

I nod as I snuggle further into his embrace. Even the scent of his skin comforts me. Jonah's arms are my fortress. His fingers brush against my cheek, and I turn my head to kiss them lightly.

Libby's voice calls out again, even louder. "Aunt Vivi, who is that? Do you know him?"

That makes me laugh, and I even see Jonah smile. "Of course I know him, sweetie. This is my friend Jonah."

"Hi," Jonah says. Apparently he reserves his hellos for little children. But I can't resent it, not when I hear how gently he speaks to her. "I came to visit Vivienne. That's all right, isn't it?"

Obviously Libby likes being asked her opinion on this subject. Her chubby little face becomes grave. "It's all right, but you have to help me color later."

Jonah gets a deer-in-the-headlights look. I whisper, "A little rusty with your Crayolas?"

"*You're* the artist," he says.

It's only a small joke. But it's such a relief to smile, to let everything else fade into the background for a moment.

On the porch stand Anthony, hands in his pockets, and Chloe, one arm slung possessively around her husband's shoulders. Neither of them seems ready to welcome Jonah with open arms—or to welcome him at all. I glance up at Jonah. "Ready to run the gauntlet?"

He picks up his suitcase and takes my hand. "I've walked through a lava field," he says. "I think I can handle this."

"Well," Chloe says as I show Jonah inside. "I hardly expected you to bring a *date* for the occasion, Vivienne."

"I'm here for moral support." Jonah holds out his hand. "Jonah Marks."

Sometimes "Southern hospitality" is just another term for hypocrisy. But those good manners are carved into Chloe so deeply that she can't resist them. With a small, pursed smile, she says, "Chloe Charles Whedon. This is my husband, Anthony, and our daughter, Olivia."

"Call me Libby." Already Libby thinks she's made a conquest. "Are you Aunt Vivi's boyfriend?"

"You'd have to ask your aunt about that." He looks away from her just long enough to smile at me.

Anthony steps forward, almost a swagger. "What line are you in, Jonah? In soybeans, myself."

Chloe chimes in, "He's so modest. Anthony would never tell you his family runs the largest soybean farms in Tennessee and Mississippi."

She always says this like growing soybeans is better than winning a Nobel Prize. Which makes it even more delicious to watch their faces as Jonah says, "I'm in volcanoes."

"Beg pardon?" Anthony says.

"I'm a professor at UT Austin. I study volcanoes and earthquakes."

Libby pipes up, "You study them in books?"

"Not only in books." Jonah smiles down at her. "I travel around the world to look at geological hot spots. Sometimes I get a plane or helicopter to take me directly overhead. Every once in a while I even have to wear a heat-shield suit, so the lava won't get me."

"*Coooooool.*" Big-eyed, Libby stares up at Jonah like he's the most fantastic person she's ever met in her short life. So he's won over the one family member whose opinion matters.

As for Anthony—it's as if he's deflating. All of a sudden he seems to realize he's shorter than Jonah, and he sits in the nearest chair, like maybe that way nobody will notice.

The formalities have been dispensed with. Jonah turns to me, and it's as if I'm the only person in the room. "When can you visit your father?"

I glance at the brass-and-marble clock on the nearest mantel. "Two or three hours from now. Mom left for the hospital right after the doctor called, but the rest of us have to wait for him to be moved to his room."

"Okay." Jonah slides his arm around me. "We'll wait."

Chloe surrenders with good grace. "Would you like some iced tea, Jonah?"

"I'm fine. What about you, Vivienne?"

"I'm good," I say, thinking, *now that Jonah's here.*

At first we all hang out together downstairs. Jonah and I sit on the long velvet sofa, me curled along his side as if we'd been together forever—as if this weren't the actual day we'd realized how much we might mean to each other.

Jonah must be as rocked by this revelation as I am, but at the moment, his attention is divided. Libby has settled her lap desk on his lap, to make it easier for them to color side by side.

"You must really like volcanoes," Libby chirps, as Jonah uses the goldenrod crayon to touch up some lava flow.

"I do," he says, then adds more quietly, "and they're the only thing I know how to draw."

That makes me smile, but still, I can't stop hearing the clicking of Chloe's boots on the hardwood floor as she paces back and forth. Anthony buries himself in his cell phone, playing some game he doesn't go to the trouble to mute. The hands on the brass-and-marble clock on the mantel move so slowly I could believe they're painted on. Jonah's presence makes me feel less afraid, less alone—but nothing can make me feel comfortable in Anthony's presence, not even him. So when Libby goes down for her nap, I plead exhaustion and take Jonah upstairs with me.

"Do you need to sleep?" he murmurs as we reach the second floor. "You have to be ready to drop."

"I am, but I couldn't fall asleep now. Just come out on the gallery with me."

Jonah frowns. "The gallery?"

"Like a balcony, except the supports go all the way down to the ground." New Orleans Architecture 101. "Come on."

Our gallery is screened in, which makes it a pleasant place to spend long summer nights. By November, the breezes are cooler, but Jonah and I are dressed warmly enough. I sink down onto one of the long bamboo "outdoor chaises," and Jonah sits next to me.

Although I expect no more than the comfort of Jonah's presence, after a moment, he speaks. "We never talked about our families. I thought I was . . . protecting myself. I never asked if you had your own stories to tell."

"You picked up on that already, huh?"

"Kind of hard to miss."

Jonah doesn't know enough, and yet he knows too much. So I shake my head. "This isn't the time to get into it. I just have to get through this, okay?"

"Okay," he murmurs, pulling me down into his embrace. We lie there quietly for a while before he says, "Do you feel all right? After last night."

The memory makes me blush. "Oh. Yeah." Some of the most intense sex of my life was less than twenty-four hours ago, and yet it feels like a fever dream. "Only a little sore. And I scraped my wrist when I fell in the woods."

When I point out the red place on my wrist, Jonah rubs just below it with his thumb. No idea why that diminishes the pain, but it does.

I murmur, "I feel kind of guilty. You came all the way down here, and we already know my father made it through surgery. I didn't mean to waste your time."

"It's not a waste of time." Jonah brushes my hair back from my face. A breeze outside rustles the oak leaves, but I don't feel the chill. "I meant what I said on the phone."

"About things being different for us?"

He nods, and I feel a wave of almost inexpressible tenderness for this strong man hiding so much vulnerability, so much pain. Maybe that's what he sees when he looks at me.

It's so hard to believe that someone might want me—*all* of me—fucked-up sexual desire, tangled family history, book-hoarding tendencies, everything. I never looked for that. I never even dared to dream about it.

Now, with Jonah, I can finally start to ask myself what it would mean to be totally honest with another person.

Right now, I know only one thing for sure: Whatever dark secrets Jonah has to tell, whatever his past has held, I can hear it. I won't flinch, and I won't turn back.

"It's going to take a while to get there," I say softly. "You know that."

"I know." Jonah's lips brush my hair. "We'll get there."

Finally I can begin to believe that might be true.

When we go back downstairs, Chloe is suddenly occupied with the question of where to put Jonah—as in, tonight. "We haven't that many guest rooms, and Anthony and I won't want to drive Olivia all the way back to Metairie—"

I give her a look. My room has a double bed, after all. It might be a tight fit for me and Jonah, but if we made do on a backstage table, I bet we can manage.

Undeterred, Chloe continues, "No doubt Vivienne will ask our mother if you can stay here, but I'm not at all sure what she'll say. Momma's old-fashioned, you see. Even after Anthony and I got engaged, he still had to sleep in the guest room, or on the sofa when Grandma visited. Didn't you, hon?"

I remember Anthony on the sofa, and I flinch. Jonah catches the movement, perhaps from the corner of his eye, but he doesn't react. Instead he calmly answers, "I made a reservation at a nearby bed-and-breakfast. Only four or five blocks away."

Normally I get a little weary of the touristy trappings of the Garden District, like the endless walking tours of sloppily dressed gawkers who shamble along the sidewalks. At this moment, however, I'm profoundly grateful. I know the place he means; it's so close, I could stay there with him and not even Momma could take it as an insult.

That means I won't have to spend the night under the same roof as Anthony.

When we finally head to the hospital to see Dad, Jonah goes to check in at the B&B. "I wouldn't want to intrude," he says, which is gracious and polite and makes even Chloe smile in approval. Even now, I'd rather have him with me—but this much, I can manage.

The hospital is both better and worse than I thought it would be. Better, in that Dad seems more or less like himself, just tired. I'd braced myself for the sight of my father semiconscious, delirious, frail, and waxen. He does look a little pale, but otherwise, switch out the hospital gown for a polo shirt and khakis and he could as easily be lying back in his recliner at home. "They won't let me eat anything yet," he grumbles. "Not a bite!"

"You know they have to watch that stuff right after anesthesia, Dad." I pat his arm. "But I bet they're going to bring you something soon."

"Applesauce and Jell-O, probably." Dad scowls, deliberately over-the-top to make me laugh. "How about you run by Bud's Broilers and sneak me out a number four?"

"Maybe that should be your welcome-home meal," I say. "Give your arteries at least one day off, okay?"

Probably I should encourage my father to take up lean chicken and fish, lots of greens, and no more alcohol. The thing is, that will *never* happen. Dad without burgers and barbecue shrimp and po'boys is . . . not Dad. He's never going to order sparkling water instead of a Sazerac. He truly would rather live large and die at sixty-five than count calories all the way to ninety. That's not what I want for him, but he wouldn't listen to me.

Mom brushes my father's graying hair away from his face. "You look a sight. I should've brought you a comb."

"Nobody cares what I look like in the hospital, Renee." But he pats her hand fondly. Whatever deficiencies Mom has as a parent, she makes up for as a wife; my dad has always been devoted to her, to the point that he's blinded to her faults—still, after thirty-two years of marriage.

Mom and Chloe decided that Libby could manage a visit, which makes me happy. Libby piles up in the hospital bed with Dad and shows him her new sticker book, which makes him laugh.

Just the sight of her in his arms helps me relax. For once, it seems like things are going to turn out okay.

That night, everyone else in my family wants to rest, which means I have a good excuse to leave and spend some time only with Jonah. Thankfully some of my clothes still linger in the back of my closet, so I'm able to change into a fresh outfit, a sheath dress and cardigan that can go anywhere.

Forget finding a table at a fine-dining restaurant at the last minute on a Saturday night, but New Orleans is even richer in cuisine options than Austin. I take him to one of my favorite neighborhood haunts, a little place with tile floors and cane-backed chairs that serves the kind of dishes you can't find anywhere outside Louisiana—crawfish etouffee, shrimp creole. The clatter of silverware and chatter of other patrons echoes slightly off the tile, but I don't mind the noise. It gives us a paradoxical privacy.

"You're sure you wouldn't rather be at home," Jonah says. It's not a question. I shake my head, and he adds, "You don't get along with your sister and her husband."

Despite everything, I laugh. "Small talk isn't your wheelhouse."

"Never saw the point." Some of the steel has returned to his voice. "We might as well tell the truth. How else do we get started?"

We're supposed to open up to each other. Jonah's method is about as subtle as dynamiting a locked safe—but he's right. For two people as skilled in silence as we are, only the direct approach will do. "No," I say. "I don't get along with them."

"Why not?"

The truth hangs above me, heavy and sharp, a Sword of Damocles. I'm not ready for that, and even if I were, I wouldn't blurt it out in a restaurant. So I start with the pettier reasons. "They're— status obsessed. Shallow." I have to smile. "You saw how quickly they started bragging when you came in."

"I noticed," he says dryly.

"You shut that down pretty fast, by the way. Good job."

Jonah shrugs and smiles, but he sticks to the subject. "That's not the only reason you don't get along with them, though. You're not a judgmental person. You wouldn't react to that on its own."

It takes me a minute to decide how to answer. Telling the full truth remains impossible, but I don't want to lie. "Anthony's a . . . horrible human being," I finally say. "He wasn't faithful to Chloe when they dated in college."

The only proof I have of that is what he did to me. Equating my rape with sex, suggesting even momentarily that infidelity is Anthony's worst crime—it kills me a little inside.

A place to begin, I remind myself. *It's only a place to begin.*

I continue, "Right before they got married, I told Chloe what kind of man she was marrying. She didn't believe me. Ever since then, she's thought I was a liar, or jealous of her, or just plain crazy—I don't know. Anthony has fed her resentment, of course. Mom took Chloe's side."

"That's not easy," Jonah says. I can tell he senses there's more, but maybe he thinks he's pushed enough for now. "Were you two ever close?"

"When I was little, I thought Chloe hung the moon." To my surprise, I have to swallow a lump in my throat. "She was so grown-up, and glamorous. So beautiful. You saw for yourself."

"I didn't notice."

Most guys would be flattering me. Jonah means it.

He hesitates, as if he doesn't know what to say next, but finally comes out with, "Sibling relationships are tough. I get along with my sisters and my brother, but—let's call it a negotiated peace."

Jonah knows I read the article online; there's no point in pretending I don't know a few basic facts about his family. "I thought you only had one sister."

"Maddox and Elise are technically my stepfather's children,

but he married my mother when I was very young. Elise and I barely remember life without each other. Maddox and my biological sister, Rebecca, are even younger—as far as they're concerned, there was never a time when we weren't a family. We all consider ourselves brothers and sisters, close as blood, full stop."

That sounds like loyalty. Like love. "Then what's the negotiation about?"

He stares out the window at the busy street, unwilling or unable to meet my eyes. "As you know—as half the damned country knows—our parents' relationship is troubled in the extreme. My mother isn't well. The four of us don't agree on how to handle that. However, we all understand there's no easy answer."

"It's good that you don't blame each other," I say softly. "Chloe and I do, sometimes. I wish we didn't."

Jonah nods and turns back to me. "Maybe we get better at this over time."

"Knowing people? Or loving them?"

"Both." His hand covers mine, and we fall into a comfortable silence.

Yet I cannot forget how much more I have to tell. How many secrets I still keep. Even today, when Jonah has traveled here to stand by me—when we've agreed to learn how to love each other—I still can't bring myself to tell him the truth.

My secrecy grows heavier during the evening. Darkens.

Changes shape.

"You're sure you wouldn't rather sleep at home?" Jonah asks as I park my car in front of the B&B.

"No. I'd rather be with you."

He opens the front door with a heavy brass key, and we climb the carpeted stairs quickly, hoping not to attract attention from either the hosts or other guests. Neither of us feels like making small talk about the city for another thirty minutes.

The bedroom here is done in grand style—an enormous four-poster bed carved out of wood polished until it gleams, a marble-fronted fireplace, and an armoire so tall it nearly reaches the twelve-foot ceiling. Lace curtains cover the window, so we're hidden away from the rest of the world. Good.

Jonah puts my bag beside the armoire. "You didn't have this much stuff last night. Did you find some things at home?"

I nod absently as I step out of my shoes. Then I slowly pull off my cardigan and unzip my dress, which crumples to the floor. As soon as it's off, I look Jonah straight in the eye as I begin to unhook my bra.

He takes two steps toward me and kisses me, long and deep. As I shrug my bra off my arms, his hands find my breasts. His touch is gentle. Too gentle.

"We would have to be quiet," I whisper against his lips. "But we can still play."

Jonah goes still. At first I think he's already there with me, preparing to unleash his darker side. Then I recognize the confusion in his gray eyes . . . the hurt.

Tonight he didn't want to play. He wanted to make love.

I remember how he was in Scotland, the strange distance between us when I insisted on bringing my fantasy into our bed there. He obliged me, even though I could tell he wanted something else from me. Jonah doesn't need this fantasy the way I do.

But I do. Right now I need it worse than ever. I don't know why, and I don't care. I just want Jonah to take me without mercy.

"Come on," I whisper as I slide my hands under his shirt. "Last night we were interrupted. Don't you want to pick up where we left off?"

That makes him smile—the dangerous smile that makes me hot in an instant. "I knew you wanted it."

Then he shoves me onto the bed, hard.

I gasp in genuine surprise. Jonah's with me in an instant, standing by the edge of the bed to peel off my panties. He tears them from me roughly, then leans over my body and bites my breast—not hard enough to break the skin, but hard enough that I have to stifle a cry.

He hears the moan in my throat. His palm covers my mouth, fingers hard against my face. "Don't you fucking scream. Do you hear me? *Don't scream.*"

Jonah rolls me onto my stomach. I hear the zipper of his jeans, and I realize he's not going to get me ready. He'll fuck me right away, as hard as he can. It will hurt. He wants it to hurt.

There's a price to pay for demanding our game tonight. I want to pay it.

His hands clutch my waist and pull me down until my legs dangle off the bed. He parts my thighs roughly, then grabs my hair and tugs hard enough to bring tears to my eyes. The whole hot length of him fills me as he thrusts inside.

"You're already wet," he says, as if it disgusts him. "You're such a filthy slut."

Jonah starts taking me hard and fast, every stroke meant to punish. His grip on my hair tightens as he pumps into me. My blood has rushed to my clit, my cunt, and already I know I'm going to come hard, soon.

"That's right," Jonah pants. "You know you have to take it, don't you? Don't you?"

Yes, yes, I have to take it, no matter what you give me, no matter what—

And then Jonah says, "Good girl."

This room vanishes. Jonah vanishes. The past decade of my life is gone. I am a fourteen-year-old girl; I am lying on the couch; Anthony is raping me. He is inside me right now.

Within one breath I know what this is. A flashback. I'm having a flashback. I haven't had one in years, not a real one—a moment where I am back there, and Anthony's on me, and *it is real*. It is completely real.

I gasp, "Silver."

Immediately Jonah stops moving.

"Silver, silver." Tears have begun to flow down my face, and even as the nightmarish image of Anthony fades, the horror remains.

Jonah pulls out. He rolls me over, and at first the sight of him frightens me. He's naked; his still-hard cock stands out from his body, ready to fuck me again. But then I see the expression on his face—concerned. No, stricken.

He's not going to hurt me. Jonah would never hurt me.

"Are you all right?" he whispers. I shake my head no. He begins to lie down beside me, then pauses. "What should I do?

"Hold me. Just hold me."

Jonah stretches out by my side and pulls me into his embrace. I start to cry—deep, racking sobs that hurt my throat. When did I last cry like this? Have I ever let go so completely? I can't remember. I can't think.

All I know is that Jonah is with me, pulling a blanket over me and holding me close, and it feels like the only safety I have ever known.

THIRTY-ONE

"What's wrong?" Jonah whispers once, late at night, after I've stopped sobbing but before I can fall asleep.

"I can't. Please. I can't."

"You can tell me."

"It wasn't you. Please, Jonah, not now, not tonight."

I drift in and out of sleep, never truly losing consciousness for more than a half hour at a time. Jonah holds me all night long.

First thing Sunday morning, I decide to start the drive back home just after lunch.

"I'll be back for Thanksgiving," I say as I towel-dry my hair in front of the mirror in Jonah's room. "If anything happens before then, I can get back PDQ."

He nods, but says nothing. We dress in near silence; I slip on my jeans as Jonah buttons his shirt, both of us aware of each other yet never meeting each other's eyes. The weight of unasked questions fills the room.

Jonah wants to take care of me. He wants to understand me in a way no one else has. He's knocking at the locked door nobody else ever even found. My famished heart hungers for this, for him. But I am still not ready to speak the words. I am not ready to tell Jonah who and what I really am.

Somehow it seems as if when I say the words to him, when I say, *Anthony raped me*, all of it—the rape, Anthony's power over me, the true depths of my sexual compulsion—will become more real.

Which is ridiculous. It's pretty fucking real and always has been. Still, that's how I feel.

Jonah says, "Would you like me to drive back with you?"

"But you bought a plane ticket."

He gives me a look that reminds me his dad owned an airline. "It's not a big deal. Besides, you might need someone to change a flat."

That makes me smile for the first time this morning. "Okay."

I text Mom and Chloe my decision about leaving today before we head to the house to say good-bye. This saves me the angst of a face-to-face confrontation, but means they'll have time to prepare their most withering put-downs before I even get there. The lesser of two evils, I figure.

Fortunately, when we arrive, the first family member out the door is Libby, her bright yellow overalls as sunny as her smile. "Aunt Vivi! Uncle Jonah!"

He gives me a look—but it's not the panicked face most guys would make upon inheriting the title of uncle after just one meeting. Jonah's not scared, not at all.

I think, *I'm in so deep.*

So I swing Libby up into my embrace. With a pang, I realize she's already almost too heavy for this. I'm missing this little girl growing up. "Where were you this morning?" she asks. "I had to eat Cocoa Krispies all by myself."

"Yeah, but Jonah's bed-and-breakfast had waffles." I smile at him, and finally, the two of us are once again at ease.

"Waffles?" Libby's face falls. Obviously she feels she got cheated. So I quickly add, "Next time Jonah's in New Orleans, you and I will take him to get some beignets. How about that?"

"Ohhh-kay," she sighs. I am being forgiven, but barely.

Which is better than I'm going to do with the rest of my family.

Inside, my mother accepts my introduction of Jonah politely, though without ever leaving her seat in the high-backed armchair. Her blue eyes scour him as roughly as steel wool. She's never trusted my judgment about anything—least of all men. Geordie they liked well enough, but he was an exception to the rule of disapproval. "A professor, you say? Were you one of Vivienne's teachers?"

How blithely she accuses Jonah of a massive ethics violation. Before I can reply, Libby does it for me. "MawMaw, I told you, Jonah teaches volcanoes!"

She raises her eyebrows. "I assumed that was a story."

"I'm an earth sciences professor." Jonah meets my mother's eyes steadily, even searchingly, as if he's looking for the truth I won't tell him. "Vivienne and I have mutual friends."

Which is a pretty neat way to sidestep the question of how we started going out in the first place. I'm impressed. "Jonah flew down yesterday morning," I add, "and he'll drive back with me today, so I don't have to go alone."

"Very kind." Mom sounds like she doesn't believe her own words.

This is when Chloe makes her appearance, coming in from the kitchen in a sweater dress and, Jesus H. Christ, high heels. "Heading back already?" The way she smiles at Jonah makes me realize why my sister went to all the trouble to fix herself up this morning. No, she's not actually flirting with him; whatever Chloe's other flaws may be, she's not a cheater. She'd never go after a guy behind Anthony's back. But she still has this need for men to notice her as the most beautiful woman in the room.

Jonah hardly even looks at her past a polite nod. "It's a long drive." Chloe's smile tightens as it goes from genuine to artificial.

"I'll be back for Thanksgiving," I promise. "Just a couple of weeks. And I can arrange to spend a few extra days at home, with Dad."

"What about Christmas?" Mom says it like I've never deigned to stay with them, when in fact that's the one holiday I've never skipped. Granted, I spend as little time at home as possible, and I always make it back to Austin for New Year's Eve.

At least, I did. This year has to be different. If being around for Dad means enduring hours or days of Anthony's company, then that's what I have to do. "I'll be here, of course."

My mother sweetly says to Jonah, "And will we be seeing you again over the holidays?" Obviously she expects him to dodge any solid commitment, thus simultaneously proving him unworthy and humiliating me. Mom never could pass up a two-fer.

Once again, Jonah doesn't flinch. "I expect so."

"Of course." Mom settles back in her chair, satisfied—even pleased with him—but there's a definite sense of surprise at my having found an interesting man. Like, *Look what the cat dragged in.*

The gauntlet is all but cleared. Now we just have to get into the car.

But then we walk onto the porch, where Libby is playing under her father's supervision, and I amend that. We just have to get past Anthony.

"Y'all should have good weather for the drive," he says as he strolls up to us, standing just a bit too close to me—not enough to stand out as weird, but enough to give me the creeps.

My response is clipped, almost harsh. "Hope so."

Anthony's grin widens. "Are we going to see you during the holidays, Vivienne?"

"Absolutely. Longer than usual this time." *For Dad*, I remind myself.

He nods, as if I need his approval. And then he says, "Good girl."

I don't have another flashback, thank God. But the memory of Anthony saying this while I lay there on the sofa, crying, still shaking with fear and pain—it lances through me, sharply enough to drain the blood from my face.

Just walk away, I tell myself. *That's all you have to do.*

But as I turn, I see Jonah. He stares at me, then slowly turns his head toward Anthony. Horror seizes me in its cold fist.

Jonah knows. He *knows*.

The sick silence of this moment is broken by Libby's laughter. She's still playing on the swing, innocent of everything.

Jonah says, "Libby? Go in the house and get your coloring book. I want to take one of your pictures with me."

Her eyes light up, and she jumps from the swing to run inside. Anthony, aware something has changed but not what, frowns at Jonah. "What is this about?"

Jonah has not taken one step forward. He does not raise his voice. But in this moment I am reminded of why, when we first met, I thought he was dangerous.

Because he is.

"Listen to me," he says to Anthony. "If you ever touch Vivienne again, if you ever say anything to her about what happened, if you even *stand too close* to her, you're going to regret it. Deeply. Painfully. And permanently."

Anthony laughs, but there's a nervous edge to it. This is the first time anyone has ever called him on what he did to me, and he doesn't know how to handle it. "What are you talking about?"

"Don't play stupid either." Every muscle in Jonah's body is tense. "Just this once, you have to deal with the truth."

I should speak, but I can't. My shock is too complete. Shame, anger, wonder, gratitude, love—they're all bubbling up, boiling over, and I am in a place beyond words.

Finally Anthony takes a step back, getting out of the range of Jonah's fists. "I don't know what Vivienne told you, but there's two sides to every story, buddy. You know how women get."

"I know what rape does to people," Jonah says.

Anthony holds up his hands. "Whoa, whoa, whoa. That's a hell of an accusation to throw at somebody. Vivienne and I were teenagers. Hormones all over the place. You remember how it is. So we got busy one night, and then when I stayed with Chloe, Viv couldn't stand it—girls get jealous, and sex mixes up their heads—"

"Anthony?" says a tremulous voice.

Only then do the three of us realize Chloe had stepped out onto the porch. I don't know exactly how much she heard, but it was enough.

Anthony had been defensive; now he's almost panicked. "Sugar, you know there's nothing to this."

"You said she flirted with you." Chloe braces one hand against a white column. She's shaking so hard I can see it from here. "You never told me you *slept with her.*"

Finally my voice returns to me. "He didn't sleep with me, Chloe. He raped me. Anthony told you a lie, and I told you the truth."

I can tell she doesn't believe me. At least, not yet. But for the first time, Chloe has to accept the fact that Anthony Whedon is a goddamned liar.

"I meant what I said." Jonah takes another step toward Anthony, which is enough to make Anthony skitter back to the steps. "Leave Vivienne alone."

Seeing Anthony like this—exposed, foolish, scared—is a thousand times more satisfying than I ever dreamed it could be. Someone finally stood up for me. Someone finally believed.

I take Jonah's hand. "Let's go."

Jonah only glances at me for a moment; his laser glare remains focused on Anthony. "Okay."

As soon as we turn toward the car, though, we hear Libby's footsteps on the porch. I turn to see her dashing toward us, a page of her coloring book in one hand. "Here, Jonah! I picked you out a picture!"

He bends down to take it from her. None of the adults says a word.

"It's a princess, see? I made her dress yellow, and red, so maybe it's like a volcano dress. Do you like it?"

Jonah nods. "It's fantastic."

Libby beams up at him, trusting and adoring. But Jonah can't smile back. I know that he's seen what haunts me most about Libby. She has her father's eyes.

I don't trust myself to speak again until I've steered the car onto I-10. "Jonah—thank you."

"For what?" He sounds strained.

"For taking Anthony on. For seeing what nobody else ever saw."

He stares out the window at the dull jumble of chain stores that lines the interstate. "Why didn't you tell me?"

This conversation was inevitable—I knew that—but I'm not ready. When would I ever be? "It's a hard thing to say." True. Obvious. Meaningless. Jonah deserves more. "The only people I ever told were my mother and Chloe, and they didn't believe me. I mean, the only people not counting my therapist. Because, wow, I have done some time in therapy."

"It never helps." Jonah doesn't get sidetracked. "Your mother . . . didn't believe you?"

"Anthony's rich. He wanted to marry Chloe. Mom would never let herself believe anything that got in the way. Even what happened to me."

"And your sister? That's what you told her the night before the wedding, wasn't it?"

Concentrating on the road is difficult. "She only heard part of the story before she shut me up. Anthony had convinced her I was jealous of her. As if."

Jonah shakes his head. "I would have believed you. Don't you know that?"

I think I always knew, though I never realized it until now. Jonah would have believed me, and that's why I didn't tell him. "It would have—complicated things."

"You don't think I deserved to know?"

"What? Where my sexual fixations come from? Do I need to bring you in to talk to my therapist before every date?" I sound hysterical, even to myself. So I take a couple of deep breaths. "You keep your secrets too, don't you?"

"This isn't about me."

"Isn't it?"

Jonah turns his face from me. "This is the way to the airport, isn't it?"

"Uh, yeah—"

"Drop me off there."

"Jonah?"

"You should have told me." The words burst from him, so angry I wince. He sees that, and speaks more quietly, but with an effort. "I needed to know, Vivienne."

"It's a difficult thing to tell." That sounds so inadequate.

"You didn't think I needed to know that before I did these things to you?"

Humiliation scorches me from the inside out. "We both wanted that fantasy. It was your idea!"

"If I'd known you were a rape victim, that would have changed everything." Jonah won't even look at me now.

I'm crashing. Burning. And from a greater height than ever before, because only moments ago I dared to believe that Jonah was truly on my side. For the past couple of months, I've been trying to make peace with my sexual desires. Now all the shame has returned in an instant. "You think I'm sick for wanting it after what happened to me. Don't you?"

"That's not it."

Of course it is. "You hate me for giving in to the fantasy, even though you wanted it too—even though it was your idea."

Finally Jonah turns to me again. I wish he hadn't. The fury in his eyes makes me feel sick inside. "You turned me into the last thing I ever wanted to be. You turned me into someone who abused a rape victim."

"It wasn't abuse. Not if I wanted it."

"Your wrists are still raw!" he shouts.

I wince and turn away.

When Jonah speaks again, his voice is calmer—but in the tight, controlled way that tells me it's mostly an act. "We can't keep doing this."

Does he mean we can't play our games any longer? No. He means that this is the end of him and me.

"All right," I say. The words come out cool and polite. I sound like my mother. In our worst moments, we often revert to our worst selves. "Let's go to the airport."

Jonah doesn't speak as I drive him there, though I sense he's waiting for me to say something. What? It doesn't matter. The man I showed my most secret self to has rejected that part of me. The one person who looked deeply enough to find the truth turned against me because I didn't tell him myself.

And something about my secret feeds the darkness inside him in ways neither of us can bear.

I pull up in front of the airport, by the sign for Oceanic Airlines.

We are surrounded by people dropping off friends and family members, hugging each other tightly around the backpacks they wear, exchanging kisses and laughter amid nests of luggage. Jonah opens the car door, then says, "Good-bye, Vivienne."

It sounds so final. But I can top it. Without looking at him, I say, "Get out."

THIRTY-TWO

"This is the part where you say 'I told you so.'" I wipe at my eyes with the Kleenex Doreen always has waiting on the end table. "Go ahead."

"That's not what I'm thinking, and it shouldn't be what you're thinking either."

"Why not?" My eyes actually ache from crying. I don't think I've stopped weeping since I broke down driving past Shreveport yesterday afternoon. "The most fucked-up sexual arrangement ever has now blown up in my face. Not like a grenade, like an atomic bomb. You saw it coming."

Doreen shakes her head. "Not this."

All last night, I kept staring at my phone, waiting for it to chime with a text from Jonah. I didn't expect an apology, much less an explanation. But I can't stop wondering what he's thinking.

Jonah may have left my life, but his shadow will linger for a long time.

"Someone finally learned the whole truth," I whisper. "And he hated me for it."

"You don't know that he hated you. You only know that Jonah had to stop."

"Why else would he stop?"

"You tell me." Doreen gives me one of her looks, which means it's time to dig deep.

And I remember Jonah's words: *You turned me into the last thing I ever wanted to be.*

I tuck a lock of hair behind my ear. "Whatever darkness that's within Jonah—whatever fuels that fantasy for him—he doesn't want to turn that on someone who's actually been hurt."

"Jonah spoke harshly. He shouldn't have done that. But he gets to have limits too."

She's said this to me before, but about Geordie, when he absolutely could not play along with my fantasy. Those two men have drawn their boundaries about a thousand miles apart, but they're both within their rights.

Still. "Jonah was angry. He was *furious*. I froze up just the way I did when I was a little kid and Mom would start screaming."

"Did you feel threatened?"

"Not physically. It just . . . hurt so much. Jonah had stood up for me, and finally, finally Chloe knows Anthony's full of shit, and it could have been one of the best days I'd ever had. Instead everything fell apart."

Doreen nods. "Let's focus on the good part of the day for a bit. Somebody finally believed you. Somebody finally put the blame where it belongs, on Anthony. How does it feel?"

Beneath all my sorrow, all my anger, that tiny light still glows. "Unbelievable. Like—like the whole world turned upside down."

"In a good way?"

"Yeah." Whenever I think about returning home for Thanksgiving, or Christmas, I feel apprehensive, but it's not the dread that has consumed me for years. Anthony will never have as much power over me again, even if Jonah's not at my side. I saw him humbled; I saw him humiliated. That memory will feed me for a long time to come.

"What about your father?" Doreen says.

I have to laugh. "Apparently he already talked one of his golf buddies into sneaking him some jambalaya. He hasn't changed."

"Do you wish that he would?"

"I try not to wish for the impossible."

And yet I can't stop wishing I could roll back time, wind it back on a spool until I reached yesterday morning. Maybe I couldn't change anything, but at least this time I'd understand exactly what went wrong.

Even understanding wouldn't be enough.

Later that day, as I sit in my office manually inputting grades, my phone buzzes with a text. Electricity crackles along my skin, and I have no idea whether the sudden flush of energy comes from anger or hope.

But when I look at the screen, I see it's only an invitation from Shay to come over and watch Netflix with her tonight or tomorrow. *And how was your romantic weekend in the woods?*

I never even told my closest friends about Dad's heart failure. Major omission. So I send out a few texts, then spend the rest of the afternoon answering frantic questions from Carmen, Arturo, and Shay. I tell Kip, too, and within minutes a caramel macchiato has appeared on my desk as if by magic.

"Caffeine doesn't solve everything," I say to him, even as I accept it with a smile.

Kip sighs. "A macchiato can only solve your problems if you *let it*, sweetie."

The one person I don't hear from is Geordie. He's incredibly busy at the moment—papers are always due at the end of the semester, and LLM papers are to undergraduate papers as World War II is to the invasion of Grenada. Still, for something like this,

I would expect him to text at least. Geordie was the only guy I've ever been with who won my mother over; he launched a full-scale charm offensive on my parents, to such good effect that they sent him a birthday card two months after we broke up. So Geordie would be worried not only about me, but also about my dad.

Sometimes cell phone reception sucks in the library, I remind myself. *Plus he might have shut off his phone to be sure he'd be productive.*

Which isn't a bad idea. I snap off the phone, and just like that, I'm not waiting for Jonah any longer. It should feel triumphant, or at least decisive. Instead it only feels sad.

That evening I go to the studio. Some artists find it difficult to work when they're upset, but sometimes that kind of emotional energy fuels me. Don't knock sublimation until you've tried it.

So I sit there, Bettye LaVette on the radio and chambray shirt rolled to my elbows, preparing to ink my latest plate. But just as I'm about to get started, I notice an indentation in the plate. Once it was just a nick in the wax, but now it's a reservoir for ink, a blotch waiting to happen.

Some prints look good—even better—with a bit of random "noise." Not this one. I swear under my breath and prepare to study the plate closer. Sometimes you can fix something like this; sometimes you have to start over.

Although there are several different etching techniques, and I've experimented with most of them, every method of etching involves the same fundamental process. You always start with a metal plate; you coat that plate with a waxy, acid-resistant material; you carve the design or picture you want to make into the wax, all the way down to the metal; and then you pour the acid. The acid bites into the metal, cutting your lines into it permanently. Then, when you ink the plate, you reveal a pattern you can print over and over— each piece of art identical and yet genuine, never faded by repetition.

But when you make a mistake, the error lives on and on. The ink catches it every time. No matter how many more prints you make, the blot will always be there, replicated a hundredfold.

Sometimes I think my life is the metal plate. Anthony carved the lines into me. But my toxic relationship with my family—and now the way Jonah turned on me—that's the acid.

And the same stains, the same errors, repeat themselves every time.

Disquieted, I step away from my work. A minute's break might be a good idea. I go to the water cooler and get a drink in a tiny paper cup, then recall that I haven't turned my phone back on since midafternoon. Might as well see what's going on.

As it powers up, I tell myself, *You will not expect a text from Jonah. You won't. It's not happening.*

This proves to be true. He didn't text me, but Geordie did. Five times.

OMG Viv I'm so sorry is your dad okay?

Carmen says he's all right but jesus you must be freaked out want to meet up for a drink bet you could use one

Hey I'm at Freddy's Place if you feel like coming out

Theiyre beng total shitheads Viv fuck this place

If you know the owner of this phone, can you come pick him up?
He is not allowed to remain on the premises.—Management

The time stamp on that last one is only ten minutes ago. I groan and grab my purse.

Most people think of Freddy's Place as "the one next to the

Mexican restaurant that turned out to be a front for the largest
drug-running enterprise in town." (No offense to Freddy's, which
is awesome. But when they busted the Mexican restaurant, it was
pretty big news.) The food at Freddy's is good, but when I come
here, it's usually for a drink or dessert after a movie, sometimes
both. I love their courtyard, strung with lights, filled with laughter, and always visited by a few dogs dozing under their masters'
tables.

The person I've come here with most often is Geordie, and as I
see him slumped on the porch, I wonder if we'll ever be allowed
on the premises again.

"Viv!" Geordie holds both hands in the air, like he just scored
a winning soccer goal. "I told you she'd come!"

The manager standing next to him, arms crossed, scowls even
more deeply. "You know this one?"

"Yeah, sure thing." Oh, my God, Geordie's so drunk. It's not
like I haven't seen him messed up before, but it's weird to see him
this trashed this early in the day, especially when he's out on his
own. "I'll take him home. Has he paid his tab?"

Geordie laughs. "O' course I paid! Whadya think I am, luv?"

That much Scots accent means bad news. "Sorry," I mutter to
the manager as I scoop one of Geordie's arms around my shoulders.

The guy shrugs. "He can't keep doing this. That's all I can say."

"What do you mean, 'keep doing this'?"

This wins me a disbelieving snort. "He shows up here at least
once a week. We told him a while ago we weren't going to allow
him to drive away—so most of the time he takes taxis. Today he
drove here, though, and I can't allow him to leave. We could get
sued for millions if he had a crash, and frankly, it's just a matter
of time."

"I'm not tryin' to drive!" Geordie bellows. "If you'd let me
order some more food I'd be fine."

The manager doesn't even glance at him. "If he ever comes here alone again, we won't even serve him. Maybe remind him of that tomorrow. That way he might actually remember it."

With that, the manager walks away, leaving me standing there with Geordie's weight heavy against my side. He smells like rum. "Thanks, Viv," he murmurs, giving me his goofiest, most endearing smile.

"Just get in the car." I can see his Fiat in the parking lot. Tomorrow morning someone will have to bring him back here to pick it up; probably that's going to be me.

As I head toward his apartment complex, Geordie says, "He's exaggeratin', you know he is. Two times I've been there. Maybe three."

"But you were going to drive like this, Geordie. You can't do that."

"I didn't want to drive like this. I wanted to eat and wait another couple of hours! I'd've been fine then, y'know I would."

Maybe he would have been. Maybe the manager was in a shitty mood. And Geordie's always partied hard without it screwing up his life.

Yet I can't help thinking over the last few times I've hung out with Geordie. He drank heavily every single time. Halloween, he even lost consciousness at Arturo and Shay's. We're not eighteen-year-olds experimenting with alcohol for the first time; Geordie is thirty. He should be past that by now.

"You Americans." Geordie leans back in my passenger seat. The city lights flicker behind his handsome profile. "You're Puritans, every one of ye. In Scotland, they'd call me a teetotaler."

I went to Edinburgh one summer when I was eighteen, on one of those "if it's Friday it must be Belgium" lightning tours of Europe. Plus I watched the fishermen at that inn where Jonah and I stayed on the Isle of Skye. Geordie's not lying about the way they drink. Every pub fills at five P.M. with Scots from all walks of life. Over there, the day isn't complete without a pint or two.

You're overthinking this, I tell myself. *This is basically a cultural difference. Besides, Geordie's been working so hard on his LLM. You know the pressure he's under. Why shouldn't he knock back with a drink once in a while? So he got carried away one time. It happens.*

I've said things like this to myself before. But tonight is the first time I realize what I sound like.

I sound like my mom. I sound like Chloe.

I sound like someone working very hard to deny the truth.

We get to Geordie's apartment complex. As I put the car in park, he says, "Thanks, luv. Sure you won't come up? Oh, no, that's right, it's all Jonah now, isn't it?"

Jonah's name feels like a lash against my skin. Yet I stay focused. "Geordie?"

"Yeah?"

I take a deep breath. "You drink too much."

He laughs. "I told you—"

"I know what you told me. But you've been drinking harder the past few months than you ever did before. You've been drinking alone—and not, like, a glass of wine with dinner. Drinking hard."

Geordie groans. "Ah, Christ, the morality police."

"Listen to me," I plead. "Geordie, we may not be in love anymore, but you know I still love you as a friend. I care about you, and I want good things for you, always. So I have to say this."

"Say what?"

Telling the truth is terrifying. It's a leap off a cliff. I'm going to hit the ground hard. All I can hope is that afterward, Geordie will think over what I've said and listen.

So I look him in the eyes as I say, "You have a drinking problem."

I expect him to laugh at me. Instead Geordie only stares. He's not used to my being that blunt; that makes two of us. Only now am I finally learning how to be honest even when it's hard.

"Please," I say more softly. "You're the most incredible person. You can have a wonderful life and do so much good in the world. Don't let this own you. Stop and think about what's happening. Get some help. And know that I'm behind you no matter what."

A long moment of silence passes, one in which I imagine him laughing at me, or cursing me. He does neither, only sighs deeply as he buries his face in his hand. "Christ, Viv."

"I wouldn't say this if I didn't love you." Only as the words come out of my mouth does it hit me that the truth can be a gift of love. That no other gift can possibly compare.

But Geordie simply steps out of the car and slams it behind him. He trudges into the apartment complex without ever looking back.

Even our greatest gifts sometimes come too late.

THIRTY-THREE

After dropping Geordie off, I don't return to the studio. My concentration is shot. Instead I head home, take a long shower, and go to bed early. Since Friday night, I've been riding various adrenaline rushes, from desire to terror to fury; by this point, I'm ready to drop.

I slide into bed and turn out the lights, but sleep eludes me at first. Too wired. So I lie there on my side, wearing an oversized T-shirt from a charity 5K I ran two years ago, exhausted, unsexy, and very much alone.

Alone isn't the worst thing, I remind myself. My sister is probably lying in the same bed as Anthony right now. I'll take my fate before hers any day. Besides, at the moment, I need the kind of silence only solitude provides.

Someday soon, I'll figure out what to think of all this. I'll come to terms with losing Jonah, and find out if my friendship with Geordie is going to survive, and hold my own within the new dynamics of my family. Doreen will help me. So everything's going to be okay.

I tell myself this. For the most part, I believe it. But I remember how I fell asleep the night before last—how safe I felt in Jonah's arms. It seems as if I'll never feel that safe again.

Right now he's in his fancy downtown apartment, as alone as I am. I wonder if he's already taken down my etching.

Probably he has. Yet I hope he hasn't. That way one thing I gave him—one message straight from my soul into his—that would live on.

My phone rings not long after four A.M.

Fuck, I think grumpily. Just when I'd fallen deeply asleep. *If this is a wrong number, I swear to God—*

But then I remember Dad's surgery. Panic grips me as I lunge across my bed to snatch my phone from its charging dock. Dad could be okay—Chloe could be calling just to yell about Anthony, or maybe this is Geordie telling me to sod off, or—or it could be Jonah—

None of the above.

Frowning, I answer, "Arturo?"

"You were asleep, weren't you?"

"At—four seventeen in the morning? Strangely enough, yes. What in the—" My voice trails off as I realize the answer to my own question.

Arturo says it out loud. "You told us, when Shay went into labor, you wanted to know first thing. Well, we're heading to the hospital now."

"Oh, my God." As weary as I am, I laugh out loud. "Is she feeling okay?"

"She's doing great so far."

In the background I hear Shay yell, "What do you mean great? Something the size of a watermelon is trying to come out of my— *ohhhhhhhhhh—*"

"We gotta go," Arturo says hastily. "Come to the hospital when you can!" With that he hangs up.

Labor can take a long time. Sometimes even days. I've spent some time leafing through Shay's dog-eared copy of *What to Expect When You're Expecting*, so I know the average length of a first-time labor is eight hours. I could certainly go back to bed and get some more much-needed sleep, and I'd probably still make it to the hospital before Shay gives birth.

Instead I text Carmen. Which one of us is picking up the coffee?

Immediately she sends back, I've got it. See you there!!!!

Seton Central is all the way on the other side of town from my house, but at this time of night, the roads are empty. I get to the hospital within twenty minutes to find Carmen already pacing in the waiting room. Her outfit makes me giggle—a silver and black San Antonio Stars jersey and hot pink sweatpants—but I'm one to talk in my oversized fleece top and faded jeans. Carmen knows why I'm snickering and sticks her tongue out at me. "Laugh it up."

"Sorry, sorry, I'm tired. Everything's funny."

And it is. A few hours ago I felt worn out and hopeless, but I guess the baby decided to remind me of all the good things still waiting in the world.

We drink our coffees and walk up and down the halls, watching the sun rise. Carmen tells me about the conversations she's had with Arturo over the past few days. "When he finally understood how freaked out I was about my graduate work, he told me I was being an idiot. Which was not exactly a helpful thing to say—but I knew what he meant. And Arturo said neither of us would let anybody down."

"Because you're both smart, and determined, and probably the two most together people I know," I say.

But Carmen shakes her head no. "He said it was because we were the most bullheaded people on earth. If we say we're going to do it, it gets done." She pauses. "Unless, like, a meteor hits the earth or something."

"I think we can give you a provisional meteor exception."

"Thanks."

Shay's baby might have gotten an early start this morning, but is apparently in no rush. Carmen and I breakfast on reconstituted orange juice and stale pastries in the hospital cafeteria. You'd think a place dedicated to health wouldn't serve this kind of junk. (Maybe they're trying to drum up future business.) We leaf through "women's magazines" that are all about fugly crafts and baking and seem to be an average of eleven months old. We pace around the waiting room like Ricky Ricardo in that old episode of *I Love Lucy*. None of it makes the baby come any faster.

At one point, just to make conversation, Carmen says, "So what's up with you and Jonah?"

All my exhaustion seems to descend on me again in a second. I sigh and lean back in my chair. "I don't know."

"You guys seemed pretty into each other at the party." Carmen bats her eyelashes, deliberately over-the-top, in an attempt to make me laugh. "What's wrong?"

"He came home with me this weekend."

She sits upright and stares. "Jonah Marks went home with you after your father's heart attack?"

"Yeah."

"Vivienne, that's *major*."

"I know." I hug myself tightly, my fingers buried in the cranberry-colored fleece of my sleeves. "And having him there helped so much. But—"

"But *what*, after that? You can't agree on the chapel for the wedding?"

It's a joke, of course, but Carmen's so far off-base it hurts. She understands that I don't get along with my family, even if she doesn't know exactly why. This means she knows something of what Jonah's support meant to me. How can I possibly explain that it all fell apart within an hour? "I think maybe we rushed things."

How inadequate. It's all I've got.

Carmen frowns, and I know I'm about to get the full third-degree treatment from her—but that's when Arturo appears in the doorway. He's wearing blue scrubs and an enormous smile, and while he's still the same guy I know, he's someone else now too, somebody new.

We both get to our feet, clutching hands. Tears well in Arturo's eyes as he says, "I have a son."

Then we're all crying, and hugging, and the weary, bitter world somehow feels brand new.

Visiting Shay and holding the baby have to wait for a little later in the day. Carmen stays at the hospital, but I run a few necessary errands—picking up food for the new parents to keep in their room, putting out their trash at home, et cetera. I even buy a few pale blue balloons and tie them to their doorknob, so the neighbors will know the good news.

And they'll realize they need to buy earplugs now, I think as I smile. *A newborn is moving in.*

It's almost lunchtime before I return to the hospital. As I look around for someone to ask about visiting hours, I hear a cheerful voice say, "Hello there!"

I turn to see Dr. Rosalind Campbell in her white coat and scrubs, looking nearly as tired as I feel. She wears a luminous smile nonetheless. "Hi," I say. "Everyone's okay?"

"Right as rain. A good, easy birth."

Bet Shay doesn't describe it as easy. Then again, an obstetrician probably has an entirely different frame of reference for this sort of thing. "When can I go in?"

"On the hour. But the baby's in the nursery now, if you want to see."

Just the thought of seeing this child—a brand-new person who is half Arturo, half Shay—fills me with delight. "Okay, I'll head that way."

"I've got another mother coming in any minute," Rosalind sighs. "How do all the babies know to be born on the same day?"

She waves as she heads off. From her friendliness and ease, I can tell Rosalind still has no idea that Jonah and I have split. He wouldn't have gotten around to telling anyone yet. It's hard for me to remember that Jonah and I had our last terrible argument just over forty-eight hours ago. The safety I felt with him already seems to belong to another lifetime.

No. I'm not going to let anything drag me down right now. This is a special day—the birthday of someone I already love— and that should eclipse everything else.

I walk to the nursery, which is filled with infants bundled tight in white blankets, their tiny pink faces peeping out. Every single one of them is adorable, in the squished way that newborns are adorable. Like miniature Winston Churchills. They seem identical to me, until I look at one baby and recognize him. Because I know him already, even though he's hours old. He has Arturo's nose, and Shay's stubborn chin, and I would know this kid anywhere.

When I tap on the window, one of the nurses looks up at me, amused but tolerant. They must get this all day. I point and say, "Can I see him?"

In response, the nurse lifts the baby up and holds him close to the window. He blinks in the weary confusion of the newborn.

Nicolas Gillespie Ortiz, I think. *Welcome to the world.*

They settle him back in his crib after only a few moments, but I stay where I am. Until he's taken up to Shay's room and I can visit with the whole family there, I might as well enjoy the sight of a dozen infants, all exhausted by their long journey into this life. Yet they sleep peacefully, and something about this sight quiets the anger and fear inside me as few other things ever have.

At one point, a young Chinese man stands there for a moment, looking at a tiny girl very near the window. I remember hearing the nurses whisper about him and his wife earlier: *This baby's a citizen. That means they get to stay in the United States.* Which is great for them, I guess. But right now, that's not what this man is thinking about. Instead he gazes down at his newborn daughter as if astonished to discover just how much love he can contain.

Someone else walks up not long afterward and comes to stand only a few steps from me. Nicolas is yawning his first yawn, so I don't turn to see who has come close. Then I hear, "The baby looks just like his parents."

I turn my head to see Jonah. His hands are jammed in the pockets of his navy blue coat; dark circles shadow his eyes. He stands there, awkward and uncertain. Probably that's how I look too.

The difference is that I've never seen Jonah like this. His confidence defines him; his command of himself is as absolute as his authority over others. Now, though, he stands before me and lets me see how vulnerable he truly is.

I always thought of Jonah as a strong man, but this is the first time I've realized he is also brave.

"They're all so new," he whispers.

"Well, yeah." My voice sounds calmer than I would have expected.

"I meant—the world breaks so many of us. Maybe all of us, in the end. But everyone starts out like this. Untouched, happy. Perfect. And we put all our hopes on children, all the hopes we can't believe in for ourselves any longer."

"Not all," I say, but I know what he means. "It's not really fair, is it? We expect so much of them, even when we let ourselves down."

"Who knows. Maybe they'll do better than we ever have. Eventually someone has to get it right."

If only Nicolas could have that kind of life. For today, I refuse to think of all the disappointments and dangers ahead. Right now his world is only about food and warmth and love. Let him enjoy it.

Jonah doesn't seem to have anything else to say yet, so I ask, "Rosalind called you?"

He shakes his head. "When I came into the office this morning, people were passing around a card for Shay. I signed it, did what I had to do, and then came straight here."

"I'm sure she'll appreciate that."

"You know I'm not here for Shay."

I hug myself more tightly. "Are you here to . . . what . . . take it all back?"

"No. I'm here to explain, if you're willing to listen."

What could Jonah tell me that would make everything all right? Nothing, I realize. But that's not why he's here. We can't fix this; we were smashed up long before we ever met. Jonah only wants to tell me the truth. His truth.

And I should tell him mine.

I've come to realize that speaking the truth can be a form of love. Maybe listening can be too.

THIRTY-FOUR

Seton Central is located in a major urban area, not far from a highway—and yet, right next to it stretches Seider Spring Park. It's a long, skinny green space that runs alongside the winding Shoal Creek Trail. Within a few minutes of leaving the hospital, Jonah and I are walking between trees, next to the water, seemingly away from the rest of the world—even though the distant roar of cars sometimes mingles with the rustling of leaves.

Pale skin, shadowed eyes, stubble, beat-up jeans beneath his coat: Jonah looks like hell. No doubt I do too. We're long past worrying about appearances, yet I can't help but notice.

Mom's lessons die hard.

"I'm sorry I was so abrupt in the car," Jonah says. "It was a difficult time for you, in many ways. I should've held it together for your sake."

"You told me what you were honestly feeling. You don't have to apologize for that."

We walk on together, side by side. Our footsteps crunch on fallen leaves and drought-dry grass. In Austin we don't get autumns of crimson leaves or winters of brilliant white snow. The year ebbs away into colorless cold.

Jonah finally asks, "Do you want to tell me what happened with Anthony?"

Once I thought I could never say this to anyone, least of all him. Yet now Jonah's the only person I can imagine telling. "I was fourteen. He and Chloe were in college, dating. One night when he was visiting, Chloe went to bed early, and my parents did too. Anthony raped me on the couch."

After a long moment, Jonah says, "He came on you. Didn't he?"

God, graphic. But true, and nothing less than the whole truth will do anymore. "Yes, he did. I've hated that ever since."

"You said you told Chloe and she didn't believe you?"

I shake my head. "I told my mother and she didn't believe me. Anthony told Chloe I tried to flirt with him, and she got angry with me for trying to steal her boyfriend. The week before her wedding, I made one last attempt at getting her to see who and what Anthony really is, and I tried to explain the whole story to her, but she didn't want to hear it. Now my rapist is in the family, and he's half of Libby, whom I love *so much*. That means he's part of my life forever."

Jonah's gaze has turned inward, as if he's studying my story from every possible angle. "I thought most rape victims couldn't stand seeing even allusions to rape. Much less . . . what we did."

"You're right. Most rape victims have a very different reaction. But this is what it did to me. Who I am now."

He nods, still deep in thought. "I should've realized," he says quietly. "When you never wanted to fuck any other way—some of your limits—I should've known."

"You have your limits, just like me," I say. It's mostly me parroting what Doreen and I talked about.

But then I find myself remembering that first night in the wine bar, when Jonah and I negotiated the terms of our arrangement. He asked me to defend him, not to injure him too badly, and—not to call him Daddy.

My stomach drops; nausea sweeps through me. My voice sounds strangled as I ask, "Jonah, did it happen to you too?"

"Was I raped? No." But Jonah stands still, weighing his next words. "It was—so much more fucked up than that."

What in the world could be more fucked up than that? I can't imagine.

But I don't have to imagine. I'm here, and I can listen. "Will you tell me?"

He doesn't answer for a long time, long enough that I begin to think he'll say no. Instead, he turns away from me, stares at the brook, and begins to speak.

"I was four years old when my father died. Not quite six when my mother married Carter Hale. Elise was five then, and both Rebecca and Maddox were two. They took formal portraits of the new family—you know, little suits for me and Mad, velvet dresses for the girls, Mom and Carter smiling. The money, the children, the airline, the real estate. They wanted the whole world to know they had it all." He shakes his head. "No one ever guessed what was really happening behind the doors of Redgrave House."

"Which was what?"

Jonah takes a deep breath. "The first time—the first time, it was late at night, and I heard my mother crying. I'd heard that before, after my father died. Sometimes it helped her if I came to her, gave her a hug, something like that. So I went to her bedroom. And Carter was . . ."

"They were having sex?" I say. That would freak out almost any kid, but surely even the archetypal Freudian event wouldn't leave Jonah so deeply scarred.

He says, "Carter was raping my mother."

"Oh, my God." I can't imagine seeing that, ever, much less as a small child.

"I didn't understand." Jonah's voice breaks. "I had some idea of what they were doing, but my mother was crying. Bleeding. And then Carter saw me, and he was so angry. I thought he would beat me, but he did worse than that."

"What?"

"He made me watch."

Bile churns in my gut, and I think I might actually vomit. Who the hell does that to a child? Whose mind works that way? A monster. Only a monster. All these years I thought Anthony Whedon was the worst thing that could ever happen to me, but Carter Hale is another level of evil altogether.

"Carter took his time. I think I was in there an hour before he was done with her. He told me that—that this was what it meant to be a man. That this was what women wanted. What they deserved."

All this time, I thought I was working out my darkest demons while Jonah just played our games for fun. Never did I dream what secret burden he might be carrying.

But even if I'd spent hours psychoanalyzing him, guessing what might underlie his own desires, I would never have guessed this.

"I didn't believe him," Jonah says. "I knew it couldn't be right, the way he'd hurt my mother. But the next day, when I was alone with her, I asked her if we would run away. Mom said—she said it was just that way between men and women sometimes. She pretended everything was all right. I told myself that must be true."

By now I remember how this story began. "Jonah, you said— you said, 'The first time.'"

Jonah's smile is sharper than any blade I've ever seen, maybe as sharp as the blade Jonah wishes he could hold to his stepfather's throat. "Maybe it turned Carter on. He likes humiliating my mother, and what could be more humiliating than bringing her child in the room to watch? So he started coming into my bedroom when I was trying to sleep. He'd carry me into their room and wouldn't let me leave. He made me say out loud all the things 'Daddy' was doing to her."

I picture a small boy in his PJs, maybe with rocket ships printed on the cotton, having to speak those words. It's as if the pain from that moment leaps through the distance and the years to pierce my own heart. "Oh, God, Jonah, I'm sorry. I'm so sorry."

He doesn't seem to hear me. Now that this terrible story has begun, he can't stop until he's gotten it all out. "At first Carter made me watch from the corner. After a while, he started making me sit on the foot of the bed. And a couple of times—he—Vivienne, Carter made me ride on his back."

Jesus Christ. I've gone from feeling nauseated to feeling faint. If it's this terrible for me to hear this, what must it have been like for Jonah to grow up this way?

"Eventually he made Elise watch too," Jonah says. "We were able to keep him from ever starting in on Rebecca and Maddox, though. We protected them. Sometimes I think that's the only truly good thing I've ever done, protecting them. So they get to be the normal ones." He runs one hand through his hair. "If you think I'm screwed up, you should meet Elise."

I imagine little Jonah and Elise suffering to keep the two babies safe, and their bravery tears through my heart. "When did he stop?"

"When did Carter stop raping my mother? Never, as far as I know. But when Elise and I got close to puberty, he stopped wanting us in the room while he did it. Maybe he had a touch of pedophilia mixed in with all his other psychoses. Or he thought we might finally be big enough to challenge him. At the time, I didn't analyze the reasons why. I was just glad it was over."

"And your mother never left him?" Of course not. They're living on different floors of Redgrave House. I remember the news stories now—Jonah's mother's insanity, her violence.

No wonder the children haven't turned on her. They know she's mad because Carter Hale drove her mad.

"I used to ask her why she didn't go," Jonah says. "When I was little. I said she shouldn't let Carter hurt her. But she told me—over and over, she told me, that's how things are between men and women. She pretended nothing was wrong. And so in my head, that kind of violence, that kind of humiliation—to me, that was what sex was."

He's been reliving his worst memories. Letting his demons out to play. Each of us assumed the other was simply indulging a kinky fetish, when in fact we were shepherding each other through our nightmares.

"Obviously I learned the difference between sex and rape." Jonah turns back to me. When our eyes meet, it feels like we're looking at each other for the first time. "I knew I would never, ever do to anyone what Carter did to my mother. That I would defend any woman in that kind of danger, to make up for the times I wanted to defend my mother and didn't. Yet deep inside, on a level I couldn't consciously reach—I wanted something I could never allow myself to have."

"Until we found each other," I say.

"No. Knowing what happened to you . . . it changes everything."

"Why?" I want to shake him. "You haven't hurt me, Jonah. You've *helped* me. For some reason, what we do helps me work through this. I've felt so ashamed of myself for so long. So dirty. With you, I could let some of that shame go." Why do I feel so much freer when I've surrendered to Jonah in that way? I don't know, and yet I do.

Our games are the only escape from that shame I've ever had.

Jonah looks torn between anger and tears. "I'm glad it meant something to you. Something good. But the things I do to you—I can't do that, knowing how you've suffered. Knowing that when we're together, you're reliving an actual rape—I just can't."

I cannot handle any of this *for-your-own-good* bullshit right now. "You're leaving me to protect me?"

"No. I'm protecting myself."

He gets to have limits, Doreen's voice reminds me. Maybe I should restrain myself for Jonah's sake, too. We're dealing with horrible experiences, probably not in a very healthy way. Yet I still feel like I could scream, or shout, like I would do anything to keep him from walking away again.

"What we have goes beyond sex," I say. "At least, it does for me."

Jonah won't look at me. "For me too."

"So shouldn't we at least try to love each other?" I take one step toward him. "We found each other—two people broken in the exact same way. That's pretty rare."

"And you think our broken edges would fit together, make us whole?" He looks so sad. So lost. "It doesn't work that way. I wish it did."

Is Jonah right? Maybe he is. Despite everything, I can't make myself believe that.

But I also can't make Jonah stay.

"Is this good-bye?" I ask.

Jonah opens his mouth to say yes—I can sense the word on his lips—but instead he says, "I don't know."

Hope seizes me. *He wants things to be different. He doesn't seem to know how they could be, and I don't either, but if we both want that, maybe there's still a chance.*

"You know where to find me," I say. "Even if it's not, you know, about *us*. If you just want to talk."

He gives me a look. I don't think Jonah makes a habit of sharing his troubles with anyone. However, after a moment he says, "You can talk to me too."

Jonah has now become the only person besides my therapist who fully understands what's going on with me. I've needed someone like that in my life. But Jonah and I will never have the kind of transition to friendship that Geordie and I have—or had, before I confronted Geordie last night.

What we have cuts too deep. Matters too much. Jonah and I will find our way back to each other, or we'll drift apart forever. We won't wind up with anything in between.

In either case, our future won't be decided today. It will take a long time for us to weigh the truths we've learned, and told.

"I should leave," Jonah says.

Don't walk away. Don't go. But this intensity is too much to bear for both of us. We have to leave the wreckage of our pasts and go back to the lives we've built. "Me too. I'm supposed to go see Shay and the baby."

"Tell them congratulations."

Does he mean it, or is it just something to say, words to fill the silence? Both, probably. "Okay. I will."

We walk together through the park, the only sounds our feet crunching on dry grass, the distant rumble of traffic, and the water flowing next to us. Neither of us is walking very quickly. Jonah wants to stretch this moment out as much as I do, I realize. The difference is, he's willing for this moment to be our last.

I'm not. But how do I change that, if I even can?

Only when we reach the edge of the park does Jonah speak again. "I'll never forget you."

Goddammit, now I'm going to cry. "I won't forget you either. Like I ever could."

He smiles unevenly at me. "I'll think of you every time I see your picture on the wall, of the man capturing the dove."

"He's not capturing the dove."

"But his hands are cupped around it—"

"He's protecting the dove. Keeping it safe. In a minute, he's going to open up his hands to let it fly."

Jonah looks at me for a long moment, his gray eyes searching mine. Then he nods and walks away. Yet again, no good-bye.

This time I'm glad he didn't say it. Because it's not good-bye for us. When I told him about the dove flying free, I saw something in Jonah I've never seen before.

I saw hope.

And that's how I know that somehow, someday, Jonah will find his way back to me.

From the author of *Asking for It*

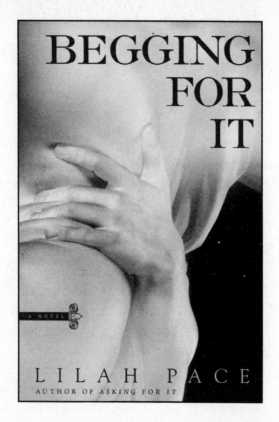

Some secrets should only be shared in the dark.

Jonah and Vivienne's bond started as a no-strings affair
between strangers who shared the same desires.
Now their passion has turned into love, but when a secret
about Jonah's twisted past comes to light,
Vivienne will learn how dark the truth really is...

COMING SEPTEMBER 2015

lilahpace.com
penguin.com

T479-0315